The Wicked Lord Byron

RICHARD DEAKIN

Achilles Books
(Achilles Productions)

First published in 2018 by
Achilles Books (Achilles Productions)
www.thewickedlordbyron.com

© Copyright Richard Deakin

The right of Richard Deakin to be identified as the author of this work has been asserted by him in accordance with the Copyright, Designs and Patents Act 1988.

Epigraph: Robert Graves, 'Narcisuss', Greek Myths, 2001. Copyrighted by The Trustees of Robert Graves Copyright Trust. Reprinted with permission from Carcanet Press Limited, Manchester, UK.

Hardback: 978-1-912572-00-7
Paperback: 978-1-912572-01-4
Ebook: 978-1-912572-02-1

Printed and bound in Great Britian by Clays Ltd, Elcograf S.p.A

At Donacon in Thespia he came upon a spring, clear as silver, and never yet disturbed by cattle, birds, wild beasts, or even by branches dropping off the trees that shaded it; and as he cast himself down, exhausted, on the grassy verge to slake his thirst, he fell in love with his reflection. At first he tried to embrace and kiss the beautiful boy who confronted him, but presently recognized himself, and lay gazing enraptured into the pool, hour after hour. How could he endure both to possess and yet not to possess? Grief was destroying him, yet he rejoiced in his torments; knowing at least that his other self would remain true to him, whatever happened.

– Robert Graves, *Greek Myths* (Narcissus)

Foreword

By Robin, Lord Byron

When Richard Deakin first asked me to read this book, I confessed to him that I was apprehensive; I am not generally a fan of fictional versions of Byron's life. In the event, I surprised myself by how much I enjoyed it. Sometimes hilarious and sometimes moving, it has the great merit of sticking closely to the known facts whilst imagining what can only be imagined.

After a beguiling magic realist opening which suggests what we all might experience on our deathbed – a conflict between different aspects of our character – the novel morphs into a vivid recreation of the life of the Poet Lord Byron. It's a life which has long held a fascination for students of English literature, for biographers, for film makers and for writers of fiction. Not surprising, perhaps, as the Byron story is hard to beat.

A ten-year-old boy from Aberdeen inherits an old English title and comes south with his mother to find his inheritance to be an ancient abbey – magnificent but crumbling and decayed. Writing poetry from an early age, he has a tempestuous adolescence, falls in love with both sexes, and at the age of twenty-one sets out on a grand tour of the Eastern Mediterranean. Two years later he returns with a poem which – when published – catapults him to instant fame.

Life in London society involves him in high profile love affairs – as with the mercurial Caroline Lamb – as well as a clandestine but not entirely secret affair with his half-sister Augusta. A highly unsuitable marriage soon ends in disaster and amid increasing debt and rumours of all manner of sexual shenanigans he is forced to flee abroad.

From the shores of Lake Geneva, Byron moves to Venice and thence to Ravenna and Pisa; it's a high-octane existence with a lot of sex, a dash of politics, deep friendships and terrible tragedies - but above all a prodigious output of writing. Eventually tiring of his life in Italy, he throws himself wholeheartedly into the cause of Greek independence and dies a martyr's death in the marshy swamps of Missolonghi.

Both as poet and personality, Byron was one of the most famous men of his age. Identifying himself with Napoleon, and conscious of his own celebrity status, he seems to have lived his life as if he was forging an epic story that he knew would be told long after his death.

More than any other English poet, Byron wrote from experience: "as to Don Juan," he said about his poetic masterpiece, "it may be bawdy – but is it not good English – it may be profligate – but is it not life, is it not the thing? – Could any man have written it – who has not lived in the world? – and tooled in a post-chaise? in a hackney coach? – in a Gondola? - against a wall? - in a court carriage? - in a vis à vis – on a table? - and under it?"

My only reservation about this work – which I acknowledged immediately – was the title. The "Wicked Lord" label has invariably been applied to the Poet's predecessor, his great uncle, who killed his cousin in a duel. I tried but failed to persuade Richard to change the title; he has now persuaded me that both literal, ironic and indeed humorous interpretations are permissible.

It is certainly true that the Poet's life was deemed scandalous by contemporaries and in the Victorian era well-bred young ladies were forbidden from reading his poetry. Many, however, disobeyed this injunction – and how could they not? There is so much that is fascinating and paradoxical in Byron's life and work that it lends itself not only to straightforward biography but also to fictional interpretations. Byron well knew that different writers would interpret his life in different ways – and often deliberately provoked contradictory reactions.

Based on this well documented story, Richard Deakin has created a highly original and entertaining work of fiction, with a host of colourful characters including the dandy's dandy Scrope Davies, the piratical Trelawny and the wild and tragic poet Shelley. Byron would surely have been amused.

Robin
13th Lord Byron
President, The Byron Society
London, England, 2018

Chapter one

Why I came here I know not — where I shall go to it is useless to enquire. In the midst of myriads of the living & the dead worlds — stars, systems, infinity — why should I be anxious about an atom?

Great bellies of black cloud hang, darkening the air, above the wretched little town on the fetid marsh. The month is April, the fierce summer heat of Western Greece not yet to be felt. But the sombre cloud, damp, warm, threatening, hovers like a pall over the town, which seems to be yearning for the release of lightning and the accompanying downpour that will refresh the exhausted air below.

In the bedroom of the principal house of the town George Gordon, Lord Byron – LB – is arguing, as he dimly realizes, for his life. The two doctors stoop like carrion birds over their victim. The bed, vulgarly ostentatious, has a lurid bloodred counterpane and a tremendous carved headboard with the letter 'B' cut in heavy gilt. On the stained pillow lie the heavy dark curls, now greying and receding, but the famous chiselled beauty of the pale face seems only the more emphasised by the ravages of the uremic fever that rages in the man's body. The sick man makes vague gestures of refusal as the two vul-

9

tures crowd around him, stooping over, touching him, fussing, tormenting, asking. 'Not now. Not just this second, don't-ye-know. Not yet.'

The first figure mutters relentlessly in Italian: 'No remedy is possible if milorde will not consent to being bled.'

'Not now. Not yet.' He chuckles at his own words, then, his mood abruptly changing, begins to flail the air around his head, as if troubled by a swarm of wasps. In a moment he regains control, snarling at himself in disgust, and says, in tones he has been practising all his life for this moment: 'Come – no snivelling at the end. Here on the rock and the vultures tearing at the liver.' The second doctor tries to take his pulse. He shoves the fellow away with a shout that takes the last of his strength:

'IN THE BOWELS OF CHRIST LET ME BE!'

Doctor Bruno's face registers shock; the victim's tone becomes conciliatory. 'I shall doubtless continue cursing quacks a good year or two yet. You may tell Death to come himself if he wants to speak to an English peer. I'll not treat with his seconds.' Bruno's hovering face does not register the joke. LB turns savage. 'Piss in the face of such – KNOWL-EDGE, d'ye call it, that tells you to do this! This foolish bleeding of a poor invalid!'

The English vulture, Dr. Millingen – is scandalised. 'My lord!'

'If you had but a pound of good brains in your head, you would see that your leeching a man draws out the life, makes the heart beat feebler and feebler until it is quite gone out, gone out altogether...'

The English surgeon affects the manner scientific, hooks his thumbs in his fob pockets. 'My dear Lord Byron, I am afraid that I am forced to agree with Doctor Bruno in this particular case. It is a simple and, I assure you, most scientific process. The fever stimulates the blood so that it swells and swells in the veins, and the pressure – by virtue of what we may call venal osmosis – mounts upward toward the cranium. I cannot answer for your reason once the pressure of that excessive quantity of blood has mounted to the brain.'

The patient groans. Millingen, sensing weakness, pounces, leaning over his victim: 'Why, the pressure has even been known to rupture the essential part of that organ and deprive a man of his very wits.' He pauses for effect. 'I must insist that you be bled, my lord, or you will certainly go mad.'

Dr. Bruno makes a gesture between his thumb and forefinger to indicate the tiniest of amounts, and tries out his English. 'Chesst litta bitta bloodss...'

Stifling both a laugh and the fear that catches at his heart, he looks from one to the other with a dawning comprehension of defeat. 'I would not go mad, end like a grinning idiot... like Swift.' He turns indignantly on the English vulture, the peppersalt moustache. 'You KNOW me, do you not, Millingen? You are a hyena crafty enough to prey on the dead flesh of a man's greatest fears.'

'My lord – my lord!' Dr. Millingen's feelings are hurt. Damn the fellow!

'Like the old king says, let me not go mad, sweet heavens, I would not be mad...'

Bruno rubs LB's hand with Mediterranean intimacy: 'Milorde...'

He is grateful for the smallest gesture from this man who has hitherto been merely an agreeably subservient employee, this Charon to ferry him over the Styx...

'Signor Bruno?'

Millingen has had enough. A patient – even Lord Byron – must know his place. Damned foreign lot of doctors and their soft talk.

The patient picks this precisely wrong moment to appeal to his fellow Englishman. 'Just a little space for peace, Mr. Millingen, I beseech you. Let me sleep for a little, and if I am no better you may draw off a pound or two of blood in the morning. Only let me sleep now.' He pauses, panting. 'I BEG you, gentlemen, if you could allow me to rest...' If I had my strength, he is thinking, I should give them both a damned good punch in the guts for this impudence.

Bruno informs the patient in bad English: 'But we dare not let you to ssleep, milorde. If you were but to ssleep now you might not again awaken.'

Sleep. To sleep. Will there be no end to this waking? Reaching up for Bruno's proffered hand. 'O Bruno, Bruno...' Slyly: 'My dearest Bruno...

'My lord!' Millingen's words ring with a final authority. 'If my lord will consent to lose a pound or so of blood tonight, he will wake up a sane man. Otherwise...' He shrugs. 'Dean Swift, for example, in his last years lost his wits entirely.'

LB, defeated, releases the Italian's hand. His head falls back on his pillow and his eyes close. Our revels now are ended. Let be. He speaks directly to darkness. 'You are, I see, a damned set of butchers. Very well. Take the blood. I care not, only if you would allow me to sleep afterwards...'

'Of course, my lord, of course.' Dr. Millingen is always willing to endure a patient's whims, insofar as they do not cross his own. Bleeding is the only cure. With much professional display of doctor's bags, instruments, and washing of hands, the two vultures proceed to remove the patient's nightcap and apply leeches to each temple.

The patient shudders as the leeches bite home, but drifts gratefully toward the black vacuum of sleep, murmuring still: 'They draw out the life of a man, slurp it up dark and red, like the last of the wine in his glass – can you not see that...? Though God he knows I have wished for such an end long enough...'

'Only a single leech upon each temple my lord,' the English doctor says, softening his tone. 'We must take the scientifically calculated amount, not an ounce more or less.' Another patient saved in spite of himself. He signals Bruno to continue applying the creatures out of his medicinal jar.

Two dozen leeches are applied around his lordship's body.

The Italian vulture beams approval, winking at the man on the bed with affection, making the 'tiny' gesture again between forefinger and thumb, and hissing in his abominable English: 'Chesst litta bitta.' The physicians withdraw to let the leeches begin the cure. In a few moments they will return to snip off the creatures' tails so as to begin to extract the blood in earnest.

He sleeps gratefully, shouting from time to time at the empty room. 'Augusta. Augusta, dearest one? Teresa, carissima, mia amica! Where's Loukas? Loukas? Ah, monstrous bitch, Annabella, Lady, bitch, did I deserve so much? See, Prometheus on the rock, the vultures tearing at the liver...' And so on.

Suddenly he senses that he is not alone in the bed. He wills himself to open his eyes. Others have done it – why not me? The eyelids open. The whitewashed mud walls seem to be bathed in flickers of red and blue light. But the light is not what has aroused him. He looks down at the foot of the bed. Under the blankets something is threshing wildly, not his legs. Something slithers out from under the blankets down to the floor. He is reminded of sights he has seen in the East – a lizard being born, a snake shedding its skin.

The creature rises to its feet like an exhalation from the ground and stands staring at him. Dull terror fills his breast. 'AUGUSTA!!!' he screams feebly, a child calling for its mother in the night. His gorge rises, his stomach spasms. To his inexpressible horror the figure staring down at him is himself, down to the nightgown and the fat leeches flopping about the temples. But the resemblance is inexact. The being staring down at him is a little younger and plumper, from an earlier period.

The man on the bed has had problems with his weight all his life, and it is partly as the result of a severe bout of fasting motivated by an absurd passion for the Greek youth Loukas – and only partly from, as he himself believes, riding on a wet saddle in the rain – that the present fever has managed to get its black grip on him. He has retained his slim figure at the cost of his life. But, he is thinking, as a little of his native courage begins to return, if this is a doppelganger the resemblance is inexact. The creature gazing down at him looks like the careless LB of Venice, of a few years past, the face behind Don Juan – fat, lecherous, happily drowning its griefs, copulating with a different woman every day. Plenum et optabile coitum, as he boasted in the letters to his cronies, detailing almost every expenditure of seed. In the final room the plump figure from that luxurious period shakes its head to clear it, shakes its limbs like a newborn colt, backs from the bed, and gazes down at the terrified LB dispassionately.

'LOUKAS! AUGUSTA! LOUKAS? TERESA...!'

The other snickers with laughter, making the leeches on his temple flop about from side to side. His tones are predictably intimate. 'Do calm yourself down old boy.'

At the intimacy in the tone, the familiarity of a voice he has heard all his life inside his head, the stricken man on the bed calms down.

'That's better. We've been rather a noisy devil for the past 36 bloody years haven't we?' He nods to himself. 'Bloody years. Speaking of which...' – he plucks the leeches off his temples, throwing them into a corner of the room where they leave red smears on the floor – '...the genuine blue blood of the genuine lord. Discarded by his lordship's very own ' – he bows – 'Nightgowned Spirit! Who is now brought with his lordship to a very obscure corner of this Earth.'

LB believes he is dreaming, and calls for the boy asleep in the next room, upon whom his heart has perched, as the nearest perch within reach. 'Loukas?' he mutters. If he can talk to the boy, ruffle those amiable dark curls, be jealous again because the boy does not love him, he will escape this dream and live.

'Not Loukas old boy,' the other responds gently. The newcomer has been looking around the wretched untidy room, filled with weapons, harness, maps and bandages. He passes a chubby hand curiously over the dirty whitewashed walls stained with the red traces of crushed mosquitoes. Not a good place to die, the Spirit is thinking.

He feels a sudden rush of pity for the forlorn figure on the bed. He extracts a gold snuffbox from somewhere in his nightgown, opens it, deposits a pinch on his hand, sniffs it up, and puts his snuffbox away. 'It was waiting for us all along, this little corner. Everyone has their own little corner – nothing special, as a rule. But I must be off now. Better late than never, pal, as we were fond of remarking in our youth.' He turns away. The unnaturally lit room seems to LB to darken as the other steps toward the door.

Terrified, he calls out: 'Augusta. Teresa mia amica. Carissima mia amica....'

The Spirit stops and looks back at the prone figure. 'I'm sorry, but I really do have to trot along.' He pauses, hand to mouth, considering. 'Though I must say I'm really not fully aware of the etiquette in these matters. This is the first time for me as well. Perhaps I do owe you a little time.' He smiles, and nods at the door. 'Besides, there's plenty of time – too much as it might be – where WE are going...'

'AUGUSTAAAAA!!!'

'Be it so, old body of mine. To hell with the future. The past shall be now, for the Time Being. You SHALL see Augusta again. Teresa too. Aye, dammit, Matthews, Hobby, Scrope, and Shiloh – why not? But especially Goose.'

The beloved name brings an instant response: 'AUGUS-TA?'

'She's not here.' The Other glances around the room with distaste. 'She has a little more sense than THAT, pray God, though God he knows not much. You see – Augusta, Teresa, Annabella – they couldn't come today. Not even Loukas can come, not even that pretty boy you long for, and he only in the next room.'

'Loukas? LOUKAS!'

'Not even him. And you and I must quit the stage so soon.' The Nightgowned Spirit extracts a silver flask from inside the folds of his gown, takes a leisurely swig. 'Seems a bit pointless, don't it' – he replaces the flask – 'popping off here and now in this stinking shitehole of a village. Nowhere, in the back beyond nothing, in the veriest stinking arse of nothing. With no taste of battle to be had. No matter, 'tis a tale will grow in the telling.'

He sniffs, abruptly thoughtful. 'I wonder what the party is doing in Lady Holland's House this very hour? Taking tea, no doubt...'

A hopeful voice from the bed: 'Scrope? Hobby? Shiloh?'

'Yes, we did linger in a few more colourful settings than this, did we not? I tell you what, if you're feeling sentimental, we've just time for a quick look at some of 'em, aye damme even see poor dead Shiloh again if you like. I shall have to rearrange things a little in the interests of clarity and brevity of course, because time is limited...'

'Augusta? Teresa?'

The Other sighs. 'Our women too – both of them. Why not? Let's see...' He takes a chair and sits facing the wall, pulls out a cigar from the nightgown, lights up and smokes, staring at the wall. Having made a calculation as to size, he gets up and tentatively rubs a space on the wall, outlining a rectangle perhaps ten feet by six.

To the man on the bed's astonishment a picture begins to materialize in the rectangle. Aware that he is lying on the bed all the while, he is absorbed into the sounds and sights of that box of light. He is unaware that, with a little practice, he will be able to dissociate himself from the picture at will, and at first feels imprisoned. He can still see the picture when his eyes close, and this realisation makes him nervous. He is unable to tell if he is experiencing or remembering the past, which flows into the Present in a most confusing fashion. Am I then or am I now? Am I THOSE MEN or am I...

The Other's calm tone. 'It's only the 36 years, but it seems like we started so very very long ago, with the amount we have crammed in. And it seems, as in the philosophy of Calvin, that even before we started we were foredoomed to be the wastrel that we were.' The picture takes on crystal hardness, the sounds begin to make sense in relation to the image. 'It was in our Byronic makeup. Great Uncle Willie, par exemple – the first Wicked Lord B, who don't write no verses.'

Chapter two

I have been concerned in many duels as second, but only in two as principal.

A cool green English landscape, the sky reddening toward dawn. Mist hangs above the ancient oaks bordering the great lawn. The trees form a Cathedral framing the front of Newstead Abbey, ancestral home of the Byrons. The watching man on the bed notes the magnificent oaks. 'We had not the benefit of these trees,' he mutters indignantly to his other self. The Wicked Lord had long since cut them down.

The birds sing the dawn chorus, in accordance with unbreakable traditions. The eighteenth century men face each other, pistols dangling from their fingers, twenty paces apart. Each lifts his bottle of brandy, takes a final toast, lays his bottle down, two overgrown schoolboys on an allnight spree in the age of Reason.

The watcher in the bed recognises the participants and not the circumstances, hears the inexorable voice of his Other self, explaining, formulating, inescapable.

'Now, as you will recall, great Uncle Willie's best friend was also called Willie – Willie Chaworth. One would have thought that it was only *reasonable*, to use a word much in vogue at the time, that two friends, lifelong neighbours, should sit up all night over their brandy. But the problem with *reason* is that it is not so robust a faculty as to preclude the clouding of it by prodigious quantities of strong spirits.'

The argument has finally come about in a small difference of opinion as to the best way to hang game. Chaworth favours hanging the dead beast in the cellar, in the traditional fashion, but Great Uncle Willie, being of the Byronic persuasion, is convinced you simply *have* to hang it from a tower, in a bag. He is fond of towers, and in the end there is only one reasonable way of deciding such a dispute.

The duellists settle themselves into aiming position. Willie Chaworth's hand is as unsteady as Willie Byron's, as each sways drunkenly, trying to get a bead on the target as his barrel drifts past it.

'Are you quite ready, dear fellow?'

'Absolutely, my dear Byron, absolutely.'

'Does there seem to you to be enough light?'

'Quite enough.'

'Well then.' Willie Byron fires an instant before Chaworth, knocking him backward so that Chaworth's shot goes over the Wicked Lord's head. The roaring echoes of the shots fade, the smoke begins to disperse slowly in the still dawn air. Clouds of crows from the great oak trees explode in all directions into the affrighted sky, and William Chaworth lies bleeding into the forest floor, as if to make the plants grow.

Willie Byron, who is henceforth to be known to his neighbours as the Wicked Lord Byron, lays down his expensive pistol carefully and walks over to his prone friend. He kneels and cradles Chaworth's head in his arms. Seeing the way things are, he lays Chaworth's head down, squats astride him, and slaps his friend's face brutally in an effort to bring him back for a moment from the dark place he is on his way to. A last word... to settle the matter. He shakes Chaworth's limp body roughly. 'Can you hear me, Willie? From a tower in a bag, d'ye see? It IS the only way.'

Chaworth's eyes flick open. Air whistles through the shattered lungs as he fights for breath to frame his reply. 'I can merely suppose God... if he exists...' A cough racks him with agony, but he recovers a moment, though there is blood and spittle on his lips, which his friend wipes off helpfully with his silk sleeve. 'I still prefer... the traditional method...'

Willie Byron is piqued. 'Ah, my friend, the old ways are not always best... Towers, don't you know, are wonderful things.'

'Your hand is damned steady under brandy and soda. I had hoped it had been wobbling, like mine own.'

The Wicked Lord waves his hand negligently. 'O, it was wobbling, it was wobbling. 'Twas but luck and chance.'

'Twas a damned fine shot in this light.'

'Nothing. Nothing at all.' Willie stands up and lights a cigar with a strangely familiar flourish. 'Please don't mention it.' He glances at the horizon, squinting. The sun is beginning to come up and hurt his eyes. The brandy has begun to turn to headache, and the landscape around him, the deed itself, begins to look real. *Dear me*, he thinks, *what have I done?* Chaworth is also his cousin.

Chaworth coughs politely to attract the Wicked Lord's attention. 'There is – my dear Byron – one other item we ought to discuss. I hesitate to raise the matter but it would seem somewhat urgent in the circumstances...'

'O do, do.'

'I congratulate you on a fine shot, Willie. Fair is fair. But you do keep going so very black, d'you see... I do believe I'm pegging out, and there are those that will turn the hard eye on you for it. One's wife, say, might complain to the House, do you see? I only hopes yer don't swing for it.'

'My dear fellow, don't worry about a thing, not a thing.'

Chaworth can no longer hear. The survivor looks down at the body, puffing on his cigar. 'Well, I'll be damned.'

The Nightgowned Spirit snickers. 'Possibly the understatement of the eighteenth century.' He smiles in fascination at the fading image of Great Uncle Willie he has created.

The man on the bed is outraged enough to mumble: 'Damn your lying eyes. That's not how it was at all. The duel was fought with sabres, in a locked room in London, by the light of a single candle, till one of the friends should be dead.'

'Well – I wasn't there, old boy. I'll try to be a little more accurate with the stuff we've actually seen. Please remember I'm reworking this for speed. And there was a time that we believed the pistols version of the duel, before we knew about the sabres in the locked room. There was a time when we dreamed this version, so that it became a part of us...'

'Take more care... show respect for fact, damn your eyes...'

'It is a little too late in life for you to set up as a critic. You're seeing it all through my eyes, do you understand? There were always the two of us: you, the body who suffered, to scribble about the early things – the passion and the blood and all that – Childe Harold, the brooding Hamlet figure, hand to brow, staring moodily out to sea. And me, I was the brains of the outfit.'

The Nightgowned Spirit leans and puts his hand to his

brow in a grotesque parody of the brooding Harold, bursting into laughter. 'And me the poor chap that had to cheer us up, every time, with the funny edge of the world. To make us laugh at our ridiculous self and fellow creatures.' His chuckling subsides. He takes a pinch of snuff. 'Aye, there was always myself there, to giggle and make giggle, to force us to stand back, as it were, at a respectable distance, from the harsh images of life. While you were always there inside us too, so tragic. We were born tragic, eh, old boy, what with the limp and all?' He gives a monstrous imitation of LB's limp, slapping his thighs laughing, then sits, trying vainly to control a giggling fit. 'O God – even our poor bloody lusts and desires got off to a simply terrible start...'

Chapter three

My passions were developed very early – so early, that few would believe me, if I were to state the period, and the facts which accompanied it.

Our innocence was stolen from us at an early age, by a sort of lovely species of religious maniac, and we may be permitted to detest the Cant of religion all the rest of our life, for we have seen the Cunt that espouses it in her unguarded moments, frigging herself to ecstasy as she perverted a little boy to serve her pleasure.

All day long we had been learning to read the Good Book with the pious *Maid* (for so misleading are words) May Gray. Our sleep was deep and pleasant. our dreams exciting. But greedy hands were taking us, cupping us in their soft, urgent clutches. We woke to find the Maid, Delilah come to life, lying next to us frigging herself and murmuring, pious Miss May Gray: 'Lamb, lamb, lamb of God, lamb, lamb, lamb of God...'

Which confused us almost as much as what she was doing with her other hand. Her long brown hair spread all over the pillow. The girl, finding her hand not doing the trick, stooped and took us in her mouth, but her efforts rewarded only herself. We were nine years old.

After a year of May Grey's nocturnal attentions, our body came awake. Puberty – that which in boys should be a period of self exploration – in us was the establishment of the Bitch Goddess over our earliest dream of Sex. 'Lamb, Lamb, Lamb of God, washed clean by the Lamb,' the girl would moan, fingering herself as, gripped in her other hand, we came our baby come over her hairy belly, spurting with all the jet pressure of boyhood.

Our nights passed in this delirium of sensuality, but our days passed in no less of a delirium of a boy's lonely exploration of the ancestral seat of the Byrons. What it is to be an only Childe...

Having come into our inheritance unexpectedly like a fairytale (the other heir of the Wicked Lord having been slain by a cannonball on the island of Corsica) we were now, after the Wicked Lord's death, living at Newstead, our ancient Abbey near Nottingham. This noble mass of yellowing stone, its Great Stairs and towers and tall mediaeval windows, had been our family pile since Henry VIIIth stole it from the monks and gave it to the first Baron B. Back in the time of Henry the Abbey had a roof. In our day rain poured into the bones of the great structure through broken roof and tower, as if to wash Newstead into the earth. The Abbey and its lands were all in decay.

Mother and I had little means, despite our title and expectations. Mother had been a Golden Dolly, a woman one married for her money, but our Byronic father had managed to gamble and drink away most of her fortune before he died. A very small portion of the great Abbey had been fitted out for human habitation. For the rest we roamed over the broken ruins like a little monkey in a jungle temple, hiding in little nooks where the monks must have smoked their hams, or digging in holes where they had buried a mountain of monkish skulls, the tribute of the thousands who had died through the long slow-burning centuries of the Middle Ages.

An ideal playground for a small boy.

Death was very close, in that place. Often enough we had dug into the soft consecrated loam and turned up skulls. We had found, too, the pair of pistols (as we wrongly believed) with which our predecessor the Wicked Lord and Willie Chaworth duelled to the death. When we found out the truth, that the friends did the deed in a locked room in London, with cutlasses, fighting until one should be dead, we did not rest till we found the Wicked Lord's cutlass in the jumbled booty of the faerie castle.

Procuring money from our reluctant mama, we sent old Joe Murray the servant (who served our Wicked predecessor) into Nottingham for powder and shot. From that time on we roamed the Abbey armed with the Wicked Lord's pistols, practising our shooting. We have never since ventured forth from a house without a brace of pistols about us.

We have always had a horror of being slain by some assailant. But with pistols we feel safe, for we can blow a half crown out of a cane at twenty paces, a proper duelling distance and a target smaller than a bad man's heart. (This trick we learned as a boy. We try not to frighten people with it. As Scrope the Birdmore saith, the best part of duelling is the kissing and making up.)

We did not have the Abbey completely to ourself. There were a few servants – old Joe Murray our 'grandad' the favourite, the holy whore May Gray not excepted – and there was also Mother. Avoiding the rages of our outrageous

Mama was the chiefest worry of our boyish days, not a difficult task in that great Abbey, until the fated day we met May Gray in her cups, with her friend Agnes, and our little world was shattered.

We were attracted by the noise the girls were making. Our beloved pointed at us drunkenly as we limped into the kitchen, dressed in our Sunday best riding outfit, a horsewhip in our little hands. Her friend, we saw, was very plain, so we were not afraid, and knew we looked damned well. 'Now, Geordie, now...' May mumbled.

We had been struck dumb at this sight of our beloved rolling in her cups. We recovered ourselves to offer our broad Scots politeness: 'A guid day to yai ladies...'

'That's his Sunday suit. Ain't he the little dandy? What a picture you are today, Geordie. Would you have a kiss now for poor May?' She opened her arms. The memory of the previous night, the whispering girl's hand on us, holding us *there*, pulling, kissing, inflaming, babbling her delight at the sweetness, that night, that passed between us like a dream. Our little boy's sense of honour forbade us to display any hint of this private love in front of the other girl, this secret world we and the Maid had shared.

We went to her haltingly. Kissed her chastely on the cheek.

The bitch transferred the kiss, opened our boy's lips with her tongue, lingered over us with a sidelong glance of triumph at her friend. The joke over, she let us go and clasped us to her ample bosom in genuine affection, as we are able to see the scene now. 'And who is it in the world that you love most, my sweetness?'

The never-before-uttered truth. 'I do love you *more* than all the world, May Grey.'

'There, Martha. Do ye doubt me now?' She released us, patted our head, pushed us toward her friend.

We bowed gallantly over the slut's hand as if she were Lady Jersey. 'And a guid day to ye, I'm sure, Martha. We are vewy pleased to meet you.' We would retain a Scots burr all our life, and never learn to pronounce the letter *r*.

Martha reached out to stroke our hair as if we were an animal. 'O May, May, what a beautiful little boy...' – she remembered and glanced down – '...if not for the funny leg.' The bitch took her hand out of our hair, reaching down to touch our reinforced boot curiously. 'Looks like a little 'oof, do it?'

Never insult a Byron carrying a horsewhip. Her next foolish thought was that her face was on fire, and she screamed. 'Dinna speak of it, you, dinna speak of it, you...!'

We managed two or three slashes across the cheek before May leapt up and grasped our arms, clamping us to her, and we wept hysterically on the beloved bosom, still a child after all, as a sobbing Martha, hands on her cut stinging face, ran off into the passage to scream for help. 'O Mrs. Byron! Mrs. Byron!'

The Dragon woke. Mother came into the kitchen leading the sobbing Martha with the red stripes across her face. Seeing the cowering May Grey and we, Baby B. still holding our whip up, Mrs. B. ran over to grab the whip off us. Before poor May had the chance to explain or even get out of the way she lashed out with the whip again and again at us.

Our agony was not so much pain as the sight of that heavy jaw, that jowly face that looked like ours all gone to some hellish mode of fat, worked up into a fury to match our own.

'Evil spirit of my life! It is a wastrel you are, just like your FATHER!'

Suddenly she calmed down. In the aftermath of violence she must have taken note of the cowering maids and her sobbing child, and the glasses of porter, and guessed the truth. 'O, Mrs. Byron...' May Grey began.

'OUT!!!' The maids went.

We were weeping streams, our eyes on the man in our imagination, the dead man we had not seen since we were two years old, and so had no actual memory of. 'My father was... my father was a...'

'There, wheesht, Geordie my only boy.' Mother grabbed one of the chairs and sat on it, perching us on her knee, and rocked us gently on her massive breast, back and forth, back and forth, rehearsing the familiar tale. 'O, but a handsome man he was, Geordie, a handsome man... but a gamester he was, a gambling man. Such a beautiful man as he was made, when he was walking above the earth... and soon, so soon, all the Gordon gold is gone... so *dashing* a man...'

'Dashing...'

'It were worth every penny... to have so beautiful a man, even for a year only...' Baby B. calmer now, sucking his finger, rested his head quietly on his mother's breast, contemplating the dead man's exciting image. Mother sang the ballad her Scots tenants had made about her man, her voice issuing pure from the girl's spirit in that disillusioned lump of flesh:

'The youth is a rake, frae England is come,
The Scots dinna ken his extraction ava;
He keeps up his misses, his landlords he duns,
That's fast drawn the lands o' Gight awa'....'

'I will be a *dashing* man too, mama. They will not laugh at me for the eternity of a lifetime. I will make them MARK me. I will make them mark.'

'Aye, my only one, the ladies will not always be laughing.'

'I will make them mark.'

Chapter four

*I have got a new friend, the finest in the world, a tame bear. When I
brought him here, they asked me what I meant to do with him, and my
reply was, he should sit for a fellowship.*

'...make them mark, make them remember...' The dying man
repeats the refrain of youth as the image on the wall fades.

But the Other is out of humour. 'O, how could we ever
forget?' He lights another cigar, biting off the end savagely.
'And all those poor women after May, all going through hell
to prove something to one whore from the past. Dead centre
the concupiscent bitch got you. I grow BORED with this.'
In high dudgeon he starts for the door to be stopped by a
despairing cry from the bed.

'AUGUSTA! NOT YET!'

The Spirit feels the agony in the cry, and stops. 'O fear me
not. I don't mean nothing too sudden. We still have plenty of
time to see Goose.'

'Goose... Goose at least...'

'Certes, certes... Cheer up. Remember how we used to like
College?'

'College?'

The Other resumes his seat, pulls out his silver brandy flask and drinks happily, taking a pull on his cigar. 'Ah. Aye. College. It is well that College cannot see YOU like THIS. Put the damper on the fun a little, eh? The best years of our life. Swimming in the Cam – diving for coins in the Pool – they call it Byron's Pool these days, old boy.'

The dying man can hear a low rumbling animal growl. It is the Bear, at Cambridge – who lives in the hexagonal tower above our rooms...

The Nightgowned Spirit bursts into laughter. 'Getting drunk and baiting the Bear. Arguing revolution with Hobby and 'Citoyen Matthews.' Sometimes drinking later than Scrope Berdmore Davies himself, God rest his soul, wherever it chuckles at present. Old Scrope! The drollest man alive... to see him was to want to BE him. At least it seemed so the glorious year of 1807...'

We had been in the country, making underage love and publishing underage verses, the previous year, and were not happy, but could not afford to return to College. When we got back from our involuntary year away, we found that all our Harrow friends were gone from Cambridge, and wrote Mama that she must never expect us to stay at Trinity now. We were more surly in our rooms than our bear, whom we had brought with us from the Abbey, and who was our only friend in Cambridge for that first long week of the new term.

We discovered that a Mr. Matthews had been occupying our rooms in our absence. Matthews, whom we hitherto knew but slightly, had been kind enough to leave a note on our table hoping that the room was as we might have wished it. Mr. Matthews trusted that he and his friends had not damaged Lord Byron's furniture, as they were unable to determine afterward what they had got up to on some of the nights they had used it. Matthews, in the same note, invited us to a dinner party of his intimate friends, on Saturday. These would be other boring undergraduates, and NOT alas our lost friends from Harrow, who had left College...

We had decided not to go when some nuance of wit in Matthews's note sent us along to meet our departed lodger. On such trifles do lives turn. Nothing we found in Cambridge has stayed with us as enduringly as what we found in Matthews's room that night. For Matthews himself – but that is another matter.

The evening opened with a discussion on the topic of our rooms. It seemed that Mr. Jones our tutor – I mean the tutor we shared with Matthews – in his odd way, had said, on putting him in, 'Mr. Matthews, I recommend to your attention not to damage any of the moveables, for Lord Byron, Sir, is a young man of *tumultuous passions*.' Matthews was delighted with this; and whenever anybody came to visit him, begged them to handle the very door with caution. Jones's phrase had put him into such a good humour, that I verily believe that I owed to it a portion of his good graces.

Matthews had been telling his friends that the young man of *tumultuous passions* was to come that night to Supper. It was on that account that I received the respect I was first granted by the other gentlemen present, one of them a Fellow of the College so much my senior in *haut ton* as to have already become an intimate acquaintance of that Dandy's Dandy, Brummell himself. Besides, the Fellow, Scrope, was five years older than us, and no doubt thought us callow enough at the time.

Scrope Davies was a harder drinker, wilier gambler, and faster seducer than we could ever have been, had not our fame somewhat subsequently influenced the cooperation of the fair sex in regard to the latter vice. If not for Matthews' introduction to the man, what interest could such as I have held for the inimitable Scrope, or even the other fellow – the arrogant, serious, radical reformer, Mr. Hobhouse? Since neither of them admired our lordly rank for its own sake.

The memory of Matthews, the cleverest young sodomite in Cambridge, sinks like smoke into oblivion, like memories of childhood, unreachable. The two other friends could be sitting across the death room from us now, here in Greece, they are so close still. But Matthews is quite gone.

'Careful,' the Spirit remarks. The dying body on the bed is trying to sit up, tries to look at the picture of the young Scrope and Hobhouse more intently, but finds itself falling into the frame of light... WE ARE THERE NOW, NOW, NOW...

Somewhere the Bear is snuffling, and growling softly. At the top of the stairs is uproar, seen in the dim light from the candles in the hands of the three young men. The Bear roars again. The young men's voices begin to shush each other. A bottle is dropped, scattering broken glass across the floor. LB's young, light voice: 'For Christ his sake be careful, Scrope. He ain't had breakfast yet.'

In the gloom, Scrope's voice. 'Let him try some of this. I breakfast on it every day.'

We see Scrope. Scrope! He leans toward the bear, holding

out his flask. The heavy growl of a large animal someone is pestering. A licking, slurping sound.

'Come, come, Alphonso. Just another drop, now.'

The next growl angry.

Hobhouse. His voice. Hobby! 'Slop it up, now. There's a good grizzly.'

Scrope, curiously: 'But why have you christened him Alphonso?'

'He is named for Sir Alphonse, the Dean of Studies.'

'I have it on good authority that he IS the Dean of Studies.' Scrope's voice coaxing: 'Come on Alphonso – force it down. Just another drop.'

The great beast, roaring, leaps and crashes to the floor.

'For God's sake Scrope, he'll break his chain...' – Hobby, anxious as usual.

Suddenly there is chaos in the near-darkness. 'Jesus he's got me Scrope!' The Bear has pinned LB's jacket to the ground with a hairy paw, snarling into our face.

Scrope, calmly: 'Now come along Alphonso, let go of Lord Byron's coat like a good grizzly, or he won't take you for your morning constitutional.' Scrope leans forward and does something to the bear's head. The Bear yelps in pain, retreating in fear from the small hard figure of Scrope, and lets go of us. 'Drink this, sir, it will calm your nerves...' – Scrope, by way of apology to the Bear. The Bear accepts the apology. Slurping sounds. Pleased with each other, Scrope and the Bear lean their heads together like old comrades. 'There, see, it's real Frog stuff ain't it? Pre-war stock. Drink it up. Why, it'll put hairs on your chest, man...'

Scrope's arm over Alphonso's shoulder, comrades again.

Hobby and ourself laughing. The Bear roars its reply,

laughing back at us, demanding more brandy, pawing at Scrope's flask. Scrope passes the beast what is left of the flask and has done with it till he judges the bear has finished. Then, despite the protests of ourself and Hobby, Scrope goes back for the empty flask, somehow managing to get it out of the huge animal's clutches. Before the Bear begins to protest more seriously the loss of the flask, we leave the Bear's room and descend the spiral iron stair to the main chamber.

We three. Scrope Berdmore Davies – the Birdmore – small, hard and handsome, and already, at Cambridge, a hard work-ing gambler by profession. Behind Scrope the more faithful, but duller companion – Mr. John Cam Hobhouse. We all display the bright crazy manner of young men drunk, rather than the cynical bitter fatigue of the older toper.

Scrope may, in his accustomed fashion, already have preceded his two friends in this matter – there is already a sense of deadly languor about all his movements, as if he is too bored to go through the motion of breathing. He pokes up the fire in the grate and turns his flask upside down glumly. 'Was there a hole in the flask or did that ursine swine get the lot?'

'He appreciated it Scrope. Our Alphonso has superior taste to your common or garden Dean. His is the very aris-tocracy of bearhood.'

'I could never abide a bear that could not hold his drink.' Scrope tosses the flask carelessly aside. He reaches inside his coat. 'Medicinal supplies. An emergency, I think.' Taking out a second flask, he toasts us: 'Gentlemen: Scrope drinks to you. Good health and a short sweet life.'

Scrope passes the flask to us. 'Good health and a short sweet life.' We try to pass the flask to Hobhouse who makes a gesture of refusal. We passes the flask back to Scrope who with a flourish puts it away. He takes a pinch of snuff, in a familiar gesture of the Nightgowned Spirit (which both have learned from Brummell), offers a pinch to us, and gestures at Hobhouse. 'O have we drunk enough, fides Horatio?'

Ourself and Scrope laughing at Hobhouse, whose duty now is to refuse to be discomfited. 'Satis sum, satis es, satis est. It seemeth to John Cam that when gentlemen retire, the drinking ought to be refined rather than otherwise.' Hobby walks over to our sideboard of decanters and glasses. 'Gentlemen: we are not in the field.' He pours three overlarge brandies and seats himself facing us.

Hobhouse breaks the silence. 'Where did Matthews go to? Were we not drinking with him in Town an hour ago?'

Scrope laughing. 'He met a young man outside the inn with whom he claimed an earlier acquaintance.'

'I doubt not it was a pretty young man enough.' John Cam's distaste for such activity is as evident as his fascination with its perpetrator Matthews, the French revolutionary 'Citoyen,' to whom the political Hobhouse is as devoted as a dull moth to a bright star.

Scrope takes snuff. 'The Citoyen might have done better to tell his friend Lamb of the advisability of an apology. To kiss and make up is always the best part of duelling. However, it is too late to pass the matter over. I did little enough to provoke the fellow.'

We coughs. 'Poor distressed Lamby said you 'hinted at his illegitimacy,' Scrope.'

'In a manner of speaking.' We look up, waiting for the Word. 'I called him a damned adulterous bastard.'

The others laugh, but concern shadows Hobhouse's face. 'You called Lamb out?'

'I should have remembered not to speak to the cur, for I am much annoyed with him. He *is* a damned adulterous bastard, you know. I doubt he will come to the appointment when he has a chance to think about it sober – too windy to try his aim 'gainst the Birdmore, sir.'

'You think him windy?' Hobhouse, who dislikes duels, is hopeful.

Scrope yawns. 'I do not expect to give myself the pleasure of seeing him on the field of honour at dawn. He will have to leave College, however, if he is not there, for Matthews will not let such a good story go by without telling it all over Cambridge.'

'You never know. Lamb may still be drinking.' We pulls out from our jacket a small pocket-pistol. 'Have you seen these? I always carry a pair – you can settle matters on the spot. Why wait till dawn, for seconds and apologies and suchlike shite?'

Scrope takes the proffered weapon. 'Loaded?'

'Of course.'

Hobhouse vainly tries to prevent what happens next. 'In the devil's other name, Scrope, it is three of the clock or after...' as Scrope, snapping out of his drunken languor for a moment, turns expertly with the pistol, cocking as he turns, and fires, the noise excruciating inside the room, at a bottle which is on a high shelf on the opposite wall. The bottle explodes, a shower of red wine deluging the mess of books and clothes in the unfortunate corner. Acrid smoke hangs in the air as Hobhouse's heart pounds in his ears. Scrope hands the pistol back to LB and relapses into his languid posture in the armchair.

Loud choruses of: 'In God's name, Byron...' and so on begin from the adjoining rooms on milord's stair. In time the protests die away, and Scrope remarks, apropos of nothing: 'Damn.'

'What matter, dear fellow?'

'I was trying to knock off the neck only. I grow old, my dear fellows, old.'

We takes out our other pistol. We turns and fires at another bottle, this time succeeding in shooting away the top third – approximately the neck, as Hobhouse puts his hands over his ringing ears. 'Like that?'

Scrope languidly turns to look at our bottle. 'No. Just the neck.'

A renewed chorus of protest from the adjoining rooms. The Bear wakes up, roaring, choked back by the chain. The thudding and moaning of the drunken beast upstairs is more disturbing, somehow, than the protests of human neighbours. 'Perhaps it is time to draw the line, gentlemen. We seem to have awoken the Dean of Studies.'

A silence. Soon Hobhouse, recovering from the noise and the fright, is chuckling about something. Scrope is ever anxious not to miss a joke; he has no scruple in using other people's jokes, and has been known to write them down in a notebook before he goes to sleep. 'What is it, dear fellow?'

Hobhouse giggles: 'Just the neck...' His mood changes. He picks up the decanter and pours us each another drink gloomily. 'That Bear will come down those stairs and be the death of us all one dark night. Who could blame him? To share rooms with wicked lords is not fit for man nor beast.'

'O, he's a sweet-tempered Bear enough sober. You don't know that Bear as I do, Hobby. I took him for a walk around Town today and introduced him to the Fellows. *Some* of them were charmed.'

'I am surprised the Fellows do not object to your keeping a Bear in your rooms since they made you send your dog back to Newstead.'

'They have forbidden me to keep my dog here and be damned to them. But there is nothing in the college constitution concerning BEARS, as I made sure to tell them, having checked the document myself. And he is a very civilised bear.'

Hobhouse laughing, his jowly face forgetting itself, the time we love the pompous oaf best. For Hobhouse knows, at least, how to drink and laugh – no hope for them as laughs, as the preacher saith when he heareth the sniggering from the congregation. 'We shall see what they have to say tomorrow about bears and pistols in rooms.'

Scrope yawns. 'I grow old. Tomorrow you say? God keep us in good health till then. Tomorrow and tomorrow, petty pace and all that. Methinks I had better pettypace it off to mon repos for the night. Seeing as I may have an adulterous bastard to accommodate with an exchange of shots at dawn. Then a pause for breakfast and a short nap – since I grow old – before an engagement over luncheon with a foolish young man who wishes to teach me a lesson at dice that methinks will melt away his poor patrimony.'

Scrope drains his glass, takes a pinch of snuff. 'I won three hundred from the fellow on a tennis match. Does he think to best me at rolling the cube now that he has lost with the rounder ball?' Scrope shakes his head tolerantly. 'But early to bed early to rise, you know. Scrope were ever a prudent fellow.'

He gets up and walks with exaggerated care to the door, pulls off a hook a cocked hat with an enormous feather, and strolls back toward his friends. Without warning he transforms his languid posture into a grotesque parody of Edmund Kean's

Hamlet, emits a groaning roar and lurches toward Hobhouse whom he grips by the throat, screaming into John Cam's face: 'O GOOD HORATIO, I'LL TAKE THE GHOST'S WORD... FOR A THOUSAND POUND!' He lets go of Hobhouse and, po-faced, picks up his silver sword-stick from beside his own chair to run out of the door chuckling.

Hobhouse's smile follows him to the door. 'Sometimes I fear our friend must come to a bad end.'

We reach forward to pour us both more brandy. 'Have you ever wondered how and why he manages to keep busy every hour God sends? As if he could not live with the thought of an empty minute.'

'Saying – tomorrow you say, Sir? God keep us in good health till then.'

'What a man, though, Hobby, a MAN... he actually does not give a curse. A *superior man*, a SUPERMAN if he had but the inclination...'

John Cam, the ardent democrat, is scornful. 'Scrope himself would never listen to such nonsense.'

'Mind you, mind you, look at France, Hobby. The common herd first smashes down the barriers, so that the thing may be permitted to happen – then out of their mass can arise the better man, Bonaparte, out of them and over them...'

'Bonaparte?'

'Not just Bonaparte! Can you not grasp the essential principle for Christ his sake, a *man* need not follow the common herd whether the herd be of lords or ploughboys...'

'With no doubt a separate herd for each...'

'I am not talking patents of nobility! A MAN... can be above all THEIR plans for him, the plan of the well-trodden paths. Keep a bear? A MAN could keep a tiger, Hobby, a real man could do what it occurs to him to do as he crawls under the stars... as he roams the face of the planet...'

'And a real woman?'

'And a real woman too.'

Hobhouse pours more drink. 'God forbid that whole nations may not come to believe as you do, or they will sleep-walk into madness and mass murder of the lesser beings, following such a man.'

We walk to the window, draw the heavy muffling drapes and throw open the casement. Bird song invades the room. That flat cool Cambridge light. 'Dawn, Hobby. Hark at the birds. I wonder if Scrope hath shot Lamby yet for his pains?'

'What about MY pains? If I do not get another drink soon the blasted *headache* will begin.' With resigned logic, Hobhouse pours another glassful. His hand shakes. 'O God... we will suffer untold agonies for this.'

'God had little to do with it. We should only suppose that he provided the sunlight which ripened the grapes.' We walk over to pick up the pistol, and hold it thoughtfully against our cheek. 'I 'gin to grow aweary of the sun. Did you know, Hobby, that some of the fellows, the other day, were talking about playing an imaginary game, like roulette. Instead of spinning a wheel for the purpose, you would make the wager with a pistol having a dozen barrels, only one of which was loaded with powder and shot, and would fire. And hold it to your head. A sport, by Jove – a wager worth making.'

Hobhouse clutches his aching head. 'For Christ his sake don't fire it now, the blasted BEAR will come down...'

'I want you to remember something for me...'

The pain in Hobhouse's head seems to swell. 'It had better be worth it...'

'I think to take to pistols soon/And blow my brains across the moon.' Not bad?'

Hobhouse considers. 'I suppose it has a certain ring to it.'

'A man could use such a pair of lines somewhere. Do you think you shall recall them for me?'

Hobhouse belches idly. 'Indelibly forever, dear boy.' The young men grin at each other. The two lines have already vanished, sacrificed to that moment. John Cam's mood changes. 'Ah – it's just that blasted SKULL talking. You ought never to go back to the Abbey. Keep away from dead monks and live mamas. Sell the gloomy damned place. Or at least go somewhere else for the summer.'

'I have already given our holiday some thought, dear fellow. Do you remember what Scrope said as he left?'

'O good Horatio I'll take the ghost's word for a thousand pound.' What of it?'

'You do not yet know his meaning. Can you remember back to last month, in London, when we abandoned Scrope, losing heavily at dice in the Union, only to find him in the morning curled like a dragon guarding treasure about a chamber pot filled with banknotes. Thousands of pounds sterling – crammed, any way, and won, Scrope knew not how...'

Hobhouse smiling. 'I remember...'

'The Birdmore has consented to continue to service my debts with that ill-gotten cash, so that we may go abroad. With specific instruction that, after they have quit the unwholesome city of Cambridge, he take with him his prudent friend Mr. John Cam Hobhouse on an improving expedition to the East in the hopes that his lordship might have at least a decent chance of returning and, he says, and that Mr. Hobhouse may broaden his narrow opinions by seeing a little more of the world.'

Hobhouse instantly on his guard. 'Take Hobhouse? Where?'

'The Isles of Greece!' We slumps back into our chair, thinking about the logistical problems. Sleep is rushing up on us like a runaway coach.

On Hobhouse too the night has taken its toll. 'Greeshe?'

We grunts sleepily and passes out in the armchair. After a short interval, our prudent friend does the same.

Chapter five

I beg leave to observe that intrigue here is the business of life; when a woman marries she throws off all restraint, but I believe their conduct is chaste enough before.

All very well for Scrope to undertake to stave off creditors for us while we were gone. Scrope's loan underwrote our debts to the level of several thousands of pounds (God bless the Birdmore's heart and chamber pot) but that merely serviced our most pressing debts. We still didn't have enough to go abroad unless we planned on coming back in a fortnight. See us, LB, then, putting the spurs to Hanson, the family lawyer, to borrow some more on our much-encumbered estates, that have been so mortgaged by the Wicked Lord before us as to seem tied round our neck like a millstone. It was having the damned places as a PROSPECT that encouraged us to live like the lord we were. We should have been a model of prudence else.

Hanson, our lawyer all our life, was useless as ever he was and would be. However, needs must when the devil drove – and the help of Scrope's four thousand was not quite enough lucre to launch us on Europe. So we coolly took a few thousand more from a usurer, signing a promissory note to pay over the next ten years.

Anything, so long as we could get away. The party to consist of Hobby, to whom we promise to advance a thousand for the trip, our valet Fletcher, and the young boy Robert Rushton, son of one of our tenants whom God help us we fancied but never touched. Robert we planned to send home as soon as we headed into Turkey, where the natives are not so particular about the honour of young boys.

Can youth itself be compared to the feeling of going on a holiday? And going on holiday when YOUNG – why, as Mr. Wordsworth said of the French Revolution (before he turned his coat to a Tory one) – 'twas very heaven. Remember Hobby smiling then, riding for the pleasure of it up on top with the coachman as the coach rattled through the splendid rolling hills of South Cornwall, with prospects of the distant sea upon which we were about to launch ourselves. Hobby's face, smiling with the joy of youth in the open air.

Like any sailor's town Falmouth was full of whores aye of both sexes too. Hobhouse wrote from Falmouth to the Citoyen, Matthews, the only complete sodomite of our acquaintance, and thinking that Hobhouse's epistle did not get to the point of the place, we added to the letter a reference to Hyacinthus, the boy loved by Apollo (writing to Matthews, obscurely, as scholar to scholar, for sodomy was a hanging offense if proved): *I take up the pen which our friend has for a moment laid down merely to express a vain wish that you were with us in this delectable region, as I do not think Georgia itself can emulate in capabilities or incitements to the 'Plen. and optabil. – Coit.' the port of Falmouth and parts adjacent. – We are surrounded by Hyacinths and other flow-*

ers of the most fragrant nature, and I have some intention of culling a handsome Bouquet to compare with the exotics we expect to meet in Asia.

Despite our boast to Matthews, we were aware of the watchful eye of Hobhouse and left the boys to the real sailors. We followed Hobhouse's virtuous lead and made the acquaintance of some of the delightful ladies of the docklands. Thus sanctioned by the pious example of Hobhouse, we plunged into the cunts of Falmouth with a will. Plunged then through the clean sea that washed away the dirt of the English port, going as if underwater and coming up in another world...

But Lisbon was a great disappointment. After we had got over the novelty of seeing lemons everywhere on trees and tasting them in our pilaff, and biting into as many sweet oranges as we wanted, we were dismayed at the squalor of the old port. It was as if, under the strain of that poverty produced by the recent wars against the French, the whole town had been reduced to the moral level of the London docks. It was worse than Falmouth ever could have been.

A few days later Hobby and I, fired by the glorious view of it seen from our boat, set out for the beautiful town of Cintra fifteen miles from the capital. Here was beauty, we saw, staring up at the palaces and gardens rising out of the midst of rocks, cataracts and precipices. White churches and convents on stupendous heights, a distant view of the River Tagus. We climbed the heavenly hill in the golden sunshine. The scent of mountain thyme blew along the path, a cool breeze was lifting off the sea. 'Cintra is the most beautiful town on Earth,' we pronounced. Hobhouse gave us a look that said, yes, and only the second town outside of your native country you have ever seen.

We (we mean ourself – Hobhouse could not swim) decid-ed to swim across the broad estuary of the Tagus before we left the coast.

Hobhouse, standing on his rocky hill, looked out anx-iously at the dot that was us, crossing slowly, so slowly, the immense blue gulf below. The dear fellow told us later he could not repress the tears of relief when he saw the belov-ed dot gain the far shore. A fine experience for us, also. But other than that glorious swim, the whole country of Portu-gal had a dejected feel to it, like a whore somebody had been cruelly beating for too long. God he knows we had soon had enough of the place, and were itching to see more of this southern world.

Hobhouse procured the horses. John Cam's was a fiery black stallion, and ours, at our particular impulse, a more polite chestnut mare. Napoleon's generals and Wellington's levies having so lately contested the Iberian peninsula, it was with a delicious sense of our own daring that we two friends crossed Spain; the best gallop of our lives. Leaning across the pommel, gripping our pommels for safety, in an exhilaration beyond fear we pounded down the hardpacked roads, racing ahead of our luggage and servants.

At the Spanish border we found there was almost noth-ing to separate the two countries, enemies since the dawn of time: deep in the mountains, a tiny stream glittered silver in a gloomy narrow canyon. We were astounded to think of the blood that must have been shed to establish this insignificant line on the map. 'A lame man, such as myself, could step across this puddle with ease,' we remarked, fascinated. We did so.

On into Spain: where the men were not yet slaves, as they seemed to be in Portugal. So much to admire in the proud fierceness of the Spanish people. The country as well as the people grew yet more rugged, dry rocky mountains capped with snow, peak behind peak ascending to heaven. We had to get off and walk upon certain steeper parts of the ascent as we crossed the Sierra Morena. None of the mountains in Scotland had prepared us for *this*.

Each night, to the delight of ourself and the chagrin of Hobhouse, there was nothing to eat but eggs fried in olive oil, bread, and rough black wine to wash the greasy mixture down. We grinned each supper time at John Cam's discomfiture, oil and egg yoke on our lips. Accustomed as we were to dieting against our tendency to put on flesh, it was a feast. We were getting so much exercise on our travels that we knew we would not grow fat again until we reached a city. On such fare we rode seventy miles a day, making Hobby and ourself as thin as whippets. This was life.

Hobhouse complained always of the lack of beef and beer but was glad enough of the furious riding; even Hobby could not help but be a young man sometimes. We were pleased by the delightful town of Seville, and by Cadiz, so pretty and neat and clean in the winter sun. There we met our first foreign damsel of rank, a dark beauty, daughter of an Admiral, who contrived to squeeze next to us in the box at the opera. We made the usual approaches. The return offer being, to our no little surprise, that if his pretty lordship would but wait a month until the lady was married, he would have nothing denied him...

A young lady's chastity there was *expected* to perish with the maidenhead she gave to the husband, who should tolerate her amours as long as he had been the first to bite the cherry. This was a foretaste of a delightful European custom.

By the time we reached Malta, gateway to Italy, we were prepared in continental ways and able to walk straight into a fullblown love affair with a lady of our own rank, Mrs. Spencer Smith. The 'noble Fletcher', our valet, was always an encumbrance, lamenting with Hobhouse the lack of beef and beer, but Fletcher at least understood our ways with the fair sex. To Hobhouse of course we were all cynicism about the new affair. But when confronted with this married, beautiful and adventurous lady of our own rank, we could not help wonder a little worriedly if we had found ourself a reason to live after all.

It was true that Constance was married, but the husband (good fellow) was not with her. She was quite as accustomed to travelling as ourself, had been born at Constantinople, daughter to the Austrian ambassador, and had married an Englishman in the foreign service who had managed to annoy Napoleon so much that the wife had twice had to flee French custody to escape the Emperor's wrath.

Sweet Constance. A delightfully musky German smokiness in her voice... We did not pick up the joke that occurred to us – Inconstance... but scribbled her verses, wherein she became Sweet Florence.

Mrs. Spencer-Smith. The moment, at the consul's party, that we started to talk with this lady, tall, cool, dark and elegant, but with the blue-eyed paleness of the north, like unto our own, and the husky foreign voice, we were completely charmed. We could see by the glitter in the lady's eye that our feelings were reflected. It was a character much like ours, and there was only one other female we had seen who had a face more like our own: our forbidden half-sister Augusta. Love at first sight for the Narcissus that we were. Plenum et optabile coitum took just a little longer.

We got away from Hobhouse for a few days to make love to the lady a little. Sure enough after a few days of wining and dining and the sending of poems addressed to her wonderful selfregarding self (much like our own), she yielded herself up entirely, and it was outside, in broad daylight, after an agreeable ride into the countryside for the purposes of a picnic, that she smilingly disrobed in front of our astonished eyes.

The lady was beautiful. She stood there casual as a dockside whore, gazing at us with the large blue eyes so like our own. Her hair, long, black and very fine, streamed behind her in the breeze, which had perked up her nipples not a little. The silken bush at her lap was sculpted into a perfect triangle, whether by nature or artifice we could not determine.

We knelt and leant our head against the soft belly reverently. She began to remove our shirt. We unbuttoned our breeches. She kissed us, rolled on top of us, apparently in no need of further dalliance. Nothing loth, we plunged into the dark bush between the pale thighs, again and again, and, as we spent, registered with alarm that this lady our social equal was coming too, the blue eyes wild with a frenzy that equalled our own. 'Ich komme, ich komme,' she shouted in the language of her childhood.

At that time we were more used to whores and chambermaids, and found it a little frightening to make love with an equal who took an equal pleasure in the event. But we performed the act once more before we left the charming spot, under the cool shade of a tree by a stream. She would not lie with us again, once back in the town, but together we vowed eternal love and planned to meet in a year's time at Malta.

Chapter six

The mildest mannered man that ever scuttled ship or slit a throat.

L B and Hobhouse launched themselves, next, on His Majesty's
brig-of-war the *Spider*, which gave them passage across
the blue Ionian sea to fabled Greece. The ship docked briefly
at Patras to take on stores, and in order to feel the soil of
Greece under their feet they disembarked and went into a
currant ground to practice shooting.

That same day they sailed on to Prevesa. At the ship's
rail, gazing with Hobhouse across the Gulf of Lepanto, they
asked a friendly officer the name of the dismal, marshy-look-
ing place they could see through the haze, that very first day
in Greece. 'That, sir, is the town of Missolonghi,' the young
lieutenant answered, grinning. 'As godforsaken a spot as you
will discover in these seas.'

As they looked at the blurred, dank looking place, they
were overcome with a feeling of horror, the sensation commonly referred to as if someone is walking over one's grave.
The lagoon and marshes had a seedy, tropical look. 'It is
like,' Hobhouse remarked, being classical, 'the gardens full
of willows and dangling pomegranate outside the entrance to

Hades' kingdom, in the Odyssey, when Odysseus journeys to the House of the Dead...'

Homer was much on their minds. They knew that at some point they would have to sail past Odysseus's Ithaca, which LB was already talking of purchasing – one of the officers had remarked that it was for sale.

From Prevesa they rode, with their valet and a new Greek hireling called Jorgos, or as Hobhouse would insist on calling him, George, to the town of Jannina, ruled by a tough Turk called Ali Pasha. In front of the town walls was a corpse dangling from a tree. The English travellers exchanged raised eyebrows as they rode past into the town. The arm and side of the body had been torn away and the dogs below were quarrelling over the meat. 'A patriot,' LB remarked grimly, 'as was.'

Ali Pasha, the terrible Turk they had heard of, had also heard of *them*. He had good reason to want to get the English on his side, since the war seemed to be going against the French. And a strange notion of the importance of an obscure English lordling to the English government... To oblige the two obscure Englishmen, the Pasha, who was not at Jannina, had left them an escort of Albanian troops with instructions to take them to visit his castle in Tepelene, further north in Albania, or Macedonia as Hobhouse insisted on calling it. The Pasha had treated them like dignitaries of state, and they were not loth to take advantage of the man's misapprehension of their true status in England.

The sights on that mountainous route LB would relish for a lifetime, though Hobhouse could only grumble at the hardships of the journey. The precipitous roads had been washed away by torrential storms, and a distance of some seventy five miles took all of a week's travelling. 'Dammit, Hobhouse,' he complained, as Hobhouse cursed his goat meat dinner for the tenth time, 'have the goodness to reflect that you are penetrating into Albania, a region only seen by one other of your countrymen, the intrepid Mr. Leake. Why...' – he grinned wolfishly before John Cam could suggest another route – 'it is an ADVENTURE into the unknown, man! These hills – did you ever see anything so wild? Think what this Ali Pasha may be, who can hold such a land in his hand.'

'A killer of patriots, to be sure,' snarled Hobhouse, stomping off to his bug-infested bed with ill grace, leaving his friend grinning over the bottle of cloudy village wine.

At five in the afternoon the next day, with the sun sinking like a ship in the west, the party cantered into Tepelene. The bustle around the town was piquant, even to the exhausted Hobhouse. The Albanians in their white kilts and red, gold-encrusted jackets, bristling with silver handled knives and pistols and the like; the Turks with their flowing pelisses and turbans; and the grinning black slaves who came out of the town to take charge of the travellers' horses. Boys were calling the faithful to prayer from the minaret of the mosque; but the Christian travellers were politely ushered into clean cool rooms, where the vizier's secretary, bearing presents of sherbet, came to enquire after their health, and to invite them to meet his Pasha on the morrow. Hobhouse for once did not curse his dinner, which was a delicately cooked selection of meats and vegetables brought to him with an acceptable wine. As his friend pointed out to him, the soft clean beds too were all that a man might desire. 'Where be your Christian bed to compare?' LB grinned, waving a chicken leg.

Next morning the pair dressed themselves grimly in full staff officer's suits, resplendently scarlet and complete with swords and gold epaulettes, that they had brought from England for just such an occasion. The splendid scarlet 'staff officers' were taken to see the great ruler of Albania and Western Greece by an obliging little doctor who seemed to understand the travellers' schoolboy Latin well enough to translate it into Turkish.

The friends marched bravely into the Presence, impressed not a little by the white marble room hung with red ottomans, and the cooling fountain splashing into a tiled pool in the middle of the room. *An alien world, to be sure, LB was thinking. This man is as powerful as any king in the world, in his own domain. He could strike off our heads and no one in these parts could say him nay, for the British Navy is far off.*

The old killer, Ali Pasha at last, fat and whitebearded, paid his respects to the English milord. Held LB's hand lingeringly, not bothering too much with the stolid John Cam, who clearly felt the slight not a little. Ali added (to rub Hobby's nose in it) through the interpreter, that he was sure of the identity of the LORD because of his curling hair and little white hands. His lordship risked a tiny smile at Hobhouse as this was translated. 'You must visit me at night, pretty youth,' Ali continued, 'when I am more at leisure.'

The unlikely blue eyes in the nest of brown wrinkled fat twinkled incongruously.

I know that game, he thought, *and I will not play it with such as you.* Nevertheless he was happy to take a pipe of opium and a cup of coffee with the ruler, who requested that the young lord think of him as a FATHER while in his dominions. He made his retreat from the Presence, not without another smirk at Hobhouse as they walked away. 'You should have more respect, Hobby, for a patent of nobility,' he murmured. 'These Turks, now, have the right idea...'

Thereafter, throughout the afternoon, gifts of sweet-meats, sugared almonds and the like, appeared twice an hour from the ruler to the young lord. With the repeated request that the young lord visit the pasha AT NIGHT – when, Ali said, he was more at leisure from the cares of office. Much to Hobhouse's relief, the young lord always turned in early with a virtuous expression.

After some days of this it was time to leave. LB, talking to this charming (charmed) old man, could not get out of his head the thought of the hanging corpse with arm and side torn away, swinging in the wind before the gates of Jannina. This marble room with its sparkling fountain of cool water was paid for by slavery and death. Was this the meaning of wealth in a country? Nevertheless, the fascination of those pale blue eyes in the old pirate's face, that had decreed so much cruelty in the name of order. For Ali was a great general – known as the Mahometan Bonaparte thereabouts.

The pair rode out of the place with the blessing of Ali Pasha and a letter of introduction to his son Veli, Pasha of all the Morea, the Pelopponese. The old man had given them a new servant Vascilly (Hobhouse called him Basil), a brave Albanian and an old soldier. Ali was joking with Vascilly and the Albanian guard as the travellers mounted.

'What did he say?' LB asked one of the Albanians who could speak a little Greek.

The man's eyes were not smiling. 'He says if we do not keep you safe he will cut off our bollocks.' He did not laugh, for he could see that with the men it was not a matter of joking. He nodded politely at Ali for the last time as they cantered out of the town, the old man nodding and smiling benignly.

On the last day of October his lordship, a little jealous of the piling-up pages of Hobhouse's meticulous and tedious journal, began a long poem to record his impressions of the places they were seeing. He invented a moody narrator, a sort of fantasy figure of himself, and thinking of the fascination of Ali's wickedness, gave his alter ego a gloomy past he himself did not yet have. This made for fun in the scribbling. After all, he thought, no one will want to read it. He enjoyed writing it more than any satire he had yet composed, and christened the piece, a little solemnly, 'Childe Burun.'

He did not show it, for once, to John Cam's critical (generally encouraging) eye. It was too revelatory of his own fantasies, though the rhyme scheme, he believed, was respectable enough. Riding over the mountains of Albania, he had been reading parts of *The Faerie Queene* of sweet master Spenser, in a little pocket book called Elegant Selections. This stanza would do as well as another, he thought, and soon began to hear the metre in the very hoofbeats of the horses.

Ali had offered the travellers the use of an armed vessel to get the Byronic party from Prevesa to Patras. The fierce-looking troops on board and the big cannon lying around the deck were reassuring in waters infested with pirates. But here LB learned the only important lesson he would learn about sailing: never trust your lives to a Turkish crew. Only the Greeks and the English seemed to have the knack of navigating the world in comparative safety.

For God's sake, LB thought, as Hobhouse worried, this is not a storm. Hobhouse agreed, but could not help but be alarmed by the panic of the crew as the wind rose in the rigging. They did not furl the sails in time and a sail split. LB's valet Fletcher yelled for the wife in England, the Greeks called on the Saints, the Mussulmen yelled for Allah, and the Captain burst into tears and told his passengers to call on God.

Hobhouse was irritated at the sheer incompetence on display; his courage, as ever, burst out in indignation. His friend lay down in a corner of deck with his cloak wrapped about him to keep out the hissing rain. He loosened his upper garments, prepared to make a swim for it. An Albanian capote, best wool in the world, so greasy it kept out water; the great cloak flapped like a tent about him as he observed dispassionately the crew's incompetence.

Night drew on and the storm rose. At last the Greek sailors on board were allowed by the Turks to take charge, and the boat sailed free before the storm, which was after all not so very great. The Greeks were in charge of the boat. An omen, LB thought, of what could happen in this benighted country, if the Greeks could take it back. Meanwhile, the storm raged, the Turks screamed like women, and the impetuous sea was making a habit of sweeping the deck in a white froth. For a long while it seemed that the ship should be hurled onto the rocky coast of Corfu.

In the event, the boat was driven onto the coast of Suli on the mainland. He examined his courage in the cold light of day, on firm ground. He could see that Hobhouse was pleased with himself, but he was a little chilled to recollect his own sensations, lying there on the deck, waiting for the chance to disport in the tall waves without benefit of ship. *God help us,* he thought, *we did not even care about the probability of that happening but relished the idea like a fool. As if we wanted to die.*

The travellers returned to Prevesa with all their luggage, Fletcher, and the old Albanian servant. The party ambled disconsolately on muleback to the very port they had just tried to leave. On firm land, the next day, the friends looked at each other over a celebratory bottle of wine at luncheon, if, Hobhouse thought, gazing ruefully at another steaming plate of rank goat meat, you could call it luncheon.

Still and all, thought John Cam, we are alive, and may live to taste English beef yet. 'My dear fellow,' he remarked to his friend, as he pushed his dinner aside. 'You may do as you wish but I for one am not risking a Turkish boat on a serious voyage. We shall go on by land.'

'To Missolonghi by land? There are a thousand men, individually and in tribes, waiting in line to cut the throat of us TOURISTS between here and there, for our boots and our purses.' He smiled, enjoying his wine and the sensation of remaining alive for a little longer under this sun that shone so agreeably in the little garden behind the inn.

Hobhouse was adamant. 'I should rather hire us a bodyguard than risk another Turkish ship at sea.'

'To be sure, we could hire a few score cut-throats of our own, to scare away the others. Cut-throats are plentiful, and cheap in these parts.'

In a few days a wild squadron of redcoated brigands had been gathered. LB cantered out proudly at the head of his little army, long steel swords and musket barrels all a-glitter in the sun. LB's valet, the noble Fletcher, had his eyes almost popping from his head as milorde, resplendent in scarlet uniform with gold epaulettes, led his first command out of the town and into the bandit-infested mountain passes.

'After all,' said Hobhouse, 'it's safer than a ship.'

'When we lived near the barracks of Ali's Albanian troops I never found soldiers so honest, not in Gibraltar and Malta where there were Spanish, French, Sicilian and British troops in abundance. In the Albanian barracks we had nothing stolen, and were always welcome to their provisions and milk. These men are exactly like those others.'

The fifty tough-looking, well-armed riders in the band did indeed frighten all the other banditti away, so that there was not even a threat of an attempt on the party. And the Albanians were altogether a grand bunch of lads to be on a Greek mountain with. That night they had a great party by firelight, Hobhouse and LB as drunk as all the rest. A goat was slaughtered, its throat slit casually by a laughing fellow, using his bright curved sword, and amid much excitement one among their number produced a sack of squid he had bought in the port, which he chopped and fried in olive oil and wild garlic, lemon juice and *rigani*, the wild oregano that grew in fragrant clumps all around the camp. Meat, fish, wine, oil and bread: a supper that would not have disgraced Odysseus himself.

The men, being Albanians and not Greeks, sang songs rather than told stories as the wine was poured, and soon began their wild dancing around the fire. The kilted horsemen threw down their sabres and joined hands, bounding, man linked to man, in a circle around the fire, yelling their uncouth dirge. LB found out the first line, getting a rough translation into Greek from his new servant Vascilly, and mentally rendered it: 'O, who is more brave than the dark Suliote/ In his snowy camese and his shaggy capote...?' His eyes glittering in the firelight, he turned to the grinning Hobhouse. 'These men are the descendants of Alexander's soldiers, who conquered the world.' The song went on to boast of piracy, and the cutting of a glorious number of civilian throats in the name of their last Pasha.

Everyone, save two lookouts, fell asleep drunk on the open mountain wrapped only in a cloak and a skinful of wine. LB awakened at dawn and saw the brassy blaze across the rocky horizon. He turned his head and, deeply startled, found himself gazing up into the devil's eyes of a curious mountain goat that had unwisely wandered into the camp. He cried out, thinking for a second that the Devil had come for him. As the goat ran off, he turned and looked down at the mountains below and realised the distance they had travelled. The experience of a lifetime.

The two sentries were dozing over their muskets. He threw a pebble at one to wake him up.

The day of November 20th, in that year of 1809, lingered in LB's mind curiously. It was of no apparent consequence: the day they reached the miserable coastal village of Missolonghi, the marshy hellhole they had earlier seen from the vantage point of their boat. It was a miserable enough place to be sure, a town of fishermen's huts on a shallow, mosquito-infested lagoon navigable only by small boats. The travellers could hardly wait to be done with the place. One could reach a ship by prior appointment, venturing out in a boat. But the sea was empty of large ships, and cursing the town of Missolonghi, which (they thought) could not take offence, they continued to Patras. Happily a ship was waiting there, and took the whole party in the required direction, coasting east along the Gulf of Corinth.

The pair landed at one point, and stopped for a few days with an official, Andreas Londos, who, though in the employ of the Turks, and a pleasant enough young Greek noblemen, nevertheless burst into tears at their mention of the Greek patriot and songwriter murdered a generation ago by his Turkish masters. After a night of jokes and drinking and laughter, they were astonished to see this man's change of expression. 'Rhiga, Rhiga,' moaned the young man, clasping the Englishmen's hands, the tears streaming down his face. 'He was the poet of the Greek people, murdered by these butchers for writing a song...'

'Someday, soon now, these people will rise,' he told Hobhouse when they were in their beds.

'They will never do it alone,' Hobhouse said. 'We foreigners shall have to help them.'

'They do not want foreigners interfering. If a people want to be free they must first strike the blow themselves, so that they can place a proper value on freedom.'

Delphi was next on the itinerary. Hobhouse must see his damned ruins, and LB the home of the Muses, the Parnassus he as all poets must climb. Warily, the pair found a *Greek* commanded ship, and crossed the Gulf of Corinth again to the olive groves on the fertile Krisa plain, where Hobhouse had already advised LB they used to hold chariot races. As they were rowed ashore out of that numinous blue sea onto the golden beach, the black shapes of the mountains grew taller above them. In a fever of excitement they supervised the landing of the horses.

Over a hasty luncheon they checked the route with the local innkeeper. 'Take water,' the old man mumbled. 'And bring back pure water from the Spring.'

Their bellies full of hard bread, roasted goat, and sour red wine, the friends rode slowly up the broad flat valley toward the mountains. The road, scarcely a track, led them through the biggest olive grove in the world. The ancient trees, gnarled and thinly leaved, glistened with the hard green olives of the new crop, and the thin leaves provided scant shade from the noon sun above their heads. There were no dark shadows beneath the branches. Yet the stunted forest had its own effect. Spirits, if any, would flit through this dusty place light and dry, not like the dank heavy monsters one would expect to encounter in an English wood. Both men were pleased by the spirit of the place. 'The Krisa plain,' Hobhouse said pedantically, 'was the site of chariot races in the Pythian games, in honour of Apollo. In earlier times, the kings themselves took part in these races.'

'I'll race YOU now, to the foot of that hill there,' snarled his friend, exasperated at the continual lecture. He yelled back over his shoulder at Hobhouse. 'If you ever want your scribbling to be as good as your mind, you must learn to live in the here and now!' He had stolen a lead by starting before he had finished talking, leaving Hobhouse to gallop after him calling a foul.

They slowed their blown horses into a walk. John Cam was inexorable. 'The first priests of Delphi landed on the beach behind us, as we did. They came in a boat no doubt from Crete, they were strangers like us. They must have seen the potential of the spot as the centre of the world, which the ancients believed Delphi to be.'

The young men dismounted for a drink of water and to rest their panting horses before climbing the little hill. They had not seen so much as a shepherd boy since leaving the coastal village of Itea. LB handed his friend a crust of bread to chew, and a flagon of warm water to wash it down. The mountains looked, still, a long way off.

Somewhat later in the afternoon, the vague tracks became a road climbing toward the mountains. After a half an hour the village the townsmen of the shore had called Kastri became visible on the heights above. Hobhouse assured his friend that Kastri was built on the central part of the holy site of ancient Delphi. 'And shall,' he went on, 'have to be infallibly moved when the treasures beneath are excavated.'

'Easy for you to say,' grumbled his companion. 'Your family's house is not in the village.'

Both travellers were shocked at the lack of anything approaching a ruin on the famous site, this navel in the belly of the ancient world, where somewhere buried was the navel-stone, the omphalos, to mark that centre. A few marble columns, some fallen and broken, were all that remained of the great shrine. Hobhouse could scarcely contain his disappointment, and LB, growing irritated, limped off, the way being too steep for the horses, further up the mountain. He soon grew tired, his gammy foot aching, and sat down to rest. He seemed to be in some natural cup of the mountain, overgrown with wild herbs, but he saw it was not an amphitheatre – that shape he had already passed – but a long track that ended abruptly; a running track, he guessed.

Chuckling, the lame man rested his back on a convenient boulder. A running track. Something he would never find of use. He glanced up into the dazzling sky. Behind him he could see the great rocky masses that were the Phaidriades, and the steep and narrow cleft between the two mountains that vanished in thickets of scrub. Above holy Parnassos four eagles wheeled slowly in the updraft. His eyes slid off the dizzying sight and fell, down through the wooded plain to the distant Gulf of Corinth, a panorama of hazy blue. His gaze swept up again to the eagles, and he could feel through his back a sense of the ruined magnificence in the dirt beneath him. *The men of this country,* he thought, *are buried as the spirit of their land.* Greece was buried. It would be an awful mass of earth to shift. Yet eagles wheeled overhead, as they had done in the time of Pericles.

Coming back to rejoin Hobhouse he found that his friend had also wandered away. When Hobhouse came back it was clear that he too had had some sort of vision on the mountain. The two Englishmen ceased their bickering as they walked their horses slowly down the steep trail toward the foot of the holy cleft between the Phaidriades, where, the villagers said, they would find the Castalian spring.

Hobhouse explained that the priestesses and all suppliants for the oracle had first to purify themselves by bathing in the spring. Nothing loth, the two friends immersed their heads and hands in the little stream bubbling out of the foot of the cliff. It was so frighteningly, shockingly cold that they were unable to bear the touch of the water for more than a minute. Purification, the pain of the cold. The bright winter sun comforted them a little as they stared down solemnly at this snow water too pure and cold to touch. 'Well,' said LB to his friend, 'that's us clean.'

Later they came across a column, fallen out of thin air, out of history, in front of the gate of a wretched monastery that stood, very temporarily as it looked, beneath the wrathful earthquake-prone mountain and its poised masses of rock. 'The first tremor,' LB remarked, 'will sweep these fellows off the face of the earth.' Hobhouse suggested that they dismount to examine the broken pillar.

They scrawled their names side by side on the yellowing marble.

Chapter seven

The isles of Greece, the isles of Greece!
Where burning Sappho loved and sung...

Riding down from the pine covered hills of Fort Phyle, the plain of Athens, the Aegean and the Acropolis burst upon our eyes all at once. It was Christmas day in the South, a Christmas Day bright, sparkling and clear; white snow capped the peaks behind us. We cantered down through the olive groves above the city, crossed the Cephisus, and went under an arched gateway into this city that has been the mind of the Earth.

There was not an inn or hotel in the degenerate modern town of a thousand houses squatting wretchedly by the side of the Acropolis. The English consular assistant found us rooms in the home of a Greek widow, Widow Macri. Hobhouse looked at the consul's man strangely as he left us sitting with the widow. The three daughters hovered twittering in the background like hummingbirds, but even Hobhouse could scarcely believe that his majesty's consul had provided his majesty's subjects with a consular-appointed pimp.

We were soon disabused. The daughters were indeed for sale – the old lady let it be known she would take no less than six hundred English pounds sterling for each one of their hands in marriage. 'Why, the old bitch has got damn near two thousand pound of capital, Hobby. You should marry the OLD LADY and sell the gals yourself...'

Our own favourite was the youngest, Theresa, a girl of fourteen whose little buds were just beginning to swell. The presence of this innocent laughing girl – with whom we fell abruptly into mutual but unconsummated love – would provide an uneasy background for us as we made our rounds among the tiny but exclusive population of Franks, or westerners, in the city. But she was too young, so that we fought down our urges.

Dinner at the consul's. We proposed a competition among the western guests to make an epitaph upon the noble leaders of their own particular countries, and started the ball rolling with a lament for the not-yet-dead Lord Castlereagh: Ahem: 'Lines to be inscribed on the tomb of Lord Castlereagh,' or whatever it is to be called:

Posterity will ne'er survey
A nobler grave than this:
Here lie the bones of Castlereagh
Stop, traveller, and piss.'

Hobhouse roared his hearty appreciation as the table smiled uneasily, with many a glance at the consul, aghast at our jokes about the government that was providing the splendid dinner we were eating at that moment off His Majesty's very table...

Meanwhile, despite our distinct lack of £600 to spare, our feelings for the maid Theresa were growing. Her huge dark eyes, like those of a young deer, and the intensely black curls that tumbled around her shoulders, were never out of our thoughts. Theresa was helping us with our Romaic, or modern Greek. We saw her for a private lesson every day.

But somehow we always managed to keep our hands off the beautiful child and always felt ourself a better man for it. She was too pure.

There were plenty of other intrigues to engage in among the Franks in the place and all the parties. In Athens were numerous foreign women who did not stint their favours to a pretty young lord. The best harem we have ever lived in, excepting only Venice. And every day we rode out of the city with Hobby to one of the adjacent mountain peaks, with a view of Eleusis, Aegina, Salamis, names that have flashed continually in the night of time.

At last permission arrived from the Turkish authorities for us to visit the Acropolis. So we saw it at last up close, this god-built marble pile that we had caught glimpses of while slithering through the stinkingest alley of the town below. The actuality, close up, was no disappointment. We were dazzled at the aching broken beauty of the temple of Athena Nike – winged Athena, and so dazed at the Parthenon we had to sit down on a massive step and look down on the broken columns of the other temples below, as the fluffy white clouds massed over the distant hills.

We were outraged at the Turkish gun emplacements commanding the heights. The place, Hobhouse told us, was used by the Turks as an armoury. It had been a stray cannon shot exploding this armoury that had recently destroyed both the Turkish powder and a good deal of the building, including the roof.

'The damned Turks,' we said to Hobby, 'have then done more damage to this beauty in an instant than the ages could do since the time of Christ.'

We were rendered more furious by the sight of the Acropolis marbles being removed by Lord Elgin's men for transferral to London. 'When we went to see the marbles in London you called them naught but a mass of crumbled limestone,' said Hobhouse. 'You were all wrong there and you are wrong now. These stones, in London, will benefit supremely the rising generation of English architects and sculptors.'

He was so annoying that we responded in anger and said too much. 'I was wrong because I had not before seen them in their natural surroundings, and realized of what magnificence they were a part. It is CRIMINAL to take them away from here, to benefit English sculpture, an art of which the English are as capable as the Egyptians are of ice-skating.'

In a sulk, Hobby and I separated, and we scribbled, sitting in the temple of Athena, a few lines to that lady, patron of the city.

> Ancient of days! august Athena! where,
> Where are thy men of might? Thy grand in soul?
> Gone – glimmering through the dream of things that were…
> …o'er each mouldering tower,
> Dim with the mist of years, grey flits the shade of power.

The argument over the Elgin marbles was still not settled when we rode out to Sounion, lookout post for ancient Attica, the ruins of a temple of Poseidon on the heights overlooking the sea. While Hobhouse pottered about with tourist guide and compass at the foot of the broken columns trying to trace the history of each fallen stone, we settled ourself with our back on a piece of Doric pillar. We sat there an hour gazing out at the immense jewelled mass of glittering sea dotted with steep green islands as far as the horizon. Each one an isle of Greece, with a name and history and myth and spirits of its own...we were scribbling a little from time to time...

The isles of Greece, the isles of Greece!
Where burning Sappho loved and sung,
Where grew the arts of war and peace...

'What are you doing?' asked Hobhouse, coming up and interrupting us at some crucial point in the verse. Comme d'habitude.

We were still sulking a little. 'O nothing...' we muttered, covering this scribble, but seeing the hurt in Hobhouse's eyes we were sorry. Hobhouse was invited to sit and read the lines and, looking at the prospect of islands, said he could well imagine Sappho striding around one of them with a golden haired lady friend. He liked our verse. Which is what friends are for. Dear, dear Hobby.

'Ah, John Cam – these places are the abode of gods whose shrines no longer burn. I had neglected to remind you, by the way, that yesterday, January the 22nd, was the day of my own 22nd birthday. I grow old faster than I can blink.' We patted our chest theatrically. 'This temple, too, contained a burning shrine once. Soon I shall join these ruins in eternity.' Hobhouse refrained from chuckling (to his credit) and bade us a happy birthday yesterday. Peace was restored between us.

We returned to Athens. Pleasant as life was in that city, we both wanted to see the wonders of Constantinople before our time in the East ran out. We wrote Theresa a poem when we and Hobhouse left. So that she might read it herself, we penned the last line of each verse in Greek: 'My life, I love you...'

We left the grave-eyed young girl crying, clutching the piece of paper that was the poem, and a handful of our gold, and the mother gazing at us with calculation in her old cunning eyes as we fled the scene. Unfortunately for the old lady's schemes a day at sea, comme d'habitude, washed us clean of that emotion. The lines, however, live.

Maid of Athens, ere we part
Give, oh give me back my heart!
Or, since that has left my breast,
Keep it now, and take the rest...

We showed the piece to Hobhouse, remarking for that cynic's benefit that even a shallow love is sufficient to produce a masterpiece if the poet is young and in exercise.

A jolly old uncle of a Navy captain by the name of Bathurst took a shine to the pair of us, and offered us and our chattels free passage for the sake of our company as far as Constantinople. Free tickets to Turkey! But at the entrance to the Hellespont our captain's ship, the frigate Salsette, was detained by contrary winds blowing out of the gulf. We anchored. Taking us on deck, the Captain gestured at a flat plane leading up to some broken hills, or mounds, a half mile on shore from our anchorage. 'If you wish to take your horses on shore for a gallop, gentlemen,' Bathurst said, 'now would be the time. We are stuck here until the wind changes.'

'A miserable enough spot, barren and bare. Let the damned horses wait. What do they call this wretched place?'

'I do not know its current nomenclature. It is the site of ancient Troy.' He laughed as he watched our faces change.

71

We went ashore. We had fine galloping over that emptiness of sandy dirt which was once the greatest city in the Aegean. 'Or so they say,' Hobhouse remarked, always one to spoil a thing with too much brains. 'It is said by other scholars that the whole of the Iliad, and Ilium itself, this town we supposedly stand on, may be naught but a fable.'

'Not by you, Hobby, I trust? Damn their lying cretic's eyes to say that of Daddy Homer, father of all us poets.' We dismounted and threw ourself down upon a mound that we took for the barrow of a dead hero. 'Any man who imagines that Homer is not true in all essential particulars of history is a fool. He is the truest writer who ever lived, truer even than Shakespeare.' We nodded at the bare ground, studded at intervals with suggestive mounds and shapes. 'You know in your soul this is the place, Hobby; and that Achilles slew Hector under these buried walls. How can you doubt it?'

Hobhouse, not getting down from his horse, gazed about at the puffs of dust raised by the brisk and continual breeze. No sign of human habitation lingered on that spot. Despite the sun blazing above us and his good riding jacket, he shivered. We knew what he felt, looked round again, and shivered with him in the heat.

A few weeks later, still on board the wonderful ship, we were eying the cold current pouring down from the Sea of Marmora through the Hellespont. Our new friend Lieutenant Ekenhead had pointed out the two spots known as Sestos and Abydos – the European Sestos, and the Asiatic Abydos, a gap of ocean swum by fabled Leander in Mr. Marlowe's poem of Hero and Leander. 'My lord, if you are as good a swimmer as your friend boasts, you and I could do it. We could then say that we had swum from one continent to another...' the young lieutenant's eyes twinkled. 'We will have no Hero waiting for us, but it will be a good tale enough to tell the girls.'

We squinted at the distant shore, lost in a bright haze. Our eyes are exceptionally keen, but this shore was all blur and mystery. To swim between Europe and Asia. The distance not so great, a mile or so: but a fast cold current, which looked dangerous.

It was perfect.

'Well, Mr. Ekenhead, old boy, I dare say we can dispense with a Hero to wait upon our coming, since our conjugal powers will not do justice to the lady after such a swim.'

Ekenhead grinned wolfishly, looking much like another sailor from times to come, our beloved scoundrel Tre that was to be. 'O, I am sure we could manage to ravage her between the two of us, my lord.' Ekenhead. Tre. Hobby. Scrope. And Shiloh. And Parry, bless him. Our friends.

Hobhouse, while we attempted the straits, read Ovid's original of Hero and Leander, sitting in his cabin as we disappeared, young Ekenhead in the lead. Out in that immensity, with the lieutenant's head only bobbing into sight when he crested a swell, we were alone but not afraid, at one with the ocean. The misty hills of Asia looked on in the distance. We yearned for the far shore, but it was necessary to swim *slowly* toward it so that the swimmer should not become exhausted and succumb to the cold water... So cold, so very cold, that gulf, that void, that water from the frozen steppes northward. And the current so strong. We landed with relief, staggering up out of the surf, the lieutenant still ahead. He sat down on a rock in front of us, and we sat by him, glad to see him panting too. We gasped on the shores of Asia like beached whales. But alive!

To be on the continent of Asia, having *swum* from Europe...
To tell the truth we felt not a little relief that the feat was over.
To disguise our fear of the ocean to the brave lieutenant, our
poem about the feat was a joke. Comparing ourself to fabled
Leander, we wrote with tongue in our cheek about his failure
to swim the strait:

> *He lost his labour, I my jest;*
> *For he was drown'd, and I've the ague.*

The pair in the deathroom observe this light cheerful writing,
as from a soul that lived in a different world.

Chapter eight

*I hope you will find me an altered personage, – I do not mean in body,
but in manner, for I begin to find out that nothing but virtue will do in
this damned world. I am tolerably sick of vice, which I have tried in its
agreeable varieties...*

As Captain Bathurst shook hands in farewell, and the
affable Lieutenant Ekenhead slipped us each a bottle of
good naval rum, we rode ashore near the Sultan's palace.
Nothing seen afterwards in Turkey could erase the first sight
we saw in Stamboul: under the palace wall a dead body
being gnawed to pieces by a pack of dogs. Hobhouse turned
without comment, and we exchanged bitter smiles. Thus the
flavour of every Turkish delight that followed was tainted by
our remembered view of that corpse, and the repetition of
our jest on seeing the body – 'a patriot as *was.*'

Constantinople, or Stamboul, as the Turk preferred it, was
a disappointment in many ways. No foreigners were allowed
to stay in the magical old city at night; and although one could
see the external beauties of the city by day, as Christians we
were completely cut off from all society with the Turks in their
capital city. Delightful, though, to ride out and circumnavigate

the land walls of ancient Byzantium from the Sea of Marmora to the Golden Horn, and to sit and talk rebellion with Hobhouse, that lovable prig (as hot for the revolution as ourself) in the Turkish burial-grounds, '...the loveliest spot on earth,' we assured a grinning Hobhouse gravely. We were sitting on a flowery tomb in the shade of a grove of enormous cypresses, looking down at the terraces of gardens below them. As Winter turned into Spring the palace gardens along the Horn had burst out in a flame of blossom.

We rode daily to view the astonishing opulence of the Sultan's pleasure gardens in the Valley of the Sweet Water. Picnicking in this Eden, drinking red wine from the bottle, telling tales of Scrope Davies and his deeds, we consumed our noontime meal of bread and cheese surrounded by the sights and scents of a muslim paradise. All that was missing were the houris, but Hobhouse was a prig about women and not willing to share (nor even, as Scrope the incorrigible Birdmore hath no qualms in doing, to pick up our leavings of the fairer sex for his own use.) We did not, therefore, bring houris with us to our picnics. Copulation *en plein air* was probably not John Cam's style.

Despite the corpse and the dogs, we were bound to stay here among these Tory heathen for a while. But that is not right – we liked the individual *Turk* well enough, but we were coming to have a hearty dislike for the Turkish form of Government, which we were at that time too indolent to indulge in rebellion against. We meant to cut a dash among the Frankish ladies, as at Athens, and we sported our scarlet uniforms and epaulets at every opportunity.

But nothing was the same as Athens, where the rule of the Turk in that city was lightened by the presence of the Greek people. Everything in Stamboul was designed as if to displease. Invited to take part in the ceremony marking the British Consul's final audience with the Sultan before the Consul left for England, we were piqued to find out that we, an English nobleman, had been offered no special precedence in the procession. We determined to quit the city immediately, and it was only after Hobhouse's most tactful persuasion, together with the assurances of the Austrian ambassador that the Turks allowed no precedence in the procession, that we could be persuaded to remain in the city and take part in the ceremonials.

Which went like this – a hundred scented Westerners standing in their ranks, facing the Presence. The Sultan's eyes lingering on ourself, the beautiful young man in the scarlet coat, with our delicate features, black hair and piercing blue eyes. (We were somewhat vain in our youth, and know what we looked like.) This old whore, we were thinking, is at the heart of this evil. As he paused before us, to examine us.

Our blue-black eyes, locked on his, narrowed with hate.

The Sultan's eyes narrowed in response, completely misinterpreting our expression. HE nodded, murmured, walked on. From time to time his gaze strayed back to ourself, who, he clearly believed, had given him a *look*. But we were weary of Turkish foibles, and looked away, cutting the old pig at his own ceremony. It was hard for us not to smile. It is one of the funniest things, when the man you are trying to kill with your look thinks you are flirting.

Hobby had to go home. When the *Salsette* sailed with ambassador Adair, Hobby and I made sure to be on the ship. Hobhouse was to remain on board and proceed to England, after we and our servants were dropped off at Sounion Head. On the *Salsette*, much to Ekenhead's chagrin, we were gloomy despite the bracing sail in the warm summer seas. We sat at the rail for hours on end, talking to no one, staring at the water sliding past the keel, not even looking up to observe the boats or islands drifting by. Several times the garrulous lieutenant approached us with a tot of rum. Several times he was thanked, but refused.

We were thinking of Hobhouse. We could never abide a parting, despite our longing to be rid of Hobhouse for a while, to discover the delights of the East for ourself. So many partings in our life have led to death. It was as if Hobhouse, too, were dying, in leaving us, after being a companion so long. We could not bear it, and so we quarrelled with our friend to make the parting easier.

Hobhouse was worried about what would no doubt happen to his friend, alone, in the sodomitic East. The Turks, we had already taunted him, were, for all their barbarities, sensible peoples in that they preferred a pipe and a pathic (a pipe of opium and a compliant boy) to the Englishman's bottle and whore. We eyed each other sullenly the length of the deck, while our friend Ekenhead tried to get us to drink together. The tall gangling figure of the sociable lieutenant could be seen for a good part of the day walking back and forth between us and Hobhouse, like an orphan dog that had once belonged to us both.

We came together of course just as the frigate approached Sounion Head where we were to part. Ekenhead was allowed at last to distribute tots of rum, much to his obvious relief. The occasion, under the prompting of Ekenhead and old Captain Bathurst, became convivial. The five of us had a party.

As his lordship's baggage was unloaded onto the little wooden dock, Hobhouse noted in his diary: 'Took leave, non sine lacrymis, of this singular young person, on a little stone terrace at the end of the bay, dividing with him a little nosegay of flowers.' The tiny figure on the shore was blurred by Hobhouse's tears. But John Cam owed his friend more than a thousand pounds already, quite enough, he thought, for a man who had no employment and had lately quarrelled with his father.

Our own feelings were more mixed. Chagrin at the departure of a dear friend, to be sure. But it was with a delicious sense of freedom, as of entering into a new world, that we rode back along the rocky road to Athens, where we intended to spend the winter. As we cantered into the city we grinned up at the bonewhite purity of the Acropolis above us, the godbuilt marble pile seeming to leap up at us in greeting as we topped the rise that brought it into sight. Below the holy city on the heights sprawled the wretched modern town. High above this baseness the city of the mind shone like a star, the city of Plato, and of Socrates, and his beloved friend Alcibiades...

...and of a beautiful girlchild called Theresa Macri...

At the Macri house our entourage clattered to a halt. Out came the giggling older sisters and the mother slyly following behind. The old chambers were made available to 'milorde', the older girls danced attendance as of yore, but there was something amiss. The spirit of Theresa, that wild and innocent young doe, seemed to have been infected by the mother; her behaviour was not so charming nor so natural as before.

No doubt the child was primed by the greedy mother to trap us into marriage; hilarious thought. Where before Theresa would entertain us for hours with her childish prattle, joining us as a sort of sisterly companion, now she was all eyes, careful of what she said to us, so that what she said was no longer worth hearing. And of course the poor child, no longer enjoying it herself, was thrust by the mother into our company at every opportunity.

To escape these torments we made an excursion to Tripolitza to see Veli Pasha, son of the genial killer Ali. On the way, we picked up a new attendant, a Greek boy placed into our care called Eustathios. The lad immediately fell in love with this startled lord, our horses, dogs, bodyguards and pistols. The day we set off to see Veli, the worthy Fletcher, our eternal butler, was horrified to see the little tease sporting a pink parasol. We were amused by the reaction of the noble Fletcher, as ever; but we were also aroused by the bright display of the boy Eustathios, and thought it high time Fletcher, the last Englishman in our party, went home.

This little break from Athens had served to clear our head of nonsense. On returning from this excursion, our servants packed our things at the Macri house; we told our hostess we were leaving, another lodging was to be taken. The girl Theresa cried. We were sorry for her but had made our decision. It was, as is usual in such cases, the mother's fault. The mother herself, we were pleased to see, was in consternation. Pressing a little gold into the hands of the daughters, and promising to come and visit the family by and by, we moved our little party to the Capuchin Monastery high on the cliffs above Athens.

We had been invited to lodge at the monastery by the affable Abbot, with whom we had dined one night in the town below. We felt a little virtuous at our change of address and the sparing of the sweet girl both on the same day, and we wrote that evening, to Hobhouse: *I am living in the Capuchin convent, Hymettus before me, the Acropolis behind, the temple of Jove to my right, the Stadium to my front, the town to my left, eh, Sir, there's a situation, there's your picaresque! nothing like that, Sir, in Lunnun, no not even the Mansion House. And I feed upon Woodcocks & red mullet every day, & I have three horses (one a present from the Pacha of the Morea) and I ride to Piraeus, & Phalerum and Munichia...*

Sealing this innocent letter with our baronial signet in the hot wax (motto *crede Biron*), we exulted in our eyrie high on the cliffs, as night fell on the ramshackle little town beneath us. Thousands of souls below... We made a mental note to roger them all.

We rang the bell for Fletcher to come and dispatch the letter to the conveniently absent John Cam Hobhouse. Our twenty-two year-old blood beat in our ears. Looking through the window at the twinkling lights of the town we could feel all the hearts below us, beating in time with ours in the darkness.

Chapter nine

Four or Five Reasons in Favour of a Change.

'Ist At 23 the best of life is over and its bitters double. 2ndly I have seen mankind in various Countries and find them equally despicable, if anything the Balance is rather in favour of the Turks. 3dly I am sick at heart. Nor maid nor youth delights me now.

The monastery functioned as a hotel for passing Franks like ourself, and was also a school for the Frankish (or Western) boys, presided over by the old Abbot as headmaster. A sort of Harrow in heaven – if you liked boys. The half-dozen 'Ragazzi' under instruction were so riotous as to delight us with memories of our own schooldays, making us fancy we were back at school. Lonely on the mountain without Theresa, we fell in love with our favourite boy, Nicolo Giraud, a pretty blue eyed lad of French descent who was assigned to teach us Italian.

Our heart would ever perch on the nearest branch, in the matter of love. In England, where it would be a hanging matter, loving Nicolo would have been a serious problem, but in that other part of the world, nothing was simpler. The whole of the East breathed the same atmosphere as the great public schools of England in this matter, and your true ruling classes were ever sodomitic. In the monastery, one day, quite naturally, the Nicolo and ourself made love in the Italian manner.

He was not even a virgin.

Ensconced in the monastery we were able to make frequent forays into Frankish society. The Frankish women were extraordinarily compliant, and as a result all the English tourists received the same painful dose of clap together. Recovering from this stinging dose, we resolved to stick to honest whores, for if the ladies could clap you then the whores could do no worse and they were a lot less trouble.

There were even ladies who had the virtue of whores... A Turkish girl of our acquaintance, the sister of one of our servants, who was said, even by her brother, to be no better than she should be. The thought of a Turkish girl, the forbidden sex in Athens, was unbearably exciting, and displaced poor Nicolo from our rampant mind. Gold was slipped into the pretty Turk's fingers, whisperings were made in the pretty ear. The woman proved no less passionate than her countrymen were savage. We, to our surprise, became rather fond of the girl; admiring especially the dark lips of her cunt, such a contrast to the pink softness within, and her tigerish enthusiasm for fucking, which reminded us (as she bucked wildly astride us) of the attacking hordes of Saladin, assaulting our Christian tower with a vengeance.

A letter from Mrs. Spencer Smith, waiting patiently at Malta, did nothing to bring an end to this bout of debauchery. With a girl like this to hand, we were immune even to the charms of Constance. Each night we rode our girl, and each day we rode out to the harbour at Piraeus and took a swim across the bay. What a life was this. What with the nightly and the daily ride and the swim, we were well in exercise, even thin, and as happy as we had ever been when alone. Our mode of life was settled, and nothing could have been better. We were so busy with these pursuits that we were even freed for a little while of the curse of scribbling, which is in any case only a sort of relief for an overteeming mind.

Riding back from Piraeus one day in an open jacket with nothing but our purse and the habitual pair of loaded pistols in our pocket (thank God) we were startled to encounter a small party of Turkish soldiers bound for the sea, carrying a sack that was, obviously, wriggling. We stopped them, as to exchange the time of day. No doubt a lamb, or the like, on the way to be slaughtered. Perhaps, we thought, we can induce these fellows with a little gold to let the poor creature go.

'What do you carry?' we asked the three Turkish fellows. 'Can we buy it?'

A woman caught in adultery, they told us cheerfully, and for a Turkish woman the usual punishment – she was to be hurled into the sea wrapped in this sack. It was a serious matter, and gold, in this particular instance, was of no avail. We immediately offered gold; perhaps not enough. The Turkish soldiers acted as if we had insulted them. We were their friend, and should not have offered gold...

The girl in the sack cried out, recognising our voice. All the time smiling at the friendly fellows, we put our hands slowly into our pockets, slipping out our pair of little pocket pistols and levelling them at the startled men. They were outraged at this blatant insult, worse than the money as an insult to our friendship. They began protesting. Were they not about official police business? Did the foreigner think to interfere in Allah's justice? The girl was of loose morals – was the sentence not the usual sentence?

The foreigner kept hold of the pistols, but promised them much gold if they desisted, and death for at least two of the three men if they did not. A hasty consultation in Turkish, still at the point of pistols. We would shoot them in a *second* – did they believe that we would? And throttle the third man. They came to a sensible decision. A bargain was struck, our pistols lowered, everyone spat and shook hands on it, mates all around again now. The girl was cut loose, and mounted up behind us. We had promised the soldiers to make the matter good to the Governor of Athens, whom we knew socially.

The Governor was smilingly compliant in indulging us in this matter. But the affair of the girl who survived her death sentence became a scandal in the city. Our poor girl had to be sent at night to Thebes, to stifle the affront to public morality that letting her live presented. By tyranny of the Turk, we were deprived of our favourite girl. The bastards would have killed the poor woman out of hand if not for that chance encounter on our evening ride. Nice fellows enough, the Turks, taken singly. But would that they were gone from Greece, we thought, and if we could help them go we would.

The winter passed in a delirium of sensuality; no more Turkish ladies but an enthusiastic bout of immorality from the Frankish tourists, the European gels. However, at the end of the winter, the beautiful tourists began to leave. All things conspired against us. No more money forthcoming from England; only dire warnings about the need to go home and put our affairs in order. (Our attorney, Hanson, wanted to sell Newstead – which we had vowed never to do, even at the cost of returning home to prevent it.) We were dragged back to England like a bear on the end of a long cruel chain.

As the boat cruised through the blue spring tides toward Malta – where, remember, we still had to face Constance Spencer Smith, our love of a year ago – our disordered spirits were not helped by a confusion of maladies earned in Athens that still lingered in our body to plague our soul: the clap, the piles, and a tertian fever. The only quack on board remarked *scientifically* that one can suffer only one set of symptoms from each disease at a time – but to be sure they relieved themselves hourly, like sentinels.

We dangled over the rail in our hand (at odds whether to drop it or not) the manuscript of the wild new poem we were making. (For the word poet meaneth *maker*.) If only we had dropped that MS into the sea, what a difference it would have made, perhaps even saved us from a life of scribbling and celebrity – but our hand kept hold of this piece we had made, hey-ho... and the rest is history.

ROLL ON THOU DEEP AND DARK BLUE OCEAN ROLL
TEN THOUSAND FLEETS SWEEP OVER THEE IN VAIN;
MAN MARKS THE EARTH WITH RUIN – HIS CONTROL
STOPS WITH THE SHORE; UPON THE WATERY PLAIN
THE WRECKS ARE ALL THY DEED, NOR DOTH REMAIN
A SHADOW OF MAN'S RAVAGE, SAVE HIS OWN,
WHEN, FOR A MOMENT, LIKE A DROP OF RAIN
HE SINKS INTO THY DEPTHS WITH BUBBLING GROAN,
WITHOUT A GRAVE, UNKNELL'D, UNCOFFIN'D, AND
UNKNOWN...

'Wait a minute... we had not written that Canto at that time – not till we left England again – you are misrepresenting the composition of the...'

'Be silent. It was all the same poem. But to continue. Eh bien, Childe Harold. It's a good pose, Chilled Harry, but we were not really much happier with it than the affrighted gulls we shouted our verses at...'

'Must that verse forever have the sound of a hysterical boy?'

'Everybody's a critic – be still now.'

At Malta the governor kindly lent us a room for our interview with Mrs. Spencer Smith, who had been waiting for us some weeks. We had imagined that we would be feeling guilty at what we had to tell the lady – that we were going home without her – but seeing her self-possession we realised with distaste that she was no more in love with us than we were with her. The sirocco wind had been blowing, and both of us were sweating profusely. The interview was a little sullen on both sides.

Why, the bitch wanted us merely for a travelling companion, and stallion for the night. What impudence, we thought. We looked with some amazement at this strong lady's calm blue eyes. Her gaze did not give way before ours at all. She was a woman perfectly mistress of herself and of every art of intrigue personal and political. She was not at all in love, but quite willing to persuade a young man that she was if it would serve her turn. A damn fine woman, but even more wicked than our wicked self (as we never say we love when we do not.)

The formidable lady, though disconcerted at our refusal of her charms, said goodbye with a cool smile. To add to the fun on Malta, we had fever that left our linen drenched with sweat every night; and the hot sirocco wind never varied its monotonous stifling breath. The ship for England would not sail until June – weeks away. Those dog-days at Malta stretched endlessly; and the certainty of responsibility, debt and dragon mother in England offered no more cheerful a prospect. For the want of anything better to do, we sat down at our desk and resolved to write:

Four or Five Reasons in Favour of a Change.

'*1st At 23 the best of life is over and its bitters double. 2ndly I have seen mankind in various Countries and find them equally despicable, if anything the Balance is rather in favour of the Turks. 3dly I am sick at heart. Nor maid nor youth delights me now. 4thly A man who is lame of one leg is in a state of bodily inferiority which increases with years and must render his old age more peevish and intolerable. Besides in another existence I expect to have two if not four legs by way of compensation. 5thly I grow selfish and misanthropical. 6thly My affairs at home and abroad are gloomy enough. 7thly I have outlived all my vanities, aye, even the vanity of authorship.*

Thinking, we will give you, England, six months...

(In the deathroom, looking on from the future, the Nightgowned Spirit can hardly listen quietly to his younger self. Choking with laughter, he turns away to address his remarks to the dying body. 'Six months – five years my friend! –

damned hard ones at the latter end, but sweet as syrup to the vanity of authorship. Ten thousand years in experience – and they won't sweep over YOU in vain, mind you, mind you...')

Chapter ten

What is the worst of woes that wait on age?
What stamps the wrinkle deeper on the brow?
To view each loved one blotted from the page,
And be alone on earth, as I am now.

The fag-end of a holiday: the tedium of travel which is three parts of life's experience. The sailor's soft voices change, becoming more harsh and guttural as you go further north. The famous white cliffs wrapped in a blanket of fog. Christ Jesus you couldn't even see the place through the filthy mist. O, how we hated England that day we landed.

Things to be arranged: lodging and board. Lodgings at either Dorant's or perhaps, Reddish's Hotel (as to board, we could dine cheaply and well enough at our deserted unfashionable club, the Alfred). One of the dearest men to our heart in the world, I mean Scrope Davies, arrived drunk on our first night at Reddish's Hotel; we embraced each other like men returned from the wars. With the exquisite Mr. Davies, motley was the only wear. We drank and laughed all night in the hotel. He had a completely new set of stories which we had not heard before, and brought with him a half dozen of burgundy of exquisite vintage. We were so intoxicated with this fellow's wit and wine, we hardly remembered to tell him any of our own traveller's tales.

Next day we pursued the dubious cultivation of the society of the ubiquitous Robbie Dallas, a useful little slavey of a lord-loving reverend, a family acquaintance kept on to carry our new manuscript to the booksellers. Dallas was used by many a scribbling poet as a sort of literary packhorse. He knew everybody, and had been instrumental in the publishing of our previous masterpiece, *English Bards and Scotch Reviewers*. A useful fellow, fifty-odd years old, but knew all the Grub St. and a few of the more respectable publishers. All for the love of poesy.

After the usual pleasantries – Dallas was a distant friend of the family, and we had certain people in common to enquire about – he got to the point. Had we any new VERSES that he might, ah, peruse...? The satirical stuff, of course, the *Hints from Horace*. The spit and image (so we thought) of our last push through the press, *English Bards*. We thrust our *Hints* upon him, and he promised to read the thing and call on us next day, at breakfast. To praise our genius, as we thought.

But after Dallas read *Hints from Horace*, he sniffed at it over his kipper at breakfast in the hotel. And asked: 'Has my lord produced nothing else under the influence of his travels?'

Reluctantly we handed over the new thing – that was a little too private a fantasy to be published. Hastily we scribbled with a borrowed pen and changed the name from *Childe Burun* to *Childe Harold*, instructing slavey Dallas to do the same all through the manuscript before he showed it to anyone else. Chilled Harry, the story of the Byronic travels. If Dallas thought he could persuade somebody to publish, why, he might sell the copyright and keep the proceeds. But the satire, now, the *Hints from Horace*, was the thing, we insisted to the good reverend.

Being back in England, it was necessary to live up to one's position with the resumption of bottle and whore. Renewed drinking all night with Scrope and 'us Youth,' and rogering all afternoon a particularly intelligent, and expensive, and amorously talented young laughing dame in our room. Putting off the dreaded day when we had to return to Newstead and pay our first visit to our mother, who would no doubt be furious with us as to expenses occurred and monies borrowed against our estate.

We decided to buy a coach in which to travel to Mother and Newstead, and conveniently enough a good one was to be had from our friend 'Bold Webster,' whose Golden Dolly, Webster assured us, had no need of her new husband's old appurtenances. Webster testified that the spring of the vehicle was sufficient to bear the weight of copulation, and at a mere two hundred guineas (which we should borrow off the good Jews at a murderous interest) it was a bargain, Sir, a bargain.

The smooth flow of the Nightgowned Spirit's narrative is interrupted as his tones grow bitter. In the squalid death-room waiting up the road, watching this dilly-dallying in London, the Spirit shakes an angry fist at the wall. Webster and the coach fade out of the picture. We are as ashamed of ignoring our mother at this point as of anything in our life

– in which shame and pride have always been the driving forces. It is with a supreme effort that NGS restrains himself from striking his prone alter ego with his fist.

'Wanted to go to the balls in style, did we? Bought a CARRIAGE, forsooth, to transplant our rotten carcass in STYLE. Because the literary lion of the season couldn't just go visiting in any old thing. So we stayed around to buy a coach. So we forgot Mama as always – until it was too late. A coach! For two hundred guineas we did not have! O, I can hardly wait to see it...'

'Mama... Mama...' from the bed.

The Spirit snarls at the bed: 'We do not want to remember Mrs. Byron's death. We do not want THIS, and we do not want to remember the death of Allegra, our natural daughter. These things we will not address at length, by God.'

'Censorship follows me to the grave, I might have expected it,' mutters the man on the bed, so low that his other self does not hear.

The Spirit takes an angry gulp from his flask. 'Always so many things to do, until that irreversible moment too late for the dearest things that perish like blossom. Buying a coach from the idiot Webster, unfinished business with Dallas, about scribbling – this and that – a message comes that Mama is ill. O, we resolve then to set out, and borrow forty pounds for the journey – only to have another message arrive before we do so that the old lady is dead. O, by God, THEN we rush back to tell her about our years abroad. Are you proud? Do you want us to watch THAT? Well, I change my mind, damn you, you SHALL...'

'What is happening...?'

'We are in the present, now, we will feel this do you FEEL it now...? We are there, in in that room with poor dead Mama – we deserve to relive this, God help us both...'

LB is in his mother's deathroom, cradling the body of the loved/hated dead woman in his arms. He is sobbing. 'I had but one friend in the world, and she is gone.' His voice is muffled in his mother's long hair, as he strokes that pale fat cheek he never stroked in life.

Chapter eleven

Come to me, Scrope, I am almost desolate – left almost
alone in the world...

Mama dies on the 1st of August, 1811, before we are able
to see her alive again after our two year absence. When
we get to the Abbey only a corpse is there. On the 7th of
August, before she is buried, we receive a letter from Scrope
Davies that we assumes at first is merely Scrope's condolences. We were wrong. It never rains but it pours.

My dear Byron

Matthews is no more – He was drowned on Sat-
urday last by an ineffectual attempt to swim through
some weeds after he had been in the Cam 3 quarters of
an hour – Had you or I been there Matthews had been
now alive – Hart saw him perish – but dared not ven-
ture to give him assistance. Had you been there – both
or neither would have drowned – He was indeed a man
of talent – My soul is heavy – I can do nothing – I wan-
der about in despair – I shall never see his like again

– His body was found 12 minutes after he had sunk –
They tried every effort to restore animation but in vain
– Such was the end of the man whose mind appeared
to be possessed of greater powers than the mind of any
man I ever knew –
    God bless you –
        and believe me ever yours

               Scrope Davies

This from Scrope before the funeral, with Mother's body still in the house with us. Matthews is gone from this world before we can see him again. Our friends fall about us. The Citoyen, the Revolutionary, is vanished forever. We can hardly recall his face, now.

The day after Scrope's letter on the 7th we receive a letter from Matthews himself, despatched on the Friday (he died on Saturday, the following day) – and received by us from beyond the grave. During the delirium that follows we cannot keep ourselves away from the room where poor Mrs. Byron lies dead, but must visit and revisit her unfeeling corpse, as if it will do any good to either of us now, or to poor dead Matthews, the greatest of us if he had lived. There is to me something so incomprehensible in death, that I can neither speak nor think on the subject. Indeed, when I look on the mass of corruption which is the being from whence I sprung, I doubt within myself whether I *am*, or she is *not*. And now my Mother and the revolutionary Citoyen in the same breath.

So how odd it felt to receive Matthews's letter on the 8th, full of jests and a brilliant good humour – so *alive*. It was as if dead Matthews wrote to us from Hades.

Hades is much on our mind. On the 9th, idly, we set ourself to translate the Hades episode from Homer, for a Homeric drama we have in mind; the Greek is hard to parse, after being so long away from school (at Cambridge one learns nothing). After the supreme effort of translating we are too indolent even to make it scan as decent blank verse. It winds up very rough, like a piece of Old Saxon.

Odysseus sails to the Island of the Dead, where Circe has told him to dig a ditch and fill it with sheep's blood, to summon the dead spirits so that he may question them.

I made the men hold the sheep, and I
slit up their throats, and held their streaming throats
over the trench, till it was filled with blood.
There sat I on a stool, with my sharp sword
before this bloody feeding-trough for the dead,
as hungry spirits gibbered towards me, gathered round
squeaking like bats. I set my soul
and drew my long bright sword
and sat me down before the fosse
and none would I let pass
before that blinded and all-seeing man, Teiresias.
The souls swarmed around me, craving blood...
whispered to me. Among them warriors, weary of wounds,
besmeared with blood and bearing still-bloody arms...
whispered. In front of them, to my amaze,
first comes my comrade Elpenor his soul,
Elpenor, a man not strong in war or wine
but a good fellow for all that,
Elpenor – who slept the night on Kirke's roof
and missed us in the morning as we sailed.

(as the spirits of the dead throng and gibber around him,
he speaks to one)

Elpenor, how did you thus outpace us to this Island,
and we swift sailors on the hissing sea?
Or have you learned to walk on water nowadays?

ELPENOR: *Odysseus, subtle, cunning one*
it was bad luck and too much wine.
With vomit in my throat I crawled me out
apart from still hard-drinking friends to spend the night
on Kirke's cool roof: but in the morning
when I woke and saw you launch the ship without me
I hurried down to you, and in my haste
forgot the ladder to the ground
and tumbled off the roof, a perfect dive
– to hit head-first.
The shock shattered the spine's nerve,
wrenched askew the neckbone
– the soul sank to Hades' house.
When you get back to Kirke's island
I beg you there to burn my bones
till they are purged of flesh, snowy and white
and heap my barrow high.
I have no monument, had yet to make me a name,
but stick my good oar upright in the earth
– the one I used to pull beside my friends. (he weeps)

ODYSSEUS: (weeping with him) *Old friend, it's gladly done.*
So we sat there on either side of the trench,
my friend and I, eying each other sadly,

unable to touch, and weeping bitterly
across the ditch of death.

We cannot finish the passage. We burns on our fire this terrible poem before any one sees it; before we have put it into proper blank verse even. We had wanted to write like Homer, but he is too terrible for modern humankind, which cannot bear very much reality. We commit the pages to the fire and watch our unknown masterpiece curl and blacken on the flame, gone with the rising smoke, like the ashes of heroes, fit sacrifice for our dead loves, our Mother and the Citoyen.

The only real company in the house is old Joe Murray and the page Robert Rushton, who is a good enough boy for a sparring partner, but of no more use than poor old Joe to converse of such things as death. Hobhouse is away with the regiment he has foolishly joined after a quarrel with his father; and we are not yet reconciled to our tempestuous half sister, Augusta, with whom we had some trifling quarrel about insulting our common uncle, puling Carlisle, in our last published verses. (Carlisle is lucky we did not call him out. And to HELL with her for supporting him. Or so we felt at that time...)

There is only one man in England who can bring comfort to us now. We pick up the pen and write to him.

My dearest Davies, – Some curse hangs over me and
mine. My mother lies a corpse in this house; one of my
best friends is drowned in a ditch. What can I say, or
think, or do? I received a letter from him the day before
yesterday. My dear Scrope, if you can spare a moment,

do come down to me – I want a friend. Matthews's
last letter was written on Friday – on Saturday he was
not. In ability, who was like Matthews? How did we
all shrink before him? You do me but justice in saying,
I would have risked my paltry existence to have pre-
served his. This very evening did I mean to write, invit-
ing him, as I invite you, my dear friend, to visit me.
God forgive Hart for his apathy! What will our poor
Hobhouse feel? His letters breathe but of Matthews.
Come to me, Scrope, I am almost desolate – left almost
alone in the world – I had but you, and H., and M.,
and let me enjoy the survivors whilst I can. Poor M., in
his letter of Friday, speaks of his intended contest for
Cambridge, and a speedy journey to London. Write or
come, but come if you can, or one or both.

There are few things that God hath created so sweet as a
good friend. Scrope the Great – a busy man, for he *lives* by
Gaming, having no fortune of his own – abandons his com-
plicated and dangerous affairs and rides the weary miles to
us at Newstead, giving up a week of his life to save our own.
I am not sure if it was worth his trouble, but we have always
been grateful to him for making the effort.

The Birdmore comes not before time. A terrible sickness
is upon us. On the day of Mother's funeral, with Scrope not
yet arrived, we cannot bear to follow the funeral procession
to the family church at Hucknall Torkard, which shall no
doubt contain our own carcase shortly. We cannot say goodbye to the body that bore us. We can only stand in the door
of the Abbey and watch the procession of servants and family friends till Mother is out of sight.

Young Rushton stands with us on the Great Stair, our only companion in this watching. Apart from ourself and Robert everyone else is at the funeral. We ask the boy to fetch the sparring gloves, and proceed to our exercise. But after a few half-hearted blows, we can bear to box no more. Mumbling we know not what to the poor boy, we fling away the gloves and go to our room alone.

Sit in our room with the loaded pistol in our lap, our hand on the trigger, rocking on our rocking chair, thinking thoughts we should prefer not to recollect even now. And constantly the Devil whispering in one's ear – it is all one, why wait, do it now, a ball clean into the brain pan as good a death for a man as any, the spark, the powder, the explosion, the ball in the brain pan.

It is only the thought that the good Scrope is already on the way north, and what HE will have to endure if he finds our corpse, that stays our finger. We must maintain good manners to our friends, it is the cement that binds civilisation. It might be a trifle to blow one's brains out, but it would be no light thing to offend Scrope Berdmore Davies Esquire.

No man had a more amusing friend than Scrope the Great, who could outwit Brummell himself in a war of words. Before Scrope, Matthews, myself, and Hobhouse, firing together were outgunned, to the very nines, and sunk like a bunch of Froggies at Trafalgar.

He arrives sitting his dappled grey pony (a perfect match to Scrope's other clothes) with a supple grace. A small man, thin and wiry, but one whose muscles are like steel wire. The best tennis player in Cambridge. And the best thrower of dice. A gleam from those grey eyes, the colour of silver, flashing across the yard at Newstead, reaches us on the Great Stair – Scrope's glittering sharp eye.

Scrope's *eye* in any ball game, at shooting, or even boxing, is uncanny. Once when Scrope was indulging in a game of hazard at College I saw a sturdy young buck think he could elbow this little fop out of the play. The fellow grabbed the dice from out of Scrope's hands in his eagerness to be first to throw again. Scrope gripped the thick wrist in his little hand and stopped the man taking his dice. When the young man swung at Scrope's chin with his other fist, Scrope, a keen student of sparring, warded the blow, stepped back, set himself coolly, and punched the fellow, so as not to do too much damage, in the wind. The lout had to be helped from the table, and was lost to the world for some moments. He did not venture to return to the baize that evening. The just deserts of bad manners.

Yet Scrope is the gentlest of men with those who keep their manners, and has been known to spare a young man who has lost everything the paying-up of his debts. (He did however keep that young man's *dormeuse*, a sort of gentleman's sleep-ing-coach or caravan. Scrope, when he hath nowhere else to stay, doth travel to the races sometimes in this famous vehi-cle, now known to the gentlemen of the turf as 'Scrope's dor-meuse.') He is proud that the dormeuse reminds him of his own charity.

Not a cruel man. A dead shot and a nerveless duellist, he always prefers to kiss and make up a duel if possible, though he is never afraid to spill blood if he feels honour demands it.

See the Birdmore, then, springing lightly from his horse. The best dressed Fellow in Cambridge. Alvanley or Sefton or Brummell could not be better turned out, for it is neces-sary for Scrope to spend a considerable fortune of his gaming income upon clothing in order that he, a country vicar's son, may move in the circles where *high play* is common. Where the pheasants gather for plucking. It is to be remembered that Brummell reduced the Prince of Wales to tears by criticizing the cut of his jacket. Scrope Davies, Among The Dandies, is accounted as tastefully dressed as either the Regent or the Beau. His favourite colour is grey, to match his horse. His friends, though they do not say so, think that it is to match his eyes, which are of a peculiar shade of grey-silver, with no blue to them.

He walks over to us and we embrace, without words, and walk arm in arm up the Great Stair into the house. The first thing that Scrope does is discharge our loaded pistols at the nearest game that present itself through the window, to the great distress of old Joe Murray's chickens. He then cleans each piece, lays it with its brother weapon, and locks the pistol case. 'These things are but toys,' Scrope says, putting the case of pistols away in a cupboard before opening the wine, 'but it is better to play with them carefully.'

Though Scrope will often *finish* himself with wine or spirits of a night, he will only drink *in the day* on some special occasion. He evidently considers today to be special, for that first afternoon we immediately address the half-dozen of fine burgundy he has brought in his saddle bags. Scrope bids us drink deep, and the rest of that day is a blur.

Next day Scrope is up with the birds, whistling, while we nurse our aching head. He makes us eat a little breakfast (we rarely see mornings, so this is an unaccustomed meal) and then proceeds to drag us around on a tour of Newstead Abbey. As if we were a boy again, with pistols and powder and shot to amuse us on the way, as he makes up imaginary histories and mythic Byronic ancestors to bring the place to life.

'D'you see, dear boy,' says Scrope, turning to shoot a late-blooming plum off an old tree in the Abbot's garden, 'it is as I have always told you. Droll thing life is, scarcely worth the bother – and yet what is one to do except act as if every detail of existence were vital? To *bother*, to show style, is the only mark of a man of spirit.'

We manage by dint of good luck to duplicate Scrope's extraordinary shot with the plum, though our hand shakes alarmingly and our head still aches from Scrope's wine. Scrope nods with approval as our plum explodes with bloody execution across the garden. 'A plum is no larger,' Scrope says, 'than a bad man's heart.'

He keeps us occupied. He laughs with the living, though he don't weep with the dead. 'To be busy,' Scrope says, 'is the thing.' If we are not riding we are sparring with the gloves, if we are not sparring we are shooting, and if we are not shooting (he is careful to lock away the pistols at night) we are drinking. On those drunken evenings, after a day of strenuous exercise, we talk a little of the eternal verities. Scrope has always seemed to us to have most of the answers to life's questions, but what he told us that first night comes to us through a veiling mist of wine and brandy and we wish we could remember it better.

We tell Scrope a little about Harrow, our childhood school. Scrope tells us tales that make barbaric Harrow sound the soul of the Enlightenment. He had been, as a *Colleger*, or clever boy designed for a King's College Fellowship, obliged to live since the age of eleven in the Long Chamber at Eton. This was a world all its own in which the boys were locked up every night alone, some from the age of seven onward, so that the boys had as it were gone wild and formed a society of their own, of a savagery which may well be imagined by those who know anything of small boys.

'It was in the Long Chamber,' Scrope yawns, 'that I first acquired a taste for drinking, and where I first realized that a man with a brain good enough to calculate the odds on the fall of a pair of dice could make a good deal of money betting against unthinking dolts at hazard. It is also the place where I first learned to be a *hard hitter*. One's fists were all that saved one's virtue from the larger boys in Long Chamber.'

'The masters of the school did nothing to prevent this abuse?'

'The masters, d'ye see, locked us in alone there all night. We were our own primitive society, and what we got up to might perhaps have inspired Dean Swift to have incorporated the Country of the Long Chamber into the fifth and most horrific book of *Gulliver*. It was terrible, man. But one survived.' We laugh, and Scrope opens another bottle by knocking the head off neatly with a poker, a particular trick of his which we have ourselves taken up. But no one can knock off the neck of a bottle with a poker as neatly as Scrope.

We rally him a little by recalling the time HE had wanted to shoot himself, and we had been instrumental in preventing it. For answer, he pours the bottle of burgundy into the skull cup. 'Wine and weapons do not mix.' When Scrope gets out the skull cup it is almost as if we drink with the ghost of Matthews, for we recall our former buffooneries as a foursome with Hobhouse at Newstead, when we used to dress up in old monks' costumes and frighten each other in the dark. The cup is made of the skull of a monk we found in the garden, plated with silver inside for more sanitary drinking. It holds a bottle and a half, which is the size of a man's brains.

Newstead is a haunted-looking place, at night, and Scrope and I laugh as we remember the night Citoyen Matthews hid in a stone coffin in the Long Gallery and rose up out of it to blow out Hobhouse's candle as he passed by, so that Hobby, who was on his way to relieve himself, almost did so on the spot. H. and M. then *had words,* and the matter finished by Matthews's threatening to throw Hobhouse out of a *window,* in consequence of I know not what commerce of jokes ending in this epigram. Hobhouse came to me and said, that his 'respect and regard for me as a host would not permit him to call out any of my guests, and that he should go to town next morning.' He did so. It was in vain that I represented to him that the window was not high, and that the turf under it soft. Away he went.

Scrope recalled how when a wild Irishman, named Farrell, one evening began to say something at a large supper at Cambridge, Matthews roared out 'Silence!' and then, pointing to Farrell, cried out, in the words of the oracle, '*Orson is endowed with reason.*' You may easily suppose that Orson lost what reason he had acquired on hearing this compliment. Poor Matthews had the same sort of droll sardonic way about every thing. His opinions were very revolutionary, like the blessed French, so that we called him 'the Citoyen' for sound reasons.

In this way, joking with Scrope about the dead, we heal each other of the death of Matthews, and perhaps of the death of Mama. It is to be hoped that this is a fitting memorial for our brilliant friend the Citoyen, for though he had voluminous writings that I know of, none of them were ever found.

Once, when the Newstead party broke up for London, Hobhouse and Matthews, who were now the greatest friends possible again, agreed, for a whim, to *walk together* to town.

They quarrelled by the way, and actually walked the latter half of the journey, occasionally passing and repassing, without speaking. When Matthews had got to Highgate, he had spent all his money but three-pence half-penny, and determined to spend that also in a pint of beer, which I believe he was drinking before a public-house, as Hobhouse passed him (still without speaking) for the last time on their route.

They were reconciled in London again.

Mathews was better in theory than in practice. One of his passions was 'the Fancy;' and he sparred uncommonly well. But he always got beaten in *rows*, or combats with the bare first. In swimming, too, he swam well, in theory and in a calm pool; but with *effort* and *labour*, and *too high* out of the water for reality; so that Scrope Davies and myself, of whom he was therein somewhat emulous, always told him that he would be drowned if ever he came to a difficult pass in the water. He was so; but surely Scrope and myself would have been most heartily glad that,

'the Dean had lived,
And our prediction proved a lie.'

Matthews was leader of that profane band of scoffers who used to rouse the Master, Lort Mansel (late Bishop of Bristol) from his slumbers in the lodge of Trinity; and when Mansel appeared at the window foaming with wrath, and crying out, 'I know you, gentlemen, I know you!' were wont to reply to this *Dies Irae*, 'We beseeche thee to hear us, good *Lort*!' – 'Good Lort deliver us!' & etc. Lort was the Bishop's Christian name, but his replies to Matthews's gang of drunks were anything but Christian.

Matthews's head was uncommonly handsome, very like *Pope's* in his youth.

Those days of exercise and song and jokes and wine with Scrope at Newstead are, for obvious reasons, not too clear in our head now. But we remember that we twit him again on the question of his own former suicide (a topic of which we were both fond). We remind him of the time at Brighton in 1808 that after drinking a good deal and losing all our money in a gaming house Scrope and Hobhouse and I (it being high Summer), did firstly strip and plunge into the Sea, whence, after half an hour's swimming of those of us (Scrope and I) who could swim, we emerged in our dressing gowns to discuss a bottle or two of Champagne and Hock (according to choice) at our quarters.

In course of this discussion words arose; Scrope seized H. by the throat; H. seized a knife in self-defence, and stabbed Scrope in the shoulder to avoid being throttled. Scrope fell bathed in blood and wine – for the *bottle* fell with him – being infinitely intoxicated with Gaming, Sea-bathing at two in the morning, and Supplementary Champagne. Scrope's wound proved to be a gash long and broad, but not deep nor dangerous. Scrope was furious: first he wanted to fight, then to go away in a post-chaise, and then to *shoot* himself, which latter intention I offered to forward, provided that he did not use *my pistols*, which, in case of suicide, would become a deo-dand to the King. At length, with many oaths and some difficulty, he was gotten to bed.

Before he passed out that night at Brighton, Scrope had said: 'Life is dice, life is hazard; I would not have it otherwise. It were dishonourable not to play out the game to the end, for who can tell what the next throw may bring? Put

THE WICKED LORD BYRON

Scrope to bed, gentlemen. To keep throwing, to keep throwing, is the thing.' The rest was silence.

To keep throwing the dice, to keep turning up the cards, to *live* was our constant theme those dark nights at Newstead, after the death of Mama and Matthews, when Scrope Davies came to stop us blowing out our brains the first foggy night. He stays a week or more, does not leave us alone again until he has extracted two promises: firstly that we will not kill ourself without having a last drink with him, and secondly to relieve the murderous tedium of his enforced Fellow's stay at Cambridge in the Autumn by coming to visit him there in his Chambers.

Scrope's only *real* income is that of a Fellow of King's College. Likewise his only real home is his rooms at King's. But he hates Cambridge with a vengeance, and it is a blight to his life that he is obliged to spend a certain portion of his year in residence, which he does in Michaelmas Term, or forfeit his income from the College. He insists that we come up the Cam to see him in September, and promises that he will, despite the worst that Cambridge can do, show us a splendid time while we are his guests.

From Cambridge a month or two later, we scribble a letter to Hobhouse:

> *I write from Scrope's rooms, whom I have just assisted to put to bed in a state of outrageous intoxication.*
> *– I think I never saw him so bad before. – We dined at Mr. Caldwell's of Jesus coll: where we met Dr. Clarke and others of the Gown, and Scrope finished himself as usual. – He has been in a similar state every evening since my arrival here a few days ago. – We are*

to dine at Dr. Clarke's on Thursday... I like him much,
though Scrope says we talked so bitterly that he (the
Said Scrope) lost his listeners... Every body here is very
polite and hospitable, my friend Scrope particularly. I
wish to God he would grow sober, as I much fear no
constitution can long support his excesses. – If I lose
him and you, what am I? ...

Scrope mumbles to us (after Mr. Caldwell's dinner) in his delirium. He is making an attempt to answer our own remonstrances, for irritated with the task of putting Scrope to bed (not an uncommon one for his friends) we carelessly (not realising Scrope's capacity to understand us still) accuse him of destroying himself with wine after he had prevented us from destroying ourself with pistol and ball at Newstead. 'You fool, Byron. I never said life was bearable,' Scrope mumbles. 'Still, one may drink, and be alive for another throw in the morning, and drinking thus hath moral superiority over your pistol and ball.'

It were always, apprentice Hamlets all, our practice to complain of the 'almighty fixing his canon against self-slaughter.' But perhaps Scrope may have a valid excuse for drinking. He is particularly maddened, at regular intervals, by the torments of imminent insolvency, the strain of living the high life without independent means.

A *Dandy* normally becomes insolvent at the moment he comes of age. He has no coat of arms, no ancestral portraits, no obligations, no attachments, no wife, no child, no occupation and no obvious means of support. All he has is charm and luck, and the ability to reduce the upper classes to tears by sheer *style* and the criticism of the cut of their coats. To this Scrope the landless vicar's son added the mathematical brain and nerve that made him a gambler.

The Dandies in general have this to commend them: you can not join their society (as many try to do) by using rank, wealth, money or class. The only entrée to that élite is *style*. In this respect ourself, a mere baron, were fortunate to have the acquaintance of Scrope Berdmore Davies, the penniless vicar's son, for he admitted us to scenes of life with which our own standing could not have made us acquainted: from boxing matches to drawing rooms to gaming hells and the like, to every thing. We owe it to Scrope that the Dandies were always very kind to us, though they do not as a rule take to literary men.

Your Dandy is not merely a suit of clothes; he is your only natural revolutionary, for he has nothing to lose except everything. But we have always admired Scrope's courage in his resolve to seek the comforts of death *slowly*. To drink oneself to death is sometimes an act of courage and rebellion.

We added a mountain to the strain upon our friend by committing him to sign for the loans we made with his miraculously gained 'chamber pot money.' That matter is now settled (we paid Scrope some £4800) but it has been only a temporary solution for him. Financial ruin stares us both in the face at regular moments. Scrope himself does not have the possibility of selling his ancestral home, as we do. But he has forbidden us from weakening, and has been known to be above £20,000 *up* on his gaming accounts in a year.

A tidy sum in 1807 and years following, the high life before the fall.

Chapter twelve

'Tis to create, and in creating live
A being more intense, that we endow
With form our fancy, gaining as we give
The life we image, even as I do now.

The poem *Childe Harold* is published; we go to London
to see it through the press; Mr. Murray the publisher
hath launched the book upon the waters; and Scrope Berdmore Davies has been sent out into Society, to see how it is
received. He is enfuriatingly casual about it when he calls,
and seems more concerned with the welfare of the basket
he is carrying on his arm. He puts his basket on the floor
gently and fusses with it to our great annoyance. 'How do
they receive my poem, Scrope, my Childe? Come, come, to
the business in hand...'

'...Mmmmm, dear boy? The thing is, old boy, the business
in hand... ah... I had been meaning to have conversation with
you concerning your mode of living... it seemed to me when
I were sober last, a week last Thursday I think... I remember turning to myself and saying, Scrope, somebody ought
to direct young Byron toward a more temperate, provident,

steady and thoughtful life, a mode of life in fact, dear fellow, like mumumu... ahh...' Scrope stutters rarely, but regularly, to dandy effect.

'Good God! Like you?'

'Precisely so. Like mu-mu – me. Observe – ' – Scrope gesturing – 'the foresight I have displayed today in bringing luncheon in a basket.' He whips away the check cloth over his basket to reveal four wine bottles, beautifully racked in silver.

'Ah, no, Scrope, it is hardly noon...' We are touched, though, that Scrope has deemed seeing him 'a special occasion'. He is strictly a nighttime drinker; he has much business to accomplish by day. We are flattered that this infinitely *busy* man should deem us worthy of drinking with in the daytime. 'Very well, Scrope, if you think I need a bracer to face the bad news... Let us drink on it.'

Scrope yawns. 'But we mustn't be uncivilised. Would you mind fetching the equipment?' We rise to get skullcup and a poker out of a sideboard drawer. Scrope takes the poker off us, leaves us holding the skullcup, gestures for us to sit nearby on the bed. Scrope pulling forward his chair – 'I'll be mother' – deftly hooks out a bottle of wine from the basket, knocking the neck off with a precise blow of the poker.

In a dazzlingly dexterous manoeuvre the bottle of wine is decanted precisely into the skullcup so that no splinters of glass are in the wine. Scrope nods to us casually and takes the skull out of our hands. 'Your very good health, my lord.' He takes a gulp of wine, shudders, hands the skullcup to us with a gracious smile. 'A liquid luncheon to clear the system of residual nourishment. And now that we have fairly commenced luncheon I feel it might be good manners to convey the news.'

'I retired from the world before the Edinburgh Review could slay my book. I am nervous, Scrope, you must not torment me. What are they saying, the fifteen hundred fillers of hot rooms? Do they notice my verses at *all*?'

'I have better news than CANT. I bring you CUNT. You can have...'

'Now, Scrope, be serious...'

Scrope leans forward and pats our arm. 'Your esteemed Piccadilly correspondent went to no less than seven different gatherings – one of which even der grosse ich should not have obtained entrance to had not Brummell been present. I danced with seventy seven Golden Dollies, beauties all, though I fear none on 'em rich enough to support the likes of thee or me.'

'Please, Scrope...'

Scrope laughing. 'The fifteen hundred fillers of hot rooms are as nothing. You will get paid a good deal more for that blasted travelogue than mere social arrival. You will be paid in cunny forevermore!'

'Now Scrope...'

'Never again will you have to fork over a guinea to a trollop, except to save yourself the trouble of speaking to a lady.'

'Dear Christ...'

'Chilled Harry is a sort of RAGE at the moment – all the ladies I spoke to were anxious to meet the poor tragic fella wot wrote it and find out what makes him so sad. You're a strange enough man – damn me if I ever saw you sad without reason. But you will have no reason to be sad again. You can roger any on 'em! Plenum et optabile coitum!'

'Now Scrope...'

'Any of the married ones at any rate and I dare say some of the virgins. I have already ascertained the distinct possibilities of Lady Dorset, Lady Oxford – Lady Oxford by damn! black hair, blue eyes, what more do you – and the Honourable Miss Weston who – here, would you care for some of this wine?' He holds out the liquorous deathshead.

Taking the skullcup off Scrope, draining it and sitting back down. Scrope gestures at the two remaining bottles. We hand them over and Scrope holds them up to smash off the necks with the poker. He finishes the process by upending precisely a bottle and a half into the skull. Replacing the bottles, Scrope notices something in the basket. 'I picked these up as I passed. There were letters on your table in the hall – dozens on 'em. Where is that rascal valet of yours? Does the noble Fletcher not, in these latter days, bring in your correspondence?'

'Fletcher? I warned him to stay away for a couple of days. He knew my temper these days of publication, he is staying with his wife. She has a position in Kensington.' Scrope upends the basket, pouring letters and calling cards on the table, where they form a tidy pile. One of the cards catches our eye. We picks it up, whistles, picks up another, riffles through the pile with mounting terror. 'What the devil am I to DO?'

'By God, look at this one. From old Tommy Moore the scribbler. The most famous poet in Lunnon town...'

'Read that one out...'

Scrope reads, chuckling. 'Well, it ain't quite like the others. Scribbler or no, Mr. Moore fancies himself one of Us Youth.'

'What is it?'

'A challenge.'

'Good Christ.'

Scrope does a stage Irish accent. "Sorr, should you fail to attend my forthcoming dinner party on the 24th inst., when we can discuss the meaning of the reference in your production *ENGLISH BARDS AND SCOTCH REVIEWERS* to an encounter fought between myself and the pig Jeffrey, I shall be obliged to have my personal representative call upon you in order that we may divine the accuracy of your remarks and settle the matter without words. At your earliest convenience, sir, I await your reply.' Why, what a name in English poesy you would make if you *Mantoned* the Irish songbird with a pistol...' Scrope laughs. 'Man, you have to do it, it would be so funny.'

'A duel with Tommy Moore! I published that little piece of bitchery before I left Europe – he don't even bother to notice the insult then. Don't suppose he even read it. Why, I used to read Tommy Moore when I were a little lad at school.'

'There is more: 'Post Scriptum. I shall await, sir, your reply with alacrity. We dine on roasted quail the evening of the 24th; it is a bird of which I understand your lordship to be inordinately fond, yours etc., etc., Moore.' He has underlined the words *inordinately fond.'*

'Let me see that.'

Scrope hands it over. 'Didn't you point out that Tommy's seconds had made sure t'other fella's pistol had no ball? He can hardly want to shoot you for it. The Beau told me he has just married a gorgeous Golden Dolly almost too fat to feed upon. Why, Alvanley himself was after her, and there, sir, is a dandy in SERIOUS need of funds – but Tommy Moore the scribbler got this particular Golden Dolly in the end. He has every reason to live. He has her fortune to spend.'

'Would it be craven to fire off a letter of reply?'

'Here, pass that receptacle. The wine should have breathed a bit by now.'

Scrope takes a pull of wine. 'I have it. The PUNCTUATION of the post scriptum is of course the out. 'It is a bird of which I understand your lordship to <u>be inordinately fond</u>, yours etc., etc., Moore.' He has underlined the words *'inordinately fond.'* The mere underlining makes it quite acceptable for you to go and eat Tommy's quail.'

Riffling through cards and invites. 'How the devil am I to know which of these evenings to attend? I can hardly go to 'em all.' We are not a little dazed. It is like a fantasy come true for a poor fellow hardly in his twenties. Baron or no, we have before now been but an obscure presence in this foggy town.

Scrope rummages through the pile. 'We must make a selection, dear fellow.' He is looking for something he knows must be there. At last pounces on a card. 'AHA!'

'What?'

'The very biscuit and tea if you're to make your mark as a young Reform Whig thruster. It's a card for supper at the house of Lady Holland – duchess of the drawing rooms.'

'Holland House! Have they heard of me THERE, too?'

'That'll be the ticket, if you really must *arriver.* All t'others will have to pass through the fat old cow's house sooner or later. You can meet 'em and then decide if visiting their other damned houses is worth your time.'

The secretly hoped-for, dreaded thing has happened. 'Before I left I was the least fashionable buck in London, creeping to my drab little club to eat my dinner.'

'My dear fellow, don't think of that no more. On est arrivé, dear boy.' Scrope drinks and passes the skullcup. 'Good health and a short sweet life.'

We take the skull and repeat automatically: 'Good health and a short sweet life.'

Chapter thirteen

But who can view the ripen'd rose, nor seek
To wear it? Who can curiously behold
The smoothness and the sheen of beauty's cheek,
Nor feel the heart can never all grow old?
Who can contemplate Fame through clouds unfold
The star which rises o'er her steep, nor climb?
Harold, once more within the vortex, roll'd
On with the giddy circle, chasing Time,
Yet with a nobler aim than in his youth's fond prime.

(The Spirit takes a grip on himself, looking round in distaste at the dirty walls in the squalid little room in Missolonghi. 'Yes, yes. We woke up one day and found ourself famous.')

The planetary movement of the waltzers performing the daring new dance. As a lamed man we could only stand and watch, pretending to enjoy ourself, as we gazed at the orbit from which we must be always excluded. The rustle of silk dresses, shining under thousands of candles, in chandeliers of precious crystal. The music ended. Lady Caroline Lamb

stopped waltzing and waltzed up. We offered her a single red
rose we had been concealing inside our jacket. 'The first of
the season. Your ladyship, I am told, likes all that is new and
rare. For a moment.'

'Would your lordship care to join the dance?'

'My body was not made for waltzing.'

'There are other kinds of waltzing.'

And so Caro invited with her eyes what happened that
night, as we took her home in our new coach, Webster's
coach, and the difficulty of getting into the woman through
all that silk, her gasps of outrage and delight when the task
was accomplished and our hands were working at the sticky
prize. Soon Caro Lamb, the great society lady, bucking like
a goat across our coach seat, and we are congratulating ourself on the performance of the coach's springs, this woman
will fasten on us like a vampire, she clutches us now with her
cunny to say never O never go away, comes, bursting, panting, like the good whore she is under the skin; our first piece
at the ducal rank. A trifle frightening, that scary bitch on the
first night.

We began to see that Scrope was right, that he had
traversed this glade in the forest of existence before us as
usual. It is hard to tell if there is a difference between a trollop and a great lady, in the heat of the night, inside her.

At the next ball as we stood talking with Caro, we were
already aware she was speaking too loudly. We burned in
embarrassment – people were looking. Caro's husband
approached. But Lady Caroline would have no truck with the
decorous fiction of respectable adultery. Before she turned
away from us to William Lamb she called out, causing several heads to turn, her two immortal lines. 'Mad, bad, and

dangerous to know.' We grinned at this glorious slander, but were not so pleased by the following promise: 'That beautiful pale face is my fate.'

Caro's wasn't ours for more than a month or so. We remember how the even greater mistake got started now. Lady Caroline had a *cousin* as *backward* in the matter of coitum as her ladyship was *forward*.

Miss Annabella Milbanke generally stood to the left of the waltzing circle, in an attitude of indifference. She would fan herself in the room's sweated heat, looking around disapprovingly. One night, after having been introduced to her by Caro, we caught Annabella's eye – not a difficult thing for us, that season. A gorgeous little prig – juiciest virgin in the room. Perhaps the ONLY virgin in the room. Tasty little miss of twenty; one of the Blues, of course.

The bluestocking would write that night to her parent: 'My dearest mama, the subject of every conversation here is the young, noble and justly celebrated poet Lord Byron. I am convinced he is sincerely repentant of the evil he has done, though he will need, I perceive, the aid of some more upright person than those with whom he habitually associates' – meaning her cousin Caro – 'to help him maintain his resolution toward a new course of conduct and feelings.'

We changed course to speak to Annabella. (A fly going to fresh blue meat.) Shook her hand politely. 'Your ladyship cannot know how much your freshness serves to charm my weary, stale and unprofitable existence...'

'O my lord...'

We pointed at the fashionable circle waiting for the next waltz. 'Observe how they revel in the merry-go-round. Up for anything so long as it is no more than another sweep around the room. And are you standing aside from it all, Miss Milbanke? So much the better for your judgment.' A suitably dramatic pause. 'Do you think there is one person here who dares to look into himself?'

Alas, she was thinking, my poor suffering Childe, the handsomest man in the room. She had read our poem and is positive that she can solve our problems toute sweet. 'I have not a friend in the world,' we said, doing Childe Harold for her, almost as a matter of practice. We took her hand again, bowed farewell. Perfect performance.

The fatal fish was hooked. What fools we both were.

That night she would write: 'Mama, at that moment I vowed in silence to be a devoted friend to this lone being.'

Caro Lamb's face working in fury as she rushed over to us following the performance with the Milbanke. 'You... you...' We gave Caro a glance on our way toward the group surrounding Lady Oxford. Caro's lip curled back at her cousin Annabella in a feral snarl. 'The wheyfaced little chilled pudding. A Milbanke! He will never endure the taste,' she muttered.

'MY LORD!' she shouted then, embarrassing us.

We hissed to her softly: 'We don't want *you*, my charmer. Look to yourself before accusing Miss Milbanke of being *cold* – your very anger is made of ice.'

Caro crying out in pain: 'But WAS I COLD in your carriage when first you made me yours – when first you told me to kiss your mouth and I durst not – and after thinking THAT such a crime I could prevent nothing afterwards – you drew me to you like a magnet and indeed I could not I could not have kept away...'

The onlookers whispered to each other, scandalised, scandalising. Born into the highest, Caro is starting the process that will result in losing caste and, in the end, sanity itself. But we were turning away. *We will be revenged on the whole pack of you, you ladies who laughed at the little lame boy. No hope for them as laughs...*

To Caroline's fury we managed to reach the group around the Countess of Oxford. Jane Oxford was soft and smooth like a piece of velvet, juicy and mellow as the autumn season itself, a tree ripe with fruit. As a young Elizabethan, Mr. Thomas Nashe, observed of his own girl, 'it doth me good when I remember her.'

A beauty still, at forty. Married only the once – and why not? – to a very tolerant fellow called Teddy Harley. You will recall that famous collection of scribblings published from the Oxford's library, in the time of our grandsires. It was called the Harleian Miscellany – which is what folk used to call the Countess's offspring. Five brats – first by the husband, the son and heir, the rest each by a different lover. The Harleian Miscellany – yes?

So much for Teddy Harley. But Jane was clever. Hated Tories. Took her pick of the hotblooded young men in the Reform Party – the radical boyos, the wild Whigs. Like ourself.

As the Countess and I concluded our arrangements there came a messenger hotfoot from the House of Lords. We scanned the note irritably. The message requested his lordship's presence immediately on a matter of the gravest urgency. The House was exactly divided on the vote whether or not to give a limited emancipation to the Irish Catholics. It seemed that Lord Byron held the casting vote. 'I will await your return,' said Jane. 'Fear nothing, venture all...'

I quitted the ball – somewhat reluctantly, I confess – in

order to emancipate five million people. On our return from the House, Lady Oxford invites us to visit her at her estate, Eywood. 'We shall fly. We shall pass our days like the gods in Lucretius.'

We took her hand, kissing it politely. 'And the husband?'

Jane caught her husband's eye. Harley, on cue, stepped forward to shake our hand with genuine enthusiasm. 'My dear fellow, it's an honour. An honour.'

'A *pleasure*,' we corrected him.

'Quite.' Harley stepped back, bored, resumed his cigar, looking at the other women.

'What a very modern arrangement,' we observed to Jane. We was a little shocked. With the connivance of the husband!

Caro Lamb hissing like a cat at the sight of Jane and us leaving together. 'I suppose you've HAD everybody,' she mutters venomously at us as we pass, Jane on our arm.

We yawn. 'Not QUITE everybody.'

Another night. Augusta's face. Our sister's face. She is saying something we have not heard, rapt as we are by the vision of that face, so like our own.

After Mama's death Augusta had expressed her condolences so sweetly that we had quite made up our quarrel with her. (Mama was not Augusta's mother, we shared only in our father 'Handsome Jack' Byron.) We saw Augusta (who is lady in waiting to the Princess of Wales) quite often then, in Town. We were getting to know her properly for the first time in our life.

'To see your face is to look into a crystal mirror and watch my own soul peering out from a girl's eyes... Love at first sight indeed.'

'But how do you LIKE it? Not me, you fool, the DRESS.'

'Alas, 'tis bitter cold, and I am sick at heart.'

'I never understand you .'

We laughed. The main thing. To have a woman with a sense of humour.

'Ignorant bitch. Have you not seen Kean as ye mad Prince Hamlet?'

'But must you be sad on a night like this? The Princess has been reading your verses – you are quite the rage, now, Baby B.' This last a reference to the fact that she had hardly seen me since I was a baby – she was a few years older, and remembered me so.

Taking our arm, she led us outside, through the open French window. Under the Moon the white roses turned to silver and the red to balls of rich darkness. 'Smell them, Baby. You must not be sad tonight. Your Mama is smiling down on us like the moon.' She took a luxurious breath. 'Can you not smell?'

'Yes – yes...'

'Life is like this for such a short summer, Baby. Only a monthlong summer of rosebreath and sunshine – that is all we can hope for in this life. You must not waste what there is by being sad, even if it IS the fashion to be like the mad Prince Hamlet.'

'Coming through that window into Lord Holland's rose-garden is like walking into a *wall* of scent. I could swear we were in Athens of a warm spring evening...' We walked further into the darkness. Inside the great room the waltzers waltzed on.

Next day Scrope told us that, in the following musical interlude, there was a sort of *buzzing* round the hall: 'Byrr'n, Byrr'n, Byrr'n, Byrr'n...'

Chapter Fourteen

For thee, my own sweet sister, in thy heart
I know myself secure, as thou in mine;
We were and are – I am, even as thou art –
Beings who ne'er each other can resign;
It is the same, together or apart,
From life's commencement to its slow decline
We are entwined – let death come slow or fast,
The tie which bound the first endures the last!

Scrope always preferred the wrong end of the ballroom away from the dancers where the dandies were drinking as if at their club, watching the action with a catlike detachment. We found him there, among the dandies. We were wearied unto death, but not as weary as Scrope, who had just won 500 guineas by playing a tennis match and betting upon himself. (Scrope was one of the best tennis players in England, a thing that frequently surprised his opponents, who would have seen him the night before the match drink himself into oblivion.)

We noticed Scrope staring past us, and we turned around. In the distance Miss Annabella Milbanke saw our head turn. She fluttered her fan until our glance settled on her. 'Look at that! Did you see the dark one move?'

'With the fan? Succulent. I've been looking at it all night.' Scrope licked his lips.

'Aye, the fan.'

Scrope got up and peered over our shoulder to get a better view, half-leaning on us. 'Who is the gel? Why ain't she waltzing? Not TOO short in the leg. Can she afford us? We are an expensive luxury.'

'Perhaps she's the one we need, Scrope. A Golden Dolly to make us behave.'

Scrope peered. 'She looks to be a virgin. Now THAT would be a novelty.'

'We write each other letters, Sir, letters. She is very fond of arithmetic. I call her my Princess of Parallelograms.'

'And worth how much a-year? Say, in square figures...'

'Be careful Scrope she's looking...'

'Dammit I'm no judge in matters matrimonial. She ain't a bad piece of womanflesh. I have not spoke with her, so I do not know if she has a *mind*. We ought to ask Hobby.'

John Cam Hobhouse was standing nearer Annabella – dangerous ground, an exposed stag on the edge of the male covert. Annabella was hunting a husband that season, as were so many of the ladies, or tigresses, if you want to pursue the analogy. Scrope finished his glasses of sherry, got up, and moved with tipsy care to where Hobhouse was chatting with a political friend.

Hobhouse excused himself from the friend. 'I say Scrope you are not going to be drunk and sensibilitous are you?'

Scrope wagged a rebuking finger. 'Now be serious for once Hobhouse, I have been giving our friend Byron some sage matrimonial advice.'

Hobhouse laughed. 'Scrope Davies's advice on matrimony? A new thing under the sun...'

'Dammit, Hobby, this is serious...' We gripped Hobhouse's shoulder to turn him around. 'There. Look. What do you think of THAT one?'

Annabella fanned herself furiously in the renewed attention. Hobhouse was appalled. 'You would destroy the poor creature in the first week, like a little boy breaking a toy.'

We put our hand over Hobby's mouth. 'Bad luck to say so, my friend. Besides, she is tougher than she looks.'

'Then so much the worse for YOUR future peace.' Hobhouse shook his head. 'But why marry at all, except, as I suppose, for money?'

'Don't you see how Caro and the lady this, the honourable Miss that, they drain my very blood... I can take no more ladies of fashion, Hobby. They take too big a slice of you. I would be better off back with the good honest whores of Brighton.'

'And where is the harm in that?' Hobhouse was shy with real ladies: his own experiences of love had always been paid for in cash – professional sex from the lower orders, so that he understood real ladies not at all.

'I need the help of a woman's principles to regain a measure of control.'

'But man, you cannot ask a woman to be your *regulator* as if you were a *steam-shuttle*.' Hobhouse laughing now.

Scrope waxed indignant at talk of regulation. 'Now look, Cam, we have GIVEN THOUGHT to this. Damme if she isn't the very biscuit and tea for young Byron.'

John Cam glancing doubtfully at Annabella who fanned more furiously. 'And, why is she the biscuit and tea, Scrope?'

Scrope, on his mettle, squinting to get a better look. 'Upright as a yard rule, ah – not a lot taller.' Knowingly:

'She looks to have good wind, and is sound enough in the withers...'

'Are you describing Miss Milbanke or the horses you would wager her expectations upon?'

Scrope and Hobhouse patting each other's back in laughter, to our great exasperation. 'For God his sake – she's looking. Act decently, can't you?'

Hobhouse began to realize that we were not joking. 'After laughing with me about the married men, the foxes who had cut off their tails? How could you think of marrying a girl like *that*...'

Scrope was growing bored. 'O holy deadlock the only possible restraint.'

'But the problem is, Hobby – how is one to talk love to a young girl like that?' Scrope howled with laughter at us, several heads turned, Annabella's fan whirring.

Hobhouse scandalised. 'Now Scrope...' Scrope, muttering, placed himself in a nearby chair and lay his arms on the table to pillow his head, which he lowered gently until it was resting on his arms, and began snoring.

We observe this fall into night. 'Why did he laugh, Hobby?'

'Because my dear fellow, you are surely aware that since your poem became the rage there isn't a woman in this room who is not hoping that you might look her way.'

'Yet what does it matter? Look at yonder fallen fellow.' We looked down at Scrope. 'With no woman for him to build a civilisation around, or to build it around *him*, what shall pull him back from the pit?'

A muffled voice from the table. 'I shall be sure to return the compliment the next time I see you in my current condition, Your Worthlessness. How dare you look down on me! How dare you claim profligacy like to the Birdmore's!' Scrope slept then, the weariest man in England.

We pressed on with our theory. 'You see, Hobby? A man's wildness needs to be chained to some necessary rock – as a tide needs a coast, as a river needs a bank to prevent it spending itself in a thousand directions at once, in that blind craving for sensation to fill up this bitter void that is life.'

Hobhouse grinning at this. 'Enough, enough. Go and ask her.'

Despite our shyness, we found that the approach was easy – it was the meaning of the conversation that would prove difficult. 'Miss Milbanke, may we have words?'

'My dearest Lord B, it is always a pleasure to me to conduct either our conversation or our correspondence.'

We kissed politely the proffered hand. 'Since we were first acquainted, your solicitous letters have given me much comfort.'

Annabella took this as a sally and smiled. 'O my lord...'

'Madam, let us not be indirect. I wish to proceed to the point.'

'Must there always be a *point* to a friendship?'

We relinquished her hand, relaxing as battle commenced. 'There is often at least a point in conversations. The point of this one might be perhaps to remind you that the time draws on when one might wish to seek a partner through this world into the next.'

'Sir!'

'I should be plainer – Miss Milbanke, I seek a wife. If you would display an inclination to consider this vacant position I should be obliged. If your answer is no we can return to our more philosophical mode of discourse.'

She started back in alarm and rising anger. 'My LORD, I had heard that you have the power to trifle with a lady's heart – is it now my turn to be treated so after the friendship which has been ours?'

'Friend – ship?'

'I never use the word lightly.' (She never used any word lightly.) 'If I had not acquired the habit of reflecting before I act, I should sacrifice considerations of prudence to the first impulse of feeling. But REASON advises me more truly that...'

'Reason tells you things? Reason, you say?' The eighteenth century man, we were marvelling at this early example of the nineteenth century use of the word, with its piquant flavour of morality.

Annabella, who had no notion that words can have diverse meanings, was thrown off the track of her argument. 'Yes, indeed. Reason.'

'Please, please. Do go on.'

'Before I came to town for the first time this season I had reflected long and carefully upon the subject of a husband. I wrote out a list of requirements. Firstly I should require a rational tenor of affection for myself, not that violent attachment which is susceptible of sudden increases or diminutions from trifles...'

'My dear lady, may I assure you that nothing *violent* had ever crossed my heart with respect to yourself.' We grinned, foolishly pleased with our own riposte, but she ignored it.

'Secondly one should perhaps consider your personal predilections which as you have informed me have brought you to grief many times. And yet even this particular problem might not be insuperable. I cannot but feel that if you truly loved and respected a person you would be able to take a more straitened path. However: it seems clear that your lord-ship would have to know *me* a good deal better before you could say whether you could respect me sufficiently to make a change in your mode of living.'

Our head swam in confusion. 'Madam I would be grate-ful if you were to explain your explanation a little...?'

'I must regretfully conclude that we do not know each other well enough to commit ourselves to marriage at this time.'

'Madam I then humbly thank you for your patience.'

As we started to turn away we could feel our mouth twist-ing with pique. She caught our arm. 'I hope we will be able to continue our friendship. I should be sorry to relinquish a cor-respondence which is capable of imparting so much *rational* pleasure.'

We smiled at her ruefully. 'Far be it from me to deny you your *rational* pleasure, Miss Milbanke. I dare say we can stay on civil terms.'

We were impressed. The first woman to refuse us since our apotheosis into Childe Harold. It had the savour of a new experience.

Hobhouse, observing the amiable outcome, had assumed a favourable result. 'Well, dear fellow – and when is the lady to board the Byronic vessel?'

Scrope attempted to wake up, blearily raised his head from the table and mumbled: 'Woman on top by far the best position...'

'Scrope,' Hobhouse warned, with a nervous glance at the bystanders, who were starting to turn around.

We smiled at the contrast made by our friends. 'Hobhouse rebukes you, Scrope.'

'Damn him!'

'But gentlemen you have been too optimistic. The Princess of Parallelograms has drawn both our souls into two parallel lines, prolonged to an infinity of friendship but alas never to touch.'

Hobhouse amazed. 'She turned you down?' Scrope falling off his chair laughing. 'Scrope! People observe!' snapped Hobby. Scrope making one of his miraculous recoveries, got up, waving a hand to excuse himself to the company.

'Aye you can laugh, Scrope. Your prophecies are confounded. I have this day spoken to a woman who was capable of refusing me.'

Hobhouse took our arm. 'My dear fellow, it may be for the best. I had my doubts.'

'To hell with these women. A man can live neither with nor without them.'

Scrope looked down at his own swaying body with a cynical detachment. 'Gentlemen – Scrope's body is moving of its own volition. Unless the room is moving, which seems unlikely. Something must be done. Sleep is better than death, you know...'

As his friends looked on in astonishment, Scrope Davies performed a trick scarcely before seen at a ball. Without drawing the attention of a single pince-nez, he slipped to the floor and crawled under the table.

Only one old gentleman nearby turned a startled eye on the sight of the grown man crawling under a table. Scrope, almost disappeared, turned to his friends. 'And so gentlemen for a time I bid you a good night.'

'Goodnight, Scrope.'

'Goodnight, sweet prince,' said Hobhouse. Scrope beamed and vanished into his lair, pulling the cloth down like a curtain.

Augusta approached.

'And are you here, Goose? So much the better for the occasion.'

She held out her hand for Hobhouse, who bowed over it. 'Your servant, Mrs. Leigh.'

'Mr. Hobhouse.'

Miss Weston came over and reminded John Cam that he has her ticket for the next waltz – for even poor old staid Hobhouse could waltz, whilst we had to look on eternally at the dance. The lady, not without a curious glance at the Byronic siblings, carried Hobhouse away, ladylike.

Augusta, unladylike, snatched two glasses of champagne from a passing flunky. She gravely gave one to us, and made a toast. 'Baby B.'

'Sister Goose.' We drained our glasses and she snatched two more.

She giggled. 'I do believe this is my thirteenth glass of champagne. Is that unlucky? Well, they are not BIG glasses.'

'You shall drink fountains of it if you wish. A woman should only eat lobster salad and drink champagne, the only truly feminine and becoming viands.'

'O Baby, I want to know how you go on. You are quite the famous fellow – the essential guest at every gathering. Are you happier for it?'

'You sound like Scrope.'

'Ah, Mr. Davies. How is HE?'

'He is under yonder table.'

'Ah, what you men get up to in this corner of the room...'

'You would not believe how hard it has become for me to leave this corner.'

'None of your snivelling. Embrace your glorious fate. Not a lungful of your tainted air will I breathe.'

We took her arm. 'Then I shall remove you to the rose garden.'

She giggled. 'Some fresh air would not be a bad idea. It must be the bubbles...' We went out, nodding to the footman who opened the French window and let us out into Lord Holland's rosegarden. The air was drenched with scent. We snuffed. 'GOD!'

'God is acceptance.'

'What?'

'Only think how happy you could be then, if you would simply jump into the river of acceptance.' She giggled.

'You damned pagan bitch. You have lost me.'

This delighted her. 'Why not? College is not everything. And besides, you always told me you *never worked*.' The last two Byrons on earth laughing.

'You see, Baby B, there is not one person here who is better for you than your own kind.'

'To hell with other women. To walk with you is to smell roses under the moonlight...'

She staggered a little and we caught her. She stroked our face. 'Poor Baby...'

'Every time that I am privileged to walk into this wall of scent I ask myself for the thousandth time why I should not stay in a garden with *you*, never go back to the other human beings...'

'How you go on.'

'Scrope told me the Colonel has gone to Newmarket with all the money he could raise and that you had been in straitened circumstances until the Princess herself had to send you assistance.'

'O, you know, with all the babies to care for. But the Colonel must make a show at Newmarket. The Prince would expect it.'

'Warm heart and your gold so warm it runs away like molten metal – easy to see you are a Byron.' We take her face between our hands. 'I dreamt of you the other night. I was out-of-doors somewhere, your face was huge and pale, impossibly distant, floating in the black sky like the moon. For an instant I thought it was my own face, in an immense and sombre mirror.' We kissed her, lingering on her lips.

She pushed us off laughing. 'I am your elder sister, a respectable married woman... whom you have escorted but for a moment into this garden. You forget yourself, Sir.'

'Certain things were discovered in a Garden – by two who like us were of the same flesh. Only later did men call it sin.'

We led her further into the bushes, as she protested feebly: 'One cannot approve of such sentiments.'

Hobhouse finished his dance with Miss Weston, and returned to talk to his friend, who was nowhere to be seen. 'Has any of you fellows seen Byron?' he asked the bystanders.

Unexpectedly Scrope stuck his head wearily out from under his table. 'Do pipe down, Hobby. I am *tired* – can I never make you understand how *tired* I am?'

'Byron has disappeared...'

'Think, dear man – you know where he has gone without making all this fuss.'

'I don't know – where?...'

Scrope raised himself on his arm and snarled. 'Blast your eyes...'

He looked up at Hobhouse irritably but was astonished at the ignorance he saw in the other's face. He gestured vaguely after the siblings, but was unable to think of a bon mot. He backed rapidly to vanish under the tablecloth again, pausing only to bark: 'OUT!!!'

Hobhouse crossed to the great window and threw it open. The footman gave him a curious look as he stood there, peering anxiously into a darkness.

Chapter fifteen

– but really & truly – as I hope mercy & happiness for her – by that
God who made me for my own misery – & not much for the good of
others – she was not to blame – one thousandth part in comparison –
she was not aware of her own peril – till it was too late – and I can only
account for her subsequent 'abandon' by an observation which I think is
not unjust – that women are much more attached than men – if they are
treated with any thing like fairness or tenderness.

The Prince of Wales coffee house. A fine French dinner, head to head with Scrope Berdmore Davies. In came the Lord Alvanley, one of the ugliest but most exquisite dandies in London. After nodding at Scrope, his fellow beau, he seated himself at a nearby table. 'Waiter.' The man ran over assiduously. The whole company was more than a little curious to see what the great man would order. And Alvanley, in the softest and smallest of voices: 'Waiter, bring me a glass of Madeira Negus with a Jelly, and rub my plate with a Chalotte.'

A drunken Lieutenant of the Navy in the next box roars out: 'And waiter, bring me a glass of damned stiff grog, and rub my arse with a brick-bat!' The place breaking down with laughter, Alvanley's face looking as if he has eaten a lemon.

Scrope gestured at his plate. 'A splendid meal. Splendid. Thanks to that happy turn of the cards last night, I Scrope shall settle the bill.'

We looked around. 'I had hoped to meet Tommy Moore here too but he said he might have to come late. He will tell us the news.'

'Of course – the extent of the damage. I say, do they have some decent port in the place? This wretched claret of theirs becomes acid upon the tongue at the last.'

We ordered a bottle of port. The waiter brought it and poured our glasses. We are anxious that Scrope approve of the wine. 'This stuff should suit you. I believe it's older than I am.'

Scrope sipping. 'Ah, that's better. There is no point in having the gout in later life unless the port has been good.'

'Do you think you shall take as much care over what you drink at my funeral?'

'Hardly a FUNREAL, dear boy. Not quite a funreal, as I calls 'em. Quite the reverse. Commonly a cause for celebration, you know.'

'Had the Colonel not been out of the county when the child was engendered, Scrope, I might have agreed with you.'

'And where is young Hobhouse tonight? Out nosing into the news?'

'I have heard that he threatened to call men out all over town last night. Though he knows the essential truth of the charge as well as any man.' We thought of something and chuckled. 'Do you remember what Ben Jonson said to Sylvester, who challenged him to rhyme with:

'I, John Sylvester,
Lay with your sister.'

Jonson answers: 'I, Ben Jonson, lay with your wife.'

'That is not rhyme,' says Sylvester. 'No,' says Ben Jonson; 'but it is *true*.''

As we laugh at dead Ben's witticism we see Tom Moore making his way across the packed room. Something in Moore's look made us lurch to our feet even as Scrope chuckled on alone. 'Excuse me gentlemen – I did not mean to interrupt your jest.'

Scrope the Dandy was not to be impressed by a mere literary man. 'Nay,' he drawled, ''twasn't ours – 'twas old Ben Jonson's...'

A famous man, who wants all his friends to be friends, has to work with the uneasy mix of those before and after his celebrity. 'Tommy, Tommy, come in, sit down. You know my friend Scrope...'

'Mr. Davies and I are acquainted from the time he was your second and made peace between us, of course.'

'If Mr. Moore,' said Scrope, somewhat mollified at being recognised, 'will do us the honour of joining our table.' Moore sat down.

'Would you care for some of this port? Coffee? Champagne?'

'Port will do, I thank you.'

Scrope gave him port. A tall, patrician-looking Irishman with some trace of an accent yet; greyhaired, handsome, he was not yet forty. The son of a grocer, he had risen through the popularity of his poetry to the highest social levels in the land. Ourself and Moore had both been through the baptism of fire that is fame; but Moore did not hold his lightly, in the Byronic manner. It had been damned hardearned, the fame of Tommy Moore, a long campaign of knocking on the door of polite society until they let him in.

'Your health, gentlemen.' Moore downed a glass and was refilled. The formalities were over. 'I will come straight to the point. Mr. Hobhouse, so I was told at Lady Jersey's, offered to challenge one of the company last night.'

Scrope snorted, amused. 'Hobby's the game one. I hopes he can shoot straighter than when we was at College.'

'God bless him, he should not be risking his life for MY misdeeds,' we muttered. 'Who did he call out? I will fight the bastard myself...'

Moore was not impressed with our bravery. 'I hardly think that killing a man will be the best way of quelling *talk*. Please be serious. We are talking about losing caste.'

Scrope laughed. 'An old English baron does not lose caste so easily,' we ventured.

'But I can assure you both, gentlemen, it is a heavy thing not to be receivable in a *dacent* man's house.' Scrope stopped laughing. He could see Moore was so serious that the oirish accent had come out.

'O, comme çi comme ça,' Scrope replied. The Dandies were sufficient unto themselves, and were to that extent aloof from a society whose rules they did not recognize.

'Let the bastards shun me. Does Caro Lamb think she will make me as unpopular as *she* has become?' We pulled a handful of tickets out of our pocket, threw them carelessly onto the table. 'There will always be PARTIES.'

Moore did not smile. 'I try to look after your interests, because you are my friend. Sir, I have a particular care of my friends.' He glanced at Scrope, who was nodding approval.

'Gentlemen...why so sad?' We poured another glass all round. 'Life is bread, but life is brief, as Augusta says. Lees loom and doom glooms, as she puts it in her damned crinkum crankum. What is the difference who one's father is? As for the brat, it *ain't an ape*. We have confounded the world's belief in THAT superstition at least.'

The subject of having a baby with our sister at last having been broached, we all relaxed a little. Scrope Davies offered the company cigars, and we sat smoking comfortably. Moore revealed his bedrock Irishman's weapon: the streak of optimism that was the essential ingredient of his charm. 'Well, gentlemen, but the damage is NOT IRREPARABLE. No one knows enough to believe any of these stories for long. We may thank Colonel Leigh's reticence for that.'

'A spendthrift, rotten, drunken bastard. But a gentleman for a' that.'

Moore sighing. 'This will blow over. It is simply talk. There is always talk. However...' he paused, exchanged another glance with Scrope.

'Yes? However?'

Scrope mumbled through his cigar: 'Mr. Moore means there is one thing at least that you can do to remedy the situation.' White teeth grinning around the cigar, silver eyed devil.

'Mr. Davies is right. You should have done the sensible thing when you had the chance.'

We turned angrily on smiling Scrope. 'Dammitall, you saw Miss Milbanke refuse me! Why the devil do *you* not get married if it is so desirable a state!'

Moore was not smiling. 'Miss Milbanke is not the only lady of marriageable age in London. But there is one way to still TALK. You shall always have my friendship, but I speak as one who wishes to continue to see you also in Society, where perhaps you might not be readily admitted if you persist in...'

'Tommy. You may decide to marry me off if you insist. But wherefore should I take matrimonial advice from Scrope Berdmore Davies Esq.? I grant that, whenever I seem to arrive at a little open space in the forest of existence, as I limp across the clearing I look down and often see the neat prints of Scrope's boots in the mud and realise that the bastard has been there before me. But I do not see Scrope's unmarried bootprints here.' Scrope laughed out loud, even Moore smiled, we had put the table in humour.

'O, there are exceptions to every rule, you know. Exceptional men, at any rate,' Scrope offered.

'I myself have never regretted marriage,' said Tommy.

'There remains only the problem of whom to marry – a slight problem to be sure, but a MATERIAL one.'

Scrope blew a perfect smoke-ring and we watched it hold its shape for a long moment. 'I believe there's a reasonably vast selection on the market this season.'

Chapter sixteen

– I have written – yet hardly a word that I intended to say –

Augusta at table in her drawing room, in the moldering house near Newmarket so convenient for the Colonel's racing. She lingered happily over tea and cakes, rocking the cradle with her left hand. 'Come and speak to her, Baby. Come and look at least...'

We were facing away from her, in case our face as we replied did not always correspond to our tone of voice. 'I don't have a lot of use for 'em at the mewling and puking stage. I told you that with your last.' A silence, and we turned around. 'Though of course, this one is not quite like the others.'

Augusta sipped tea. 'You speak as if you were the only man in the world ever to feel shame and guilt. You speak like a little boy still.' She nibbled at a bonbon. 'You wallow in the guilt as you wallowed in the sin. Is one mistake not enough for you?'

We looked into the cradle. OUR child, the essence of the Byrons...

'Is it surprising she resembles those old pictures of Dad? And is she to blame for my loving you? Is this the curse God

puts on the world? I enter the flesh most dear to me, to con-
taminate it with a stray soul that the world says should not
be... A wild spore blown in on the winds generated by the
chaos of our passage...'

'Don't you want to hold her?'

We turned away. Augusta rang the bell for the nanny, who
came in and took the little bundle away. When the girl was
gone, we ventured: 'Have you heard any more from your little friend Charlotte?'

'O, Charlotte has always adored you, Geordie. But you
must not be too upset if her daddy won't let her have you.
There is always Miss Milbanke to ask again. Miss Milbanke
still has excellent prospects of a fortune when Lord Wentworth dies. She will be a peeress in her own right, some day.'

We were suddenly merry. 'By all means let us preserve the
blueness of our blood. Miss Milbanke let it be. She is a pretty
enough girl in her way...'

'I like Charlotte better. But there is still a chance that
Charlotte will accept you. She has got around her daddy
before now. No doubt we shall get a letter today.'

'She too is a pretty little thing. They are all on 'em pretty
little things. As long as it ain't that Arabella Forbes. SHE is no
better than a Tory. By God I could never abide a Tory. Jumped-
up, parvenu little line-toers, the beasts of the bourgeoisie...'

The post arrived. We took a letter off the tray, dismiss-
ing the servant. We read the letter, our face feeling suddenly
drained of blood, and wordlessly handed it to Augusta. Shame.
We had liked young Charlotte. Augusta read, pursing her lips.
'She does not write a very pretty letter. I would say that she
is no great loss to either of us.' Her brow cleared. 'You must
speak to Miss Milbanke again. You would love her in a week.'

'There was always something *piquante* about Miss Milbanke. But what decent woman would accept me save as stallion for the night, while the longer night cometh on...?'

'You could never refuse a pretty woman like Miss Milbanke anything.' She rang a bell for the maid, and got the girl to bring writing materials. She gestured for us to sit beside her. 'Come, Baby. Let us compose a letter.'

We picked up the steel pen, dipped it into the ink, and began to scrawl: *My dear Miss Milbanke, I trust you have shaken off the slight fever you informed me of in your last. The remainder of what you had written I must confess I am not positive I understand. You have written of moral objections to our union. Can you also conceive of some change of conduct which might, under the impetus of respect for a good woman, remove that good woman's objections? I write merely to enquire of possibilities. Yours, et cetera et cetera, Byron.*

Augusta rang the bell. 'You might have put it more prettily.' The girl came in. Augusta folded the letter, dripped candlewax over it to make a seal. We stamped the imprint of our signet ring into the cooling wax, and scribbled Annabella's familiar address, with all the flourish of a man putting a pistol ball into his brain. Augusta handed the letter over to the girl, who took it out. The deed done, we were suddenly cheerful. Augusta poured more tea, but we pushed the cup away. 'Damn tea, let's have a drink on it.'

Annabella's answer arrived within the week. Fletcher, our lugubrious valet, entered with a letter on a tray. We slit it open, and cried out so sharply that Augusta thought we had cut ourself on the knife. 'What is the matter?' We handed her the letter. She read under her breath, peering shortsightedly. 'I have long pledged to myself that I would endeavour to make your happiness my first object in life...' she started skimming silently. (No one could be expected to read the whole of a letter from Annabella). '...I will henceforward trust to you for all I should look up to, all l should love. It is a choice suitor who will undertake to reform himself for one poor woman who signs herself, yours for ever et cetera.' She lifted her head, pleased. 'Why, this is a very pretty letter...'

'Of course, of course...' we mumbled. 'I must be able to love a woman who is so amiable and can write a pretty letter. Miss Milbanke has a fine mind, and a great interest in mathematics, I believe. But I had told Hobby we should go abroad again, d' you see...?'

'You must write her a pretty reply. It will be expected.'

Augusta read over our shoulder while we composed it. *I... have become convinced... that it is in your power... to make me happy... you... have made me so already... I swear that the...* ['Don't!'] *FOLLIES, to give them no harsher name...* – we looked briefly at her but she motioned us to continue – *now plague my conscience with the knowledge that I should never have given way to those... irrational passions... so readily if I might have been sooner guided... by your example...* ['And LOVE – write LOVE!'] *... and love. Yours for an eternity, or as near as we may approach to it, B.*

She patted our shoulder. 'This is a splendid reply.'

'Perhaps we should not send it.'

'It is too pretty a letter to waste.' She rang for Joe Murray, who came and took it away.

The rest was anything but silence.

Chapter seventeen

Her favourite science was the mathematical,
Her noblest virtue was her magnanimity;
Her wit (she sometimes tried at wit) was Attic all,
Her serious sayings darken'd to sublimity;
In short, in all things she was fairly what I call
A prodigy – her morning dress was dimity,
Her evening silk, or, in the summer, muslin,
And other stuffs with which I won't stay puzzling.

By coach north, along frozen roads, to Seaham – a great house with a miserable bleak prospect out over the North Sea. It was not out of nonchalance that we stood toasting our frozen arse on the coal fire in the parlour as we waited for Annabella to come downstairs. It was damned cold in that place.

We had arrived so late that we had not been expected; the parents were out.

Annabella came down. She stopped uncertainly some yards off. Everything had changed since we had seen her last, no doubt she could see it in our face. 'My dearest Byron...'

'Miss Milbanke,' we managed to choke out. A mistake. All a mistake.

THE WICKED LORD BYRON

She held out her hand to us. Ours remained at our side. 'I can only hope, my Lord, when you do not come forward you do not mean to signify that your affection for me is abandoned so soon.'

'Madam, it was merely that I should have to stump forward on this excuse for a leg and mar forever the first impression I made upon you.'

Instantly guilty, she rushed forward and took us into her arms, which startled us not a little. 'O my poor B, never again will you bear that burden alone...'

We grunted into her shoulder, in a sulk: 'If only you could have married me two years ago you would have spared me what I cannot get over...'

She pulled away, at that. 'Why? What has happened?'

'Nothing at all.' Happier now we have stirred up trouble for ourself, we lit a cheroot. 'What do we do now?'

'I shall take you this afternoon on my special walk along the cliffs, where we shall watch the sea roll in. 'He that has sailed upon the dark blue sea / Has viewed at times, I ween, a full fair sight,' as I believe you phrased it.'

We felt ourself grinning like a wolf at such foolish talk. 'The North Sea in winter is but a dismal shade of grey. It is not to be compared to the Aegean.' At this, Miss Milbanke looked suitably abashed and parochial. She excused herself for a moment, to call the servant to bring in the tea.

Damn tea... we were thinking, but said nothing more, having said too much already. We needed a real drink.

However, our visit proved not so much of an ordeal as we expected. The parents were not so bad – the old man was a garrulous bore, but goodnatured enough. The mother we did not like at all for some reason, but she left us well enough alone, and the fortnight at Seaham was not bad once we had picked up the pattern of days. It unfolded like a comedy that could only have the one ending. We were left much to ourselves; Miss Milbanke had clearly been indulged by her parents all her life, and if this strange young man (ourself) was what Annabella chose as a road to hell, it seemed they were quite happy to let her get along the primrose path to the everlasting bonfire.

The first day of the comedy we sat at opposite ends of the sofa, looking at the roaring coal fire. The day after we were sitting next to each other and the day after that were kissing passionately.

The novelty of making love to the first virgin of our life had a piquancy all its own. We began to sense deep oceans of passion beneath that placid rational surface. In short, the Game fascinated us both, moths fluttering about our mutual flame. Soon we were openly caressing her breasts through the fabric of her dress and there was, even here, no serious objection – after the territory had been so patiently gained – from Miss Annabella Milbanke.

A few days of this, and Napoleon proceeded to the next battle, over the charming black bush which we knew lay below the inadequate protection of a half-dozen or so petticoats above those blue stockings.

Here Napoleon met his Waterloo. Following the usual preliminaries of kissing &c, with the cold detachment of the great general we judged the time right to assault the Citadel and began to grope in her skirt. In the throes of her passionate fantasy with this figure out of her – or rather, our – imagination, Annabella abruptly realised what we were doing, pushed our hand away. We were angry, frustrated, our patient balls aching, a memorable erection hidden discreetly by the cut of our coat. 'Well?'

'We have as yet no right to give ourselves utterly to each other.' She shuddered, whether in horror or passion we could not tell.

We got up and turned our back. ' I suppose you think it will be very well when we are wed but by God it will be too late then. If you had married me but two short years ago you might have spared me what I cannot now get over.'

'If you will not explain the fault you complain of I am not able to answer the complaint.'

'There are things a man cannot explain freely.'

'I can well understand that a man of genius must find it difficult to converse with a poor girl who has in the comparison seen little of this world. You are free to consider our engagement at an end if you wish.' She was doing too well at this, her unconscious player more than a match for our knowledgeable game.

'You know,' we said through gritted teeth, 'I would never permit my happiness to depart.'

Annabella's eyes brimmed with tears. 'I do not see how I am to retain your attentions, not knowing the ways of the great ladies you have known – in a year you will tire of me, in a month...'

We stepped in front of her to prevent her exit; in effect, surrendering. 'Come, Bell – forgive me. My sister would tell you that in me a fit of pique means nothing. You must learn to ignore it – in a few seconds it will have gone away again.' She ceased to sob. Mouths mashed, tongues entwined.

Our hand went to her breasts and she did not try to stop us. We began to insinuate a hand into her skirts. She pro-

tested in our ear: 'No, my love, we must wait, wait, until...'
We kissed her to stop her mouth and began to push her back
toward the sofa, until we fell on it entwined together as
Annabella wrenched her mouth free. 'My love... AAHH!' she
shuddered as our skilful finger penetrated her layered petticoats to the inner sanctum.

A babble of talk which we did not hear properly. Our
whole brain was concentrated into the sensation in our middle finger, the feel of her erect little button beneath our moving fingertip. Ruthlessly, we brought her to a spend, not real-
izing this was the first she had ever allowed herself, or how
much it was shaking the foundations within her in hot little
waves. We listened amused to her cries. Afterwards she burst
into tears, bewildering us. 'But Bell, Bell, it will never do to
cry... why, we are as good as wed already.'

The change in the distressed girl was startling, the sight of
that immense Will at work. She stood up, calm, fixed, *rational*. Confound her, we thought, I must have her when she is
like THIS. 'We must go to our rooms now, mama and papa
are asleep already. You must return to London until the wedding can be arranged.'

'The devil if I have not just travelled from London on
these mudtracks you call roads... do you wish me to perish
of pneumonia? '

She burst instantly into tears. 'If I am not a virgin bride,'
she sobbed, 'what will there be to set me apart from any
other of the ladies you have known...?'

We enjoy others' tears less than our own, and started to
babble comforts in the sort of philosophical baby language
she might understand. 'You are a new kind of woman to me
already. You will learn to manage me and make me smile. I

will fly down to London and get us a special licence from the old Archbishop of Cant himself, and sweep back north like the wind... and carry you away from mama and papa so that you will live with the wind as part of it...'

She sighed at the picture: '...and Childe Harold will find ease and redemption clinging to the hem of the skirt of a woman who shall lead him to Heaven at last.'

We took her hand, and kissed it in acquiescence. 'Amen.'

To London then, to linger as long as possible in the last wild days of our bachelorhood. Annabella sent us letters urging hurry, to which we replied with asperity: *You will recall that it was yourself who engineered this absence. If it will give you any satisfaction, I am as comfortless as charity, chastity, or any other virtue.*

We were having too good a time in London, and in no hurry to get married. Annabella started writing to Goose to bring us to heel. At last, commanded by Augusta to come to Six Mile Bottom *'on your way to marry Miss Milbanke,'* we rode reluctantly north again with the marriage licence, in the company of our best man Mr. Hobhouse, as if to a funeral.

Never had we been so sorry to leave a city.

Chapter eighteen

And there was one soft breast, as hath been said
Which unto his was bound by stronger ties
Than the church links withal...

Ibid farewell to Hobhouse as the road forks for Cambridge, where he is going to visit Scrope, with whom we have promised to spend Christmas. 'Courage, old friend.' Hobhouse shakes hands warmly, then rides off forever on the bachelor's road, turning once in his saddle to call back cheerfully: 'Scrope and I will drink deep to the match!'

After a miserable cold ride, relieved only by a stop at a warm inn for food and drink, see Sixmile Bottom loom out of the damp foggy land where some fool built it – the country home of Colonel and Mrs. Leigh. We bang on the door of the great house for a long time: the servants have all been let go, we have heard. Augusta comes downstairs with a candle and lets us in. We stand and look at each other. Moaning and cursing comes from the room above the stair: 'Who is it... in the other devil's name...'

'Leigh is here? So much for a last quiet Christmas together. You lied to me, in your letter... You used our Sign...'

'I did not know he would return.' She is staring at us uncertainly. Her dark hair is loose and floating up in the draught from the door. She puts down the candle and steps forward to take us in her arms. We embrace her fervently. 'AAAGHHH!' she recoils. 'You're freezing! Come to the fire and shake the snow away, Baby. I built it up in case you came tonight.' She takes my hand to draw us across the room into the aura of the great fire. 'Your clothes are all frozen.' She fetches a rug that has been warming in front of the fire, puts it over our shoulders, pours us brandy from a carafe on the mantelpiece, and we stretch our icy hands toward the warm flames.

The brandy is warm from the fire and the sweet shock of it in our cold throat explodes in our head. My blood is bounding and I make a rapid calculation. Leigh is here, but does not pose a threat of interruption, having drunk himself to sleep.

I know what to do. First, pretend to more calm than I feel. 'Come Goose – you are shivering.' Casually, I hold the rug open and motion for her to come inside. 'Come here and we can share the rug.'

With a little giggle Augusta steps back to the table and pours herself a brandy. 'I am warm enough here.' She brings me a low stool. I sit on it and she stands next to me, staring into the fire. I put more logs on the fierce mass of embers, and the fire blazes up. Her hand on my shoulder.

(Augusta's hand. Her hand. The watching pair in the death-room can feel the touch of it still.)

'Come down here.'

'I would have to be mad to come under a blanket with you tonight.'

'Dammit, we could TALK, at least... How ARE the children and the damned Colonel, if I may enquire further?'

Her tone changes to unnutterable weariness. 'The Colonel and I and the Children continue as before. I do not want to talk about ME. I am sick of ME. I wish to talk about you. When the Devil are you and Mr. Hobhouse to go north? That poor girl must be absolutely in despair.'

'Questions! But there may be but the one answer after all.' I brush her hand from our shoulder and move my stool closer to the fire. 'I have written a letter.'

'To whom?' She moves closer to the fire and replaces her hand on our shoulder.

'Are you going to share this rug? This damned swamp of a house will be the death of you, like Newstead killed Mama. I don't expect she would have begrudged sharing a blanket with me – but she is dead these twice two years. My last friend in the world.'

'Now, Baby... You know you are the dearest of all my babies...'

'Then come down here.'

'Presently. To whom did you write a letter?'

'To Miss Milbanke,' I mutter between my teeth.

'You have sent her many a letter these past two years. What news is this?'

'What do you care? Feeling as you do so *distant*.' I take the letter out of our shirt, but snatch it away as she reaches to take it. 'You are either legitimately a Byron, in which case you belong in THE BLANKET, or you remain outside, in which case you shall see no more of my letters.' She giggles and I round on her savagely. 'I am not joking. Your plans for me may come to nothing after all.'

Augusta comes to us and we wrap ourselves up in the blanket. I kneel and spread out the letter on the floor in the firelight, and she, in order to share the blanket, must kneel too. Heads together, kneeling together, as if we have returned to the childhood we never shared.

She begins to giggle uncontrollably. 'O, you cannot send this... it's all woggly.'

'Woggly?'

'Wobbling I mean... the handwriting you fool...'

'Of course it's wobbling I wrote it in the inn while I was drinking hot rum punch.'

'But this is only a jest...'

'You cannot believe that I would make jokes while that poor girl waits in the North for a figure compounded out of her – or rather my – imagination. She is waiting for Childe Harold, a man out of a dream, a puppet who never existed. We should never be happy. I must break off the engagement. You shall come South with me... To Europe and beyond. We will leave this silly little world behind.'

Upstairs, the Colonel groans in drunken sleep. Augusta glances at the ceiling, and says quickly: 'In a year from now you will look back at this night, from your happiness at Miss Milbanke's side, as if this were all a foolish dream.'

I snap my fingers. 'A dream can be real like THAT. We can go to the warm south, so far there will be no more English faces to trouble us.' As she starts to object about the children: 'We shall take the children. Leigh would not care if we took 'em.'

She blocks her ears, moaning softly: 'We should be cast

out altogether, we should never be able to come back into the *world* at all.'

'You would set the Colonel free – he would not mourn you a day. To hell with the world.'

Upstairs, the Colonel cries out in his sleep. Her glance turns up to the ceiling. 'I must go to him now – he might want something.' She gets up.

I seize her hand. 'You will not be long. And you will come back.'

'A minute I swear – a minute I swear to you.'

The moment is ripe. I laugh coldly, not letting go of the hand. 'Do you mean the special promise? The promise that we used to make that could never be broken?' With my fingers burning into her wrists like manacles, she nods her agreement curtly. I let her go and she trots up the stairs. I pull the rug around myself and stretch out my lame leg, which is aching damnably, to warm it in the heat of the great fire. The fire is roaring, and something inside us is roaring with it.

Augusta comes back, but we do not turn our head. In front we feel the fierce heat of the fire, but behind us we can sense the great chill of the huge room, and within it her reluctance as a further coldness on our heart. 'He speaks in his sleep at times, especially when he has been drinking. I did not disturb him.'

'Let the bastard choke on his own drunken vomit. It would solve many problems.' I turn around and stretch out my hand.

She speaks very calmly – I feel it as a slap in the face. 'We must stop all this nonsense NOW. It is only Miss Milbanke who can make you happy.'

'Is THIS how you fulfil a promise? I will discuss nothing while you stand up.'

'We must not...'

'Either we must or the letter to Miss Milbanke must... Come here.'

'Only for a minute, I...'

'Damn *minutes*.' I seize her wrist, pull her down to her knees beside us. 'Is *minutes* how you propose to keep the special promise?' She does not reply. 'Is that wretch Fletcher here yet? My man, my valet, Fletcher?'

'He arrived last night in the mail coach. Why? He must be asleep.'

'Go and wake the scoundrel – I want him to ride to Cambridge and catch the northern mail with this letter. And tomorrow I shall take myself to Cambridge too, and spend Christmas in Scrope's chambers. Hobby and Scrope will be delighted to see me. We shall go South together instead of north to Miss Milbanke, to that South you will never share with me now.' She looks at me, flames behind her eyes. I get up and start to shout so as to wake the house: 'FLETCHER? FLETCH?' Augusta puts her hand over our mouth, I pull her down with me and wrap her in the rug. Both of us listen anxiously for signs of Fletchers or Gaming Colonels.

She begins to caress me like a mother. She takes me in her arms, clasps me to her breast as one might soothe a child. She strokes my sweating face, in the aura of the great fire, smoothing the long curled hair out of my eyes. 'It is the only way. You must marry Miss Milbanke. Where could we go? You are too famous to be let alone to...'

I kiss her, open the bodice of her nightgown to reach for the mother's wet breasts inside, saying anything if I can have what I want, this minute, *now*. 'Once more, Goose, only the once more, Goose, please, and I will do as you say exactly...'

She stops my hand. 'You must promise – the Special Promise – to tear up this letter.'

'Anything, only you will be with me one last time...'

'The last time, Baby, the very last time.'

I laugh, and joke grimly like a god averting fate: 'That's a point of view we can at least discuss.' I push up her gown above her very breasts, I must see everything, do everything, know her, BE her...

And now she is willing. 'Come inside me.' She grasps and places me, sitting astride. We plunge and thrust at each other as if we will melt together, groaning in this final act of our love, while the gaming Colonel grunts and groans like a pig upstairs, Fletcher and the children sleep on in distant rooms of the great damp house, and two watchers in the future deathroom see all, feel all, taste all, LB and Goose together, one last time...

'O Baby...' – throwing aside the nightgown from her shoulders entirely, so that in the flames from the fire the perfect breasts bob and dance above me, and that beloved face, as it might be our own, framed in the dark curls of the Byrons. She grins down at me with a frank pleasure. *Tonight*, we are both thinking, *for the last time.*

She leans her face close to mine, her eyes meld into one eye through which I seem to be gazing into her soul. One last time, as the Colonel snores on dreamlessly upstairs.

Chapter nineteen

And he stood calm and quiet, and he spoke
The fitting vows, but heard not his own words,
And all things reel'd around him...

After Christmas we went north by coach, with our friend and best man, John Cam. Hobhouse – a man's perfect companion on the way to his execution – talked incessantly of the fine time we had had of it in Greece. Talking of warmth as the coach went dragging and bouncing further into the frozen northland. Wrapped in our travelling rugs, drinking too much from our flask, staring out at the sparkling snow crusting the fields, we were dully content that Hobby was there to talk us through it.

The ugly house appeared in its flat field of snow as the coach crested the final hill. Hobhouse was a little stunned at this barren spectacle of Puritan magnificence. 'Seaham, they calls it? Strange wet name – by God it is a bleak looking pile enough.'

'That don't signify, Hobby. I shall take her South in the end. Or if she will not go I shall take yourself and Scrope, by God.'

Good to see Sir Ralph, though – dull as ditchwater, but a good fellow for all that – with his sweet foolish smile, stepping up to shake our hand. The mother of the bride smiling too, but her eyes as always carried a look as if she means to do us harm. Strange how we – *(and if you haven't guessed it WE is the Nightgowned Spirit speaking on behalf of both of us)* – strange how we always knew that Lady Milbanke meant to do us harm.

'My dear Lord Byron!' said Ralph, pumping our hands warmly. 'And can this be Mr. Hobhouse, the best man?' Hobby got pumped too.

'Well met, Sir Ralph.' We nodded coldly at the mother – no point in maintaining illusory friendships, we are not marrying HER. 'Lady Milbanke,' we grunted.

'Lord Byron.' She offered her hand briefly. Annabella made her entrance down the grand staircase, smiling shyly as becomes a virgin bride.

We found ourself half-entering into the spirit of the occasion, though our heart was sinking within. 'My dear, may I present Mr. Hobhouse?' An imp put the next sentence into our mouth. 'He has kindly consented to give away the groom.' (Lady Milbanke winced visibly.)

What followed was like a confused, precipitously rushing dream. In that sparely furnished living room ourself and Annabella knelt on cushions. All was done as quickly and irreversibly as driving a pistol ball into the brain pan. Those present were ourself, Annabella, her parents; Hobhouse and the Milbankes' groom were to sign as witnesses. The parson, a yellow faced, shivering, consumptive poor devil, seemed more the fellow for reading the burial service. No rare matter, no doubt, in this cold flat land open to the North Sea.

The parson was an illegitimate son of Lord Wentworth. All in the family...

It was as if we were watching ourself from a parrot-perch on the high ceiling.

Annabella's responses were firm and clear. But Hobhouse noticed that our hand was trembling as he put the ring in it. He held our hand for a second, to steady it.

There was only one contretemps. The Parson: '...with all my worldly goods...'

LB (to Hobhouse, sotto voce): 'Debts in my case...'

The Parson: 'My lord, please...'

And we heard ourselves say, in a trembling voice, 'With all my worldly goods I thee endow...' The consumptive parson coughed and mopped a little bloody spittle from his lips, and continued, poor doomed devil, with our marriage lines.

Chapter twenty

I'll not gainsay the generous public's voice,
That the young lady made a monstrous choice.

In the wedding coach, things did not go on so smoothly. As we clattered along the frozen roads on our way to our treaclemoon at Halnaby, Lady Milbanke's maiden home, our new wife was startled as we began to howl like a wolf at the top of our voice.

She ventured to ask what we meant by this. 'You remember how I had spoken to you of the songs my band of cut-throats used to sing in Albania as they danced around the campfire, man linked to man...' Our histrionic mood was pleased to find an audience so receptive, and consequently our gloomy pose and dire predictions darkened the air in the coach hour after hour.

We arrived at Halnaby Hall. Burningly conscious of our limp, we did not deign to hand her down from the coach, leaving that duty to the coachman. We clumped through the mud and snow straight into the house, ignoring the old and faithful band of Milbanke retainers lined up in the drive, caps in hand, to greet their new Lord and Lady. The embarrassed girl had to greet her old friends the servants alone, under the curious eyes of the coachman, who had no doubt been puzzled by what he had been hearing from his perch above the happy couple.

Annabella was by now in something of a state. We calmed her down by the usual method, our middle finger. This toying with her spending upon our hand was a sort of hors d'oeuvres to the main course. As a matter of fact, we HAD the wife on the sofa directly before supper – she was hot-blooded enough once you got those blue stockings off. It was quite moral now, for we were married.

A night of mutual heaven – innocence and experience enjoying each other for the first time. Riding that smooth clean cunt into paradise. Until we fell asleep in the great bed and began immediately to dream of the Other Place.

The delusion began when the fire in the bedroom suddenly spat and cracked, waking us. Red flickering through the red curtains on the great bed. We lay with half-open eyes and were caught up in our half-dream and the effect of the firelight. We knew ourself to be in ancient Hades. In a golden bed hung with bright red silks, in a marble torchlit room, deep underground. Lying next to us was this pretty dark woman we had just made love to, who could only be... Proserpine, Queen of Hades. (Funny how we could not think of Hades without wanting to make love to Proserpine. Quite a girl, Miss Milbanke.)

Waking up back in the bedroom at Halnaby, we ripped the bed curtains aside gasping, held our head and screamed: 'Hell... hell... monstrous imprisonment!'

Annabella, waking, reached over to touch our back sleepily: 'What is it, my love?'

We leapt off the bed. 'Never touch me!'

She was naturally offended, and we calmed down, gesturing vaguely. 'I had a dream. Only a dream.'

She forgave us instantly, her dark hero with his painful, glamorous past – the source, no doubt, of the nightmare. 'O my darling, what dream...?' She took our hand.

'A dream that...' We suddenly realised what our dream must signify and snatched our hand away. 'Are not even my dreams to be private? I could never bear to sleep with a woman. It puts me in mind of my mortality.'

Bell angry now. 'My LORD!'

'You would oblige me, madam, by resuming your slumbers and restricting yourself to your own half of this our little red love nest, our suburb of Hell.'

She looked at us. 'Is the woman not wonderful? She asks me what she may do to help me and will not do it. I beg you, madam, if you value my soul, go back to sleep. Over THERE... on YOUR side of the bed...' The poor girl complied in injured silence, moved over, and sincerely tried to go to sleep.

We lit a candle, extracted a pistol and dagger from a box beside the bed, and began prowling the room as she lay with eyes closed under the blankets. Hearing us move round the room she could not resist having a peep, and the sight of us with pistol and candle startled her into calling: 'My dear...?'

We threw on her, God forgive us, a glance of intense loathing. 'I beg of you... for my sake... to sleep...' Annabella turned over and pretended to sleep, but she must have heard us stalking about the room like an aroused tomcat.

We took our candle and pistol outside, aware of her listening to our peculiar dragged footsteps as we limped down the dark hall toward we knew not what. We badly wanted to kill something, but of course there was nothing to kill except ourself, and we were not quite ready for that.

Chapter twenty-one

My papa, Sir Ralpho, hath recently made a speech at a Durham tax-meeting;
and not only at Durham, but here, several times since after dinner. He is
now, I believe, speaking it to himself (I left him in the middle) over various
decanters, which can neither interrupt him nor fall asleep, – as might possibly have been the case with some of his audience.
    Ever thine, B
I must go to tea – damn tea. I wish it was Kinnaird's brandy.

After three weeks treaclemoon at Halnaby, the married
couple returned to Seaham. The eternal tedium of life
with Annabella's parents preyed on us. Then, too, our financial affairs in London seemed to be going to hell in our
absence. The matter came to a head when we saw Annabella eating a hearty breakfast, while we, with our horror
of getting fat, had to endure our hunger. 'You remind me
of an animal eating. A woman should consume only lobster
salad and champagne – the only truly feminine and becoming viands.' Her look of outrage and hurt squeezed even our
sullen heart, so that we apologised: 'Come, woman – can you
not share a joke?'

'Yours is a cruel notion of a joke, Byron.'

'You should not pay attention to everything I say.' Bleakly, we picked up a sheet of paper from the table and handed it to her. It was a letter from Hanson the lawyer, who had failed yet again to dispose of our estate at Rochdale or even Newstead; meanwhile, the very Grocer's bill was unpaid. At her look of dutiful concern we felt a wave of anger rise. 'It is intolerable that a man with my expectations should have to live like this!'

'You know that Papa would have helped us already if he had not spent so much money on his last election...'

'Lack of election to be more precise....'

'...and you know too that we can expect to be the main beneficiaries of my uncle Lord Wentworth when...'

'Uncle Wentworth? I have seen him doddering about the House, not knowing if he were a Whig or a Tory. He will dance on my grave before he has the decency to vanish into his own.'

'My lord. He is my Uncle!'

'We have languished in this ice house waiting for your relative to die for too many weeks already. We must go South and put the spurs to old Hanson the lawyer. Go to London, sell the blasted estates, raise some cash .'

Annabella is shocked. 'London?'

'Until it pleases me to go further South, to the Isles of Greece, or Portugal perhaps. You may come then or not, as you please.'

'To go to London with your habitual inclinations and present means...'

'This aimless waiting for your uncle to die – no more. If I can put my boot in old Hanson I shall have funds of my own to squander – by God I am BORED with this house. Do you have a particular need to prevent me seeing my friends?'

Chapter twenty-two

*If I could explain the real causes which have contributed to increase
this perhaps natural temperament of mine – this melancholy which hath
made me a bye-word – nobody would wonder – but this is impossible
without doing much mischief.*

The married menagerie rolled south to start their new life.
'Thrift, thrift, Horatio' – travelling in the family coach,
and thus saving money, it occurred to us we might as well
turn off at Newmarket, to save even more money on inn fees
and pay a visit to Six Mile Bottom. 'After all,' we observed
to Annabella, 'you have never met Augusta, who married us
off strictly by letter.'

'Surely,' said Annabella piously, 'I must love your sister as
you do.' We gave her what was no doubt a strange look.

The two A's – Augusta and Annabella. We had hoped to
play one off against the other, but they were allies against
us from the first moment. How to contain Geordie was the
common theme. We found them in conference when we rose
at noon to our breakfast.

Seeing them at their lunch already made us irritated, and
hungry for the society of men, even the gaming Colonel, who

was away at the races. We lingered over our green tea with a tot of gin, lounging insolently, staring. Augusta, nibbling a biscuit, smiled nervously, and Annabella looked guilty. As though they had been up to something, by God... Apropos of nothing, we said: 'So you *wouldn't*, Goose.'

'Wouldn't what, Baby?'

We turned to Annabella with a bitter smile. 'She plays a good innocent, eh? She does it very well.' As Annabella's eyes widened, we reassured her blandly: 'Don't you worry my charmer, the bitch stayed innocent enough last night, even after we packed YOU up the wooden hill to Bedfordshire...'

Augusta to Annabella: 'Take no notice. In this mood he is not to be reasoned with.'

This aroused us to cold fury. 'Have you told Annabella that you wear drawers? O, nothing but the latest fashions for Goose.' To Annabella: 'You see, I *know* she wears them.'

(The watching pair in the future find that they understand now, too late, exactly what everyone was feeling.) Augusta got up, white with rage, and stalked out without looking at us. As she slammed the door she may have heard us say behind her: 'O pray excuse Augusta's moods. She is pregnant you know – one of Leigh's, this time – none of my doing.' (We see/feel a shaft of terror lancing into Augusta. She went to her room, her heart pumping. We can sense it all now, all the hearts that beat in the darkness, from our future perspective at the end of time. It is a trick we had rather our story was without.)

'I too am carrying a child...' Annabella said. She had almost said 'our child,' but stopped her mouth, lest we think she is comparing it to Augusta's. (We could see that too.)

'A quick enough breeder, our lady wife. Though not as fat as the good Goose as yet.'

'Must our life together have the qualities of a dramatic poem?'

We laughed, we warmed to her at last. 'O Bell, Bell, you must learn how to laugh at me, and to make me laugh. Augusta can make me laugh at any thing.'

Annabella smiled too, but a little too quizzically: our mood changed and the moment was gone. 'My two women are thick as thieves against me. It is time to arrange our own household matters. Mr. Hanson, my lawyer, has written that he has obtained the key of Number Thirteen, Piccadilly. We start for Town in the morning...'

'The Duchess of Devonshire's great house? How shall we begin to afford it?'

'O the rent's not so bad if you don't pay it.'

She looked at us with great eyes full of reproach. 'But dear – our circumstances...'

'Did you think that I would bring you to Town to live in a garret? Be still, woman – we must have a proper place in Town. We would *lose caste*.'

Moore's phrase, so convenient to win an argument. We stared at each other sullenly, as if we had been married for twenty years instead of as many weeks.

Chapter twenty-three

The fact is that my wife if she had common sense would have more power over me – than any other whatsoever –

That wonderful house in Piccadilly – all you could want. Annabella and ourself dining very happily by candlelight in the great hall. Having a fine time despite a deplorably tough joint of beef. We lifted a glass to her. 'You see? We were right to come here. We have done better here in Town these past weeks, have we not?'

Tipsy with champagne and happiness, gesturing around with her bubbling glass. 'Such a GRAND apartments.' She sipped her wine. 'But I had heard the Duchess's terms were extortionate.'

We gestured airily. 'O, the rent's not so bad if you don't pay it.' We were not the man to waste jokes, and had forgotten that she had heard this one already. She smiled dutifully at this, and we almost loved her for it. 'O Bell, Bell, we shall pull together yet. You have only to learn from Augusta the way to make me laugh.'

'Do you know, I almost feel as if she were my sister too.'

'I am glad of it. We are a happy enough family, if better

apart. I will drink this glass to the good Goose – you will please write and tell her I do so.'

Radiant, she announced her surprise. 'We have no need to write. I have written already to invite her to visit us. It is time she had a rest from that dreadful man.'

Our glass shattered explosively on the table. A great red stain of wine spread down the white front of our shirt. 'Why, you little fool...'

She was baffled. 'My love...?'

'It will make a great difference to YOU in all ways.' We limped out before we could see the usual tears begin. She was ever a fool in matters of the heart.

Chapter twenty-four

I have great hopes that we shall love each other all our lives as much as if we had never married at all.

The table in the great room set for tea. The women sitting in a peaceful world of tea and chocolate cake, delightful. An outside door slammed, with the sound of the voice they were coming to dread, and all their peace was at an end. 'You took your time – it is COLD out there, you wretch, Fletcher, come in here with me and help.' LB came in, trailed by his hapless valet, and looked at his two women, who were avoiding his gaze as if guilty.

'Afternoon tea! How cosy! May I help myself?' He walked over to the pot of tea to pour himself a cup, without milk. He was following a severe diet, which did not help his temper. He sat next to Annabella. 'Did I tell you that I encountered a DUN upon the doorstep as I entered? I doubt not one will want to move in with us next.' He could sense Augusta trembling with suppressed rage, and turned to her pleasantly. 'You see, Sister Dear, how tiresome these people can get about the money I owe them? One cannot explain why the much-longed-for decease of my wife's uncle Wentworth should not put his funds at her husband's disposal.'

Annabella spoke with spirit. 'Byron, I have made it perfectly clear to you that my parents are unable to release the money at the present time. The terms of Lord Wentworth's will are quite specific; the estate must rest with Mama for the present. The duns must be made to see reason...'

'You cannot make a dun see *reason* – it smacks to them of evasion.' He grinned nastily at Annabella. 'I was told, Miss Milbanke, that you was a *Golden Dolly*. It seems I was misinformed.'

'Baby! Hold your tongue.' Augusta had had enough. One did not behave like this in front of servants. She motioned with her head for Fletcher to leave, and he went, his face a respectful blank.

Annabella tried her charmless tact. 'O, don't oppose him in this mood, Goose.'

'O, let the bitch oppose me if she can. She has known me a good deal longer – and more intimately – than my wife ever will.'

Augusta winced at this remark; Annabella ignored it. 'But Byron, if there are legal reasons why Uncle's Will cannot...'

'You may explain your *legal reasons* to the duns. I stumble over four or five every time I step out of my carriage. One fellow is given to lurking in front of the Theatre for me. He has taken to eying my carriage a little too pointedly for comfort. If they take the car I shall have to *walk* home from Drury Lane and get my throat slit by a footpad...' He rose and bowed. 'Well, ladies, thank you for tea. I must be off to the Theatre. A new play to discuss with the Committee. Art is all, ladies. Life, dear ladies, must wait.'

Annabella carefully avoided his eyes. 'When may I tell Fletcher to expect you?'

'O, so late, my dears, that it would pain me to disturb you at all. I shall dine with Mr. Kean and some of his fellow theatricals. Pray do *not* expect me.' With another curse for the hapless servant who opened the front door for us, and a further oath at the dun on the step, he was gone.

The happy world of Darjeeling and chocolate cake lay shattered. Augusta was furious. 'How can you tolerate this? He had not even the excuse of being drunk!'

'Do you know, Augusta, I believe he has not been quite right in the head since the brandy he drank on Saturday.'

Alarm bells rang in Augusta's head. 'Saturday?'

'He came in on Saturday at five in the morning after drinking brandy all night with Mr. Kinnaird's party – with that infamous man, the actor Mr. Kean, and... women of the theatre, as he told me...'

Augusta asked carefully: 'You think him... ill?'

'Insanity IS a form of illness. He should not be held morally to blame for his actions. His brain has doubtless suffered organic damage from the brandy he consumed on Saturday...'

Augusta stood up, dazed. 'Mad?'

Tears sprang to Annabella's eyes. 'O Augusta, you must believe me, or I fear I shall go mad myself.' Annabella took down a heavy volume which she placed on the table in front of the older woman. She opened it and pointed to a word. 'You see?' Augusta's eyes could not quite focus on the page, as she heard, from a great distance, Annabella say: 'You know, I could never leave him, if he is ill.'

Augusta was frightened. 'Do not speak of leaving him. He would blow his brains out.'

'I shall not leave him so long as I know he is ill.'

The women looked at each other for a long time, as if making an unvoiced bargain. Annabella dropped her gaze to the page and pointed again to the word. 'You see?'

Augusta tried to read it. It was a hard word and she was not very literate. 'Hydro... hydro... syphilis... '

'Hydrocephalus. Water on the brain. The pressure mounts and mounts until it is capable of depriving a man of his very wits...' *(The Nightgowned Spirit bursts into laughter as the body on the bed begins cursing.)*

Augusta's head was reeling. 'You must not speak of abandoning him! I do not know what he would do!'

'Yes, we must be very careful. Dr. Baillie has not yet had a chance to examine B – but he seems to allow I may be right.'

'Do not trouble at what Baby *says*. Men in their cups will say anything – all of London says what a fine brain he has...'

'Brightly they fell, like falling stars, as Mr. Milton says. It is always the higher archangels who are given the power to ruin themselves most completely.' From very far away Augusta heard the utterly confident voice go on. 'O Augusta – I should hate to have to leave him. But with a child coming, what can I do? Now if he is *ill*, we may still hope for a cure. But otherwise...'

Augusta looked down at the page swimming in front of her. 'Hydro... hydro...' She looked up helplessly, eyes glittering with tears, at the distorted blur of Annabella's face.

Annabella caught Augusta's watery eye, and held it. 'Hydrocephalus.'

Chapter twenty-five

Is thy face like thy mother's, my fair child!
ADA! Sole daughter of my house and heart?

The air punctuated by a squeal of agony, dying back into a rhythmical groaning. Annabella on her childbed, attended by Doctor Baillie and two nurses. (LB in his bedroom below felt his nerves tearing at each cry that pierced his ceiling.) Baillie did something under the blankets. Annabella reached another crescendo, then slumped back a little before the pain built again.

LB smashed the neck off another bottle of soda water with a poker. The stress had given him a raging thirst. The bottle, hit without Scropean exactitide, shattered and exploded noisily onto the floor. 'Damnation!'

There was no corkscrew in the room.

Annabella flinched. 'Lord protect us – he is throwing bottles at the ceiling now...?'

'My dear Lady Byron you must remain calm,' urged Baillie gently, doing painful things to her innards.

The nurse interrupted: 'O my Lady I am sure my Lord would not...'

'Always he will have us poor women on his side... cats, after him – cats of the Theatre, cats of the ballrooms, poor girls he is able to take advantage of... because we all, when we see him... but Dr. Baillie he will murder us yet...'

'There, there, Lady Byron. I never met a man who did not love his firstborn.' A rush of agony; a wave of a pain such as she never knew existed. Annabella screaming, screaming, screaming.

Doctor and nurse bent down, disappearing to do some mysterious and painful business she could not identify. A last tearing agony pulled out of her and Baillie slapping something red that he dangled in front of the too-small-hipped mother, still weeping with the pain. Seeing Annabella's condition, Baillie gave the red thing to the nurses to wipe and wrap. 'You have a daughter madam – a healthy daughter.'

Annabella took hold of the child, as LB downstairs smashed open another bottle with the poker. His wife sat up in bed, almost dropping the baby. 'O we are not safe here, Dr. Baillie, not safe! He is smashing bottles on the ceiling now!'

Baillie motioned to one of the nurses. 'Pray show Lord Byron his daughter.' The nurse took the bundle off Annabella and went downstairs.

LB put on an air of studied nonchalance as the pretty girl came into his room. Upstairs the older nurse was giving Annabella a draught of laudanum, to help her to sleep. Baillie's work was done. He washed his hands, preparatory to coming downstairs to speak with his lordship.

In the room downstairs his lordship was doing his best to shock the young and susceptible nurse. 'Come, girl – out with it. Of what sex IS the little monster?'

'A girlchild, my lord. A beautiful little girl.'

'A girl! Can the woman get nothing right?' The nurse thrust the baby at him. He peered at the little face, stroked the cheek with a finger. But when Baillie came into his room he instantly stopped, as if caught in an unmanly act. 'Doctor Baillie – my thanks for... ah... THIS item. And pray, how is my poor wife?'

(You must always remember that we never saw our own father after the age of two.)

'She sleeps, my lord, after her long struggle with your daughter. She will sleep now for many hours. As is natural.'

LB sniggered nervously, stepping over to a table laden with bottles and glasses. 'As is natural! Aye, I forgot – nature can be allowed to hide no secrets from a quack...' He poured two large brandies, offered one to the somewhat insulted physician.

'My lord, you...'

'No offence, man, in the world. She has taken no injury and my daughter lives and I thank you.' Pressing the glass of old brandy into the doctor's reluctant hand, irritated with Baillie's confusion. Did the fellow not know how men are supposed to behave? He nudged Baillie and winked, so that Baillie had to drink. At a gesture from the doctor the nurse took the child out.

When Baillie had drunk a toast to the newborn, LB refilled the glasses. 'Just to wet the baby's whistle. We'll just let the women sort themselves out. I'm sure they always know what to do for the best in these matters.'

He rested his hand on the doctor's shoulder affably as Baillie, regarding him levelly, considered his diagnosis.

Chapter twenty-six

...for the mind recoils
Upon itself, and the wreck'd heart lies cold,
While heaviness collects the shatter'd spoils.
It is not in the storm nor in the strife
We feel benumb'd, and wish to be no more,
But in the after-silence on the shore,
When all is lost, except a little life.

The expensive experiment of having a house in Town came to an end. Annabella had still not obtained Baillie's final diagnosis of her husband. Augusta was at Sixmile, but Annabella kept her informed by daily letter of the progress of the doctor's investigation of the poet's mind.

As for the Child, she had survived her first Christmas, and was a month old. She was about to be taken on her first journey – to Kirkby Mallory, in Leicestershire, where Annabella could join her parents for the journey northwards.

Annabella invited Augusta to visit the London house before she went north. In the drawing room it was already late afternoon. Augusta sipped out of a liqueur glass, shivering slightly at the rich flavour of oranges on her tongue. 'Scarcely

ILL, my dear,' she remarked. 'A little out of sorts, perhaps. Under a strain, you know...'

'I shall reserve final judgment as to the nature of B's malady until Doctor Baillie can complete his diagnosis. He was somewhat violent in speech toward the doctor during their last meeting – and this is making an exact diagnosis difficult.'

Augusta feared, vaguely, the sound of final doom in the doctor's diagnosis. For Annabella, she knew, was capable of final dooms, which did not exist in Augusta's moral universe. 'Surely the doctors will be able to treat his complaint. I have a great faith in doctors.'

'I think,' Annabella observed, 'that I begin to understand his case. His misfortune is a *habitual passion for excitement* which is always found in ardent temperaments, where the pursuits are not to a sufficient degree... organised.'

Augusta luxuriously tipped the last drops of golden liqueur. 'Could Baby be... *organised?*'

'The love of tormenting arises chiefly from this same source, the passion for excitement. Drinking, gaming, etc., are all of the same origin.' She smiled modestly. 'Did you know that Doctor Baillie said that I seemed to have a talent for such subjects?'

He pushed open the door and came through. Dressed to go out, in greatcoat and boots, he was in a cheerful mood, and beamed at his women, causing Augusta to think, you fool, be careful of her now, be careful.

'HA! Liqueurs in the afternoon. I have caught you moral monsters in a mortal sin. May I join you?' He sat down and helped himself to a glass of liqueur, which he threw down in a gulp. He was looking forward to a short holiday from Annabella, and poured another glass for each of them jovially. 'Come, Ladies, it is a wicked cold night I must walk out into. Let us have a toast.' He stood and raised his glass.

Augusta stood, forced herself to smile, held up her glass in good fellowship. 'We have heard enough of Mr. Scrope Davies's wild and wicked toasts – do you not know something decent?' She looked imploringly at Annabella, who stood up, raising her own glass nervously.

'Shakespeare! What could be more decent than that? Even old Scrope himself would approve. Ladies, I give you: 'When shall we three meet again?''

'In Heaven, at least, I hope,' said Annabella quietly. She drank, very serious.

'Ah, Bell, you seldom wish to joke like this. We should do it more often.'

(The eyes of the watchers in the deathroom can see through flesh and all, see deeply into what we only looked at the surface of then, which was Annabella's intention to leave us.)

With a complex inward shudder Augusta sat down, forgetting to drink the toast. He turned on her. 'If by not drinking you mean to express your disapproval of my absence tonight, Goose, kindly withhold it. I am not going out merely to indulge myself in drink at the Cocoa Tree. The Drury Lane Theatre is in grave danger of going under unless we gentlemen on the Committee can decide on the new production – and the fools will inevitably choose the wrong play, without my expert hand to guide them.'

Augusta, bitterly: 'O, the *Theatre* may go under, the *Theatre,* he says...'

Annabella interrupted quietly. 'Will there be... drinking?'

'O, late rather than much,' he protested innocently. 'I don't expect you pair to wait up for me. I shall seek the pleasure of solitary repose in my own chamber – not yours, nor yours,' he joked, laughing at his girls. Women – can't live with 'em, can't live without 'em... Annabella not amused. 'Come, Bell – give us a smile to go out on, at the least.'

She burst into tears and rushed forward to hug him, burying her sobs on his puzzled and embarassed shoulder: 'O may you come soon and safe, soon and safe...'

He patted her shoulder awkwardly. 'Madam – I shall, in a few weeks, I shall.' He pushed her a little away so that he could look at her. He was quite baffled – her face was a mask of panic. He kissed her reassuringly, as he thought, on the lips. 'May God keep you and the little one safe. As soon as I have wound up our little experiment in Town I shall come North. Only a few weeks, for God his sake.' He looked at Augusta, smiling, amazed at the hysteria of women over such trifles. 'And you, too, sourpuss – cheer up!'

Augusta stood, her eyes glittering tears. 'Go with God, Baby. Go with God.'

'You act as if I were going to the Devil! I am only going to meet Kean and Kinnaird!' He started to leave, but turned at the door to see Bell's reaction, joking to the last: 'Don't listen to her, Goose. She is always acting as if poor Edmund Kean were the Devil himself I go to.' Exit smiling.

In the room in Missolonghi, the dying man is wondering why he didn't pay more attention to this scene the first time around when it was still within his power to change everything that was to follow. The Nightgowned Spirit observes: 'That was the last we ever saw of Annabella on this planet – or little Miss Legitimacy – our only legal child.'

'Ada,' the dying body mutters. 'Ada. My child.'

The Spirit shrugs. 'Aye, our Child. We did not see HER not no more, after she was a month old. Droll thing life is.'

Chapter twenty-seven

You are much changed within these twenty days or you would never
have thus poisoned your own better feelings – and trampled upon mine.

L B smiled down at Scrope, who had just made a joke. Hobhouse poured port at the table. While the cat's away the mice will. LB relaxing, a bachelor again, in the great house for which the rent had not yet been paid. Having received nothing but friendly letters from Annabella, he was easy on the subject of his family and had left the chore of writing to Augusta. 'Dearest Duck...' &c, Annabella had been writing to him.

Then (after she had told all to her parents) the tone of the letters changed.

Augusta decided to suppress Annabella's first letter proposing a separation. Hoping, as always, for the vague best. The Milbankes were unable to get past the barrier of Augusta to her brother. Sir Ralph was obliged to travel to London and have a similar letter delivered by hand. When the familiar Milbanke servant brought Sir Ralph's note round to No. 13 Piccadilly Terrace it was a bolt out of the blue.

In the first shocked seconds LB's reaction was, absurdly enough, indignation. What, he thought naively, have I done to deserve THIS? (*'...with your opinions it cannot tend to your happiness to continue to live with Lady Byron...'*) Suppressing the fear in his heart he wrote back to Annabella immediately, wasting no time – as usual – now that it was too late.

In the dining room at Kirkby Mallory Annabella was sitting between her parents. The dragoness with the hard, cold, closed face (and a bouffant wig of too-black hair) was watching her daughter balefully. Sir Ralph was not convinced that the letter he had delivered to his son-in-law was for the best – at least as regards the happiness of his daughter. He could see the pain she was in, and LB's reply had been very reasonable, thought Ralph, very reasonable. Always liked the young fellow myself...

The servant brought in the letter on a tray. He offered it to Annabella, whose name – Lady Byron – was scribbled under the Byronic seal in a familiar hand. With a sidelong glance at her mother, Annabella picked up the letter. The mother spoke. 'Go on, girl, open it.'

Sir Ralph a little shocked at his wife's display of poor manners. 'Come, mama, surely we can let the girl read her own correspondence in private...'

'Don't interrupt, Ralph.' The mother's eyes, slivers of flint, bored into Annabella's.

She started to read, her hand trembling. 'My dearest Wife, I can make nothing of your father's letter. Will you explain? I shall eventually abide by your decision; but I request you most urgently to weigh well the... probable consequences... the...'

'If the Child cannot continue I must.' The dragoness took the letter.

'My dear, please...' Sir Ralph murmured.

She quieted him with a gesture. 'For the Child's own good I must.' (The Nightgowned Spirit and his fellow watcher are thinking of Medea.) The mother turned to Annabella. 'You must think of your duty to God always – you must learn to do it without flinching.' She read out the letter. 'I request you most earnestly to weigh well the probable consequences, and to write to me in your own hand. I cannot sign myself otherwise than yours most affectionately...'

Annabella buried her face in her hands. 'O God he was ill these last months. He was ill!'

'Doctor Baillie has ascertained that he was NOT ill.' She signed to her husband to be quiet as Annabella sobbed. 'Take up the pen. Write what I tell you.'

In London, receiving the confirmation of the death-sentence to his marriage, LB sat desolate in an armchair with Hobhouse's comforting hand upon his shoulder.

Scrope, helping in the only way he knew, poured drink.

Chapter twenty-eight

When fortune changed – and love fled far,
And hatred's shafts flew thick and fast,
Thou wert the solitary star
Which rose and set not to the last.

Augusta entered the ballroom, paused, and had a word with her hostess Lady Jersey at the door. Lady Jersey kissed Augusta on the cheek, and sent her on her way. In late pregnancy, Augusta moved forward like a stately ship into the crowd.

Mrs. Lamb, sister-in-law to Caro's longsuffering husband, William, was standing in her way. 'Mrs. Lamb – how perfectly exquisite you look, my dear. Such a distinctive style of dress.' Mrs. Lamb gave Augusta the cut direct, turning on her heel with a swirl of petticoats and walking off.

The drone of voices round Augusta ceased. A vortex of silence began to grow, with a terrified Augusta at its epicentre. She stood there swaying in shock at a sudden understanding of what was happening. Astonished heads began to turn to look at her.

Suddenly the situation was saved by a pretty little redhaired woman. Miss Mercer Elphinstone stepped forward from a nearby gathering to take Augusta's arm, give her a polite kiss on the cheek, and lead Augusta into the protection of her group. 'Why, Mrs. Leigh, you look quite pale,' offered Miss Mercer. When Miss Mercer – the richest heiress in the room – started speaking to Augusta, the eyes around stopped staring and normal talk resumed, the loud buzz of many tongues.

'Why, yes, I feel better now, I...'

'You must be careful. How long now is it before the new little Leigh is to arrive?' She offered Augusta a chair.

Augusta declined. 'No, no, my dear, I prefer to stand here with you other ladies. I am to Sixmile in a few days, for the lying-in, you know.' As the painful pumping of Augusta's heart receded, she forgot her fright. It was one of the benefits of a nature that dwelled resolutely in the present that it could go on so quickly from near-disaster. Her only income was as a member of the Queen's household, so that it was not mere social disaster she had escaped.

But as her confidence returned, she looked boldly around the room again. 'You know of course that my brother is here. You were very fond of him once, I believe, dear Miss Mercer,' She broke off as she felt another silence begin to grow in the room, as noticeable as a sudden noise. Miss Mercer looked around to see what was happening.

We walked into the crowd near them, and a channel opened around us. We encountered a lady standing in our way. The lady was paralysed, like a rabbit caught by a stoat. Seeing the panic in the her face we took her hand and kissed it, grinning. She snatched the hand from us as if it had been defiled, and walked past us to the other half of the room. At this cue a general exodus began and the crowd moved after the lady into the adjoining half of the room. The cut direct, from the whole company.

Backed up to the mantelpiece, playing the wolf at bay, we grinned sardonically at the troop filing past, ready to punch the first man who dared to grin sardonically back.

Sensing Augusta's confusion, Miss Mercer calmly led her over to us. Miss Mercer offered us her hand. Our own hand, we saw Miss Mercer notice as we took hers, was trembling a little. She gave us a cool friendly glance. 'Alas, my dear Lord B. You had better have married ME. I would have managed you better.'

'And had you done so Miss Mercer I would have become so happy as to make me positively unfashionable – as now my unhappiness makes me so.'

'Courage – you shall endure.' She raised our hand to her lips and kissed it. 'But I am afraid, my dearest B, that I have given somebody the next waltz.' With another smile Miss Mercer, whom we should have married instead of Bell, was gone, like a memory of something that might have been. For we never saw that lovely girl again.

The music started up like some awful thunderstorm around us, and we clung to each other on the edge of a bright circle of dancers. It was as if we had to protect Augusta with our body from the scowls as they swept past. Face after hateful face.

But the watching pair in the deathroom see the furious dance slow as brightness falls from the air around the dancers, as they fade into history, darkness, dust – as we never will, by God, fade like those others did, to oblivion...

In a dim room in western Greece the Spirit grows restive. He picks up a lamp, takes a stroll over to the body on the bed. 'The memory of all those days becomes now the memory of a night and a day. Remember?'

'O night and day must I remember...'

The Spirit is delighted with intelligence where he had expected delirium. 'Shakespeare! Now that's the spirit! Hamlet to his Father's Ghost. Scrope would be pleased...'

'AUGUSTA!!!' The lips frame a hoarse whisper: 'Augusta... don't go...'

'O, she had to go, man, she had to. She could not have borne a child in the strains of Town that season. Do you not remember?'

'...seeing her for the last time on this planet...'

'Being awake with her early in our Garden of Eden, as it might be, before we left it... in a town garden in our House in Piccadilly for Christ his sake – where the rent was not so bad if you didn't pay it – and the sky blowing open and the stars hanging among the clouds in a dawning firmament...'

'Goose, Goose, in the name of God once again...'

The Spirit laughs. 'I see you are not satisfied with mere words – you must have the real Goose for the last time – very well. We shall be THERE, in that moment, NOW...'

CITYCitycity... against a dawning sky. Under the oak tree in the Garden, Augusta is sitting up on LB's bench. LB is dozing with his head in her lap. The warmest night in the year. LB sits up, yawns and stretches, shakes his shoulders, and she leans forward for her kiss. She comes to herself, looking around sleepily.

In a slightly dazed voice, to her brother's utter astonishment, she begins to declaim:

'The world was all before them, where to choose
Their place of rest, and Providence their guide;
They hand in hand, with wandering steps and slow,
Through Eden took their solitary way...'
'Milton? YOU...?'

She ruffles his hair in a motherly fashion. 'Don't you remember where you read me those lines of Mr. Milton?' Absently, she snuffs a great breath of air in through her nose. 'How I have loved this Garden. Ever since my first season as a young girl. Imagine, Baby, your apartments in town, the great house of the Duchess of Devonshire – how splendid!'

'O, aye, splendid...'

'And after all, what a Season it has been. What a Season!' She giggles.

He leans his head on her shoulder, trying to ignore the racket of the awakening birds. 'Aye – the Duchess's splendid house. When I leave for Europe I shall owe the old cow six months rent, I am happy to say.' His smile disappears. 'Well, it is over, now, the season. Consummatum est.' He remembers what she has just said. ' 'Through Eden took their solitary way.' Paradise Lost. When did you learn that, Goose?'

Augusta giggles. 'When we were cut off from the world for two weeks at Newstead. That Christmas that it snowed. You read me the whole blessed thing, over and over again. God throwing Satan down from the heavens, and so on...'

His smile returns; he is already learning the importance of memory as the source of happiness. 'Now that was a way to spend a winter – cut off from the world in our own planet of two. Damme if we have not had our moments, Goose...'

She slips her arm round his shoulder and gives him a squeeze. 'O Baby – they can never hurt you to death because in your heart you are better than all of them...'

'...except Napoleon...'

'Except Napoleon. And there will be men in the South you will be delighted to meet... minds fit to associate with...'

'...thoughts fit, hands apt...'

'...and within a year or so you may come back to Town again as before...'

He looks at her as if at a child, saying gently: 'To be sure, dear, they will soon forget this scandal... and I shall come back...'

'When we were under the snow at Newstead you told me of other lands – other rooms in God's house – warm lands where men believe in pleasure... you would enjoy that...'

He holds his head in his hands. 'O Augusta, I shall be outcast from the edge of the earth.'

'Say, then, that you will be outcast.' She seizes his wrists in a fierce grip. 'You will become Childe Harold in truth. Did you reach beyond yourself only to shun what was there?'

He looks at her coolly, guessing her strategy is to rally his strength through arousing his anger. As if from a long way away, he hears his lips saying: 'I suppose it is child's play for you to understand your evil mirror – I mean myself of course.'

With a laugh Augusta jerks his hands to pull his head forward. She kisses him on the lips. 'If I were a man I should never complain. I would claim my freedom to pursue sensation upon sensation until the grave claimed me... Which reminds me, I am dying of hunger.'

A rush of despair. Their final moments together on Earth. He is sure of it. 'O if we are to go inside and wake the servants I will say my goodbyes now.'

She turns and smiles at him. 'Foolish Baby. You always

behave as if you were never to see me again.'

'I swore the first time I went abroad that I should never come home. How much the more reason have I not to come home now?'

'Nonsense. You are a young man still.'

'I have cast the dice of youth and the wager is lost. It seems a familiar enough story. As you say it is one I wrote for myself long ago.'

Augusta chuckles, walks a little way into the rosegarden, stops. 'I always loved your pretty verses.' She turns and gives him a look. 'I wonder if you have made any for me these last months? Or have you been too preoccupied with the spectacle of Miss Milbanke dancing like an elephant on your heart?'

'All my verses are for you. Even those addressed to the others. "I have been cunning in my overthrow. The careful pilot of my proper woe." That was for you.'

'A pretty song. Let us hear the remainder.'

"With false Ambition what had I to do?
Little with Love, and least of all with Fame,
And yet they came unsought..."

Her laughter, like music. 'Liar! You're such a liar!'

"...and with me grew
And made me all that they can make – a name."

'YOUR name? I thought these were to be MY verses?' She lets go of his hand. 'I suppose you promise verses to all your ladies.'

He stands up. 'I would not say that.' They look at each other. 'You know, with this blasted twisted-up hoof of mine I have never waltzed – not once, no, not once, with another woman. Nobody else shall be allowed to see me try.' He puts his arm round her. They execute a few clumsy steps around the garden. 'I have a poem for you but you must let me explain it first. I have never, I will never write it down. It is for thee and me only, in this moment of ours.'

'O, I adore explanations, especially if I do not understand them.'

He smiles. 'You see, Goose, the Universe itself is waltzing, the stars dance around each other in patterns evolved according to the laws of Mr. Newton's gravitational theory – why they say the very atoms may be dancing in such a fashion. In the poem I am trying to explain that to dance with you is to be connected to this dance of the stars.'

'Yes, yes, go on.'

"I have seen Suns come tumbling, seen them fall,
Galaxies pass in the Dance majestical,
And swung like a Star, a patterned part of all.
Now I belong to Chaos and must crawl."

They waltz. 'I am dying,' she repeats, 'of hunger.'

He lets her go. 'Time has caught up with us. Damn time to Hell.' He takes her arm and they start toward the house.

Far up the road in time and space, the Spirit takes his last sight of Augusta on this planet. Her movement seems to slow at the intensity of his minute examination. Time stops. He gazes at the frozen Augusta on LB's arm. Soft cheeks, soft eyes, soft curls, soft beloved brain. A cut-crystal profile, perfect as his own.

Something about the scene has dissatisfied the Spirit. He turns with an appeal to the body on the bed. 'Pah,' he spits. 'Verses! He calls that verses! For an occasion like this, we need a little more detachment. And I am the boy to provide it. A sonnet, I think. Are you listening, there on the bed? I shall not write these lines down neither.'

A groan. 'Spare me...'

'I shall call the piece: 'The Third Observer.' Do pay attention, old boy. It's never too late to improve one's technique.' He clears his throat and declaims quietly:

'A man is not a unit: god and beast
Contend within, and body's doom confines;
'With what he most enjoys contented least'
And yet stores pleasure in the mighty lines
As some place else the Third Observer sits
Calmly at ease, paring its fingernail.
And it the soul that dwells beside our fits
Unquenchable as flesh and spirit fail;

Eternal as a jewel in the night
Burning for you along the edge of time,
Bathing in memories of a softer light,
Indulging itself to close in perfect rhyme,
To speak of that in me which cannot die
But, chained to you forever, still must fly.'

From the bed a single cry: 'Goose?'
The Spirit whispers, 'Aye, Goose.'

On the wall, the crystal profile fades out as completely as if it had never been.

Chapter twenty-nine

I had a dream, which was not all a dream,
The bright sun was extinguish'd, and the stars
Did wander darkling in the eternal space,
Rayless, and pathless, and the icy earth
Swung blind and blackening in the moonless air;
Morn came and went and came, and brought no day,
And men forgot their passions in the dread
Of this their desolation; and all hearts
Were chill'd into a selfish prayer for light:
And they did live by watchfires – and the thrones,
The palaces of crowned kings – the huts,
The habitations of all things which dwell,
Were burnt for beacons; cities were consumed,
And men were gather'd round their blazing homes
To look once more into each other's face...

'Hell, hell – we travelled across Europe breathing flames...'

The Spirit considers. 'Hell? Purgatorio, perhaps. I always rather enjoyed that aimless wandering across the Alps, meself.' He changes the image with a gesture to snow and ice and rocky pinnace, the world above the boiling Alpine cloud, those mountains out of dreams, those Alps.

'We are there now.' he mutters. 'To breathe those frozen flames again.'

Hobhouse has rejoined the party: staid, unimpressably English Hobhouse, the best and dullest friend a man ever had. Scrope, the worst and most interesting friend a man ever had, has already been and gone, abjuring an expedition further into the Alps out of a peculiar desire 'to see a boa-constrictor.'

We always liked a holiday. If we only didn't, even with Hobby, feel so alone and down in the mouth, as if the gigantic vistas of rock and ice were a depressing sight... emptiness, waste, desolation, exactly as the spaces within us. Amusing, though, to watch Hobhouse, first thing in the morning, abusing the local excellent Swiss fare because it is not English stodge and grease, and grumpily readying himself for the day. It being Hobby's habit to trudge on gamely ahead while we follow up the rear, lame duck that we are, on horseback.

Except, of course, when we reach those very astonishing paths where the guide leads us up such precipitous terrain that we are forced to abandon our horse and simply CLIMB using hands, knees, twisted feet, O any thing... sinking, at times, up to one's neck in snow, slithering by the edge of yawning precipices that exceed one's dreams of furthest space.

The weather that first day like the day the World was made. That infinity of blue sky. The trotting gentle young mare (we like our horses tame, being quite crippled enough thank you) overtakes the walking Hobhouse, who is a little tired. We resume the journey in an open carriage together.

That glittering day, with the beloved friend, and the view of the holy mountains in the distance.

We stop to look around the little town of Vevey, a particu- larly fine Protestant Church there. We find the grave of anoth- er English exile, General Ludlow, the regicide who had signed King Charles's death warrant for Cromwell, and was forced to leave our dear country when the Royalist scum returned. Lud- low! Excellent fellow! To kill a King, aye, and an English one to boot. O, for a Republic of England! Hobby and I smoke a reverent cigar above this political ancestor's tomb.

The Castle of Chillon. One has a poem which may be con- sulted, and this only may be said further to the point: we see an English lady, in the very eye of Mont Blanc, fast-asleep in the most anti-narcotic spot in the world – excellent; and her travelling companion, another worthy English, observing to the party: 'Did you ever see anything more RURAL?' As if it were Highgate, or Hampstead, or Dulwich.

RURAL! O English bourgeois eternal – as the white bro- ken teeth of the mountains grin down at her brief shadowy existence, as we gaze up at the pinnacle of rock where the trees and all life end, where begins, ten thousand feet over our heads, the eternal, dazzling, deadness of the snow, so attractive from down here.

At Mont Davant we stop the carriage and breakfast on bread, cheese, excellent local hard sausage, tea, and white wine. Thus fortified, we proceed immediately on horseback upwards into the other world.

When the ascent steepens we leave our horses and trans- fer to mules. We falls off our mule and off the path (courtesy of the rotten leg) followed by the mule and all its baggage rolling down after us through the rocks and snow until a pine tree stops our precipitous roll with a bruising thump. The mule, fortunately, comes to rest against a different tree.

Only a finger split open, and the mule is still alive. Having been taught respect for the mountain we remount the righted mule, a bloody handkerchief round our stinging finger, and follow the dogged Hobhouse up the winding track.

We dismount, having to leave even the mule, now, and climb, exhaustedly climb, forcing ourself to go on, never to be outdone by a dogged Hobby-horse. Around the last turn, upon the highest height, we realize, finally, where we are. Under the aching blue of that infinite sky we have reached a lake glistening like milk in the very nipple of the bosom of the mountain. Hobby and I turn to each other with wild looks of surprise and delight, not unmingled with terror. A shock of recognition, as if we have been here already, as if it were some space inside us.

We descend a little, leave the beasts tethered to a tree, and bear on to the next peak. Higher and higher we go, hey ho – our sweat dropping off our faces like rain, making the same dints as water from a sieve on the patches of snow we bend above, groaning, cursing, climbing. 'By God we were fitter than this once,' we grunts, happy to hear that Hobhouse can only pant back at us.

On and up to the highest pinnacle. John Cam Hobhouse stands on top of it with an unusually wild grin, surveying a prospect of mountains in every direction. We are content to shelter in a fissure in the rock, five feet below the summit, out of that biting wind, that aching void that artless Hobby so blithely breathes the air of, knowing not what it is.

On the way down, we spots a shepherd on a high steep cliff playing honeyed tones on his pipes. This place is much more like the fabled groves of Arcadia than your actual Greece, where your shepherd generally carries a musket rather than a stick or a dog, in accordance with the warlike nature of the place. But before us on that rock sits an image of Pan carrying no more weapon than his humble instrument. The effect of this scene in Switzerland has nothing to do with violence, and generates a feeling a hundred times removed, pure, like unmixed joy in Heaven. This calm creature, as it were goatfooted, seated on a rock, piping unthinkingly into the Void, as if to fill that emptiness with music.

We have repeopled our mind with Nature.

Down in the villages the people of this fortunate Republic seem free, happy, and rich. On our walk the next day we meet a girl selling fruit by the roadside. Hobhouse buys some grapes and pears and we pinches her pretty red cheek. A healthy strong blonde, with a delicately beautiful face, and a smile dazzling white, goodnatured, unafraid, not in the least coquettish.

Pure maid of the Mountain.

The image of this girl's face stays with us till we gain the prospect of the divine waterfall, curving over the rock like the tail of a white horse streaming in the wind, like the pale horse on which death is mounted in the Apocalypse, the tail neither mist nor water but something between, nine hundred feet high. Can a human heart bear more than this? 'This has,' says Hobhouse, 'been the best two days of my life.'

Aye, even as they mingle with the worst inside our heart.

Next morning, the silver tooth of the Dent d'Argent shining like truth, and at the same time on our *other* side the Jungfrau with her massed glaciers, one piled atop the other till they reach heaven. Every few minutes we hear the dull roar of an avalance falling, thankfully, past us – as if God were pelting the Devil down to Hell with snowballs.

Nothing loth, we makes a snowball and pelts Hobhouse with it, shouting, take that you devil... Hobby tries to duck behind a tree and we land a good one that slides down the back of his neck. The woods ring to our laughter and his curses as thousands of feet below a sea of cloud begins to fill the cup of the valley, curling and flowing and lipping the precipices underneath us, the foam of the Ocean of Hell in a Spring Tide – a sulphurous, boiling ocean of cloud.

The World, waiting for us below.

On the way down we pass whole woods of pines all withered – brown foliage, trunks stripped of bark, and dull lifeless branches. We point out the desolate prospect to Hobhouse: 'The appearance of these trees reminds me of me and my family.' More avalanches roar by, thankfully always in other parts of space and time than those we occupy, and the pair of us manage to sweat home safely in the red eye of the evening sun.

That same evening we go to view the great green Grindenwald, very fine glacier, like a frozen hurricane – by now all in starlight – snow and ice glowing like dreams under the clear high stars. But a Devil of a path down again, slipping and slithering past deathly falls in the dark, while the occasional crack and flash of a bolt of lightning slashes down into the valley below. A relief to be safe home to hot suppers and rum toddies, tight clean Swiss inn, best in the world, where we sleep the dead, empty, dreamless sweet sleep, no opiate in the world like exhaustion.

Before ascending the next mountain we pass the following morning a torrent like to the earlier waterfall; the Sun at seven in the morning forms in the roaring mist a rainbow of all colours, but principally purple and gold. The bow continues drifting with us before that prospect of mountains as we ride along the path. I never saw any thing like this.

On past the Black Glacier, keeping the Mountain Wetterhorn on the right – then crossing the Scheideck mountain to the Rose Glacier, glowing tower of pink in the morning light, the largest and finest glacier in Switzerland.

The Reichenback waterfall, about two hundred feet high. This is not as tall as the other, the streaming tail of the Pale Horse, and in any case the rain is slanting down now with a fine powder of snow. Time to shog.

In this weather Hobhouse and I are soon drenched and shivering and longing for our beds. Arriving at last in the village containing said beds, we pass in our open carriage four peasant girls, walking home in the snow from their day's work and singing the airs of their country. We call to the driver to stop as we register a tune they are singing, a Tyrolese air which Augusta always loved. The girls smile up at us and sing on sweetly. *Dear heart, if you could be here with us tonight, to listen to the pure voices of the mountain girls sing your song.*

Leaving Hobhouse at his beef and beer, climbing the stairs to our dark cold room, we lay the candle down on a table. We sit down, open the Journal we have been keeping for Augusta, and write:

> *I am a lover of Nature and an admirer of Beauty. I can bear fatigue and welcome privation, and have seen some of the noblest views in the world.*
>
> *But in all this – the recollections of bitterness, and more especially of recent and more home desolation, which must accompany me through life, have preyed*

upon me here; and neither the music of the Shepherd, the crashing of the Avalanche, nor the torrent, the mountain, the Glacier, the Forest, nor the Cloud, have for one moment lightened the weight upon my heart, nor enabled me to lose my own wretched identity in the majesty, and the power, and the Glory, around, above, and beneath me.

I am past reproaches; and there is a time for all things.

Chapter thirty

I stood in Venice, on the Bridge of Sighs;
A palace and a prison on each hand:
I saw from out the wave her structures rise
As from the stroke of the enchanter's wand...

The body on the bed moans: 'Cold flames...burning light...'
'You are always complaining.' The Nightgowned Spirit
shakes his head, and the shining Alps vanish like Augusta,
as if they have never been. 'But at least, now, we can bring
Manfred down off the mountain and into the city. Venice!
The greenest island of our imagination...'

'But Shelley... we met Shelley in Switzerland, damn you,
before Venice, before the climbing of the Alps with Hobby...
Give us some of Shiloh for Christ his sake...'

'On the shore of Geneva, aye, we met Shelley. A famous
episode, our physician young Dr. Pollydolly stealing our idea
and inventing the Vampyre, and Mary Shelley inventing
Frankenstein's monster on the very same evening. Not a bad
evening's work – the two greatest monsters of European fiction, both conceived on the same night...'

...and ourselves, that same dreadful, laudanum and wine-soaked evening, rogering the awful Claire for the want of anything better to roger in the mist. She was already pregnant with our natural child-to-be... hey nonny.

Mind you, without Claire we should not have met Shelley, or as we call him, Shiloh, who was married to Claire's stepsister Mary. We had first fucked Claire in England, when she wrote us a letter proposing to MEET us, after the Separation. We had no idea then that the bitch would seek us out in Switzerland, with her notorious step-brother-in-law Mr. P.B. Shelley in tow.

A famous time at Geneva, apart from the almost-unwanted attentions of Madam Claire. We had just received from England Mr. Coleridge's wonderful Christabel (which we later encouraged him to publish) wherein he had invented a new system of versing that WORKED BY THE COUNTING OF STRESSED LINES ONLY, damn near a new thing under the sun... (Except they say it is the principle of Old Saxon verse too.) We read the verses to the company. Mrs. Shelley (who was an altogether superior woman to her stepsister, Claire) listened to Mr. Coleridge's Christabel quite magnificently, with an eye full of understanding that rivalled Shiloh's.

I remember Coleridge! A gentlemen whom we have passed a little money and favours along to in our time: which only shows how unjust a world it is that one such as us could be placed in an unmerited position to help the greatest genius of the age. I have seen Coleridge in full flight of talk to some of the chief men of the age, and to do so was to watch an adult talking to children: all our brains were that far below his in the comparison.

All this was very well; Shelley and I, new friends at Lake Geneva, discussed the wonders of Mr. Coleridge, too, but all the while Madame Claire sat with her simpering smile, and our dago doctor Pollydolly enthused, pretending to understand what only Shiloh and I, and, I suspect, the gravely silent Mrs. Shelley – a remarkable woman – could understand. Then we resumed our reading. When it happened, everyone was watching us read *Christabel*, and only I was watching Shelley, who was growing increasingly agitated at Coleridge's verses.

As we read the description of the witch's horrific tits (or whatever it was) Shelley fainted clean away, his thin skull striking a corner of the marble hearth with a thud the memory of which sickens me to this day. When we brought Shelley around – and for a minute he looked as though he was gone – he said that he had had a vision of his wife's nipples turned into eyes, and staring at him blankly. Shiloh had not yet recovered, and was speaking as if from beyond the grave, his face deathly pale and his eyes full of dark knowledge.

'Go on, Shiloh,' we said, feeling like living Odysseus, talking across the ditch of blood to Elpenor's spirit in Hades.

Dr. Polidori fetched a glass of brandy, and, as the only quack present, insisted that Shelley drink it, which Shelley, as an abstemious man, was reluctant to do. At this Madame Claire with some silly remark intended as a joke dragged us into the bedroom, just when Shelley was about to say something else of import.

That we did not lose our temper and push the woman away is to be attributed to our respect for Mrs. Shelley, whose stepsister the girl was. We fucked Claire with a certain savagery in the bedroom, but she took our anger for ardour, as was natural enough. It was Claire's sole virtue to take a great deal of joy in our fucking; increasingly we ourselves were taking less and less.

Still, to fuck is to fuck, and a man needs a good fuck once a day. At Lake Geneva we fucked Claire. She never meant any more to us than that, and we constantly reminded her that WE were the one being ravished by her lecherous intentions, but it was to no avail, so that we had given up thinking about the problem the woman posed as she became more possessive. The only solution we could foresee was not to see her no more.

We acted upon this decision not before time, after she had driven us almost mad with her inability to leave us be. If we do not revisit at length that famous time at Lake Geneva, then, it is because the memory of it, save for the delight of finding a mind to equal our own in the airy Mr. Shelley, is entirely spoiled by the unpleasant memory of being stalked by our natural child's future mother, Claire Clairmont as she called herself (not her real name and be damned to her).

'Shut your lips about Claire. Let me see the child... Allegra my child... Let me see her alive again, damn you, you nightgowned bastard...'

'Aye, Geneva was a damned bore compared to what is waiting for us in Venice. We were not truly Shiloh's friend until we decided to be, at Pisa: let us by all means go to Pisa, and first let us see Venice, but in God his name let us skip the villa in Switzerland, the opium, the Vampyres, Victor Frankenstein and his creature, and the damned bitch Madam Claire.'

The man on the bed tries to reach for a flagon of water, has not the strength, desists. Without opening his eyes, he moistens his lips with his tongue. 'No time for more of Geneva? Venice, then.'

NGS begins to waltz himself around the drab death-room, humming a popular tune of the period. 'Venice... To the balls... where we were to relieve OUR balls not a little... to the ladies all masked, and all carrying that same delightful instrument between their legs, as if designed expressly to accomodate our own. It was my favourite part of our damned life, you old sobersides; Venice was ME. Venice was where I first came truly alive in you, after you had pretended to be me all your life...'

'Hell, hell...'

NGS stops for a second, looks over at the bed almost apologetically. 'Though no doubt you were burning in hell at the time. Yet what a time it was! Do you not remember? At the end of a party when we could drunkenly walk outside and step straight into the water, and swim home through the canals...'

That warm night, those streets full of murmured Italian promises and the smell of honeysuckle and wine. Walking through the open door of the palazzo, to the end of the landing, and, to shrieks of amusement from the departing guests, falling deliberately into the Grand Canal to sober ourselves up a little. Which the shock of the warm salt water – full, no doubt, of the unfragrant waste of Venice – always manages to do.

A servant comes with a torch, leans out over the canal and gives a light to LB, bobbing down there in the water. The servant is smiling. These milordi inglesi. A torch, to swim in the Canal! But it is simply good sense. One does not want to be run down by a gondola. We swim home drunkenly torch-lit, one-handed, through those warm, soupy, stinking canals, through the richest siftings of Venice, to our own ridiculous-ly cheap and magnificent palazzo.

In the room that stinks of death NGS sniffs the length of his middle finger, joyously, in a gesture both delicate and crude. 'And the girls, the girls. Or rather the married women – for in Italy they will do nothing under adultery.'

The faces, the images of half-remembered bodies float by on the wall of our memory.

'A different one every night for a year – and each with a mask on. Some professionals, most not... Aye, Manfred came down off the mountain and there lay the town spread out before him like the open legs of a woman...'

The colours – even in candlelight – seem brighter than London. Because Venice, sunken, provincial, an aging pox-pitted whore compared to what she had been in the days of her glory – Venice is a brighter world than London. A world in decline where the waltz of love moves not in rigid circles but in chaotic random swirls of direction, couples changing part-ners as often as the most bored voluptuary could wish, and all done with the most perfect tact and forbearance, as in the last days of the Roman Empire...

Look, that watchful fellow there is M. Beyle, the Froggy writer, alias M. Stendhal. The fellow is damned clever, was an officer under Napoleon, and will no doubt one day be a great author in his own right.

All of Europe's bohemia. And from all sides a barrage of lovers. Which is not even to count the whores and the fierce baker's wife we eventually have to throw out, that Fornarina of glorious erotic memory...

In Italy a woman has to be a virgin till marriage, and will do nothing under adultery. But after marriage...! The contessas smile boldly, as woman to man unafraid. For – save that regular treatment for the Clap featured a little more prominently in one's considerations – who cared? Good friends all, in one great glorious fuck.

To get by, in society here, a lover must have proper respect for the institutution of lady, husband, and cavaliere servente. This last is an approved 'amico' of the lady, whose official function is to hold her shawl at parties and the opera but whose real purpose is to roger her every orifice when the husband can no longer be bothered. (He would rather spend his time with his mistress.) There are your *regular* cavaliers and your *floating cavaliers* so to speak. A capital custom for the strictest adultery.

Observe our hand, then, scribbling that boastful letter to Hobhouse, a whore sat upon the desk (who finds her way into the letter), naked and uncaring, legs apart and moist cunt gaping near our inkstand (so that we are almost tempted to dip our pen in it to give our letter a bit more character). A host of faces, a varied host of bearded orifices at the other end – who remembers now which body was attached to which face? But as we write the letter each face is at least attached to a name, and the memory of each face, loved for a day or a month, swims into our mind's eye:

Lord Lauderdale, says Murray, reports that Lord B's

current PIECE has been fished out of the canal where-
in she threw herself in a fit of temper over a rival & c...
PIECE! Damn Lauderdale's eyes! Which PIECE does
he mean? Since last year I have run the Gauntlet. Is it
the Tarruscelli, the da Mosti, the Spineda, the Lotti,
the Rizzato, the Eleonora, the Carlotta, the Zambie-
ri, the Eleonora da Bezzi (who was the King of Naples'
Gioaschino's mistress, at least one of them), the Ther-
esina of Mazzurati, the Glettenheim – and her sister –
the Luigi & her mother – the Fornaretta, the Santa, the
Caligara, the Portiera Vedova, the Tentora and her sis-
ter – cum multis aliis. Some of them are countesses, and
some of them are cobblers' wives, some noble, some
middling, some low, and all whores; which does the
damned old 'Ladro et porco fattuto' mean? I have had
them all and thrice as many to boot, since 1817.

As the watchers watch, a drop of sweat falls onto our
paper, smudging a word. We sway slightly in the fatigue
brought on by such an outburst – even on paper. The girl
seated on our desk decides that we will go on writing, now;
she knows our way. Bored, she yawns, goes to the mirror and
begins to comb out her long sweat-tangled hair.

A little frightened by a peculiar pounding in our heart, we
decide to continue the letter in a calmer but more sardonic vein.

(A change of tone which the Nightgowned Spirit approves
wholeheartedly. 'The boy,' he remarks, 'grows more and
more like me every day.')

We put the pen in the ink, scratch on the paper:

> *Whatever brain-money you get on my account from Murray, pray remit me. I will never consent to give away what I earn, that is mine, & what I get by my brains I will spend on my bollocks as long as I have a tester or a testicle remaining.*

We stop writing for a moment, and gazes around our room. The candle on our desk throws up shadows around our eyes, so that they look to the invisible watchers, our future selves, like holes in a skull. The girl, seeing us look up, smiles an invitation. Sighing, we bend again to finish our letter.

> *I shall not live long, and for that reason I must live while I can – for the night cometh.*

Chapter thirty-one

I have fallen in love with a Romagnuola Countess from Ravenna...

A conversazione of the Contessa Benzoni. The rich sound of cake-forks tinkling against plates, a general hum of polite but animated conversation. The lady sitting on our right was trying to explain why we should meet the contessa Guiccioli, who was about to make an appearance with her ancient husband – a man long past due for a pair of horns, said the Benzoni.

We had no doubt changed for the worst in the year or two since raving across the Alps with Hobhouse. Our hair was greying, we had put on weight. We had weathered many indulgences in food, women, drink, cigars... We had lived ten years in one. We felt as stale as we seem to have looked.

But the Benzoni was saying: '...I can assure milorde that she is the freshest beauty to be had in Venice. Why the old devil the Conte married her but a year ago – at his age he can hardly have touched her. She will make you the most perfect mistress in Italy – the Da Mosti and I will introduce you when the Guicciolis arrive...'

The Da Mosti smiled and nodded as she caught our eye. 'And then, milorde, we shall see who is too tired to make love.'

We yawned. 'My dearest contessa, you must bear with me when I say I do not wish to make any new acquaintances with women: if they are ugly because they are ugly, and if they are beautiful because they are beautiful.' The two ladies giggled at the divine wickedness of the crazed Englishman. 'Your true milorde inglesi will always try to do his worst for his country's reputation, madam, because... because...'

A golden haired young woman came in, disappearing into the little crowd who welcomed her at the door. Augusta all with ringlets of gold – blackout in the head... We became aware of the world about us once again, aware that the ladies were laughing at our openmouthed absorption. The Da Mosti was almost hysterical. 'O che bella – the thunderbolt – the wicked milorde has been struck down at last!'

We made our face smile. 'I thought I had recognised someone. A trick of the light, no doubt. You ladies always forget that I am a married man.'

When the laughter at this had died down, we took a chance. 'And pray, who is the signora? Since I am detected in my approval of her earthly surface.' This started them laughing again. We could grow quite tired of this.

Seeing our irritation one of the ladies nearby explained the joke. 'Milorde it is the Contessa Guiccioli, the lady of whom we speak. That ugly old man over there is her husband.'

The Da Mosti took our arm. 'You will see – she is ripe for love.' She made a contemptuous gesture at the ugly, redfaced old man who was already being skilfully separated from his wife at the other end of the room. 'With a man like that, what woman would not wish for a cavaliere servente such as you would be? The old fool himself should be grateful for the duties you perform for him. And the wife is very beautiful.'

We laughed. 'A cavaliere servente! I do not think an English-man's vanity would stand it.' We shrugged. Nobody, we were sure, would ever bring our interest in the world to life again.

The Da Mosti shook her charming head of curls. 'Your accent, milorde, is perfect Venetian, but...' she wagged her fin-ger warningly '...he has not known love, *Italian love*, who has never been a cavaliere servente.'

The pretty young girl with blonde ringlets was presented to us, we kissed her hand; the husband too was presented, and shook our hand affably, but in a few minutes the helpful contessas had drawn him away, allowing ourself and Teresa to converse freely.

We observed her – not Augusta exactly, and yet a face... gold curls, blue eyes, eighteen years old: a flawless face, soft, smooth, delicately carved. A brain fine enough, but not too complicat-ed. An apparently sunny nature. And looking like that. We smiled at her gently. 'I never before thanked my stars that I bothered to attend a party – not before this day, at any rate.'

Enormous eyes, clear as the Aegean, grew wider at the compliment. 'You do not remember me. A whole year has gone by since we were introduced at the house of the sculp-tor. But I remember *you*. My father has told me that you left England to come and help us make the revolution – to help us make a free country out of Italy.'

'I had other reasons, contessa; your father was wish-ful-thinking.'

We have met this charming child before this! How embar-rassing! We feel our face flushing in confusion – and then we remembered. Count Gamba's daughter – Count Gamba who helps to lead the revolutionaries, the 'charcoal burners,' the Carbonari, who meet deep in the Ravennese forest! This is the pretty girlchild of that patriotic family – Teresa Gamba. A woman, now, the Contessa Guiccioli. No longer the child we saw. 'You have changed, contessa, in the year since your marriage.'

She frowned. 'It is your eyes which have changed, you are ready to talk to me now as you would not before.'

'Perhaps you are right, contessa. Perhaps I have changed.' *Perhaps*, we were thinking, *the wound has scabbed over at last...*

She took our hand. For some reason we could not fathom, there was no further need for words between us. She held our hand for what seemed like an eternity, a bright presence entering the dark well of our loneliness, murmuring two words that would become a litany: 'Mio Biron.'

Chapter thirty-two

Those movements, those improvements in our bodies
Which make all bodies anxious to get out
Of their own sand-pits, to mix with a goddess,
For such all women are at first no doubt.
How beautiful that moment! and how odd is
That fever which precedes the languid rout
Of our sensations! What a curious way
The whole thing is of clothing souls in clay!

We have then a new lover, the Contessa Teresa Guiccioli, who is, unfortunately enough, married to an ugly old man, the Count. But this is Venice, and ladies do not mind that they are married. And so we are in love once again, after all these years and against our better judgment. She has conquered us, damn her.

She does not have it all her own way at first. We – LB – have been long schooled in the debaucheries of Venice, especially during Carnival, and it is a thing much to our liking, believing as we do that the alternative, which is to remember Augusta our sister and Annabella our wife and the rest of it, is a gaping mental Hell (and as Marlowe has so justly observed, hell is merely a state of mind – why this is hell nor am I out of it etc.)

So that we are quite accustomed to the cut and feel of a different cunt every day, with a plentifuly supply of wine and spirits of wine to numb the pain of the encounters, and the devil of it only is that the consequent uproar of women coming and going and *coming* does tend to bring wear and tear upon soul and body alike (and there are those of us who hold that they are but different aspects of the same thing).

Our hair starts to look grey and our teeth become rather looseish – at thirty... What, I pray you, is the *mind* within this sorry skull become?

The goldenhaired Countess even resists for a little while. Can it be true that such a girl would not WANT a man of thirty who LOOKS forty... But it seems the thunderbolt that had struck us down was mutual, and that Teresa was willing enough – only a little shy at first. She is to tell us later that she had considered it quite past time for her to take an *amico* – a year after marriage is considered polite in the Italian system, where the women will do nothing under adultery – but that she never thought to love her *amico* as much as me, and so consequently to hate her poor unoffending husband, this once-loved ugly old man, and determine never again to make love to him. They are an ancient peoples, these children of the Romagna, and they have their traditions.

We ourselves are a creature of tradition, and we have been at loose in Venice a year or two, and picked up a few traditions of our own. The first day in the gondola Teresa would kiss and go no further; this, I believe, for politeness' sake. There was in all this the unspoken assumption – a *feeling*, really, that we should take each other bodily at our next meeting, and so I did not hesitate to make certain arrangements in advance. I even forewent my evening with my favourite whore, and curtailed my evening intake of gin and water so that I would have my head clear and body fresh for the campaign on the morrow.

According to invitation, then, while the husband is taking his evening nap (as old men should) a strange gondola shows up with LB's letter to bear Teresa away on her first night's adventure. Within a furlong or two, down a dark watery alley, the gondola stops, and Teresa is ushered into LB's own private gondola where his lordship impatiently awaits. Much whispering and kissing in the enclosed back of the vessel, milord's gondolier knowing better than to make a sound, and the pair are soon deposited at a little room we keep in these days for our more private assignations – when we want to escape the hubbub of the Palazzo Mocenigo, our own place.

Wine and little cakes have been laid out. The room and wine and cakes are pink; the lady is romantic; talks of Dante and a few other suitably noble subjects – the revolution that she and her family wish to see, for example, the freeing of Italy from Austrian subjugation. A subject that had already begun to appeal to us. And we, LB, here behind our eyes, watch the lady intently, watch ourself even more intently.

Could this delicacy of feeling be love? Could the anticipation of taking the clothing off that beautiful young body be love? Could the enchantment of gazing into the lively violet eyes of an intelligent young girl be love, if one can listen to her quote Dante, if one can delay Sex, if one does not immediately wish to roger her every orifice? Which, of course, one would like to do eventually... These sweet red lips breathing soft syllables of Dante. Is love merely to be prepared to wait? (We never waited for Augusta but rogered her as soon as the decision was truly made, Augusta as usual being one with us in the decision).

Is love the ability to wait? It is a good question. My lord is out of practice with being in love and with waiting, and is not sure. In any case, the lady is returned safely home. Another assignation is arranged, for the next day, at the same hour. My lord sleeps sweetly, but, having fasted one night in vain does not dispense with the services of the creature that arrives, regularly, at the evening hour, to see if she is required. The whore is tall and well built and beautiful, a fine young animal, though human enough.

It is usually a pleasure to sleep with the beautiful English milorde, and the girl seems disappointed that LB does not seem to want her, even though the requisite fee is not denied her. Thinking, is it not enough that I pay the woman, must I roger her too? – LB's vanity, given his doubts about his hair and teeth, is flattered, which, comme d'habitude, arouses his lust, and he obliges the trollop with an enthusiastic fuck.

As the Venetian woman, all dark hair and eyes and dangling breasts, so different from her countrywoman Teresa, mounts astride him, her eyes slitted in a fierce ecstasy, he lets himself go immediately, selfishly, but she is evidently experiencing the same feelings and they come together, as if the woman were a lover and not a whore.

Almost immediately the relief of the eternal pressure at his groin turns to melancholy, to a kind of empty remorse, not for his betrayal of Teresa but for the realisation that he has no longer truly enjoyed it. He shrinks and withdraws from the still-murmuring girl. He has a premonition that this will be the last such casual girl of his life, and it makes him begin to feel his mortality.

Waking after noon the next day, comme d'habitude, LB cannot wait for the night. He writes a letter to Teresa from the mouldering Renaissance bedroom. Then, having dressed and breakfasted on a raw egg in a glass of wine, he goes to feed his menagerie, that luckless assortment of animals which he keeps on the ground floor in the dank sea-smelling rooms where his carriages stand rusting, useless in watery Venice. For the great city has sunk not only in fortunes but indeed into the sea since these rooms were first in use, and ground floors are now considered uninhabitable.

The day drags on, the longed-for night apparently not willing to come. My lord plays billiards with himself, listening grimly to the clack of the balls in the echoing cool room, and Fletcher fetches him a cup of green tea with a tot of gin in it. He smokes a cigar to quell a raging hunger for food; the years of sensuality in Venice have left his body fat and greasy and he would like to repair the damage if he can. Weight he can always lose, he enjoys punishing his body, but it seems to him that his teeth feel loose in his head and that there is more hair – and silverthreaded hair too – in his comb of a morning, and it seems to him that his hairline is receding. He makes liberal use of macasar oil in an effort to darken his hair. He is lonely, but he is always lonely. He is bored, but he is always bored. Why should he long so for an assignation with an eighteen year old girl? Can this, he thinks, this boredom, this loneliness, be love? At times he resents the implication.

The pattern of the night before is repeated, Teresa is taken to milorde's private *casino* for the wine and the sweetmeats. Here, now, the man considers himself on his mettle, and begins to kiss the girl. As he senses her growing excitement, after an hour of concentrated attention which has left him so tired in the kissing tongue and so much in control that he is not really enjoying it, he caresses her breasts through her gown, willing his hands to make the sensitive motion of brushing all four fingers lightly across the nipple, watching his hands detachedly as they take what should be their hands' pleasure and then, aided by her, proceeds to take off her clothes. To see that beautiful white body for the first time.

Except that the girl will not wait, one would fain simply rest one's head on her soft round belly in worship and study her more minutely. A thing, which later, we are able to do, and will describe now in advance of our lovemaking, but please to remember this examination took place an hour later; this examination of her person was made *afterwards*, when in the lull after love our love lay sleeping.

To begin with: the breasts, those objects for the Child that men still love and worship. La Guiccioli's breasts, as we have suspected they would be, are firm, but heavy and pendulous, especially when she sits and bounces astride and above us, and yet, when the lady lies in repose, as now, upon her back, they are somewhat flattened against a rib cage. The nipples are large, pink, roseate, but one defect we thinks (from our conception of the ideal nipple) is that the pinkness merely BLENDS INTO the pinkness of the surrounding breasts, so that there is no clearly defined joining line, a border 'twixt nipple and breast.

We kiss one of the soft buds, and the lady stirs, smiling, in her sleep. We trickle our tongue slowly, to make a snail-trail, from the breast to the belly button, into which we has to insert our tongue. Then we raise our head to get an overall perspective on the neat golden triangle of fur that waits below. Gently, so as not to wake the girl, we leans forward and prises apart her thighs a little, so as to examine the thing more closely. Despite the youth of the girl, her blondness and her relative innocence, the lips of her cunt are as it were *virile*, projecting and full, ruby leathery flaps of skin that part at a touch to admit our tongue, where we taste our own salty ooze melting into the soft sea-taste of the womb.

And this was only a cursory inspection.

You may keep, aesthetic-LB is thinking, (back in the present now, the first lovemaking) your Venus de Milo, the fat old dame one praises only in public. Ourself, we will take a living woman any time, and to hell with visual art, to which in any case we find ourselves peculiarly indifferent compared to the rest of the tourists in Venice. True, the pictures and the museums in one's neighbourhood are agreeable, but spare us, please, the tourist's enthusiastic whine.

The lady is rather short (her only defect) but her legs, short or not, are soon wide open and long enough to wrap round us. The splendid young breasts are full, firm, upright, with the pure pink nipples of the demi-vierge, erect after our caressment as any whore's. Eyes closed, mouth lifted for our kiss, the girl moans like a cat as we carries her to the couch. We buries our face in that golden cunt, tongue seeking salt pink lips in the curly blonde fuzz, and the girl reacts as if she has never felt a tongue before, her thighs threshing madly about our ears so that we are obliged to come up for air for a moment.

Of course, we thinks, nibbling the little button at the top of the cunt, that old man would not condescend to give the girl this pleasure. When LB straightens up, kissing the pink tips of her breasts and then moving to her lips, when, unable to stand it any longer, he plunges into the warmth and wetness of the girl, and they commence fucking in earnest, there is yet something piquant about it all – much more than the mere excitement of a first fuck. This, he is thinking, as he drowns in the wide-open blue pools of her eyes, is innocence, and is done in all innocence. This is what God has called Love.

With all the enthusiasm and the moaning, making love to her is almost like making love to a virgin. She is – unless, like a whore, she can pretend – shocked, wide-eyed with pleasure, as if she has never known such pleasure before, which MUST mean she has only made love with the ugly old man her husband, surely? And husbands don't count – at least, not in Italy. As near as dammit a virgin. She admits in soft Italian that it is so and only asks how she may best please him. She has no experience in these matters beyond her husband, who, she says demurely, will only make love in the dark.

Talk to me, he says, cara, talk to me even as you wrap your legs around me, even as you hook them over my shoulders in an effort to get closer, talk to me. I am a lonely man, and I wish to be alone no longer.

Chapter thirty-three

*– What shall I do! I am in love – and tired of promiscuous
concubinage – & have now an opportunity of settling for life. –*

The new lovers – I had almost said newlyweds – soon
work out their methods. They have need of haste, for
the idyll is to last only ten days, when the countess finds
out she must travel with her husband to visit his estates in
the Romagna. By the fourth day they have established a
reliable method to arrange their loves, still unknown to the
husband, though there is no reason to imagine that he will
be angered at so conventional an arrangement as his wife
taking an *amico*.

For those first golden days an understanding governess
in the Guiccioli household, a particular companion of Teresa's, is engaged as confidante and go-between for the lovers. In Fanny Silvestrini's company Teresa is able to take her
gondola rides into the city, meet LB's gondola, and change
boats. Still with La Silvestrini in tow, they are poled out to
the Lido or one of the other islands near Venice to pursue
their own poling. La Silvestrini and the gondolier obligingly
take a walk along the sands as the lovers urgently conclude

their business behind a dune. Who knows what the servants get up to together?

And is this love? LB is thinking, as that splendid head and ripe but firm torso sits astride him, bucking him like a she-goat among the sand dunes of the lagoon. He is thinking of his gondolier, who is little better than a pimp, getting to take La Silvestrini for a walk. Even as the golden child moves on top of him, he is not unaware that he also wishes to roger the becomingly dark young Silvestrini, but he has not yet dared suggest it to this innocent who, even as he thinks these thoughts, opens her body to him like a flower, until at last, at last, he is able to stop thinking.

Count Guiccioli announces to his wife that they must leave Venice. Teresa cannot hide or keep to herself her chagrin, and with great Italian fuss goes directly to LB's box at the opera, so that she is seen delivering the tearful news of the coming separation by half of polite Venice (to the great scandal of that lecherous town where adultery is done strictly in accordance with certain sacred traditions.) LB, toying with the sensation of being in thrall once again, this novel and unexpected sensation in a life that had seemed all but over, writes to Hobhouse after Teresa has gone: 'I am in love, and tired of promiscuous concubinage, and have now an opportunity of settling for life.'

But old Venetian habits die hard. We makes an assignation with the fair Angelina, a young unmarried girl to whom we have been paying court for months, before the Guiccioli arrived on the scene. On our way to the rendezvous our foot slips as we step into our gondola and we tumble, owing to the cursed slippery slimy stairs of the damned palace dock, fully clothed as we are, into the Grand Canal, to be hauled out dripping by our gondolier, who is doing his best to suppress his mirth. We glance back at the house. The clock strikes on the Rialto, booming the time out over this sea-sinking, sea-stinking city of light and liquid crystal. There is no time to lose – the girl has said she has only an hour when her suspicious parents are elsewhere.

Dripping wet as we are, then, we are poled to the outside of the girl's bedroom on a darkened side-canal of her family's palazzo. The gondolier – a resourceful chap we have trained ourselves – props his pole on the girl's balcony, and LB shins up and enjoins the fellow to return within the hour and then begin circling past the house. Soaked as we still are, the girl comes out to us. A half hour of talking to the virgin, clinging shivering on the balcony, and we are admitted at last to the bedroom and, theoretically, a mere ten minutes or so of rogering her in the darkness. The girl cries out in pain as we go in: nevertheless bucks strongly upwards and we feel the hymen give a little and then break on the tip of our cock.

A virgin. One had forgotten what one felt like. If we stretch a point and include Teresa, it makes for two in the one week. Two in one year, in fact, for they are rare as hen's teeth in Venice, and grow rarer daily.

Afterwards, lying in the darkened room, our shirt is still wet from the Canal and we are still shivering a little, even in the girl's bed. But it seems inadvisable to disrobe entirely inasmuch as one might have to leap back into the Canal at need, should someone other than ourselves come. The girl speaks to us out of the darkness. She proposes to us to divorce our mathematical wife, and I tell her that in England we can't divorce except for *female* adultery. 'And pray, (says she), how do you know what she may have been doing these last three years?'

I answer that I cannot tell, but that the state of Cuckoldom is not quite as flourishing in Great Britain as with us here.

'But,' she says, 'can't you get rid of her?'

'Not more than is done already,' (I answers). 'You would not have me *poison her*?' She makes me *no answer*. Is this not a true and odd national trait? It speaks more than a thousand words, and yet this is as little, pretty, sweet-tempered, quiet feminine being as ever you saw, but the Passions of a Sunny Soil are paramount to all other considerations.

In the virgin's bedroom the designated time passes, we plunge our loins together into the darkness, the girl saying she is not sore, and in the darkness the girl becomes Augusta to us. God he knows who the girl was thinking of; but there is no sign of restiveness from her at the passage of the agreed time of an hour. Evidently the parents are not coming tonight, though the daughter does. But why did she say that the parents would come? In case she wanted, at the last minute, to change her mind and get rid of us?

We are glad she did not. A noble fuck. A worthy farewell to our youth.

As the hours pass, not knowing if it is for the last time, we feverishly plunge into and, in the intervals, talk to the sixteen year old, all night, all night, all night, one last time now... On the way home from the last successful adventure of our life, exhausted, shivering in our still-wet clothes like a damned clown, we think: aye, the Passions of a Sunny Soil. We have sought them, we have found them, but they have damn well near done for us, so they have. WE are frightened by our old bones shivering, and dreads pneumonia from the wet clothes, like any middleaged man.

(In the future, the watchers watch their earlier self as if from outside, now.)

Only when he is comfortably warm, LB in his dry nightclothes and gown, gazing out of his window as dawn breaks above the Rialto, his groin still tingling and a little bloody from having come three times inside a virgin, his heart as drained as his bollocks, does LB at last remember Teresa Guiccioli.

Despite the delightful tightness and enthusiasm of the divine Angelina, perhaps, he is thinking, only because we did everything in the dark, to his astonishment he finds that after a thousand cunts he wants that one golden cunt, Teresa's cunt, again. And the intelligent, amiable and sensible golden head, to be fair, on the girl's shoulders. His heart, which has seemed to be flapping from perch to perch like a vulture in a feeding frenzy, has found a branch at last upon which it would like to settle.

Several things coalesce in his mind at once. Strangely resigned, he observes the processes of light growing upon the water. Dawn is slipping into the room quietly, on light feet, like a dancer.

He takes a sheet of paper, dips his pen in the ink, and scribbles without blotting a line, eager to get it done and get to sleep:

So we'll go no more a-roving
So late into the night
Though the heart be still as loving,
And the moon be still as bright.

For the sword outwears its sheath,
And the soul wears out the breast
And the heart must pause to breathe
And love itself have rest.

Though the night was made for loving,
And the day returns too soon,
Yet we'll go no more a-roving
By the light of the Moon.

He puts down the pen, his mind as drained, now, as his body, his thoughts at peace. The first rays of the sun begin to penetrate his window off the water and glitter in the blue-black eyes.

LB gets up from the desk, yawning, and takes himself off to bed, as Dawn unshadows the Rialto.

Chapter thirty-four

Dearest Augusta – The health of my daughter Allegra – the cold Season – and the length of the journey – induce me to postpone for some time a purpose (never very willing on my part) to revisit Great Britain.

We filed the poem, which, discovering the next day, we considered a damned good one, made a copy, despatched it to Murray, and forgot the sentiments expressed, at least insofar as they related to the Countess Guiccioli. And then, too, our own little love was oftentime in the house, our little natural child Allegra, newly rescued from the clinging bitch who ravished us at Genoa, that sister-in-law of Shelley's – the mother, that misery Madame Claire.

Despite the knowledge that the child is half-Claire, we could not help but take to the lively whelp as she dominated a series of governesses and even made her mark over the chaotic ranks of the rowdiest set of servants in Venice. To make her mark upon *THEM!* At *FIVE!* A proper baby B, she was... Allegra.

We had been learning to love the child, spending more time with her than any of our other pets, trying to stop the whores spoiling her with sweets, wondering, as any parent would, what sort of a woman she would grow up to be. This little bundle that leapt into our arms and looked at us with our own eyes, and said: 'Bon di, papa...' like the good Venetian that she was grown, this creature of English stock...

Allegra was conceived in England, and Claire already with child in those days at Lake Geneva, in the first flush of our relationship with Shelley. Shelley went back to England, taking the pregnant Claire with him. We got afterward to Venice, after climbing an Alp or two with Hobby as told already. And then, with Hobby gone, we heard that Shelley had returned to Italy with our child.

In vain did Shelley invite us to leave our Palazzo Mocenigo at Venice and visit him and the mother and child at Milan. We were not going near Madam Claire not no more, and besides, we always disliked moving. So that, in accordance with sense, and after we promised that Claire could see Allegra whenever we were NOT PRESENT, the child was despatched to us, for our protection and subsistence. Which was just as well, since the Shelley children seemed to perish like flies of green fruit and raw vegetable-eating. We wrote to Augusta: '...she has very blue eyes, and that singular forehead, fair curly hair, and a devil of a Spirit – but that is Papa's...'

Throughout all the riotous rogering at the Palazzo Mocenigo, the child played on the sidelines like our other pets. And, whatever else the Italian women were, they were kind to the child. A little too kind, perhaps, and she began to be spoiled. Also, the rather riotous goings-on, what with whores, gondoliers, women-fights, and pimps and contessas coming in and out, tended to disturb Allegra's peace (so her Nurse claimed). We passed her and the Nurse onto the Hoppners (the respectable British consul and his respectable German wife) where we could visit the child whenever we pleased.

(When Teresa, a noble lady, finally met Allegra she overwhelmed her with sweetmeats, as badly spoiling the child as any of the whores. Perhaps this is simply the style of motherhood in Venice; and perhaps this is what leads to such extraordinary women, and be damned to a more rational mode of education.)

The 'schild' remembered her Mama, Claire, which was no bad thing in a child, even though she tended to call the Nurse her Mama also. What is the point of speaking like this? We loved our daughter. Like any rich man (since the sale of Newstead and the death of Annabella's uncle Wentworth we were become rich) we had plans for the child: to send her to England and live with Augusta and be raised with her cousins as a lady. We had signed a codicil to our will, leaving £5,000 to our natural daughter, to make her a lady of fortune.

The house was lonely after Allegra went to the Hoppner's; when Teresa returned to her husband's estate, it was more so. We wrote a drivelling letter to the absent Teresa, and tried to carry on as usual. But we were thrown into blind panic by a letter that arrived from the Romagna (the Guicciolis not yet having reached Ravenna) from the lady herself. She had miscarried the Count's foetus (was THAT deliberate? we shall never know) and was ill with a consumption.

Our heart misgave us. We could never keep alive a Dog that loved us...

On May 17th, 1819, we wrote to Augusta:

My dearest Love, – I have been negligent in not writing, but what can I say? three years absence – and the total change of scene and habit make such a difference – that we have now nothing in common but our affections and our relationship. – But I have never ceased nor can cease to feel for a moment that perfect and boundless attachment which bound and binds me to you – which renders me utterly incapable of real love for any other human being – for what could they be to me after you? My own XXXX we may have been very wrong – but I repent of nothing except that cursed marriage – and your refusing to continue to love me as you had loved me...

When we had despatched this letter to the unreachable Augusta we were free to rattle off in our coach in pursuit of the reachable Teresa. But we were resolved to go no further than Bologna, if we could help it.

She had to come to us a little, too, if she could.

Chapter thirty-five

I have seen a thousand graves opened – and always perceived that whatever was gone – the teeth and hair remained of those who had died with them. – – Is not this odd? – They go the very first things in youth – & yet last the longest in the dust...

On the road to Bologna, stopping at Ferrara to water the horses, we ventured into a decaying graveyard, strangely beautiful, with its overgrown marble headstones shining out in the harsh southern light. One of the graves set our heart to pounding.

Martini Luigi
Implora pace.

A companion grave said:

Lucrezia Picini
Implora eterna quiete.

Can any thing be more full of pathos? Those few words say all that can be said or sought: the dead had had enough of life; all they wanted was rest, and this they *'implore.'* There is all the helplessness, and humble hope, and deathlike prayer, that can arise from the grave. And then, in Italian, the words are absolute music.

When we arrived at Bologna the first thing we visited was not the lady, who had already gone on to Ravenna, but the graveyard. No such wonderfully poetic inscriptions, though the style of grave was richer, as befitted a more prosperous town.

But something quite wonderful happened, something straight out of *Hamlet*. The old *Custode* of the graveyard had a collection of Capuchins' skulls, labelled on the forehead, and taking down one of them, said: 'This was Brother Desiderio Berro, who died at forty – one of my best friends. I begged his head of his brethren after his decease, and they gave it me. I put it in lime and then boiled it. Here it is, teeth and all, in excellent preservation. He was the merriest, cleverest fellow I ever knew. Wherever he went, he brought joy; and when anyone was melancholy, the sight of him was enough to make him cheerful again. He walked so actively, you might have taken him for a dancer – he joked – he laughed – oh! he was such a Frate as I never saw before, nor ever shall again!'

Was this not piquante? It is pure Shakespeare.

We were within the split of a hair of returning to Venice when word came that Teresa was ill again. Settled in truth was our fate. We proceeded immediately for Ravenna. For she will die, and we will die, and all shall die, so that we must try to be happy like the Frate, while still roaming above the earth. Like a man jumping off a cliff, we gave ourselves over into the possession of an eighteen year old girl.

Cavaliere Biron
implora pace.

Chapter thirty-six

Out of chaos God made a world, and out of high passions comes a people.

...glittering watery light above our bed Fletcher has left the damned curtain open and be damned to it not even noon as yet... Remembering suddenly what day it is – why we must get up early, to travel – and waking up with a sweaty start.

Who would spend summer in the steam of the Romagna when we should be in the mountains? Wondering, as the coach bumps along the dusty summer roads, if to go to cuckold a Papal count said to be responsible for two murders already, in his own home, and make love to his wife under his very nose, is altogether wise, seeing they have a reputation for being handy with the knife in Ravenna.

But when we get there Guiccioli is all bland concern for his sick wife's welfare: the man would make a great gambler, you can tell nothing of what he is thinking. He invites us immediately to the house, to revive his poor dying wife. The lady makes a miraculous recovery (I believe it is my friend Mr. Coleridge who first coined the word 'psychosomatic') and we indulge her desire with a good rogering the next day. I suppose it must weaken her (it don't *strengthen* me) but she insists upon it, and convenient ways have been found out to get the business done.

Nerve-racking thing it is to be deep in your beloved, tooling on a sofa, with most of your clothes on ready to leap up and apart from the sick bed, then getting up to fasten one's breeches like a naughty schoolboy as the lady brushes her dress down and tries to look as if she is wearing knickers. If a younger man should have tooled OUR wife almost before our eyes we should have blown his brains out. But Guiccioli don't even send a servant to spy on our amours. We can't make *him* out at all.

In a few weeks the lady is well enough to ride about in a carriage, and it is then that our honeymoon proper begins, so different from our treaclemoon with Annabella. We drive to the forest of umbrella pines that extends to the sea behind the city, the endless wood that goes all the way to Rimini. Lost in the quiet breath of the forest, without fear, here, of a stiletto in the gizzard from one of the Count's servants (your Italian bravo always preferring to operate on home territory) we make love in the open air. On our greatcoat and a carpet of pine needles, in the shelter of the trees.

To roll with this laughing honey-coloured girl on the forest floor, in that pinescented air, as the squirrels and birds and little lizards carry on their own affairs all around us, is to be transported into heaven, a taste of immortality. Untutored in the act of love, Teresa is an eager student and her enthusiasm and obvious love of our attentions have the usual magnifying effect, so that we love where we are loved. Burying our aging body in this young body and afterwards, those delicious breasts resting on our breast, to feel our hearts thudding as one among the scent of the pines.

THE WICKED LORD BYRON

Zeus, in the *Iliad*, when he masterfully took his wife Hera and caused a thick carpet of grasses to grow up beneath their bodies and a cloud to shower cool dew upon them, could have had no greater days of love than these in the forest.

The husband remains indecipherable. Old Guiccioli has taken recently to calling for ourself at our hotel and taking us out for a drive, exhibiting his wife's famous lover to the town like Whittington and his cat, as if he is incapable of shame.

By the end of July we decide we will move out of Venice entirely, to sleepy old Ravenna. (The wretched place has been not even a *backwater* since the sea retreated from its walls). In the uncertainty of this latest adventure, we leave Allegra in Venice with the Hoppners. When the Hoppners leave she is put in charge of the wife of the Danish consul at La Mira, Mrs Martens.

We can rest easy about the child, at least. But when Teresa has to go away with her husband to tour his estates we are so bilious that we nearly lose our head, and so nervous we cry for nothing. Is this not passing strange, after THIRTY such years? To find a fresh spring somewhere about our heart, to reach under the scars and discover a part of that leathery bloodpumping muscle still capable of grief.

In our loneliness at the absence of Teresa, Allegra is sent for, and arrives in August. She has a good deal more of the Byron about her now – can't articulate the letter 'r' at all – frowns and pouts quite in our way – blue eyes – light hair growing darker daily – and a dimple in her chin – a scowl on the brow – white skin – sweet voice – and a particular liking of Music – and of her own way in every thing. Is that not B. all over?

Our beloved and her husband return, and the plot thickens. Guiccioli asks to borrow a thousand pound (request refused; the man shall not play the pimp with the woman that I love). And then asks us, as an English milorde (little knowing how outcast a lord he asks) to use our influence on our friends in London so that the Conte may be appointed honorary English consul hereabouts, to be safe 'in the event of changes' – i.e. if the Revolution comes and the Austrians start arresting the Italian leaders.

We duly writes to our (doubtless astonished) publisher Mr. Murray, the only influential Tory we know, begging Murray to ask his connections to obtain this post for the Conte, though with no great hopes, sir, no great hopes. Unsurprisingly, Murray is not able to obtain the boon.

After the denial of the Consulship and the thousand pounds to the husband by the lover, relations between husband and wife cool a little at the Palazzo Guiccioli. The Count announces abruptly that his household, including of course his wife, will now visit the Guiccioli estates in Bologna. Teresa announces that it is, of course, to be understood that her beloved shall follow the Guicciolis in his own Napoleonic coach. What can we do but comply? Damme, here we are, we are thinking as the great Napoleonic coach bounces along behind the Count's, trailing after the girl like a puppy.

At the hotel in Bologna we tool as we please, while the husband disappears for the day about his mysterious business with a benign wave. As if to say, an honour, sir, to have one's wife fucked by such a famous man. We do not trust him but our throat is as yet unslit, what can we do but oblige the lady? We feel it bitterly that a man should not consume his life at the side and on the bosom of a woman and a stranger, a wife to another; that even the recompense, and it is much, is not enough, and that this Cicisbean existence is to be condemned. But we have neither the strength of mind to break our chain, nor the insensibility which would deaden its weight.

We wants to fly; we wants to go back to England and begin life again with Augusta; we wants to go to South America and found a dynasty with our daughter Allegra, to live in that primitive heroic continent and write her epics. Both projects, in all logic, seem hopeless propositions, so we stay in Italy, and play the cavaliere, and make love. On our return from the Bolognese idyll the Conte, as if overcome with gratitude for his horns, invites us to *live* on one floor of the palace. Cheaper, he says, than a hotel – though we have to pay the fellow rent – and more convenient, between friends.

We leave our Ravennese hotel (a fleabitten place) with relief, our love of comfort almost as much a motive as our love itself. With trepidation we move in upstairs at the palazzo Guiccioli and... nothing happens! We carry on our loves as before, and the skies do not fall, there are no knives or bravos in the night.

Teresa has a convenient relapse and it is declared by all and sundry that she has to return to Venice, to the care of her illustrious physician, il Dottore Aglietti. With the Conte's permission (and with the Conte himself being so busy about his estates) his English guest is requested to accompany her. All Venice (that hypocritical pool of purple sin) will be scandalised at the flouting of the adulterous conventions.

'One must be a little careful,' remarks LB to his beloved, having been hounded out of one city already.

'Of course, mio Biron,' replies the lady, as she is deposited, alone save for servants, at the Palazzo Malipiero with her luggage; an hour later she declares Malipiero dangerously damp and already bringing on her consumption, and proceeds immediately to install herself at our Palazzo Mocenigo.

She has moved in on us. The old Conte (you must excuse the sound of THIS SYLLABLE in English) is still bafflingly calm as ever over all this, which is more than can be said for Venice, all a-bubble with scandal now.

Unfortunately the girl's father now suggests to the husband that letting his wife *live* with a handsome young man in front of the town is asking for trouble. So the lady moves to our country house at La Mira, to await the return of her husband the cuckolded Conte chastely. We has to pretend, for the honour of Count Gamba, Teresa's father, to be in Venice. But we slips in and out of nearby La Mira with the same ease with which we slips in and out of the Contessa.

We contract a fever, and Teresa moves back into the Mocenigo again to nurse us. A few weeks later the old Conte comes to visit and, in an effort to quell the seething tongues of Venetian society, moves in with us too, along with his wife, as our guest. All very strange, but it seems the crisis is about to break, both in our fever and in the marriage. The Conte insists that his wife shall choose either her lover or her husband. Teresa opting instantly for the lover, the Conte comes crying to US about it, so that we are obliged to tell Teresa to go back with her husband to Ravennna.

Reluctantly – after extracting the usual promises of eternal devotion – the lady returns to Ravenna with her husband. We promise to follow when well enough to travel.

We have other concerns, not least the fate of our latest masterpiece, being shot at betimes even by our friends in England, Doug Kinnaird at Drury Lane, Hobhouse and Murray and the like. Even, one hears with a grin of disbelief, the noble Scrope thinketh some of the ribaldry of *Don Juan* a little too excessive for publication. Kinnaird is selected for the Byronic blast; the others, Scrope and the rest, are cronies and are sure to see this, the best literary letter we ever write:

> *As to Don Juan, confess – you dog – and be candid – that it is the sublime of that there sort of writing – it may be bawdy but is it not good English? It may be profligate but is it not life, is it not the thing? Could any man have written it who has not lived in the world? – and tooled in a post-chaise? – in a hackney coach? – in a gondola? – against a wall? – in a court carriage? – in a vis a vis? – on a table? – and under it? I have written about a hundred stanzas of a third Canto, but it is a damned modest – the outcry has quite frightened me. I have such projects for the Don but the Cant is so much stronger than the Cunt nowadays, that the benefit of experience in a man who had well weighed the worth of both monosyllables must be lost to despairing posterity. I want to go to South America – I have written to Hobhouse about it.*

The prospect of England, where 'Orator' Hunt, that pampered and dinnered blackguard, seems about to foment a revolution (thus prompting the most dreary and wearisome of Tory reprisals – the massacre of the poor folk at the Peterloo fields at Manchester). And on the other hand the prospect of Brazil or Peru, where Giants fight in a land of fevered jungle and exploding volcanoes – where a man might carve himself a share of gold, emeralds, darkness, silver, disease and death.

An empire, by God, in a fierce and primitive world, a Homeric world, a NEW world as it might be.

The two prospects beckon us away from this marital
chaos (it ain't even *our* marriage.)

England, thwarted revolution and all, seems more practi-
cal on the surface – but Augusta has been intimating that she
don't even want to *see* us, for fear of the scandal. We could
see our friends – but in the middle of May in the good year of
1820 (and it IS a good year for us, damme, for once) our best
friend Scrope, finally unable to gamble his way out of debt,
has to flee England, and we are able to say to ourself: What
point to return to England, after all? For Scrope is gone, sir,
gone, down-*diddled*. Gone to Bruges where he will get tipsy
with Dutch beer and shoot himself the first foggy morning.

And Hobby is unavailable there also. Hobhouse, now an
M.P., is in prison for writing a radical pamplet that has been
voted a breach of privilege by his fellows in the House. We
write to Hobby: *Brummell at Calais; Scrope at Bruges, Buona-
parte at St. Helena, you in your new apartments, and I at Ravenna, only think! so many great men! There has been nothing like
it since Themistocles at Magnesia, and Marius at Carthage.* We
grins at our own grandiosity even as we scribbles.

But England, without Scrope, without Hobby, and with
no encouraging word these two years from Augusta, does
not call us home to her as she did. To go there to find our
best friend gone, our other best friend in gaol, and our sister/
love forbidding us her presence? There is no salvation in it.
We have no choice now.

We rejoins Teresa in Ravenna. The husband welcomes us.
The father is particularly glad to see us. The die is cast, and we
have chosen to stay in Italy. We do not know if we are to stay

a day, a week, or a year. In society – in dull provincial Ravenna – we drill how to double a shawl for our contessa, like the
other *serventi*. Diddling the blonde girl with the freckles on
her plump firm breasts while the husband dodders downstairs
is, while not quite relaxing, at least STIMULATING. And
then, of course, there is the Revolution.

The Revolution in Italy is somewhat more to our fastidi-
ous liking than in England, even as la Guiccioli is more tasty
than all English ladies (save one). The mob in Italy tend to be
reactionary, to back up the tyranny of the Austrians, betray
patriots, etc. etc., and the real revolutionaries are gentlemen
almost to a man. The Count Gamba (Teresa's father) and
the no less Count Gamba her brother Pietro for example, of
whose band we have become part.

There are various revolutionary clubs or gangs, the *Cac-
ciatore Americani* (American hunters like noble Indians etc.)
and *Bersaglieri Americani* (of similar forestwalking ilk) and
we of the *Carbonari*, we 'charcoal burners' who burn our
charcoal – 'tis a pretense, sir, and keeps us warm of a cold
night – in the densest depths of the gloomy Romagnol forest, out of the way of Austrian spies. What fun, sir, for 'us
Youth.'

By the middle of April the row is starting to come to a
head on both domestic and national fronts. We write to our
publisher, Murray: *I shall think it by far the most interesting
spectacle and moment in existence, to see the Italians send the
barbarians of all nations back to their own dens. I have lived
long enough among them to feel more for them as a nation than
for any other people in existence; but they want Union, and
they want principle; and I doubt their success. However, they
will try, probably...*

The old Conte G., Teresa's husband, is supposedly a liberal, but is ready to blow with whatever wind to hang on to his fortune, and does not want to offend the Austrians. He is a little disturbed to be harbouring an eccentric English outcast who seems intent on fomenting revolution. And further disturbed (the FACT obviously being harder to take than the mere knowledge) when he returns home unexpectedly one evening and finds (almost – it is a matter of seconds) Teresa and ourself tooling on the upstairs sofa.

Apparently when discovered quasi in the fact it is much the WORSE if the lady don't deny it, which she refuses to do. In the row that follows Teresa is for *planting* the husband and fleeing the house then and there. As usual, for her sake, we take the old Count's part. Counsel prudence. Ask her to talk to her father, who will advise her better than us.

To our consternation the father says, to hell with that old man, he makes my little girl cry, we shall see if the Pope will not agree to a separation. Shockingly, the Pope *does* agree. The girl, says the Pope, is to live with her father and the Conte must pay what amounts to a couple of hundred pounds p.a. for the lady's upkeep. 'It is no longer possible,' writes the Pope blandly (imagine the Archbishop of Canting-very saying so!) 'for her to live in peace and safety with her husband.'

Which makes us the Cavaliere Servente of a 'respectable and noble Lady separated from her husband.' It is beginning, even in Italian, to have a serious ring to it. We are, as near as dammit, married.

When Teresa leaves her husband we do not move out immediately from our apartments in the Conte's palazzo. Once we have settled into a place we dislike to disturb our comforts except after long procrastination. With things being what they are we have to take our evening ride into the forest bristling with pistols and holsters all over our saddle. In a strange sort of way we are looking forward to shooting the Count or the Count's men, and having them try their luck at us, but, interminably, as we stare grimly into each shadow, nothing happens, and the horse trots along the forest path in peace.

The other little affair, the revolution, fails to ignite into action. The rain, sir, the rain, goes on and on in this dim old town, and still NOTHING HAPPENS. The authorities seem to know what we are about, but are reluctant to touch an English milor' for fear of consequences. (Since no English Tory government would shed a tear at MY incarceration or demise, I am glad of the Austrians' ignorance on this point.) However, the Gambas are not immune: there is a movement to shut Teresa up in a convent, which is only another way of trying to get LB and his troublesome friends to leave the Romagna.

As for the revolution, I question not that the Italian parties have left it too late to free themselves from Austrian subjugation. I question if they could get together twelve thousand men of their own, *now*. If they had only struck some months ago it would be a different story.

The local police open all letters it is supposed. I have no objection, so that I may write especially about the cursed AUSTRIANS, to let the letter-openers see how I hate and utterly despise and detest those *Hun brutes*, and all that they can do in their temporary wickedness, for Time and Opinion, and the vengeance of a roused-up people will at length manure Italy with their carcases. It may not be for one year, or two, or ten, but it *will* be, and so that it *could* be sooner, I know not what a man ought *not* to do.

But their antagonists (which is to say, we of the Carbonari and the rest) are no great shakes neither. This is brought home to us the night the first man dies: one of our enemies, but a gentleman and a human being still, is shot from ambush by one of our brave charcoal-burning colleagues. Shooting round-corners is much the style here, and be damned to it. The Military Commander goes down to gunshot at 8 o'clock of a cool winter evening, about two hundred paces from our door.

We are putting on our great coat to pay a visit to the Countess when we hears the shots, and on going into the hall, find all our servants on the balcony exclaiming that 'a man is murdered'. As it is the custom here to let people fight it through, they want to hinder me from going out; but I run down the street.

My brave servant Tita follows me and we make our way to the Commandant, who is lying on his back, with five wounds, of which three in the body – one in the heart. There are about him Diego, his Adjutant, crying like a Child; a priest howling; a surgeon who dared not touch him; two or three confused and frightened soldiers; one or two of the boldest of the mob; and the street dark as pitch, with the people flying in all directions.

As Diego can only cry and wring his hands, and the Priest can only pray, and nobody seems able or willing to do anything except exclaim, shake and stare, I make Tita and one of the mob take up the body; sends off Diego crying to the Cardinal (the chief authority in the town), and the soldiers for the Guard; and have the Commandant conveyed up the stairs to my quarters. But he is quite gone, poor fellow.

We examine the body curiously. It is good, we think, to see to what end we may all come – viz, a corpse. He has bled inwardly, and very little external blood is apparent. One of the slugs had gone quite through – all but the skin: I feel it myself. Two more shots in the body, one in a finger, and another in the arm. His face not at all disfigured: he seems asleep, but is growing livid. The assassin is not taken; but the gun is found – a gun filed down to half the barrel, for concealment beneath a coat.

He said nothing but O *Dio!* and O *Gesu!* two or three times before the end. Our heart goes out to the poor fellow. He was a brave officer, but an unpopular man. No doubt this officer, who had a wife (the poor woman is not to be told till morning) would have preferred to live, but to ourselves it seems a neat enough way to die, and infinitely preferable to growing old and ugly and fat as we seem to be doing. From this day we positively itches for the Row to begin.

We have not, it seems, got long to wait. It is apparently settled that the Revolution is to break out on the 7th or 8th of March, in which appointment I should trust, had it not been settled that it was infallibly to have broken out in October 1820, i.e. last year. But one must not be particular, but take rebellion when it lies in the way.

What is the reason that I have been, all my lifetime, more or less ennuyé? I feel a something, which makes me think that, if I ever reach near to old age, like Swift, 'I shall die at the top' – go mad – first.

On January the 7th of 1821, the weather is miserable – rain, mist, slop, snow, drizzle – go that evening not to see Teresa *solus* but to a *conversazione* – a party! – at 8 o'clock, where we will see the lady and her noble family. Pietro her brother takes us aside to say that the Patriots have had notice from Forli (twenty miles off) that tonight the government and its party mean to strike – that the Cardinal has orders to make several arrests immediately, and that, in consequence, the Liberals are arming, and have posted patrols in the streets, to sound the alarm and give notice to fight for it.

I offer my house – to be exact, my apartments in Teresa's husband's house – to be the fortress where we shall make our stand – it is defensible, and Pietro has already had the good sense to lay up an arsenal of arms there – guns, bayonets, powder, and shot. If the damned Huns come to arrest us, we must fight for it, I tell them, rather than be taken separately.

At midnight we are at home listening to the rains, waiting for the shots that will signal the row has begun. If the row don't happen NOW, it must soon. But I hear nothing as yet, save the plash of the rain and the gusts of the wind at intervals. Don't like to go to bed, because I hate to be waked, and would rather sit up for the row, if there is to be one. A strangely peaceful night alone in our room, where we can relish a brooding excitement.

Mended the fire – have got the arms – and a book or two, which I shall turn over. I know little of their numbers, but think the Carbonari strong enough to beat the troops, even here. With twenty men this house might be defended for twenty-four hours against any force to be brought against it, *now* in this place, for the same time; and, in such a time, the country would have notice, and would rise, – if ever they *will* rise, of which there is some doubt.

In the mean time, I may as well read as do any thing else, being alone.

Chapter thirty-seven

...It was one of the deadliest and heaviest feelings of my life to feel that I was no longer a boy. – From that moment I began to grow old in my own esteem – and in my esteem age is not estimable.

By January 21st nothing has happened. Except that it is my birthday on the morrow. Tomorrow is my birthday. That is to say, at twelve o' the clock, midnight, i.e. in twelve minutes, I shall have completed thirty and three years of age!!! – and I go to my bed with a heaviness of heart at having lived so long, and to so little purpose.

It is three minutes past twelve. – ' 'Tis the middle of the night by the castle clock', and I am now thirty three!

'Eheu, fugaces, Posthume, Posthume,
Labuntur anni';-

but I don't regret them so much for what I have done, as for what I *might* have done.

Through life's road, so dim and dirty,
I have dragged to three and thirty.
What have these years left to me?
Nothing – except thirty-three.

When we get up, next day, our birthday, we writes the epitaph for the year.

1821.
Here lies
interred in his Eternity
of the Past,
from where there is no
Resurrection
for the Days – Whatever there may be
for the Dust –
the Thirty-Third Year
of an ill-spent Life,
Which, after
a lingering disease of many months
sunk into a lethargy,
and expired,
January 22d, 1821, A.D.
Leaving a successor
Inconsolable
For the very loss which
occasioned its
Existence.

A few days later. The Gambas... GO OFF A-HUNTING! That is, a-hunting game, for sport, in this our supposed time of war, Jan. 24, 1821. If it were like a *'highland* hunting', a pretext of the chase for a grand re-union of counsellors and chiefs, it would be all very well. But it is nothing more or less than a real snivelling, popping, small-shot, water-hen waste of powder, ammunition, and shot, for their own special amusement: a rare set of fellows for a man to risk his neck with.

From this single incident we have a strange feeling in our bones, that the thing is all off, now. The Revolution, like any thing you give your heart to, will break it in the end.

On January 28th we sits down to write ourself a:

Memoranda.

What is Poetry? – the feeling of a Former world and Future.

Thought Second:

Why, at the very height of desire and human pleasure, – worldly, social, amorous, ambitious, or even avaricious, – does there mingle a certain sense of doubt and sorrow – a fear of what is to come – a doubt of what is – a retrospect to the past, leading to a prognostication of the future? (The best of Prophets of the future is the Past.) Why is this? or these? – I know not, except that on a pinnacle we are most susceptible of giddiness, and that we never fear falling except from a precipice – the higher, the more awful, and the more sublime; and, therefore, I am not sure that Fear is not a pleasurable sensation; at least, Hope is; and what Hope is there without a deep leaven of Fear? and what sensation is so delightful as Hope? and, if it were not for Hope, where would the Future be? – in hell. It is useless to say where the Present is, for most of us know; and as for the Past, what predominates in memory? – Hope baffled. Ergo, in all human affairs, it is Hope-Hope-Hope. I allow sixteen minutes, though I never counted them, to any given or supposed possession. From whatever place we commence, we know where it all must end. And yet, what good is there in knowing it? It does not make men better or wiser. During the greatest horrors of the greatest plagues, (Athens and Florence, for example – see Thucydides and Machiavelli) men were more cruel and profligate than ever. It is all a mystery. I feel most things, but I know nothing except _____ _____

___ ____ _____ _____ ___ _____

_____ _____ _____ ____ _____

_____ ____ _____ _____ ____ ___

_____ ____ ___ ____ _____

Chapter thirty-eight

As to poor Shelley, who is another bugbear to you and the world, he is, to my knowledge, the least selfish and the mildest of men – a man who has made more sacrifices of his fortune and feelings for others than any I ever heard of.

At first the row looked promising. The Neapolitans broke a bridge, and slew four pontifical carabineers. Then the sovereign of Naples went whining to the damned Austrian Metternich, and in March the massed and drilled armies of Austria were sent to destroy the patriots. At Rieta and ill-fated Novara, the stink of Kingship and monarchy smashed the Republican movement back twenty years, to where it had been before the French showed what could be done to monarchy (and invented the perfect instrument for the disconnecting of kings from crowns, Madame la Guillotine.)

Although the authorities still did not dare to touch an English lord, Italian patriots were seized and arrested, the lucky ones merely banished. In July Teresa's family – she was now officially a ward of her family – were expelled from the Papal domains. They moved at first (with Teresa) to Florence. The plan was that they would later move to Pisa.

We ourselves did not attempt to leave the palazzo Guiccioli to join them until October, defying all the Austrians (and the poor Conte G.) could do to shift us – out of mere indolence to be sure. We dislike to move almost as much as we dislike to *be* moved.

And on that holiday from our mistress, we used our time well. We wrote the fifth canto of Don Juan – a damned good canto it was – three tragedies, and the funniest short piece we ever did, *The Vision of Judgement*, which ain't like Southey's original, to be sure.

In August, Shelley came to see us. He had previous to this sent us a copy of his effusion about poor dead Mr. Keats (a fellow we had ourselves scanted when alive). Thinking Shelley's poem a piece of brilliance, we looked at one of Mr. Keats's books that Shelley had left us which we had hitherto refused to read. To our surprise, along with much that was brash and callow (the poor fellow dying at 26, I believe) we found a mighty piece of Miltonic, epic verse, or better, as if written by Marlowe or Shakespeare, having even some of the virility of Homer – *Hyperion*, or some such, Mr. Keats called it, what time he walked above the earth.

Shelley arrived at ten of the clock on the night of the 6th August, and remained talking and drinking with us (though HE hardly drank) till five next morning. We had been almost totally cut off from any ENGLISH conversation at all; now, speaking our native tongue better than we did ourselves, came this tall pale angel with the gentle eyes, Percy Shelley. A gentleman well enough, knew Homer better than ourselves (knowing Homer being the chief definition of a gentleman.) Knew how to write a verse, or to criticise our own scribblings in such a manner that we would take note.

We talked of Homer, and of Shakespeare, and of Mr. Coleridge's notion that only the artist, after God, is capable of Creation (he calls it Secondary Imagination to distinguish it from Primary Imagination, by which we perceive the Universe that God has created). Shelley agreed with this except to deny that there was a God intervening in the argument. To illustrate his points Mr. Shelley quoted Keats and Dante (the former strangely NOT being at a disadvantage) and WE held up our end with reference to Pope and Homer (the former to irritate Shelley, the latter to delight us both.)

We were both perfectly agreed as to the necessity for the Revolution in Europe.

Shelley was dismayed when told of a certain scandal about HIM (it amused us to see so airy a being embroiled in scandals, like ourselves) but his reaction was all nerves and we saw it had been a mistake to mention it. So we talked about Homer, and Shakespeare, and Coleridge, and Dante, and Johnny Keats, and Pope, till the Cows came home and the Cock crowed, and Shelley went to bed. (It was our custom to stay awake all night, and sleep betimes all day, but Shelley was not used to it, and did not stay up to greet the dawn with us.)

We had, in the absence of Hobhouse, in the absence of Scrope Davies, found a man who could be a friend.

Shelley was to live at Pisa, where the Gambas were to reside. He told us he had been busy assembling an alternative society – poets and such – for us there. We disliked to move, but it was obvious what our next move, in all providence, should be. It might be that there was yet happiness to be wrung from this wretched voyage, existence. At Pisa waited a man who could be a friend, and a woman who could love us.

A man needs two or three reasons, perhaps, to wish to remain alive.

Chapter thirty-nine

*I was not, and, indeed, am not even now, the misanthropical and
gloomy gentleman he takes me for, but a facetious companion,
well to do with those with whom I am intimate, and as loqua-
cious and laughing as if I were a much cleverer fellow.*

Shelley hopes to form for ourselves, at Pisa, a society of
our own class in intellect or in feelings; and to connect
ourselves together with the interests of that society. So, after
resisting friend, woman, woman's family, woman's estranged
husband, and the government of the Papal States to boot, we
finally ups stumps and moves out of the Conte Guiccioli's
house to Pisa, where Mrs. Shelley has predicted we will be 'a
nest of singing birds.'

Allegra has been despatched to a convent at Bagnacavallo,
near Ravenna. When we travel from Ravenna to Pisa, we are
leaving the little girl behind, but in safety, as we think. Shelley
visited her at the convent in August, and professed himself dis-
pleased with the 'nonsense' the nuns were teaching the child about
the Deity, but even he could see that they treated her kindly.

We stayed silent under the provocation of Shelley's dis-
approvel of our little girl's education. Though it occurred to

us, we did not mention the fact of the Shelleys never having *reared* a child, a tactless thing as they had recently lost another. Some god, as Alexander might have said, stayed our arm, or rather our tongue.

To Pisa, then – to a life of routine. Three years now with the Countess Guiccioli. Has a woman (save *one* alone) ever so ensnared us? We leave in Ravenna, besides Allegra, a sad deposit with our banker, Sr. Ghigi – to wit, a Goat with a broken leg, an ugly peasant dog, a bird of the heron type which will eat only fish, a badger on a chain, and two ugly old monkeys.

Installed in our golden marble pile, the elegant Casa Lanfranchi, we can see the Shelleys' house across the turbulent little river Arno. The Shelleys live with another couple: an officer on half-pay, who has seen action, Edward Williams, and his 'wife' (whom he has by God stolen from a brother-officer) a beautiful girl called Jane. Jane is a woman of many attractions (her hair has the curl of Lady Oxford's) and it is clear to see Shiloh is in love with her. Since Williams is himself in love (in essence, a manly and pure essence) with both Jane *and* Shelley, Mary Shelley it seems must make of this what she will, and the pair of couples pursue their multiple marriage in the one house. Even Mary seems to be in love with the fair Jane, which must complicate matters not a little.

We will leave them to it. We too should like well enough to roger the fair Jane, but we prefer to stay out of the moist complications of that household and be on visiting terms only with the Shelley party. Mrs. Shelley is a woman worth talking to: even so far as to be an intellectual companion for that strange and airy Genius that is Shiloh. We have evolved with Shiloh a project to bring over Leigh Hunt to edit a paper for us, *The Liberal*, that will be the scandal of England (if such a thing is still possible) and that should give our little society SOMETHING TO DO, which we take to be a necessary uniting force for any such 'pantisocracy' as ours.

There are other friends of lesser interest. There is Medwin, Shelley's impossible cousin. There is Taaffe, of whom the littlest said the better. And soon arrives the strangest character of all – a friend of Williams who looks like Childe Harold come to life, and sleeps, so he tells us, with the poem under his pillow. Edward John Trelawny is a former pirate (so he says) and navy man, and the only man's man among the lot of them, for all that he is something of a scoundrel. With the rascally Tre we are soon thick as thieves...

('I want to see my friends again... Shiloh, Tre, Mrs. Shelley, at Piṣa...'

'Yes, yes, dear boy, pray observe the wall. See, a shooting party...')

The crash of a pistol shot, the sharp stink of gunsmoke, the sound of the soft waves washing the shore. A seascape near Pisa – an abandoned house. A walled garden with a sandy floor – our shooting-gallery. The party consists of LB, Shelley, Trelawny, and Teresa's younger brother Pietro. The ladies – Teresa, Mary Shelley, Jane Williams – are standing segregated, at the insistence of LB (despite the protests of Shiloh) to the left of the shooters. The ladies have been instructed to keep behind the firing line at all costs.

Edward Williams is obediently erecting the targets – coins

inserted into split canes – at the far end of the garden, in front of the wall which serves for a stop to the bullets. The men have been firing in turn. LB has been winning. His friends are beginning to call him 'Albé' now – an Italianised corruption of his English nickname 'LB.' Every one of the party has their nickname.

The shots proceed, LB continuing to get the best of it. As his turn comes round again Pietro is loading his pistol, which he passes to its owner. LB, his hand wobbling alarmingly, fires across the garden to knock a small silver coin spinning out of a cane. The ladies and Shelley produce murmurs of applause and a few claps. Williams retrieves the coin, and LB gives the pistol back to Pietro to reload while he takes a pinch of snuff, as Trelawny steps up to fire.

Trelawny is a handsome, muscular, darkbearded giant of a young man, who affects a piratical dress and air. He levels the heavy pistol at the coin in the split cane as Williams, rather comically, scuttles hastily out of the way. Trelawny snarls, squinting: 'What the devil is it – a shilling?' He fires and misses. 'Blast its eyes...'

LB chuckles, ungracious in victory. 'It is not the eyes of the *shilling* are to blame, Tre. And to think I began to worry when you managed to hit that hugeous half-crown.' He hands the snuffbox to Pietro, who hands him the reloaded pistol. 'Here – take some snuff, my boy. It is a sovereign remedy for preserving the TEETH – the only sound item still left in my own head...' – turning, in the Scrope Davies manner, firing and hitting the coin, sending it spinning away – 'apart from my EYE, of course, in these sad times.' He smiles at Trelawny suavely. 'A hit, by God, Tre, a very palpable hit.'

Trelawny will not be baited. 'You went out of turn – it was Shiloh's turn.' Shelley, a dishevelled figure, tall, thin, sunburnt, curiously stooped, has been wandering near the shooters. As Trelawny approaches he kneels to examine a beautiful pebble. 'Come, Shiloh,' Trelawny says. He pulls Shelley up by the hand. 'Only you can put an end to Albé's boasting now.'

The three women exchange giggles at the remote prospect, and Shelley rewards them with a radiant smile. From the other side of the garden Edward Williams calls out, as he sets up the targets again: 'I have lost your shilling, Albé, and have no smaller coin. Shall we leave the decision to whichever one of you or Shiloh can first split the cane?'

Trelawny hands the bemused Shelley the reloaded pistol, drags him up to the firing line, and calls back: 'Our side is agreeable.'

Shelley protests gently at being manhandled. 'You speak as if it were an affair of honour – now Tre, you KNOW I never duel.' He raises the pistol carelessly – a frail figure that towers over LB despite distinctly rounded shoulders. He fires and splits the distant thin cane. The women behind applaud and cheer. There is an astonished silence from the men. Shelley's face a huge grin of delight. 'Mary – did you see that?' He turns toward the women. 'Did you see that, Mary? The finest shot I ever made.' Handing the pistol back to Trelawny, he turns to pat LB's arm. 'Perhaps, Albé, you have succeeded in teaching me to shoot at last.'

LB smiles warmly at his strange friend, but takes the pistol off Pietro and loads it himself, carefully. 'I see my reputation is at stake, Shiloh. As I believe I once remarked to my friend Mr. Hobhouse – you poor fool, they are my *pistols*.'

Shelley laughs. LB turns to Trelawny. 'Did I tell ye, Tre, that Hobby has been challenged by Major Cartwright, the old duffer he disputed for the Reform nomination for Westminster, at the last election?'

Shelley, losing interest in this men's talk of duels, goes over to speak to the three women.

'I wrote back to Hobby that he should pick the Major's gauntlet up – were I there I should MANTON the old boy myself, for presuming to challenge his youngers and betters, by God.' Having finished loading the pistol, LB returns it to the attentive Pietro.

Trelawny laughs goodnaturedly at the bravado – as a man who has fought more than one duel himself – and pats LB's back. 'You are always boasting of your marksmanship at this Manton's – it must have been a shooting-gallery of note.'

'It was more a sort of shooting-academy. A MUSEUM of shooting. Joe Manton's guns were its art works. Scrope Davies bought one of Manton's guns that was a beauty to behold. Cost him seventy guineas, but worth every penny, with a gravitating stop. The shooting capital of the world, Manton's...'

'I can't say I ever visited it...'

LB's thin grin. 'Old Joe would not have let you in. But if we can teach you to wash your hands and comb your hair we will make a gentleman of you yet.' He hands Trelawny a cigar. 'O, you should have seen Joe Manton, in his day, Tre. Now HE had an eye – and he would have told you that between 1809 and 1814 with HIS pistols it was my luck to split walking-sticks, wafers, half-crowns, shillings, even the eye of a walking-stick at twelve paces with a single bullet – and all by eye and calculation, for my hand is not steady, and apt to change with the very weather.'

Trelawny grins wolfishly, shakes his head at this bragging, and calls over to the target – erector. 'I say, Williams? Can we have another cane for the peerless Albé?'

'Ha! Tre! You are not listening – it is the truth. To this prowess Joe Manton and others can bear testimony; for the former has taught me to shoot, and the latter have seen me do these feats. No boasting like a fool, as the worthy Macbeth remarks.' He takes the pistol back from Pietro. 'If I can repeat my performance and split the cane twice, perhaps I can earn your respect. Two canes, please, Mr. Williams – two, I think.'

LB aims, as Williams hurries comically out of the way, holding on to his straw hat. In the little moment of tension before firing, Teresa's excited cry of 'Viva Biron!'

LB lowers the pistol in exasperation. 'Perhaps Shiloh should fire first.'

Mary Shelley calls out mockingly 'Albé shall not have it all his own way – Shelley will uphold the family honour.'

Shelley leaves the group of women and strolls in his gangling, loosejointed shamble back to the firing line. He accepts the pistol offered by Trelawny, giggles, and says: 'No doubt Apollo steadied my hand, before.' In one careless movement he raises the pistol, aims, fires, misses, and smiles. 'Apollo has deserted me, it seems.' He hands the smoking piece to Trelawny who pats him on the back affectionately. He abruptly leaves his friends, running off to stoop over a stone on the ground near Williams, and afterward, ignoring Williams, wanders toward the break in the moldering wall which serves as a gate into the disused garden.

As the others watch him curiously, Shelley drifts slowly out of the garden and out of their sight. 'Where has he gone off to?' LB wonders.

'O, he comes and goes like a spirit,' Trelawny mutters.

LB aims, Williams gets out of the way. 'Shelley,' LB says, firing and splitting the new cane, 'is a much better shot than I am, only he was thinking of metaphysics rather than of firing.' The women and Pietro applaud as Trelawny and LB look at each other, puffing on their cigars. LB looks around at the little band. 'I propose we return to shooting half-crowns. I should not like to endanger the effect of making two such fine shots by missing the third shilling. Perhaps Mr. Williams would like to try his luck?'

Jane Williams speaks up eagerly: 'Yes, do, Edward, do.' She is anxious for her husband to be seen as an equal among these glittering folk.

LB takes a small bag out of his pocket, and hands it to Pietro. 'Here, my boy, half-crowns. It so happens I brought along a supply of that amiably large piece of silver.' Pietro goes up to take Williams' place by the targets, as the young man approaches shyly with an endearing smile. 'Mind you, Tre, a half-crown is no larger than a man's heart – even so half-hearted a man as that bastard of a poetaster, Southey the mouthy.'

Trelawny laughs. 'O, have you challenged poor old Bob Southey at last? You will have to return to England so as not to disappoint him.'

'I wrote to the whore – for a whore to the Tories is all the bastard is – but despite my expressing myself in the gentlest of terms he has so far proved too windy to send a reply. Mind you, that would be a reason to go back to England – to blow out Bob Southey's brains before I die. What a service to English poetry THAT would be. Aye, we should return to the nasty foggy place to perform that good deed. There are one or two others in the vicinity that need shooting, also.'

Pietro sets up three half-crowns in three canes as LB and Trelawny and Williams reload their pistols. Trelawny turns, raises and fires at one of the half-crowns. The coin spins humming away, and he looks at LB with satisfaction. 'You dwell on the past too much, Albé. Why, you are still a young man!' (LB laughing, shaking his head.) 'I should have thought you would have just a LEETLE interest in the polly ticks of Greece, which promises US YOUTH such a good scrap. Greece is the Revolution now. It is all up for 'us youth' in Italy.' (LB's face twists momentarily when he hears his own favourite phrase, 'us youth.') Trelawny nods at Pietro, who is trying to find the shot coin. 'That young brother-in-law of yours is going, he tells me – just looking for a damned good row. Win or lose, we shall have THAT to remember, eh?'

LB holds his finger to his lips to tell Trelawny to watch his tongue, and nods to indicate Teresa, who is talking with the other women. 'Unfortunately, Tre, I do have certain – ah – *domestic* responsibilities. But where is Shiloh? Surely it is his turn to fire? Although...' – he turns politely to Williams, who has been waiting humbly for his turn – 'Would you care to try a shot, Mr. Williams?'

Williams accepts LB's pistol – Albé's pistol! – gratefully. 'Thank you, Albé.' Williams turns, aims, fires, misses. LB exchanges a look with Trelawny. This is no kind of competition. The second best shot seems to have gone missing.

'But where IS Shiloh?' LB asks the company.

Trelawny laughs. 'God love him, only he could say.'

Williams calls over to Mary Shelley: 'Mary, shall you and I go to find your husband? Since I am not in luck here...'

'Yes,' comes the reply from the tall grave girl. 'I will come with you.' She walks over to join Williams, and they go out of the garden through the gap in the wall.

Trelawny watches them go, grinning. He catches LB's eye and nods toward Williams's wife Jane, who is trying to talk to Teresa – with difficulty, as the two women have no great ability in each other's languages. Trelawny mutters softly: 'Did you know Shiloh was in love with that piece over there?'

'What – is our angel become a devil? Jane Williams, eh?' He chuckles, elbows Trelawny in the ribs. 'Shiloh must be encouraged in this wickedness – he has been far too *good* of late... and I dare say the woman is wasted on the husband. But come, Tre – how do we know this? Your reasons, sir, your reasons.'

'He is the strangest of angels, if angel he be. You know that he cannot swim?'

'I know it.'

'Well, one day, you know, he is watching me practise diving into the river Arno and sporting about in the water. Look here, I says to Shiloh, it ain't so hard, this swimming lark, why don't you let me teach you the trick of it? At the word he dives off the bank, straight into the deep water – and on the moment falls to the bottom of the pool. There he lies on the river bed, all draped out like a conger eel, not making the least effort or struggle to save himself. He would have been drowned if I had not instantly fished him out. When he recovers his breath he says' – Trelawny leans forward to whisper in LB's ear: 'I always find the bottom of the well, and they say Truth lies there. In another minute I should have found it.'

Trelawny takes LB's pistol off him, turns, fires, hits. LB hardly notices. He is strangely moved. 'Good God! Can he be in that much of a hurry?'

Trelawny reloads the pistol nonchalantly. 'He says it would be an easy way of getting rid of the body.' He nods across the garden at the splintered targets. 'And life IS all canes and coins, I suppose...'

'Bah! If my limbs were as sound as his I should not complain. Why, HIS body is young yet. But come, Tre, what about this Mrs. Williams...?'

Trelawny delivers the wolfish grin, happy to be making an effect. 'Did I ever tell you about the time Shiloh was lost in the wood?'

'Come, Tre – Mrs. Williams – does not his good lady Mary object?'

'O, they are not LIKE that – Mary don't care – but, ah... did you ever see that poem of his? Something to Somebody, take this slave...'

' 'Ariel to Miranda: – Take/This slave of Music, for the sake/Of him who is the slave of thee...' Aye, you might say, Tre, that I had seen it. Do you mean to tell me that such trash of spirit as she has could inspirit Shiloh to write like that?'

'Even so.'

'He must be bedding her, or else he is an angel after all.' LB takes the reloaded pistol from Trelawny and in one dazzling motion turns, fires, and hits, the coin humming close past the head of the startled Pietro. Pietro crosses himself. Only one coin remains standing in its split cane.

Trelawny demands abruptly: 'Do you want to hear the tale of the woods or not?' LB nods. 'Well,' says Trelawny, 'Master Shelley is disappeared, frank disappeared, don't you know, in the Cascine forest – dark, evil place that it is – do you know it? – full of wolves, they say. Mary sets off to find him, but the loose sand and sun soon knocks her up. But I has an idea. I runs out of the forest down back onto the beach, and along the beach a mile or two before cutting back into the forest to look for Shiloh's sign.

'I walks up one wrong path after another – endless, endless – but after a time I bumps into an old old lady – an old witch she looks – gathering pinecones in what she is pleased to call the 'accursed wood.' She offers to show me where 'l'inglese malinconico' hangs his hat of an afternoon, and I offers her a shilling for her trouble. After the most cursed walk she leads me into a little glade, where the first thing I sees is a Pool, round, small, deep, black as your heart...'

'Aye, a good tale, a good tale, go on...'

'By the side of the Pool is hat, books, a few scattered sheets of paper. For a moment or two I cannot see Shiloh at all, so that you may suppose I jumped clean out of my skin when the old lady shouts' – he points dramatically down at the remembered Pool – 'ECCOLE!' Trelawny closes his eyes, at the terrible memory, opens them again, a shadow of knowledge across his face. He rubs his beard reflectively. 'I thought he was even then beneath the surface. But it turns out he is simply lying behind a fallen tree. When he catches sight o' me he sits up and says, right off, 'Poor Mary!'

'Good God.'

'He had with him his Aeschylus, his Shakespeare, and the poem to this Jane of whom we speak.' He rams the ball into the pistol savagely. 'Fresh scribbled and scrawled, it was, Sir, fresh scribbled and scrawled.'

LB looks carefully at Tre, wondering how much he can explain to the man. 'You can be sure where that poem came from, Tre. Shiloh dredges his materials from deep in that same Pool where you feared him lost.'

Shelley, Mrs. Shelley, and Edward Williams walk back

into the garden. Shelley is gesticulating wildly. 'I tell you I saw it, Edward, I saw it! Tell him, Mary, tell him that I saw it...'

LB limps over to meet them. 'What have you seen, Shiloh?'

Mary's expression is blank. She says dully: 'He has seen the spirit of little Ca – our child that perished a year ago. He was looking at the waves on the beach...'

Shelley jumps in the air, claps his hands excitedly. 'I tell you Albé I saw her clap her hands at me and smile, in the very thick of the foam she sported.' Shelley looks about himself at the others staring. He is dazed, swaying. 'She was sporting naked – she was all made of foam...'

LB is shocked, remembering his own daughters, Ada and Allegra. Trelawny, recovering first, steps forward to catch Shelley by the arm, to drag him back into the land of the living. 'What – I believe you, Shiloh,' Trelawny snaps gruffly. 'But come now...' – putting the loaded pistol in Shelley's hand – 'it is your turn to fire. A man should not be idle when duty calls.'

LB nods politely. 'There are more things in heaven and earth, as they say – but my dear Shiloh, steady, man, you look pale...'

The angel shakes long sunbleached hair. 'O, I will suffice, I will suffice.' He cocks the pistol absently, raises it, turns toward the target slowly, indifferent to where and at whom the cocked pistol is pointing as he turns.

Trelawny winces as the charged barrel drifts past the women. LB says calmly to Mary: 'Mrs. Shelley – out of the firing line if you please – it is scarcely safe for you here.'

Mary replies, a little acidly: 'If you think it best, Albé.' She walks reluctantly over to rejoin the other women, turning for a parting shot of her own: 'As you so frequently remind us, they are YOUR pistols.'

Shelley fires, hits the coin, and turns, exultant, toward his wife. 'Mary – did you see that, Mary?' Mary is talking volubly to Teresa in Italian and does not turn.

'O, leave the women be,' says LB.

Trelawny chuckles. 'You don't want to bother about THEM, Shiloh – they amuse themselves.'

Shelley hands over his discharged pistol to the attentive Williams. 'It seems wrong to me that they must take a carriage to meet us here. Why can they not ride with US? Mary can ride better than any of you...'

LB laughs. 'Shiloh, Shiloh – have you ever seen the contessa ride? There is more danger in the performance than it is worth – I do not care to risk that amiable neck.'

Shelley frowns. 'As to that, I should have thought there was an even greater danger in boring them to death – though I would not suggest, Albé, that you should invite them to your weekly dinner party. It is scarcely fitting that they should watch you men turn yourselves into vats of claret.'

Trelawny's booming laugh makes the women turn. 'Why, Shiloh, if you think poets can drink you should see the gentlemen of his majesty's navy perform the business.'

LB joins in the laughter with Trelawny and Williams. 'Aye, I was a real drinker myself, once – a long time ago, alas, and in other places than this.'

Shelley grows shrill: 'In any case it is not right to leave the women out so often – THAT is scarcely right...'

LB puts a hand on Shelley's shoulder. 'Why, man, they manage these things far better in Turkey. They lock the women up altogether, and they are much happier for it. Give a woman a looking glass and a few sugar-plums and she will be satisfied.'

Trelawny, Williams and LB hoot with laughter. 'By a man's jests shall you know the quality of his mind,' Shelley mutters. As he sees the other three stare at him open-mouthed Shelley giggles at their expressions and skips over to join the women, his mood changing to levity. The three men at the firing line pause, watching Shelley speak with the ladies: whispering something to Teresa which makes her giggle, kissing Mary, squeezing the hand of Jane. The four heads are very close.

Trelawny clears his throat. 'Look – Count Pietro has set up the coins again. Well done, my boy!' He turns with his wolfish grin to LB and Williams. 'He goes to Greece, eh? See-ing that the revolution in Italy is finished, he goes to fight the revolution THERE. What a grand adventure that fine young man will have in Greece, to be sure...'

LB nonchalantly takes a pinch of snuff, offers some to the other two. 'The Greek Committee, you know, in London, has made me an honorary member.' He sniffs. 'They talk of appointing me their representative there – but I am afraid that I have domestic commitments, and shall not oblige them.'

Trelawny, laughing, turns, fires, hits, while Williams looks questioningly at his reluctant hero. LB glances at the smiling Pietro, then down at the pistol in his hand. He cocks the weapon thoughtfully. When he looks up he sees Trelawny and Williams looking back at him. He meets their gaze defi-antly for a second, then turns and raises the pistol at the tar-get, and stands there holding his wavering aim as best he can.

Chapter forty

In memory of Allegra –
daughter of G.G. Lord Byron –
who died at Bagnacavallo
in Italy April 20th, 1822.
aged five years and three months. –
'I shall go to her, but she shall not return to me.' –

2d. Samuel 12. – 23. –

See Shelley *now*, that noble bony face contorted into what in *him* passes for fury. The damned bitch Madame Claire is behind this, we think, as Shelley glares at us with what in one so peaceful must be the equivalent of wild rage. We watch this prodigious anger wash over the angel's face with much curiosity. See it go now as rapidly as it came, the eyes clearing, the benign smile beginning to play about Shiloh's lips once more.

An angel. Ourselves, in a similar rage, would have done one or both of us a mischief. As if reading our thoughts, Shelley says: 'Byron, a moment ago I could have knocked you down.'

'I would have let you, my boy, I would have let you,' we murmur gently. We are not so well supplied with friends that,

277

though trained in boxing by the world champion Gentleman Jackson (the man who beat the great Mendoza), and used to sparring with Scrope Davies and other *hard hitters*, we should have demonstrated our prowess on Shiloh.

'Claire maintains that the convent is unhealthy in both physical and spiritual aspects. I must agree with her as to the *second* point, at least.'

'I have a great respect for the Catholic religion. Teresa was the product of a convent education. The woman is good enough for me.'

Shelley frowns in distaste. 'Do you know, Byron, sometimes I think you are little better than a Christian.'

We laughs so loud and long at this even Shelley cracks a smile. 'Why, Shiloh, the child will be safer there in the convent than with 'Us Youth.' Allegra is five years old. She needs a measure of stability in her life, even if it be provided by ignorant nuns – they are kind women, if nothing else. She is having a happier childhood than you or I. Think back to your own childhood, as I do to mine. Are you confident that to be brought up by one's *parent* is the healthiest thing?'

Shelley looks pained, we have touched him on a sore point, the memory of his own hated father. Then too, there was the question of the dead Shelley children, which we had not meant to refer to. Then – you can see it clear as day dawning over his face – Shelley endeavours to remember why he has come. 'But Claire says...'

We have had enough. 'I think Madame Claire a damned bitch. What think you?' Shelley rises and begins to walk off, forcing us to limp rapidly after him to beg his pardon. After he leaves, somewhat mollified, but not having secured his purpose, the 'release' of Allegra, we can give way to a little suppressed anger at Madame Claire for coming between us and our friend. The noble Fletcher receives a few curses even he, rascal that he is, does not deserve, as he pulls off our boots that night.

At the next shooting party, we are still irritated by the breach that appears to be made by the thrice-damned Claire between us and the divine Shiloh. And are obliged to resist the Graecophiles, Pietro and Trelawny, yet again. Let them go to Greece and be damned to them.

Our thoughts are black as we ride back from the garden outside the town. Unspeakably dull thing life is, as Scrope has always said. Yet lacking his cool head, we could never, like Scrope, seek our salvation from ennui in gambling, and have had to make do with the more mundane excitements of love. The only redeeming note to our idle life is that a good friend of ours from the old days in London, a certain Captain Hay, has joined us, and has given us a little sport, since he is an experienced officer and can shoot and sail.

Taaffe, God be thanked, has absented himself from the shooting, to explore the woods for game. Here he is now, resting his charger, waiting for us in the road, preparing to show us his game-bag full of little corpses. Myself, Tre, Shelley, Pietro and the Captain stop to speak to him. We are vaguely – a little uncomfortably – aware that the carriage in front containing Mrs. Shelley and Teresa is pulling away from us. There may be enemies in the woods... *Come on, Taaffe, hurry up your description of the unfortunate creatures you have murdered in the forest...* Shelley is soon disgusted at the account of Taaffe's slaughtering, and is about to ride on.

The drum of hoofbeats behind. In that moment, as Teresa's carriage approaches the gates of the town, we still do not realize what is happening. We look around. A dragoon in a green tunic with flashing golden epaulets is galloping up. We have an uneasy feeling about it, as if we already know that the impact of his charge will shatter our little group.

The fellow does not stop, it seems he wishes to go past us without slowing down, and Taaffe, who is blocking his way, clumsily pulls his horse around rather than out of the way, so that the green dragoon shooting through us like a rocket, clips the stirrups of the idiotic Taaffe and sends his horse springing into the air. Taaffe falls half out of his saddle. 'Damn him!' he roars. 'He rode straight into me!'

'There he goes!' laughs Trelawny. 'He will overtake the ladies before they reach the gates of the city...' At Tre's words, a tug of fear at our heart – is this to be a murdering of Teresa at last, Count Guiccioli's revenge?

'The swine! Stop him!' Captain Hay yells, and in the confusion we all ride furiously after the galloping dragoon. The fellow is clapping spurs to his mount, but his horse is blown already from walloping so hard, and we soon overtake him. Teresa's driver, hearing the commotion, stops the carriage a little way ahead. The mad dragoon is safely surrounded.

We demand an explanation of the fellow's churlish behaviour. Thinking him an officer, I hand him my card, and challenge him. Trelawny too demands satisfaction. Desperately, the man spurs through us again, this time discomfiting Trelawny's horse so that Trelawny, normally a sunny, goodnatured fellow, begins to talk seriously about running the fellow through on the spot.

This would be well enough if any of us had swords, but unlike the dragoon we are unarmed save for our empty pistols. But insulted as we all are the whole party (even Shiloh) now takes off after the fellow again and, as before, we begin to overhaul him. The whole sorry procession of us is now rolling past Teresa and Mary in the carriage and racing up to the city gates. The dragoon, no doubt by now a little frightened by these riders surrounding him, begins to shout to the guards on the walls to ARREST US ALL! The affair looks to be taking a serious turn when the guard turn out and line up across the gates, holding up their rifles and calling that we are under arrest.

Pietro and I ride through the line, and the soldiers scatter quickly enough, but the others are not so lucky, or perhaps not so quick-thinking. Looking behind us we see the rest of the party surrounded by an excited band of soldiers, and the green dragoon raging accusations. Teresa and Mary are well out of it, still outside the gates, so we mutter to Pietro, 'Come, lad, to the house, for arms and men to assist us.'

Resisting the soldiers will be no light matter. At the house – which is not far from the gate – we call the steward and tell him to round up and arm our people. Leaving Pietro in charge, we pick up a sword-stick from inside the door (we are accustomed to keep such things where other people keep their umbrellas) and remount, to go back to the gates and join in the row.

No sooner are we in the saddle than we see, galloping up the street, the green dragoon himself, still, it seems, in a tearing hurry. We turn our horse in front of him so as to block his way. As the fellow and his nag slither to a stop in a cloud of dust he offers to draw his sword, but we ride close to him and slap his face hard enough to knock him sideways. We take off the glove on the hand that has slapped him and throw it at him. Perhaps the fellow has not understood, when we gave him our card – but it is, now, plain enough. A duel, if he is at all a gentleman.

At this point the bravest and most noble of our servants, the giant Tita, thrusts in between us and grabs the man's bridle. 'Let him go,' we snarl in Italian, 'he knows where to find us, if he is a man.' Having insulted and challenged the fellow in front of half the town (who are now filling the street and all surrounding windows in order to observe this spectacle) we suppose he cannot but return to salvage his honour.

As soon as Tita lets go the fellow is galloping on again (where IS he going in such a hurry?) But our people are now gathering and they stop him a little further up the road, and in the melée the green fellow falls off his horse to the ground. We get off our horse and walk over to him, but are shocked to see that he looks in a bad way, as one of our rough-handed wretches seems to have reached up and stabbed him in the breast without warning (a thing not uncommon in a people so fond of shooting round corners). No one knows who has done this base deed, and seeing our look of fury no one will own up to it now.

The rest of our party come up, not a little knocked-about. Shelley is in Teresa's carriage in a daze, having been knocked off his horse at the gate by the flat of a blade. Worse still is the condition of our old friend Captain Hay, whom the brave dragoon, when once the Captain was surrounded by the guard, has slashed severely in the nose with his sabre. Teresa is near-fainting with agitation, and covered with poor Hay's blood; Hay is in the carriage, muttering curses and clutching his nose, the claret dripping off his chin in earnest.

It is obvious, however, that the dragoon is in the most serious danger. I clear back the crowd to give him air, and send Pietro to fetch a surgeon for the fellow, who is still lying there bleeding on the ground, scarcely conscious. We get Teresa and Hay and Shelley and the others inside, for the crowd is beginning to turn ugly, thinking, naturally enough, that WE, the foreigners, are to blame. Teresa is near-hysterical, so that we begin to fear the poor girl will have a fit.

Hay recovers in a few weeks – though he will never be so pretty a man as before – but the damned dragoon looks near to perish. Poor Tita – he alone of our servants I can vouch to be innocent, for he was with me when the dragoon was stabbed – poor Tita is arrested, along with our coachman, who, we shrewdly suspect, is the real assassin. However, the coachman too is one of our people, and we will protect him too if we can.

The upshot of all this is that the Gambas are again told by the authorities to move themselves to another state. They are defined as people too dangerous to be allowed to live in Pisa. This is inconvenient enough, as may be imagined, to make us damned annoyed – for it means that we will have to move again, a thing we dislike above all things. The 'little nest of singing birds' is in grave danger of being broken up.

The 'Masi affair', named in honour of our obscure assail-ant, occurred on the 24th of March, 1822. The man, it seems, was merely a SERGEANT not an officer (which had we known we should not have challenged him, but merely administered a damned good hiding to the swine). Sergeant Masi was simply late for duty and frantic to get to his post. Strange how one's life's direction may be turned by such a trifle. But all this is as nothing in the comparison with what happens next.

A couple of weeks later we are alarmed to hear news from Allegra's convent that the child is suffering from 'a slight fever.' We send a doctor – damn these fellows! – and learn, a few days later, that the man has BLED Allegra with the idea that she is 'tending toward consumption' and must be treated... This bleeding, this foolishness of the quack, alarms us more than we can say, and we think of going to rescue our little girl from the doctors and nuns, but we are told on the 18th of April that the child is better.

She dies – at five and half years old – on the 20th. On the 22nd, the news arrives, and poor Teresa is delegated to break it to us. When we look up from our scribbling and see her pale agonised face, we know. Before she opens her mouth, our heart spurts and races, we can feel it pounding in our chest. Teresa – looking very frightened – tells the sad tale of our little girl's last hours.

'I understand,' we hear ourself say. 'Say no more.' And sit there, feeling the life flow out of us, as if it were our life's blood draining away, unable to shed a tear, for we know not how long. From a long way off we hear Teresa's voice, but we cannot make out what she says. She tries to hold us to her bosom, which does not seem to help, so we ask her, as politely as we can, please to go away.

How often does a thing have to happen, like unto another thing, before we can ACT upon the knowledge we should have gained first time, to avoid a repetition? My daughter has been taken from me, like my mother, while my attention was elsewhere. In the rush and bustle of my affairs, I have pushed the little girl to the back of my mind; although we loved her and have provided for her, we see now that we have treated her, when she was alive, as a thing of no real consequence.

How essential she seems, NOW, to the vain little heap of ashes that is our World! We had a lover, a friend, and a child: Teresa, Shelley, and Allegra. One leg of the three-cornered stool is gone forever; and the stool, which was our connection to life, is teetering dangerously. The grief for our little girl makes us ashamed to grieve for ourself, or wish to try to safeguard ourself. We decide that Allegra shall be buried in Harrow churchyard, where, when a schoolboy, in the first days of our loneliness (before we had made our friends at Harrow) we used to sit and dream the day away in solitude.

The results of telling Shelley of Allegra's death are immediate. The whole Shelley menagerie decamps for a summer house on the beach near Lerici. Afterwards we learn that this was because Madame Claire was secretly with them, and they wanted to get her well away from us before breaking the news. Poor Claire, who had plans to seize Allegra from the monastery (would that she had succeeded, so that the child had lived!) sends us a letter full of vitriol; but our heart is too calloused by the loss of the daughter to feel sufficiently for the mother's pain. We send her Allegra's portrait and her effects – such trash that we can do for poor Claire now. We need never fear the attentions of poor Claire again, for she must hate us now for ever. All is changed utterly.

Life is no respecter of occasions. The night we hear of Allegra's death, in the full rush of our first grief, we are told that our favourite servant, our friend Tita the giant, is to be banished forever, not so much for the wounding of Masi (of which he is innocent) but for the wearing of his beard, pistol and cutlass into the court (which he did like the brave and proud fellow that he is.)

This is all, along with the exile of the Gambas, part of a plot to get rid of US, but be damned to the authorities, we shall not move until we are ready. We are sitting under the spell of a great inertia, while all around us is bustle and change. Teresa's father and brother have gone to our summer house near Leghorn, near the Shelleys. Trelawny is in Genoa building our thrice-damned BOATS (a little project he has previously initiated, as a Navy man, a yacht for us and a little launch for Shiloh.)

Alone, save for poor Teresa, who is helpless to know what to do with us, we sit in our house in Pisa and brood. A little society we had at Pisa, our 'nest of singing birds,' as Mrs. Shelley called it. To think that we laughed at her for saying it.

Perhaps it was. It was. Like Allegra, it seems all gone now: the tattered rags of a dead nest hanging in a winter tree.

Chapter forty-one

I would to heaven that I were so much clay,
As I am blood, bone, marrow, passion, feeling –
Because at least the past were passed away –
And for the future – (but I write this reeling,
Having got drunk exceedingly today
So that I seem to stand upon the ceiling)
I say – the future is a serious matter –
And so – for God's sake – hock and soda water!

Towards the end of May we gave way again to circumstance, the Gambas, and Shiloh, and move to the Villa Dupuy, a low rambling country house on a little hill four miles above Leghorn. It was neither a palace, nor marble. Its walls were painted in a yellowy pink wash, no doubt meant to deflect the sun, but the place, being spread out with no lower floors, and thin walls, soaked up the pitiless rays of sunlight like a sponge. It was a hot house; a crackerbox, and be damned to it, but there was a glorious view from the garden. Sitting under a lemon tree, drinking a cool glass of hock and soda of an afternoon, we could look out on the white houses of the port down below, and the ocean filling the rest of the view up to the sky.

A tolerable way to spend a summer.

All through the dog-days we sat there reading quietly with our mistress and with brother Pietro and Teresa's father. The Gambas were unhappy at being bounced from one Italian town to another, and at being estranged from the family's estate at Ravenna: there was even a possibility they would be hounded out of Tuscany altogether. But they were resilient, and tolerable people to share a house with: the only family we have ever known.

The old man – as noble and reckless as his young son – said soberly that he knew he should never live to see a free Italy now. Pietro muttered of the proximity of Greece. Be damned to that, I told them, we shall ALL go to South America. And so our little family dreamt away our afternoons in that shady lemon-scented garden.

The best thing about the house was that it was not in Pisa, where, God help us, the affair of the dragoon had left us in bad odour with the governing forces and even the common people. We were completely private there. Bored as we were, we sought solace in scribbling, so that the saga of Donny Johnny and his hungry bollocks proceeded apace. We didn't know what Teresa thought, hearing the chuckles that came out of our room of an evening, we were doing in there. She was very jealous of Donny Johnny – the poem, rather than that side of our character, which is gone – so we didn't discuss it with her much. We didn't discuss much with her at all, any more.

Moving days always stick in our mind. A memorable day, our first arrival at Montenero, the suburb above which our new hot pink villa stood. An American squadron lay anchored in the bay. The very ships to take us to the Americas! We sent word to the commander that he would oblige

our curiosity if he gave us permission to see one of his frig-
ates. The good captain received the note cordially, and invited us to do the thing properly and dine with the officers.

As we toured the ships, we realized that the blessed fresh-
faced young officers were lovers of our early verses, currently
the rage in the United States, being a year or two behind as
that distant place inevitably is. It was a strange echo of the
fame and favour we once had, the ghost of a reflection, our
visit to the American fleet that day. One of the midshipmen
showed us a very pretty American edition of our verses. We
wonder what they will make of the Don when he crosses the
waters – if he is ever allowed to.

We returned to our new house in a strangely irritable
mood. Moving house had solved nothing. Allegra was still
dead. Teresa and the Counts Gamba were still marooned in
that place, so far from their home estates, and under constant threat of further exile, perhaps even from Italy itself.
Reading of Simon Bolivar's latest victories made us more and
more want to go and join him in South America. To see the
noble General and shake his hand, as we could not with Bonaparte. In short, we longed to go SOMEWHERE, but we
were not sure where: South America sounded much like the
other side of the moon, and would do. Anything so that we
were out of this existence.

Trelawny had succeeded in building the boats at last
(spending a thousand pound on our boat, the *Bolivar*, when
he said it would cost a hundred and be damned to him). But
nothing could shake us out of this mood, where only our art,
scribbling the *Don*, could make us chuckle, and life itself left
us cold. We were missing Shelley, who because of the extra
distance between us we did not see as often as we wanted.

No doubt he blamed us, too, for our treatment of Allegra and Claire.

By this time of course poor Teresa was thoroughly miserable and the guilt we felt at being the cause of her unhappiness improved our temper not a jot.

Trelawny had been trying out our yacht, and described its virtues in glowing terms. This new toy should have been a happy prospect but seemed scarcely of interest now. We preferred to sulk than sail.

Shiloh was delighted with HIS craft. But Trelawny – that old pirate – remarked that Shelley's boat was not to be trusted. She had been built according to newfangled plans that foolish Williams had brought out from a friend in England; she seemed to Tre to be, as he put it, ticklish to manage, and he assured us with a worried air that she was so badly balanced that she had required two tons of iron ballast to bring her down to her bearings. She was a fast enough little sailer and puller (at thirty feet) but being undecked and, as he said, unstable, was not safe on the open sea.

We ascribed his comment, at the time, to jealousy among Shiloh's friends. Tre's friend Captain Roberts had built both Shelley's little vessel and our own sizable yacht, the *Bolivar*, but the design imposed upon Trelawny and Roberts by the damned Williams's absent friend in London had long been a sore point with the boatbuilders.

The *Bolivar* however was strong, fast, and steady before any wind, like her namesake the great revolutionary, but we took little interest in the vessel after the months we had spent waiting for it. Allegra was not there to cheer us; the little girl would have loved to sail on such a craft. We were not merely suffering the aftermath of grief, but BORED, and preferred not to be amused by even this most expensive of playthings. Shelley and Williams and the women were quite aquatic enough for all of us.

The house the Shelleys and the Williamses were using for their peculiar *menage a quatre* was a lonely dilapidated villa on the beach in the gulf of Spezia. The ground floor of the place was damned near in the water, which suited Shiloh no end, as he was as fond of the sea as though it were his lost element – a strange and deadly passion in a man who could not swim. In the luminous waters of the bay Shelley played at boats – sometimes with Williams in the *Ariel* (or *Don Juan* as we preferred to call her) and sometimes in a tiny flatbottomed dinghy, a cockleshell merely, that he, a non-swimmer, would row out for miles into the sea, then let drift at random as he sat dreaming, separated from eternity by half an inch of board.

Mrs. Williams – or Jane as she would prefer us to call her (so we *don't*) told us that one afternoon Shiloh offered to row her and her children through the shallows, and as soon as they were seated dipped oars and headed like an arrow for the deep blue water. The poor lady began to be nervous at the little swell that slopped over the side, the boat being overloaded, and liable to turn over with the least rocking and drown her and all her bairns.

Shelley let go the oars and seemed to go out of himself entirely, staring with eyes glazed in front of him while Jane sweated in terror. When he came to himself a little, Jane told us, he saw her looking at him and muttered: 'Now let us together solve the great mystery.'

Naturally, she was horrified. It took her – a woman whom Shiloh loved above all things – a deal of pleading and persuasion before he would row them into the shore. As soon as they were in shallow water, Jane said, she scrambled over the side before Shiloh could change his mind, pushing the children in front of her onto the beach and safety.

Poor Shiloh was always in a hurry to see the end of the path, not wanting to tread it lingeringly and appreciatively like ourselves. Though we are the last person on earth with a right to say it, there can be too much of these poetic death-desires: it seemed to us that we all needed some occupation, to anchor us more firmly to this life. It seemed to us that we would all be better people when Leigh Hunt arrived, to start up our little journal, wherein we might cock a snook at the European restoration of monarchy, and the turncoat Tory poets like Wordsworth and Southey the mouthy.

It would at least, by God, give us all something TO DO...

Chapter forty-two

I verily believe that nor you, nor any man of poetical temperament,
can avoid a strong passion of some kind. It is the poetry of life.

The disaster, when it comes, does not affect us alone. Imagine the thing from poor Leigh Hunt's point of view. He arrives – Mrs. Hunt and the six little Hunts in tow – after months of trying to get through from England in appalling weather. And all so that he may begin work on our new magazine.

A disturbingly piratical fellow called Mr. Trelawny greets him at the dock. Nervously, the family accept a coach ride from this dangerous-looking giant to Montenero. Thinking that at last their troubles are over, the hapless Hunts arrive at the Villa Dupuy to find a sort of warfare in progress outside the Byron-Gamba residence. Our coachman has quarrelled with the Gamba's cook; an Italian fight, knives are drawn, soon a battle between the two factions of servants is taking place beneath our window. And damn it, disturbing our scribbling.

We points a couple of loaded pistols out of the window at the crowd, threatening to shoot the next man who moves, fire a couple of balls into the thick of 'em, best Othello-style performance, never failed to calm the natives down yet. Italians for once too hot to give a curse about the English milorde: a question of honour is involved, the fight does not abate. The luckless Pietro Gamba is stabbed in the arm trying to restrain one of his own servants from using his knife on one of ours.

Deciding that perhaps it would be inconvenient to shoot servants, we amiably washes our hands of the affair and gives in to Teresa's suggestion to call the police. Anything, so we can get back to our scribbling. Meanwhile the accidental Pietro-stabber, in panic, is holding the household at bay, patrolling outside with a dagger, threatening to kill the first person to come through the door. Of course, the other fellows have all run like fun at the first real sight of blood.

Up rolls Mr. and Mrs. Hunt and family at precisely this point, sitting aghast and frightened in the coach while Trelawny, on top, roars with laughter at the definitive Italian scene.

In the besieged house we have decided that OUR honour is involved. It is the infallible hour for our evening ride. At our insistence the riding party come out of the house, with us wondering if we can extract a pistol from our pocket in time should the fellow try to make a rush of it. The fellow breaks down, then, crying, begging that Lord Byron kiss and forgive. LB declines the kiss, but is inclined to forgive so long as it does not get in the way of our evening ride, and gives the fellow a small hug. The dagger-wielder is just shaking hands with the stabbed Pietro as our entourage canter out of the yard. We call a friendly welcome, doffing our blue velvet cap at the bemused Hunts as we jog past.

Then the police arrive. They are Italian, too. They begin at once interrogating the Hunts, the only foreigners in sight.

Shelley arrives the next day – a somewhat pessimistic

Shelley, hair already threaded with grey – in his twenties! – an increasingly-worried Hunt thinks. But Shelley is kind and encouraging to the impecunious Hunts – and at last Hunt's little world begins to take shape, his domestic arrangements are being looked to, and Mrs. Hunt stops nagging. But what a hellhole it is, this hot and dusty Italy that the others love!

Shelley explains that this is not really our main house, where the Hunts are supposed to take up residence, but the house where Teresa is staying with her family with LB in attendance. That day Shelley takes the Hunts, in his dangerously undecked launch, from Leghorn to Pisa where he puts them into the groundfloor of Palazzo Lanfranchi. Shelley calls in the local surgeon to attend to Mrs. Hunt, who is again prostrate with sea-sickness after the little trip across the bay. Helpfully, the quack pronounces that there is no hope for Mrs. Hunt, who will infallibly perish. With their mother indisposed, the six little Hunt children give no little trouble to all concerned.

Shelley and Edward Williams stay in Pisa a few days. Shelley organises money, furniture (putting it on our account), food and beds for the little Hunts, and pays a visit to his own bankers. Meanwhile Mrs. Hunt recovers from what, after all, is only seasickness. It is understood that Shelley will sail back to his own household at Lerici as soon as the Hunts are installed properly – there is no particular hurry, perhaps he will stay in town a few days, Shelley tells Hunt, who is beginning at last to relax. So Shelley stays in the town to look after the Hunts, and all grows calmer.

Then a letter arrives from Jane Williams, the lady whose love Shelley and Edward Williams share, dear Edward, dear Jane, dear Shiloh, and the letter is rather puzzling, expressing as it does a distress which puts Shelley in a frenzy to explain everything to her yet again, and at once.

Why, the lady demands, has her dear Shiloh written in his last of 'never enjoying moments like the past'? Is he planning to join his friend Plato in death, or is it that he expects *her* to? Or is it simply that he wishes not to see her any more?

Shelley is abruptly in an agony to return to Lerici, to talk out this crisis in his love for his friend's wife. To explain his explanation by means of his peculiar science: that death need be no permanent barrier to love, and so forth...

Williams, silent, shy as ever, is also eager to be back near his young wife, the freethinking woman who is the flame to his moth. He can forgive Shelley anything, even his love for his Jane, which strikes him as the most natural thing in the world.

To the poor radical bourgeois Leigh Hunt, the eccentric life-patterns of his fellow-artists seem verging on madness. All his life Hunt will remember the unease of those sticky days at Leghorn, waiting for a break in the oppressive sunshine. Those tedious hopeful days living in Lord Byron's splendid apartments of golden marble, under the protective aegis of Mr. Shelley, whose silver tongue paints the rosy future unfolding in front of them, as Shiloh flits in and out like a ghost.

It was all going so well, Hunt will always think, until Jane's letter came.

Chapter forty-three

*Like Sylla – I have always believed that all things depend
upon Fortune & nothing upon ourselves.*

Look at the disaster, on the other hand, from Trelawny's
point of view. Trelawny was not confused like Hunt.
There he is on our sturdy new yacht, the *Bolivar*, master of
his first command. In the absence of our interest the boat is
Trelawny's toy.

He has been detailed by us to keep an eye on Shiloh's little
skiff, to accompany the *Ariel* (or *Don Juan* as we asked the
Shelleys to call it) on its voyage across the bay. Down on the
quay, processions of black clothed priests and local religion-
ists are chanting and dancing to try and bring on the weather, sweet rain for their withering crops, begging Heaven for
a storm at any price.

'In the ancient of days, they would have sacrificed a goat,
or something worse,' thinks Trelawny, muttering curses about
the damned lot of foreign fools.

He escorts Shiloh to his bank, to serve as bodyguard to
this fragile friend with a pocketful of cash. He follows Shelley round the town where the poet makes a few purchases to

take back to both his waiting ladies. In the village square Trelawny runs into a young English seaman he knows, an unlucky young man whose name is thus immortalised – Charles Vivian. Giving way to a strange feeling of unease, Trelawny hires the sailor to go with the incompetent lubbers Shelley and Williams, just in case...Vivian is a seaman, Trelawny can see, but for some reason he remains uneasy.

The two boats are cruising side by side out of the little harbour when an Italian guardboat comes up and grapples the *Bolivar*. Are these not, remarks the officer of the port, the radical foreigners who demand the right to sail freely around these sensitive coasts? The disreputable foreigners who had the police out to settle a stabbing incident only last week? Where does Trelawny think he is going without official clearance to leave the harbour? Damn your foreign yellow eyes, responds Trelawny predictably, and, predictably, Italian tempers ruffle. The *Bolivar* is ordered to stay in harbour until the papers are ready.

Cursing, furious, Trelawny hardly notices as Shelley and Williams call out that they are going, Jane and Mary will be worried if they do not show up as promised, etc. 'We will tell Albé where you are.' Trelawny waves to them negligently from the deck of the taller craft. 'They ought to be safe enough with Vivian,' he thinks irritably. 'This damned hot weather will never break.'

He watches idly as the little boat disappears in the heat-mist blurring the distance. His anger fading, Trelawny begins to feel drowsy in the humid air, and goes below to doze in the cool of the dark gently-rocking cabin while the clearance papers are prepared. After a period of sweaty sleep, grating noises sound in Trelawny's ears and he awakens. They are hauling up the anchor, he thinks. The damned papers must have arrived.

Reluctantly he sits up and consults the ship's clock. It is half-past six on a midsummer's day.

Coming topside, he is astonished and vaguely alarmed to find that the sky is as dark and gloomy as twilight in midwinter. The sea, he thinks, leaning over the rail, is exactly the colour of lead, and boiling dully as if covered with an oily scum. Wind sweeps the surface, but does not ruffle it: raindrops falling on the surface rebound as if off a sheet of glass. He notes with mounting alarm a general exodus of Italian boats out of the bay, rushing into the harbour so hurriedly that they are fouling each other's way. The angry yells of the colliding fishermen are drowned out by the crashing of the thunder-squall that bursts like an enormous firework over Trelawny's head.

Instantly drenched in the deluge he runs for the sheltering doorway of his little cabin, and stands looking up anxiously at an alien sky belching water and fire. He can hear nothing over the sound of the great storm – not even the alarmed cries of his own sailors – and see nothing beyond the edge of the ship's rail. A series of enormous waves begin to strike the hull, rocking the still-anchored *Bolivar* so that it is all Trelawny can do to keep his feet on the streaming deck.

In twenty minutes the vicious squall has gone as if it has never been, a vortex of boiling cloud rolling on into the land. The town behind it is refreshed in the clear cooled air. The little fishing smacks are sailing gaily out of the harbour, the crews laughing noisily at the fickle weather, and the religious lunatics on the dock are hugging themselves at having broken the drought.

His heart thumping in his ribs, Trelawny climbs his own mast with a glass to see if he can descry a sail on the horizon.

Chapter forty-four

There is thus another man gone, about whom the world was
ill-naturedly, and ignorantly, and brutally mistaken. It will,
perhaps, do him justice <u>now</u>, when he can be no better for it.

The storm howls toward its crescendo. Shelley is supposed to be manning the tiller, but as the gale blows his cloak and long wet hair about him he holds out both arms to embrace the elements.

At the other end of the boat Williams and Vivian are struggling with the sail and cords as they flap madly off the masthead. Seeing the careless helmsman with the floating hair and rapt expression Williams staggers across the deck to Shelley. Shelley is looking away from him lost in some ecstasy of his own. Williams grasps Shelley's shoulder and shakes it hard. He has to scream to be heard: 'Shiloh! Shiloh! Shiloh!'

Shelley turns to him with a wild smile of delight: 'The power in the heart of the storm! I wish I could swim like Albé and Tre – to sport in waves such as THESE!'

Williams screams, shaking his beloved by the collar: 'For God's sake Shiloh! We can scarce hold the sheet still enough to reef her – and the wind is rising yet!'

At the other end of the boat Vivian loses control of the flapping sail. He shouts desperately: 'Mr. Williams! Mr. Williams!' Williams staggers back to help Vivian. Behind them Shelley stands laughing in joy as a maddened sky boils past, the cloud, the rain, and the broken sea mingling all together.

The next flash of lightning reveals the vague shadowy mass of a larger boat looming over Shelley's head. Italian voices scream Italian words, nonsensical to Williams and Vivian, who cannot speak the language.

Williams leaves Vivian to his fate and rushes over to scream at Shelley. 'Shiloh! Shiloh! Over there – it is the Italian fishing boat that was near us when the storm broke! Can you see her Shiloh? What are they saying?'

The fishing smack almost lurches against them. The Italians are urging them to abandon ship and come aboard the fishing-smack. Williams, faced with the laughing Shelley, grows desperate. 'What did he say? You know I can never understand their damned lingo! Tell him we need taking off, for pity's sake – we will never ride out a storm like this in an undecked boat!'

Shelley, holding the tiller, makes as if to throw his arm around Williams, who backs off. 'Courage, Edward! We are yet afloat! Look!' Letting go of the tiller he points over the side into the churning water. 'Do you not see the horses? White horses in the foam!'

The Italians sound more and more imploring. Williams is almost tearing his hair but cannot think of a word of Italian in his terror. 'Tell him to take us aboard before we are swamped!' He shakes Shelley, points at the struggling Vivian. 'Think of that poor boy! Do you want him to die?'

Shelley is no longer listening. 'They want us to ride them! Do you not see them Edward? Look – there is one! And there! And there!'

The Italians have finally found a man who can shout a little broken English at the foreign madmen. 'Helloa...inglese... do you want us to assistance you?'

Shelley shouts back indignantly in Italian: 'No, signori, stand away there! Stand off! Leave us! We ride the horses of the sea!'

The fishingboat fades back into the boiling mist, as if shrugging its shoulders. Williams is beside himself. 'What did you tell him? He is going, in Christ his name! What did you tell him? Shiloh!'

The luminous creature turns and hugs Williams affectionately, letting go of the tiller completely. He drags the smaller man to the side of the boat and points down into the water, as the other sobs out his grief for the life he will never live to see: 'Look, Edward! Did you see that one? The horses! There! And there!'

The white rush of a wave roars over them all.

The storm blows away inland. Trelawny, peering from high up the mast of the anchored *Bolivar* through the clearing air, is unable to make out a sail above the water.

Chapter forty-five

You can have no idea what an extraordinary effect such a funeral pile has, on a desolate shore, with mountains in the back-ground and the sea before, and the singular appearance the salt and frankincense give to the flame. All of Shelley was consumed, except his heart, which would not take the flame, and is now preserved in spirits of wine.

The deep bass voice rolling up the beach, singing some nameless dirge that sounds like Greek, which Trelawny is actually making up as he goes along. The giant bearded figure stoops, not ceasing his chant, and lights the bottom of the pyre. The heaped driftwood and flotsam has been sprinkled with oil and spirits, and in seconds the flames are licking hungrily upward at the steel cage that contains the gruesome remains of a poet.

Fifty yards away the waves roll in gently from an indifferent sea.

Leigh Hunt, stricken with grief, will not get out of the carriage. Mary and Teresa and Jane could not bear to come. We ourself are standing a little way off from Trelawny, between the burning corpse of our friend and the crowd of soldiers, officials, and spectators, mostly ladies, who have come to witness the curious sight. The local regulations maintain that any washed-up bodies must be burned upon the beach in case of plague. Trelawny has determined to make the best of this circumstance and give his friend a Homeric send-off. He is peering down into the casket, stirring something with a poker as he chants, pouring wine, herbs, olive oil and salt over the body.

We cannot but help think how Shelley himself would have appreciated the sight of the pagan ceremony. We come over to the fire to stare down at the gruesome sight. 'Dear God, is THAT what we must come to? THAT a human body? It is more like the carcase of a sheep. O Tre, my friend, poor Shiloh is taken from us. We shall not see his like again.'

Trelawny grins his wolfish grin, but can put no heart into it. Somewhere inside his gigantic pose the man's heart is weeping. 'The flame,' says Trelawny softly, 'will purify him, as it did for the men of Homer's time.'

'Aye, Tre, Shiloh loved to read his Homer. Strange thing, in a nature so unwarlike – to love Homer. As the bard says, may the fire purge the flesh from your bones and leave them snowy and pure, my friend.'

Trelawny starts to poke into the casket with his iron crow, and turns over a lump of something. 'See, Albé – the heart will not burn.'

The brains of the Great Dreamer are cupped in the broken skull, boiling. We shudder at the sight. 'I never knew, Tre, you were so much the pagan. You do it very well.' Trelawny nods, continues chanting and pouring oil, wine, herbs, salt.

'The top of the skull has crumbled, but the brains are cupped in the broken cranium. They are literally seething, boiling, bubbling – will they never burn?' Our voice sounds to us as if it were a long way off. Swallowing hard to smother an urge to vomit, we stagger away down the beach, tearing off our jacket.

'Albé? Do you not want to see the last of Shiloh?'

'My stomach is quite turned. I shall strip and swim out to my ship.'

Trelawny poking at something in the flames. 'His heart, Albé, his heart will not burn! He would have taken that little boat to Greece! His heart would not have failed him!'

We do not rise to this taunt; it is not the occasion. 'If the skull is gone, Tre, pray save me the heart!' We strip to our breeches, ignoring the crowd of onlookers, and plunge into the water, feeling the scorching heat of the sun on our back and head. 'Aye,' we think bitterly, 'we have burned Patroclus the healer. Hector must be made to pay.'

As we plough through the soft calm water that has killed our friend, we are a little uneasy at the flaming heat falling on our shoulders and back. But what can a little sunburn matter NOW? Often enough we have felt the anger of an Achilles. Now and again we must feel the pain. And still Trelawny shouts relentlessly after us as we swim out to sea.

'The heart, Albé! The heart will not burn!'

Chapter forty-six

If I left a woman for another woman, she might have cause to complain, but really when a man merely wishes to go on a great duty, for a good cause, this selfishness on the part of the 'feminie' is rather too much.

There were several keepsakes of that day. In the event, only Hunt wanted to keep the heart. Gazing at that leathery cinder, Hunt had a feeling that his days in Italy were numbered without Shelley to look after his interests in the magazine. I have, Hunt reflected gloomily, made a dangerous journey for nothing. Save for a little charity from our distracted self, all he was likely to salvage was the gruesome trophy.

In the barouche bearing them home from the funeral pyre, the three of us, ourself, Tre, and Hunt, had given way to our feelings by drinking, shouting, singing, and laughing, embracing a terrible gaiety that seemed to afford some relief. None of us could have explained why we laughed; the very subject of death had been too terrible to raise, and we had laughed and sang and joked like those about to die of the plague are said to.

Teresa's keepsake of the day was the skin off our back, which fell off in one piece as we recovered from the sunburn we had incurred in the swim out to our ship. She kept it in a box. Our own keepsake was to have been the little leather-bound book that had been in Shelley's pocket. The curious volume we had never read, by the late Mr. Keats. The night before Shelley's funeral, studying the near-illegible copy of 'Lamia and Isabella' in our room, we were soon walking up and down and muttering, trying to think through what it meant, those rotting pages of poetry that haunted our sight, that we had neglected to read when the living Shelley had tried to foist them on us.

We were thinking of the line, little Johnny Keats's line: 'I shall be among the English poets after my death.' Ha! Little Johnny Keats and his piss-a-bed poems... 'I shall be among the English poets after my death.' He was so certain. But what did he mean? That his spirit would live in a few mighty lines? In the fragmented image of that miserably brief life? Shiloh used to prophecy that little Mr. Keats would be a giant in the life to come (the life of his poetry). That he WOULD be among the English poets after his death...

Staring down at the book, we gripped it a little too hard. The cover crumbled in our hand and the book dropped to the floor, and broke into pieces, brittle as dust. We decided that the volume should be burned with Shiloh.

After the funeral, we regretted burning the book from Shiloh's pocket, except that it was rotten with the sea. Little Johnny Keats! Why not, Shiloh my dear, one of your own books? One night we got down our copy of an MS of Shelley's from the shelves. This one, 'Adonais', was a poem *about* Mr. Keats, as Shiloh himself had told us, what time he too walked above the earth. We opened the book and read: 'He has become part of that loveliness/ Which once he made more lovely.'

We slammed the MS down on our desk as if it had burned us. *Is THAT what little Johnny Keats meant? Is little Johnny Keats a part of it all? But WHAT all? The damned sunset?*

Picking up the skullcup from our desk. Gazing at it. Putting it down.

Is Johnny Keats, and Shiloh, too, now, a part of it ALL? And did Jack Keats face death a brave man because he knew that, in the final reckoning, he should be part at least of every lover of English verse... Shaking our head, silent tears streamed down our face. We poured ourself a glass of gin to which we added some soda water and drained it at a gulp. We were too self-conscious by that time to drink out of the skullcup on the desk, but we put a curious hand upon it.

What all, we were thinking, our hand on the yellowing bone and silver, *what all is Shiloh part of now? My mind, as I remember Shiloh's mind? Is that where Shiloh is now? A thought in our minds? A part of the Imagination within us, as Mr. Coleridge says that the faculty of Imagination is in itself a reflection of the thoughts in the mind of God – the Infinite I Am, the eternal Act of Creation itself, which is the eternal being or BECOMING of the Deity...*

We swallowed another drink of gin, straight out of the bottle this time.

And therefore it follows that the awareness of interior proportion which we need to have in order to make a new piece of Art – or I dare say even of Science – this awareness is simply part of the continuous reflection in our minds of the minds and Art of the other men we have studied – the other poets in my case, and their skill in the arrangement of interior proportions which we poets have to acquire.

But damn theory! Soon we will be prating of SYSTEM, and when a poet begins to talk of system he is finished.

No – but as Mr. Coleridge has said, we do echo God's mind when we touch the Reason reflected in us from the mind of God. And when we understand other men, God's thoughts are simply, to us, the best thoughts of the men themselves. Why, even little Johnny Keats, no doubt, was a thought of God, or whatever strange thing we mean when we say the word God. That brilliant little Keats we did not help was a thought of God...

In a sudden furious pique we swept all the objects – skull-cup, drinks, everything – off the desk, and stared down at the jumble. 'Well,' we mumbled aloud, half-ashamed of ourselves, 'I dare say we will be able to take none of THIS trash with us...'

Teresa rushed into the room and into our arms. She collapsed, sobbing bitterly, on our chest. 'Mio Biron... mio Biron...'

Cara, we were thinking, *you must have known it would come to this, after Shiloh had left us*. In a sudden spasm of guilt we patted her shoulder affectionately. 'Come – courage, my sweet. What has that foolish young brother of yours been saying? Do you doubt I shall return? Of course I shall – what has the fool Pietro said?

'Curse Pietro. Curse Trelawny.'

'Now, my dear, you know very well that I have received a second letter from the Greek Committee in London which I cannot ignore – Pietro and Tre are not to blame in this...'

'Curse the Committee... curse London...'

'Now now my dear...'

'You would not have considered this if Mr. Shelley had been alive, if your daughter... but I am nothing to you...'

'Recollect that only last summer I was pleased to be made a member of that same Committee. Feeling as I do about Greece. And now they inform me they must immediately have a member on the spot, to make accurate report. I am the only member within miles of the country. It would be base not to go over there for a month or two.'

We held her half away from us at arm's length. She looked accusingly up into our eyes. 'It involves my honour to go. I should have refused when they made me a member a year ago. It is too late now, however much I want to stay with you.'

It sounded reasonable, almost even to us.

'But...'

'If I resign now my enemies will say that I am AFRAID – you could bear that no better than I.'

Salt tears welled up out of those eyes like the sea. 'It is true... if you did not go... but mio Biron...' She lapsed into a bout of hysterical crying. We held and patted her awkwardly. There was no more she could try, except to show us her sorrow. It was no longer enough.

She said bitterly: 'I hope my brother and Mr. Trelawny will stand in front of any bullets that may be aimed at you.' So she blamed them, which was good, rather than doubting my love. We did not love at that moment, but we love her enough now, when it is useless to do so.

What, indeed, could the poor girl do to keep us now that Shiloh and Allegra had gone? 'There, my dear – I shall not leave for a month – you above all people should understand what difficulty I shall have in arranging all this trash. I shall not wish to be gone for long. I am too fond of my domestic comforts and your good self.'

'You will keep THAT promise no better than the promise not to go at all...'

We had a sharp picture of a similar scene of parting with Augusta. This girl, after all, had not been Augusta, and we felt a sudden rush of pity for Teresa. We gathered her into our arms, pulled her to our breast. 'There... there... very soon now you will see how foolish are all these fears.' This was not the same situation as with Augusta. We felt certain we should see her again, God and the Turks willing.

She stopped crying, kissed us on the lips. 'Si, si. Foolish. Foolish. Only...' – the tears welled up again – '...where will you be a year from now?'

Chapter forty-seven

*Is there any thing beyond? – who knows? He that can't tell. Who tells
that there is? He who don't know. And when shall he know?
Perhaps, when he don't expect it, and generally when he don't wish it.*

There must be, in the final stages, the Spirit is thinking, some breakdown in the processes of remembering. For, clearly, this display on the wall is no longer just memory. What can this image be? A memory of a dream we had, perhaps? Or some reality accessible only to memory? On the wall, a bleak wind howls out of darkness, there is a rumble of distant thunder with no apparent lightning. Pellets of rain splash on the unsteady wind. A full moon is up, filling gaps in the cloud with radiance, bursting as if by magic now and again into cleaner spaces of air. A moon that speaks with Shiloh's voice.

> ...I
> *Argued against despondency, but pride
> Made my companion take the darker side –
> The sense that he was greater than his kind
> Had struck, methinks, his eagle spirit blind.
> 'And such' – he cried – 'is our mortality...'*

(Shiloh always managed to make himself believe that, given the will and idea, almost any man could BECOME great. One's humble self usually considered that one was born great, like Scrope, or Napoleon, or ourself – one was given no choice in the matter. But it has to be confessed that we never won this debate with the ghost of Shiloh – one even began to suspect that he could have been right all along.)

> *The word you spoke last night might well have cast*
> *A darkness on my spirit – it is our will*
> *That thus enchains us to permitted ill –*
> *We might be otherwise – we might be all*
> *We dream of happy, high, majestical:*
> *Where is the love, beauty and truth we seek*
> *But in our minds...*
> *'You talk Utopia.'*

This last in LB's voice, the cynic's voice, as Shiloh rendered it in his verse. The Spirit thinks for a second it is the body on the bed talking, then realizes that it is only the voice of memory on the wall. He calls over to the bed: 'Well said, old mole. Canst work i'th'earth so fast?' Chuckling, he turns back to the Moon that has Shiloh's voice. 'O Shiloh, Shiloh – what we have not done to pacify your ghost – to be the superman you imagined we could become – or perhaps merely to please the memory of yourself...'

A fresh surge of the storm blackens the dream-sky with cloud, blots out the moon and all who sail in her. And Shiloh's beautiful verses remembering their conversations. *Nothing to Shiloh was a mystery; or rather, all was mystery and he felt it perfectly, could touch it perfectly. Thus he was mystery itself to all who loved him.*

The air in the room seems to be growing rapidly darker. The Nightgowned Spirit glances at the real sky through the window, to see if the two skies are, yet, one and the same, or if there are other skies to be seen before the end. Not long now. There has been no response from the body on the bed for some time. So he does not bother to voice his thoughts to his other self on the bed, but merely thinks them.

Chapter forty-eight

And I have loved thee, Ocean! and my joy
Of youthful sports was on thy breast to be
Borne, like thy bubbles, onward: from a boy
I wanton'd with thy breakers – they to me
Were a delight; and if the freshening sea
Made them a terror – 'twas a pleasing fear,
For I was as it were a child of thee,
And trusted to thy billows far and near,
And laid my hand upon thy mane – as I do here.

Old Count Gamba had received his passport to go home to the family estates in Ravenna at last. *Too late*, Teresa thought, *too late, my God, it is too late...*

The day before her father was to travel, the distraught contessa waited in her room for the return of her lover, busy organising his upcoming voyage. Mary Shelley, who had been sent for the purpose by ourself, came in to try to console the stricken girl.

In the end we did not manage to come back before Teresa's father's carriage departed. Not knowing whether to stay or go, Teresa was helped next morning, prostrated after a night of grief, into the carriage. Halfway to Ravenna she gathered her spirit to write to her lover: *I hoped to have the strength to bear this misfortune without dying – but the pain grows every moment and I feel as though I were dying.* But we did not come to such a summons as we had once.

On the sixteenth of that hot July in 1823, ourself, Trelawny and Pietro, having foolishly sold the Bolivar to the beautiful visitor Lady Blessington, swept out of Genoa on the English brig *Hercules*. A gale sprang up, so fierce, and so alarming all the horses, and battering the equipment, that Captain Scott put back for Genoa again.

Knowing that Teresa had left, we did not wish to go back to the empty house of our love. On the eighteenth the weather cleared, and the *Hercules* set sail, briefly touching at Leghorn and then pursuing our voyage by the straits of Messina for Greece. Passing within sight of Elba, Corsica, the Lipari islands including Stromboli, Sicily, Italy, etc., about the 4th of August we anchored off Argostoli, in the chief harbour of the island of Cephalonia, near Ithaca, off the western coasts of Greece, prior to....

'NO!' The Spirit turns from the luminous wall and raises an eyebrow in the direction of the bed. So all is not yet finished...

The dying man tries to sit up, to demand something of the nightgowned narrator.

Though the words are unintelligible, the Spirit knows immediately what LB wants. 'Yes, yes, it was indeed the most agreeable voyage of our life – like a voyage through the brightening air back into youth itself.' He chuckles briefly, and helps himself to snuff. 'Let us see that voyage again if you like. Let us experience it and be happy. For a moment,' he adds, sniffing.

As we drifted slowly into the port at Leghorn, past the vessels riding at anchor, a certain Captain Vitali of an Ionian vessel fired all his guns in salute. The Greeks, letting us know they knew we were coming before we had even left Italy. Rather than being a MILITARY sort of salute, guns firing in unison, it was a ragged cannonade like fireworks. It made the day seem like the beginning of a holiday.

A capable-looking man walked up to us us as we docked. A fellow called Browne, a Scot, God bless the race, who asked to join us on our mission. Browne and Trelawny were thick as thieves right away; the man was an ex-British naval officer cashiered for being pro-Greek when in service in the Islands (in opposition to the policy of our own Tory government, as ever, and be damned to them, as ever).

Browne spoke modern Greek and Italian and knew all about the disposition of the English Residents in command of the English naval forces which controlled the Greek Islands. Following Browne's advice, we changed our first Greek port-of-call from Zante to Cephalonia, so as to be under the aegis of Colonel Napier, the only one of the English commanders foursquare in favour of the Greek cause.

As we pulled out of Italy we felt a tugging at our heart to see that coast of our happiness fade into shadowy distance behind. But the weather was fine, the ship ran free before the wind, and everyone on deck, including God help us ourself (rushing from our brief years of happiness to who knows what) were cheerful and gay. What a cruise! Not, this time, as mere *tourists* but as companions in arms, as brothers round the watchfire...

Every day at noon Trelawny and ourself stripped down and leapt into the water to swim alongside the ship, and be damned to sharks. One day, feeling more frolicsome than usual, we took a notion to fling all the dogs and the geese on board into the water, and Trelawny, laughing in his great deep bass, joined in the caper, so that all the birds and dogs were heaved squawking and yelping overboard and were soon strung out swimming in a long line astern.

Captain Scott heard the ruckus (to be sure the beasts were kicking up a row at the prospect of being left behind in the open sea) and rushed down the deck at us, roaring like a headmaster at naughty boys. Tre and I looked at each other, burst out laughing anew, and without further ado pounced on the poor Captain and tore off the new scarlet jacket of which he was so proud.

We tied the Captain to a rail with his own ropes, as he called out hoarsely for his bosun, who had had the good sense to absent himself from deck. While the captain invented new levels of blasphemy to curse our souls, Tre and I each inserted an arm into his new red dress jacket and leapt, joined together, into the sea amongst the dogs and geese...

The Captain vowed to get even over that night's bottle. A good fellow, Captain Scott. They were good fellows all, Pietro and Tre and Browne and the rest, and ever-faithful valet Fletcher already bemoaning the hard fare he knew from memory would await him in Greece. And our fine brave Tita, who had found his way back from banishment and came with us amiably to kill Turks.

We felt like a youth of twenty again, sailing to Greece for the first time. We wrote that night: '*I don't know why it is, but I feel as if the eleven long years of bitterness I have passed through since I was here were taken off my shoulders,*

*and I was scudding through the Greek Archipelago with old
Bathurst, in his frigate.'*

We coasted the island of Stromboli on a clear moonlit
night, sitting late on deck with Trelawny and Browne and
a bottle of rum, swapping ghost stories until the apocalyp-
tic dawn broke over the luminous water. The dark hills and
twinkling lights on the island drifted past us like images of
our past life. Each man gave himself to grog and stories until
the stars paled in the East and the party broke up for bed.
As we passed Trelawny to go downstairs he gripped our arm
and intimated what a tremendous night it had been, in peace
with each other on the deck under the stars.

A good fellow, Trelawny, for all his faults. We told him
that we looked forward to writing a fifth canto of *Childe
Harold*, if we lived, to commemorate such nights as this had
been, and he should be in it forsooth, as the pirate he was.

That sweet last voyage. Afternoons on the deck, and evenings in our cabin – like any tourist we had time to read, and
took the opportunity to make a study of Swift, Montaigne,
Voltaire, Grimm's *Correspondence* and La Rochefoucald.
Excellent fare...

On August 2nd we sighted Zante, but in accordance with
Browne's advice we began tacking at once for Cephalonia.
As we approached the island the mountains of the Morea
– the god-haunted Pelopponese – rose behind it out of the
blue distance, the mainland looming above us like a future
problem, sending a pulse through our veins that recalled
our first sight of Greece a dozen years ago when we were
young, cruising these seas with old Bathurst in his frigate,
and Ekenhead, and Hobby. Beyond those mountains lurked
the complexities of the Greek situation, where the military

faction, and the civil faction, and a million other factions, could not agree.

We began to get an inkling of an idea of the muddle the Greek cause was in as we read our letters and talked to the people on Cephalonia. We should have to dally on British-held Cephalonia until a clear course presented itself, before we could sail to the mainland. More damned waiting.

But what could we do? We were bearing with us a considerable fortune, some of it belonging to the Committee in London (and not a little of it our own) and could not indulge ourselves as freebooting spirits, like Trelawny, who had to think only of his horses and weapons and individual carcase. Trelawny cursed us for causing a delay in his Great Adventure by not striking for the mainland at once.

But if we were to help at all to salvage the situation, we had first to begin to try to understand it. The revolt against the Turks was a Gordian knot. The Greeks would need the sword of some unifying principle – a figurehead, or a martyr, some common cause – to cut through the tangled knot as Alexander did so long ago.

Or so we thought at the time, hey nonny.

Chapter forty-nine

The Greeks are advancing in their public progress, but quarrelling amongst themselves.

Imagine our delight to receive a letter from Marco Botsaris, the Suliote leader, who was using his band to bottle up the Turks trying to penetrate the mountain passes above Missolonghis and take the town back. 'Let nothing prevent you from coming into this part of Greece,' Botsaris wrote. 'The enemy threaten us in great number, but, with the help of God and your Excellencey, they shall meet a suitable resistance.' The Suliote people had been exiled from their cliffs in southern Albania by the Turk and were fighting hard to restore their homeland. They were like those Albanians we once slept out on a mountain with, in that first command of our youth.

Marco, that fine old pirate, was battling against the better-equipped but more static forces of the Turk with great courage and ingenuity, using his band of fierce mountain warriors to good effect in those rugged hills. We determined at once to accept his invitation. But our hopes in Botsaris proved vain, for by the time we had received his letter he had already suffered the fate of many a brave patriot, a musket bullet through the chest cavity.

The governor of Missolonghi, Count Metaxata, invited us to that marshy bog, but we decided to try to communicate with the Government first. As we did not come here to join a faction but a nation, and to deal with honest men and not with speculators or peculators (charges bandied about daily by the Greeks of each other) it will require much circumspection to avoid taking the side of the wrong party. We had already received invitations from more than one of the contending groups, always under the pretext that *they* were the 'real Simon pure.'

One should not despair, though all the foreigners that we have met in Greece are going or gone back disgusted. Whoever goes into Greece at present should do it as Mrs. Fry went into Newgate – not in the expectation of meeting with any especial indication of existing probity, but in the hope that time and better treatment will reclaim the present burglarious and larcenous tendencies which have followed this general Gaol delivery. When the limbs of the Greeks are a little less stiff from the shackles of four centuries of slavery, they will not march so much 'as if they had gyves on their legs.' At present the Chains are broken; but the links are still clanking, and the Saturnalia is still too recent to have converted the Slave into a sober citizen.

The worst of them is that they are such damned liars; there never was such an incapacity for veracity shown since Eve lived in Paradise. One of them found fault the other day with the English language, because it had so few shades of a Negative, whereas a Greek can so modify a 'No' to a 'Yes', and *vice versa*, by the slippery qualities of his language, that prevarication may be carried to an extent and still leave a loop-hole through which perjury may slip without being perceived. Their very word for yes, NE, sounds like no...

The people have been in chains, their spirits broken. But their spirits may be mended by and by. The common people are the hope of the land, whatever some of their leaders have sunk to. The Greek people – *the people only* – are the finest on earth.

Chapter fifty

But where is the Greek fleet? I don't know – do you?

Browne and Trelawny had ridden off to join Odysseus (or Ulysses) and his band of cut-throat patriots on the mainland. With them they carried our letter to the provisional Government. By the first week of November we ourselves (with Pietro and all the train) were on the point of leaving to join the Greek government in the Morea. We were forestalled by the return to Cephalonia of young Mr. Browne, now in the company of two Greek deputies, who presented us with a request for a loan of 6000 levantine dollars to pay the sailors of the Greek fleet (in hopes of making them stir against the Turk). We gave 'em 4000 dollars, about eight hundred pound sterling, and decided that we should go to Missolonghi and see that the *fleet* should be paid, rather than any other party.

There arrived from the Greek Committee the 'typographical Colonel' Stanhope, who, when we asked if he had brought anything decent to read from London, offered us a copy of Mr. Jeremy Bentham's *Springs of Action*. 'God DAMN his Springs of Action,' the pious Stanhope was startled to hear us snarl. 'My COCK has more spring in it.'

On the 29th we sailed for the mainland – if Missolonghis can be called mainland, swamp that it is. We were on
board, (aside from Fletcher and our giant hound Lion) the
thrice-damned doctors Bruno and Millingen (good enough
fellows to be sure if you did not fall ill) and last but not least
Luke, or Loukas, a young boy from a refugee family we had
befriended, whom God help us we seemed to be falling in
love with. Strange to be distracted at such a time (gaming
not at the Cocoa Tree for pounds sterling but in the crucible
of the world for the fate of nations) by a passion at once so
embarrassing and disturbing.

The youth, of course, had reminded us of Augusta. Those
black curls, the face almost a mirror of our own as a youth,
that sweet frown and curl of lip...

Love at first sight, as usual, of our reflection in the pool
of Narcissus.

But the boy, we were beginning to realize, cared not a fig
for us. Dimly we were becoming conscious of what was more
and more obvious to others, that our famous mortal beauty,
which we once negligently relied upon to charm effortlessly
the people we drifted past on our road to hell, had no longer
the power to move the breast of an unread (unEnglished!)
Greek boy. Loukas is impressed not by our verses or our fading looks but by the horses and jackets and pistols he expects
us to provide for him when we gain the mainland.

That boy in the other room, our last (unconsummated) love.

('Loukas!'
'Be still! He does not care!')

Gaining the mainland. A thing easier to be said than done, like many a thing that trips lightly off the lips. The Turks were out. We ourself were aboard a fast little *mistico*, but Pietro and most of the horses and supplies, including unfortunately most of the weapons, were on board the heavier, slower bombard. Upon sight of a few Turkish vessels coming out of the Gulf of Corinth, the Greek ships riding at anchor before Missolonghi instantly cut their cables and flew away, leaving the Turk, unbeknownst to us, in command of the seas.

The first we knew about it was the sight of a large ship looming in front of the *mistico* out of the darkness. We thought it at first a Greek, but the Captain identified it immediately as a Turkish man-of-war, which could blow us out of the water as soon as it noticed we were there. Every man jack on board, down to the very dogs and geese, was silent with petrified fear. Close... so close that we could hear the creak of her rigging. An utterly still night. We could hear our own hearts thumping as the good Captain turned her about to creep away in the dark before the Turkish battleship spied us.

Once we were out of sight the Turks had to wait until dawn before they could pursue us; but as dawn broke we could see poor Pietro's boat being chased by one warship over the horizon, and another sitting between us and the port of Missolonghi. This ship, catching sight of us, launched in pursuit, but we were a good deal faster than the poor old bombard (whose fate, with Pietro's, we could only surmise.) We spent a merry morning dodging our heavier enemy, squeezing through the narrow straits and shallow waters around the islands where she could not follow.

Exhausted, we landed finally for the night in the Greek-occupied port of Dragomestre; we spent a miserable night wondering what we were going to write to Teresa about the death of her brother.

But if fortune is often a whore, she can be an angel too. What was happening to Pietro was as wild and strange (and difficult to credit) as any romance. The bombard, having been chased and caught, had been boarded by the Turks, and the poor captain dragged off to the Turkish ship for interrogation. Pietro (with the other terrified passengers) was watching the Turkish frigate from the decks of the bombard. When he saw a man lowered into a boat, he rushed past the Turkish soldiers into his cabin and dumped a packet of our letters and plans loaded with shot out through his window and into the sea.

On the Turkish vessel the Greek captain knelt in front of the commander, who was glaring at him coldly. The commander was not satisfied by the bombard captain's explanations, and the captain's blood ran cold as he heard (with his ample understanding of Turkish) what the man ordered next: behead this fellow, said the Turk, and scuttle his damned ship. Cut the throats of all useless passengers and impress the sailors into service.

Looking up for the first time from his prostrated position on the floor before the Oriental lord, the terrified Greek captain – O strange – suddenly felt hope pouring through his heart: he knew this man! He called out the Turkish officer's name, then his own, and the commander's reaction must have astounded his own soldiers. He gave a start of recognition, burst into tears, hauled the Greek captain to his feet and embraced him like a longlost brother (so too are the Turks and Greeks like longlost brothers) all the while weeping at the possibility that he might have harmed a hair of his 'brother's' head.

It seems that the Greek captain had, five years since, rescued this same Turk from a shipwreck in the Black Sea. The Turk remembered very well the sensation of being adrift, clinging to a slim spar, when the Greek arrived to save him, the most welcome sight in the world. He had never forgotten his terrifying day and night in the open water, and his rescuer...

Ignoring the host of clearly military supplies: guns, horses, gold, artillery and helmets (not to mention the typographical Colonel Stanhope's god-damned PRINTING PRESS, revolutionary journals for the a-printing-of), the commander, after towing Pietro's bombard to Patras, invited Pietro to come on board. Pietro, thanking his lucky gods, took presents for the Turk of rum, port, and a telescope. The Turk was much pleased with the gifts, and, with his affable arm about his old friend the Greek captain, invited Pietro to pour himself a drink, smoke the *hookah*, and join the celebrations.

When the party was over Pietro, in a daze of drink and opium, had to pinch himself to be sure he was awake. They sailed out of the harbour to friendly gunshot salutes from the grinning Turkish soldiers. So crazy war is, that men who can be brothers will kill one another.

By the time our *mistico* had reached Missolonghi after our excursion round the islands, Pietro was already installed and in a sweat of worry about *us*. But we gained the shore at last, and put on our best scarlet uniform for the landing. There to greet us, lined up in front of our new headquarters – a three-storey house in the town – was a row of Frank and Greek officers, and Prince Alexander Mavrocordatos, a funny-looking little fellow in glasses that we took something of a shine to in the following days.

But soon we perceived that good-hearted Mavrocordatos was cursed with a lack of decision-making powers which did not bode well in a would-be warrior. The Prince advised us against various other factions of the Greeks; but we were careful not to become TOO friendly with him, for we did not want to cut ourself off and make faction against other parties but rather join the factions together.

It seemed a dismal place enough, this Missolonghi. The ground – one dare scarcely call it a street – around the house was covered with water after every rainstorm (frequent at this season) or high tide. Two or three miles offshore the stagnant lagoon was divided by a long line of muddy dunes from the ocean; behind us, on the mainland proper, there were only marshes, and a huge unclimbable precipice, the snowcapped Varassova mountain, towering over three thousand feet above the sea. It was an impossible place for a good gallop. But we soon established a routine of being rowed across the lagoon to ride our horses on ground where we might gallop without sinking into mud.

Of such trifles is fate made.

Five thousand troops were gathered in the town for a conference following the death of Botsaris – of various factions, like all the Greek forces. Prince Mavrocordatos suggested that we become a chief, and take on the five hundred Suliotes who were leaderless following Botsaris's death (then we should be yet *another* faction) and assault the nearby fortress of Lepanto, which is the key to the region. But first we needed an effective artillery to breach the stone walls so that our men should not be slaughtered climbing them.

Cannon were out of the question. But Congreve rockets were promised, that should blast through the stone walls as effectively (they said). This artillery was about to be delivered, together with an English firemaster, Mr. Parry, who was to organise the battery. Hour by hour we scanned the horizon for his sail.

This was all very well, but on the morning of the 21st of January 1824 (for how the years draw on!) we woke up to find five Turkish cruisers sailing back and forth in front of the port, our own brave navy having fled once again at the sight of them. We were blockaded, and if the artillery and Mr. Parry should fall into the hands of the Turks should be completely undone.

On the 29th the Turkish vessels vanished in the night. The Greek boats, however, did not return. But Captain Parry then arrived safely with the stores. A fierce pale rain hissed into the earth and the sea: the stores had (immediately) to be carried from the beaches into the Seraglio.

The Suliotes refused to do it; it was not, they said, soldier's work, and besides, it was a holy day. It was finally too much, and our temper broke. 'Be damned to you!' we screamed at 'em then, and attempted the job ourselves.

Wherein lay our undoing...

Chapter fifty-one

...and though I am willing to do all I can <u>when</u> necessary, yet I do not see <u>why</u> they should not help a little...

The sailors had rolled the barrels off the deck onto the dockside, but now under the grey hiss of incessant rain, the chests and barrels of military stores, powder and all, lay spoiling on the ground. But the ship and the sailors were gone, and the troops would not agree to shift the stuff indoors before it was ruined.

It was a Saint's Day, they said – a holy day, a holiday...

We watch from the future ourself, LB, singlehanded trying to push along a heavy barrel. Panting, straining, wrenching it in gasps and jerks, he managed to lay it upright in the temporary shelter of a cypress tree. The Seraglio door gaped open only another hundred yards away. Water streamed over his head and body. He rested for a few seconds in the rain, limped over to another barrel, began to wrestle it toward the first barrel under the shelter of the tree. He rocked the awkward hundredweight to get the barrel over onto its side, eased it down gently, was starting to take the weight of it when a stranger in naval uniform rushed up and helped him lower it to the ground – Captain Parry, the new Firemaster, on loan from the British Navy.

'Pardon me, my lord, but you have not the knack of it.'

Seeing the near-exhausted condition of his new commander, Parry dragged him over to the shelter of the tree, and extracted a flask full of brandy from his coat, urged him to drink. 'Your good health, Captain Parry, for this relief much thanks.' He took a drink and passed the flask back to Parry.

'My lord, I am afraid that I have understood none of this business since we landed here in this damned rain. Why will the Greeks not unload the powder? Cannot they see that the rain will spoil it? Don't they WANT the damned stuff?'

'The ignorant fools are refusing to work because today is a holy day – and even the promise of double pay will not convince them to risk the bad luck they are convinced will follow such blasphemy. Superstitious fools! They are not fit to be a free people.'

Parry, laughing, took the flask, drank, and offered it back. LB laughed too, drinking in the rain with Mr. Parry, his new friend. 'You must forgive my abruptness at the dock, earlier on, my dear Captain. These people have put me in a passion.' He shook Parry's hand warmly. 'Glad to meet a man of sense. A Firemaster by God – you will be of enormous help to us here. You shall direct the firing of our Congreve Rockets at the fortress walls, the ingredients for which I trust that Bible-thumping fool Stanhope has sent us at last.'

A frown appeared on Parry's face. 'Did you say *rockets*, Lord Byron, sir?'

'Well didn't you bring the...' A comic horde erupted onto the dock towards the two Englishmen. The Suliotes – sporting pistols, daggers, sashes and earrings like so many Elizabethan ruffians – were in high humour. Food and drink abounded, along with gossip loud enough almost to drown out the noise of the rain, which they ignored. LB glared at the men around him venomously, spat at the feet of the nearest. The crowd chattered round the abandoned cargo, a few began playing cards on the barrel under the tree.

The nearest Suliote, whose shoe the gob of spit had almost besmirched, was cheerfully unoffended, waved his bottle in LB's face, trying to explain to the stranger. 'No good, Lordos Byronos, no good. Holy day...' waving the bottle – 'no work no good today.' He went over to talk to one of his friends, looked back to see the two Englishmen staring at him, and called back over his shoulder, as to idiots: 'No good! Bad luck work today!'

'I can scarce restrain myself, at times, from firing a couple of balls into the thick of 'em. But come, Mr. Parry – the rain continues. The material for the rockets will be spoiled if we do not get it ashore properly.'

The amiable Suliote who could speak a little English overheard the last remark. 'Iss Rocketsss? Rocketsss?' He jabbered something to his mates in their peculiar dialect, and they laughed, drank, cheered and scuffled amongst themselves.

'By God – I will give them ROCKETS... I doubt they can tell me the damned saint's name they are drinking to, the heathen swine...'

Parry managed to get a word in. 'But my dear Lord Byron, Colonel Stanhope was not able to load the ingredients for the rockets. He said that not everything you had asked him for could be loaded into so small a ship as ours...'

LB's eyes bulged with anger. 'Does Stanhope think that I can persuade men LIKE THOSE to scale the walls of Lepanto without rockets – those men over there are not fools, I can assure you, merely rogues. Damn Stanhope! Do you know what the imbecile has sent me? A blasted printing press no less... Do you know what is in that box over there?' Seizing an iron bar, he rushed over to another box and broke it open savagely, reaching in to scatter the contents carelessly in the rain.

Parry cannot believe his eyes. 'Books?'

'Not merely books, sir, but English Protestant Bibles.' One of the Suliotes picked up a Bible, examined it for a moment, idly tossed it away. 'If you understand that none of these fellows can read GREEK, let alone English, you will understand the usefulness of these BOOKS...' He hurled a few more books at the idling Suliotes, who cheered and waved their bottles back. 'Do you know what Stanhope offered me to read, when I asked him what he had brought out with him from England? Mr. Jeremy Bentham's nonsense-book, sir, called Springs of Action.'

To Parry's amazement, he appeared to be going into a frenzy. 'Springs of Action? Springs of Action?' Furiously seizing a nearby pickax he smashed open the top of another crate of bibles and began hurling them at the laughing Suliotes. 'GOD DAMN HIS SPRINGS OF ACTION! MY COCK HAS MORE SPRING TO IT!!!' In the midst of this fury, he began to cough and shake uncontrollably, and fell to the ground.

He lay on the wet earth, heaving fitfully. The Greeks stopped laughing, and Parry, the man of action, threw himself on top of his commander to smother his convulsions and prevent him doing himself an injury on the rocky ground. 'My lord? My lord?' The Suliotes had gathered round in a ring to observe the sad spectacle. LB stopped convulsing and Parry wiped the drenched face with a handkerchief. The man on the ground was groaning from somewhere deep inside himself, only partially conscious.

The Suliotes quiet, all eyes. The man who could speak a little English spoke for all. 'Lordos Byronos... Lordos Byronos... NOW we will work for you on the holy day.' He took out a silver fob watch from his pocket. As the startled Parry watched, he announced something in dialect to the others, then translated to English for Parry. 'Iss midnight.' There was daylight behind the stormcloud, and Parry could make no sense of this.

'Midnight?' Parry asked. 'But...'

As Parry gaped at him, the fellow dropped his watch on to the ground and stamped on it with his heavy boot again and again until it was completely broken and embedded in the mud. 'Midnight. No holy day. Iss finish.' As Parry knelt, nursing his stricken commander, the Suliote turned away and bellowed orders to his mates. To Parry's astonishment the others obeyed him instantly, and began to carry the cargo into the warehouse with bewildering speed and efficiency. The dock began rapidly to be cleared.

The rain drizzled down as Parry helped his fallen commandant toward his quarters. Behind him, quietly, without fuss, the would-be Greeks were finally working together.

Chapter fifty-two

Upon February 15th – (I write on the 17th of the same month) I had a strong shock of a convulsive description, but whether Epileptic, Paralytic, or Apoplectic, is not yet decided by the two medical men, who attend me.

The boy Loukas had been more affected by the rain than us and contracted a dangerous fever. We gave up our own bed to him and slept on the floor. Be damned to our sickbed. We should not linger there if we could help it, like a delicate lady.

Parry was such an efficient trustworthy soul that we decided to use HIM to disburse our monies to pay the troops (about two thousand dollars-worth a week – four hundred pounds worth of English gold and be damned to it). But when Parry had Pietro Gamba examine the lists of the Suliote men on the payroll, and asked to see these gentlemen IN PERSON, he discovered that there were not a few phantom troops who did not exist outside of their rapacious officers' imaginations – the extra wages, of course, going straight into the officers' pockets.

Indignant at the discovery of their trumpery, the Suliote chiefs demanded that out of their number of three or four hundred actual men we must appoint two generals, two colonels, two captains, and inferior officers in the same proportion – in short, that out of three or four hundred actual Suliotes, there should be one hundred and fifty officers and sergeants – all on appropriate scales of pay. They stood there in their beards and scarlet tunics scowling defiance.

Feeling a fury mount in us that frightened even ourself, we gave way to 'hysterica passio' and let the wretches have the edge of our tongue for some time. Roundly cursing the ringleaders, and kicking them away from our door, we wrote a memo to Mavrocordatos with a hand shaking with rage:

> *February 15th, 1824. Having tried in vain at great expense, considerable trouble, and some danger, to unite the Suliotes for the good of Greece – and their own – I have come to the following resolution: –*
>
> *I will have nothing more to do with the Suliotes. They may go to the Turks, or the Devil, – they may cut me into more pieces than they have dissensions among themselves, – sooner than change my resolution.*
>
> *For the rest, I hold my means and person at the disposal of the Greek nation and Government the same as before.*

The damned rogues gave way like butter, suddenly, and agreed to organize themselves, if only their Lordos Byronos would not abandon them, into a properly-constituted force of three hundred Suliotes under ourself and Pietro as lieutenant. 'Well played, my lord,' said Parry. 'You have united these pirates as you may hope to do for the rest of the Greeks.'

We tried to smile at the man, but his red cheerful face grew dim, the world wobbled before our eyes, and as from a great distance we observed ourself falling and perceived that Parry, with a little cry, had caught us. As Parry and Pietro carried us to the bed we felt an invisible hand pulling our mouth all over to one side, as if we had had a damned stroke like an old man. Then we knew no more until we woke and saw for the first time that awful sight, soon to become familiar, of our people gathered round our bed gazing down at us in sympathy.

Millingen and Bruno, our two quacks, told us that for over ten minutes we lay on the bed and had to be held down, we were threshing so violently. Whatever the fit was, it seemed to be a result of the same fatigue after the fit of temper on the dock in the rain, and we were left some days weak as a kitten, though the feeling in our face came back and our face reverted to its normal shape.

This weakness was enough to undo all our hopes of action. By the time we were recovered, the greater part of the forces at our disposal had left Missolonghi. Only the Suliotes and a few others remained, but none seemed keen on the assault on Lepanto, which for lack of men and artillery we were persuaded to abandon for the moment. The bitter taste of this defeat in our mouth made us think that it was all up with our side now.

Chapter fifty-three

But what is Hope? nothing but the paint on the face of Existence...

A letter came from Trelawny, accompanied by a letter from his friend Odysseus. In it Odysseus made a proposal that we thought might yet redeem our purpose here: that, all former grievances being put aside, ourself and Mavrocordatos (who trusts Odysseus NOT) should meet in conference at Salona, near Delphi (ancient Amphissa where the Delphians razed the village for impiety, if we remember our ancient history aright). That damned spectacle-wearing fat little Prince.

Ill and fragile as we were, we could not help but be annoyed at Mavrocordatos's suspicions concerning this meeting (does he think they will murder us outright? when Tre is with them?) which seems to us to afford a possibility of concord that is the only hope of Greece. What does Greece need? Unity. Or something – a figurehead – to ignite her struggle. Mavrocordatos feared that Odysseus would cut our throats at the parley, or some such nonsense. What idea or symbol can ever make these fellows pull together and look beyond themselves?

Perhaps a sacrifice, we thought gloomily, as the days of the conference drew on and we were unable to leave the town because the rains continually washed torrents over the roads. Perhaps we must find a goat to sacrifice. Can nothing ever be achieved, in this grey flooded world?

It added to our bitter feelings that we saw that not even Loukas would look at us, were it not for the horses and pistols. The boy looked up when we greeted him; but it was only to see what we had brought him. We were humiliated to find that we would have his smiles, even at the price of our pride. It was a continuing torment to have that boy near us.

A violent incident depressed us further. A nephew of Karaiskakis, one of the Greek chieftains, was knocked down in a quarrel with some of our Missolonghiot boatmen, no doubt about the size of a fare. Moral: never get into a fight with a sailor.

Had we ourself been *fairly* thrashed, we hopes we should have the good grace to go home, dress our wounds, and forget about it. Not so a Greek chieftain's nephew (we understood the boatman had given him a shiner). The nephew went to his uncle Karaiskakis. Next day a hundred and fifty of Karaiskakis's men fell on us in revenge, seized two Greek clergy, and occupied the little fort at the mouth of our harbour.

This dissension had to be stamped out quickly, before the rebel forces were reduced to chaos. It began to look like a general brawl would ensue. We loaded a few boats with Suliotes and small cannon and sent them against the fort. The brave fellows inside, when they saw our cannon, gave themselves up without a fight, and we sent them back to their leader in disgrace.

No bones broke, a little bruised pride, and the thing settled with admirable efficiency (if not quite the 'kiss and make up' that Scrope always preferred in a quarrel.) All very well, but if word of such an incident should get abroad, it would kill any support we might expect from foreigners for our cause. It all added to our growing feeling that this game, here, would never turn out well. Our life was becoming confused, dull, full of disappointed hope; to add to the strain, we had to behave in front of our people as if we were optimistic about the progress we were making. (Not.)

We were cheered, nevertheless, to get two letters from England – one concerning our daughter (our last remaining daughter, little Miss Legitimacy, Ada) and her recovery from a threatening illness. This letter of course from the good Goose, not our supposed wife. But Augusta included a profile of the child, wherein we were able to see that she was growing handsome as any Byron.

T'other letter was from Hobhouse, who wrote: 'Nothing can be more serviceable to the cause than all you have done...' It seemed our fame had a use after all, for we ourselves were becoming a figurehead for the Greek struggle.

We prayed God we were not to be the sacrificial goat, the corn king whose bones had to fertilize the earth to make the new crops grow.

Chapter fifty-four

The king-times are fast finishing. There will be blood shed like water, and tears like mist; but the peoples will conquer in the end. I shall not live to see it, but I foresee it.

This house, at high tide, is cut off by water from the firm ground where we liked to take our gallop. Pietro and ourself had to take a boat, as usual, across the lagoon to where the horses were waiting.

The ride started as normal, with a little chatter about the best form the new Greek government – if achieved – should take. We favoured the federal model, a republic of free but united states, in the manner of the Americans, but when Pietro ventured to agree with us we were adamant that the Greeks had to choose a system to suit themselves. When he ventured that perhaps the Greeks would not know what system to choose, we told him we were sure that the *people themselves* were better than their desultory leaders. No abstract government, in itself as a system, could in itself be called good, without reference to the men who were to administer it.

This took us quite a few miles through the countryside. Towards the end of our run, we trotted past some cottages.

A magnificently wrinkled old woman in black came out of one of the cottages and called out to us. We tried to reply, in our rudimentary version of the local dialect. Then our confidence in the language returned. We remembered the lessons in Romaic, or modern Greek, given us in our youth by the child Theresa, and attempted a conversation.

The old lady and ourself looked at each other with baffled affection across the language barrier. The woman called out her numerous family into the yard, and repeated all their names to us. A fine looking family. She presented us with a curd cheese and some honey. We tried to press some silver on her but she firmly refused. 'I feel,' we said to Pietro, as we rode away, 'more pleasure this day, and at this circumstance, than for a long time past. These Greeks will make a free people in the end, despite their damned leaders. The people, my boy, the people will not be defeated.'

The young man smiled. 'The people will rule themselves better than we of the nobility are able to, if it must take we of the nobility to help them to it.'

Pietro will always modify the position slightly, the boy is no mere yea-sayer. We leaned over to pat his back. 'We will see that they can do so. This weather will clear up, and when we get to the conference at Salona we must put our voices toward the leadership of a man who has no interest in becoming a king. A man with a brain clear of ambition. We will find him. That old woman has given me new faith.'

Pietro was pleased to see us cheerful for once.

Laughing at nothings, we raced on through the mud, splashing a fine brown spray over each other. Three miles from the town, heading toward our boat, we rode head-on into a cold wall of rain that slashed at our bare faces without mercy. For fifteen minutes we had to ride through this – there was nothing else to do – until we could glimpse through the watery air the boat waiting on the lagoon. We could not help laugh, as the rain doused our revolutionary thoughts with cold water. 'So much for our hopes for dry roads, for Salona.' We shivered, rubbed our aching shoulder. 'It rains so hard, this Greek spring rain, as if to wash your bones into the earth to make the crops grow.'

Pietro gave us a worried look. 'Let us ride on through the lagoon, it is shallow enough, and have someone else bring back the horses to their stables. You still have the trace of fever. You cannot risk a slow journey in a boat. You must get home and out of your wet things as quickly as possible.'

'I should make a pretty soldier, indeed, if I were to care for such a trifle.' Thanks to this whim of our pride, we spent half an hour being soaked further in the open boat that was poled with agonising slowness across the lagoon. We were shuddering with cold by the time we landed, but were able to shrug off the experience as Fletcher towelled us dry. Good old Fletch, rubbing life back into our old carcase...

Two hours later we succumbed to a deeper fit of shuddering. This gave way to fever and intense rheumatic pains in our bones, pain enough to make us curse our earlier carelessness.

'I suffer,' we said to Captain Parry, 'a great deal of pain. I do not care about death, but these agonies I cannot bear.'

Chapter fifty-five

When one subtracts from life infancy (which is vegetation), – sleep,
eating, and swilling – buttoning and unbuttoning – how much
remains of downright existence? The summer of a dormouse.

By midnight LB's sheets were drenched with the sweat of renewed fever. He slept very poorly, but insisted on riding again the next day, going out early in the afternoon in an attempt to avoid the evening downpour. We must, he thought, keep up appearances, or the rest of our damned forces will disappear altogether. His bones and head aching, he forced himself to canter cheerfully through the familiar olive grove on the far side of the lagoon. But the saddle was wet, the groom had not dried it properly from the night before. Before long his thighs and buttocks, where they touched the saddle, were aching abominably. He felt a great chill coming into his limbs from the damp leather, and cursed the groom as the boy took his horse when he got into the boat.

Later, lying on his couch with ache in his bones, LB told his alarmed doctors of a prophecy made to him when a boy: 'Beware your thirty-seventh year.' Millingen called on him not to give way to superstition. LB snapped back: 'To say the truth, I find it equally difficult to know what to believe in this world, and what not to believe. I don't, for example, believe in doctors, as a rule.' That night, the pain wandering in spasms over his prostrated body, he called Bruno for a sleeping-draught – laudanum for preference. Bruno recommended bleeding. When LB refused, as if in spite the doctor dosed him with castor oil, so that he must stagger to the cold privy in his nightshirt and squat there in all his pain.

Captain Parry had been so alarmed at the deterioration in his condition that he had prepared a boat to sail on the 13th of April and take the sick man over to the island of Zante, away from this unhealthy mudhole of a village. But – as the gods laughed – the sirocco blew up on the morning of the 13th, and all vessels were confined to port.

On the 14th, LB, rising at noon, declared he was fit enough to go for his ride. The others succeeded in sending him back to bed. The despairing Parry tried to talk the doctors out of bleeding the sick man. But the medical men were not to be thwarted The next time Parry called for his daily visit the doctors told him that their patient was sleeping and not to be disturbed.

But the game was not finished yet. Over and over again the doctors begged him to agree to be bled, Dr. Bruno using tears and the plea that LB should agree 'for the sake of all he holds dear in the world.' The English doctor, the damnable Millingen, appealed to some dubious scientific principle or other. The patient responded by asking the doctors, straightfaced, to fetch in an old witch of the town, to see if she could take off the curse he was labouring under. But what she told him left him grimfaced and shaken; he would not divulge it to the others.

In the odd moments that he was allowed in to visit, Parry was alarmed that LB was beginning to speak of Death as an old and familiar friend. To see this most defiant of men resigned and composed at the prospect of his own death imparted a peculiar horror to the hardy sensibilities of the Welsh sailor. On the fifteenth, when Parry left his side at ten o' clock to go to bed, LB was seized by a violent fit of coughing that ended in vomiting. In his weakened state, the doctors made him agree to a bleeding on the following morning; when he again declined in the morning, Millingen warned of insanity unless the pressure of the blood was relieved. 'You are,' said LB, 'a damned set of butchers...' But he was too weary to resist them with anything more effective than abuse. The anxious faces hovered above him, tormenting him with eyes, urging him to give his blood.

For the patient the vague days and weeks of illness, near-recovery, and relapse fell in on themselves so that it was one episode, though in two parts, that had seemed to provoke the sad debacle. That fatal ride in the rain. And the ride on the wet saddle the next day. That was the boy that did for us, to be sure. *With such trifles may a man be destroyed.* He began to realize, with some indignation, whose death would serve to bring the Greeks together. The sacrificial goat...

And he could remember, on the ride, his legs aching, saying to Pietro: 'It leaves a cold in the bones, this Greek spring rain. As if it would wash your body into the earth to make the plants grow.' He repeated this observation to his doctors, but they would not listen to unscientific nonsense.

'Now, my lord.' Millingen turned to his colleague. 'Dr. Bruno, may I suggest we remove Lord Byron to a more suitable room?'

'Gentlemen – gentlemen,' LB objected weakly, 'I remind you that I was able to lie on this couch during the whole of my winter confinement. Surely you cannot think that...'

Millingen brooked no argument. 'You cannot remain in your *living* room, my lord. You must have peace.'

The patient laughed, then, through the tears of realisation: 'Si... si... cavaliere Biron implora pace... where is Mr. Parry? He will not let you do this...' Dimly he was beginning to be aware, by the looks on their faces, of what they expected would happen. 'You consider me a dying man...'

Later, in brief intervals of lucidity, he tried to place the blame of his death elsewhere: 'Why was I not made aware of this? Why was I not told of this before now...?'

All very tedious and beside the point, thinks the Night-gowned Spirit, who, as the picture of the petulant sick man with two dozen leeches on his body fades off the wall for good, turns to his remarkably-similar companion on the bed. 'Just a moment – isn't this rather where we came in? No complaining, dear boy. To mangle the bard once more, as Scrope the Great was wont to do, the rest is silence.'

'Silence?'

'Even I am not certain what exactly is to happen next. Are you quite ready, dear boy?'

'I want to sleep now.'

Outside, overhead, the great storm finally breaks, and shattering bolts of lightning slash the sky above the mourning town. Without being told, the Greeks know what the storm means, the release of what spirit, what energy, into the sky.

The village, as one man, rushes out into the streets to fire their muskets: 'Ayee, the great lord is dead, the lord is dead, he is dead!'

It is very dark. The light on the wall has gone. But curiously, LB is thinking, all is not over. In the darkness, he hears himself asking his other self: 'Where next, sirrah?'

In the darkness he feels his other self take his hand, as it has always been. The Spirit is drawing him out of his bed and across the room toward the door.

Holding his other self's hand affectionately at the last, he hears the other reply: 'I have always understood this to be the direction.'

Acknowledgements

I would like to thank the following people for their kindness and help with this book. Robin, Lord Byron, President of the Byron Society, has been unfailingly encouraging and also supplied certain factual information and an excellent Foreword. Jane Ireland supplied the drawing which Charlotte Mouncey incorporated into her cover design, based on the classic painting by Joseph-Denis Odevaere. Rebecca Souster supplied her expertise and invaluable advice. Dr. Gregg Eaves read the final manuscript and provided some very useful comments. David McClay provided enthusiastic encouragement and informed endorsement after reading the manuscript. Finally Georgina Aldridge supplied much-appreciated, prompt and considerate advice. Blessings on all!